Delores Fossen, a *USA TODAY* bestselling author, has sold over seventy-five novels, with millions of copies of her books in print worldwide. She's received a Booksellers' Best Award and an RT Reviewers' Choice Best Book Award. She was also a finalist for a prestigious RITA® Award. You can contact the author through her website at www.deloresfossen.com.

Elle James, a *New York Times* bestselling author, started writing when her sister challenged her to write a romance novel. She has managed a full-time job and raised three wonderful children, and she and her husband even tried ranching exotic birds (ostriches, emus and rheas). Ask her, and she'll tell you what it's like to go toe-to-toe with an angry 350-pound bird! Elle loves to hear from fans at ellejames@earthlink.net or ellejames.com.

D0507887

Discover more at millsandboon.co.uk

LAWMAN WITH A CAUSE

DELORES FOSSEN

SIX MINUTES TO MIDNIGHT

ELLE JAMES

MILLS & BOON

First Published in Great Britain 2019
by Mills & Boon, an imprint of HarperCollins*Publishers*
1 London Bridge Street, London, SE1 9GF

Lawman with a Cause © 2018 Delores Fossen
Six Minutes to Midnight © 2018 Mary Jernigan

ISBN: 978-0-263-27395-3

0119

MIX
Paper from
responsible sources
FSC® C007454

This book is produced from independently certified FSC™
paper to ensure responsible forest management.

For more information visit: www.harpercollins.co.uk/green

Printed and bound in Spain
by CPI, Barcelona

Chapter One

The moment he took the turn to his ranch, Sheriff Egan McCall spotted the emergency lights flashing on the vehicle just ahead. He groaned. Then he cursed.

Even in the darkness, he recognized the old white truck. It was parked on the shoulder of the narrow country road, and the driver was definitely someone he didn't want to see tonight. Or any other night for that matter.

Jordan Gentry.

Egan had only wanted to get home and get some sleep since he'd just pulled a twelve-hour shift and was bone tired. But sleeping anytime soon likely wasn't going to happen if he had to deal with Jordan first.

What the heck was she doing out here anyway?

The only place on this road was the McCall Ranch, which meant Jordan had probably been going there to see him. That couldn't be right, though. Jordan hadn't spoken a word to him in two years, and Egan wanted it to stay that way.

He pulled to a stop behind her truck and dragged in a deep breath that he hoped would steel him up. He hated, too, that steeling up was even required when it came to Jordan. Once, she'd been his high school sweetheart, but that felt like a lifetime ago. Now she was just part of the nightmarish memories that he still hadn't figured out a way to forget.

Egan got out, walking on the gravel shoulder to the driver's side. Since the engine wasn't running, he looked inside, expecting to see Jordan behind the wheel ready to complain about not being able to get her truck started. But both the headlights and emergency lights were on, so this couldn't be about a dead battery. Maybe she was having engine trouble.

Jordan wasn't there, though, in the cab of the truck. No one was. But Egan spotted something he definitely hadn't wanted to see.

Blood.

It was on the seat. So were chunks of safety glass. The passenger-side window was completely shattered.

Egan turned around so he could see if Jordan was nearby. Maybe she'd tried to avoid running into an animal or something and had hit her head. Of course, that didn't explain the broken window.

"Jordan?" he called out.

No response. There were deep ditches next to her truck and a fence just beyond that. But Egan didn't see her.

He took out his phone, using it as a flashlight, and spotted more blood on the ground. Not a huge amount, but even a few drops were enough to concern him. He needed to call for an ambulance.

However, the sound stopped him from doing that.

It was a soft rustling noise at the front end of the truck. Egan drew his gun, and he stepped closer.

Jordan.

She was sitting on the ground, her back against the front fender of her truck, and she had her gun gripped in her right hand, her phone in her left. She turned, and thanks to the truck headlights, he had no trouble seeing the source of the blood. It was on the top of her shoulder, just to the side of her blond hair, and it was running down the sleeve of her shirt.

"Are you here to finish me off?" she asked.

Obviously, she was dazed and didn't know what she was saying. Egan made that call to get an ambulance out there.

"What happened?" He went closer, peeling off his own shirt so he could wipe away some of the blood and see just how badly she was hurt.

"You" was all she said. She laughed. It was hoarse and weak, and it definitely wasn't from humor. "I knew you hated me, but I never thought in a million years you'd try to kill me."

Yeah, she was definitely talking crazy. Egan had a look at her wound and saw the gash on her shoulder. He eased her hair aside so he could see if there were other injuries, and she also had a bump on her head. She'd need stitches and might even have a concussion.

"What happened?" Egan repeated.

"You tried to kill me," she said without hesitation.

Even though Jordan was hurt, it was still hard to keep the scowl off his face. He tapped his sheriff's badge in case she'd forgotten that he was the law around here and not prone to murder attempts. "And why would I do that?"

There were tears in her pale green eyes when Jordan looked up at him. "Shanna."

Everything inside Egan went still.

Shanna Sullivan. His late fiancée. Shanna was also the reason Jordan was no longer someone he wanted to see. Even now after nearly two years, he still felt the ache. It ate away at him, and sometimes, like now, the ache felt just as fresh as it had when Shanna had died less than an hour after a man had shot her.

He leaned in, sniffed Jordan's breath to make sure she hadn't been drinking. She hadn't been. "Focus," he demanded. "I didn't try to kill you and neither did Shanna. She's dead. So, what the hell happened here?"

She touched her fingers to her head and looked at the blood that was on the sleeve of her shirt. "I…uh, was driving to your place to talk to you, and someone started to pass me. At least I thought that's what he was doing, but then he shot me. Someone driving a blue pickup identical to yours."

Egan pulled back his shoulders. He hoped like the devil that none of that was true. He definitely didn't want someone firing shots into a vehicle. Especially someone who might be posing as him. But then he reminded himself that Jordan hadn't made much sense with anything else she'd said.

He had another look at that gash on her shoulder. It was possibly a deep graze from a bullet. *Possibly.* But it could have also happened if she'd hit her head and shoulder on the steering wheel. Of course, her accusation would mesh with the broken window. Not with anything else, though.

"After he shot me, my truck stalled. I couldn't get it started," she continued a moment later. "So, I got out to try to fix it. That's when I passed out and landed here on the ground."

Egan didn't bother to tell her it'd been stupid to try to do engine repairs while injured. "You should have called nine-one-one."

Despite being dazed, she managed to give him a flat look. "Right. Call the local cops when I thought it was a local cop who shot me. I called someone from San Antonio PD instead."

He supposed that wasn't really a surprise about her not wanting to alert the locals. After all, Jordan lived in San Antonio, where she'd once been a cop. She almost certainly still had friends on the force there. But it was a long drive, nearly an hour, from San Antonio to McCall Canyon, and it'd likely be a while before her friend made it out here.

"And your cop friend in San Antonio didn't convince you to call me?" Egan asked.

"No." Again, she didn't hesitate. "Not after everything that's happened."

She was talking about Shanna now. Specifically, Shanna's murder. But Egan had no intention of getting into that with Jordan tonight.

"Come on," he said, helping her to her feet. In case she was still thinking he would try to kill her, he took her gun and put it in the back waistband of his jeans. "We can wait in my truck until the ambulance gets here." Which should be in about only twenty minutes or so.

If Jordan was right about having been shot, Egan didn't want them to be out in the open in case the shooter returned. Of course, he doubted that would happen. The bullet—if it was indeed a bullet—had probably come from someone out hunting.

"Hold my shirt against your shoulder to slow down the bleeding," Egan instructed.

Jordan went stiff when he tried to get her moving, and she looked at him as if debating if she could trust him.

Egan cursed again. "I don't know what you think happened here, but I didn't shoot you. I have no reason to kill you."

"Yes, you do." She lifted the side of her top to show him something he didn't need to see. The scar. The one from her surgery two years ago.

"So?" he snapped. "Did you think I'd forgotten you had a kidney transplant?" It wasn't a question because there was no way he could have not remembered that. After all, the donor kidney had come from Shanna.

Hell. More memories came. Jordan had been shot that day, too. The bullet had gone through her side and damaged both her kidneys. It'd been somewhat of a miracle that Shanna had been a match. Of course, that miracle came with a huge price tag since Shanna was dead.

"No. I didn't think you'd forgotten at all." She swallowed hard. "In fact, that's why I thought you wanted me dead."

"You're not making sense." He hooked his arm around her waist and forced her to get moving again.

He helped her into his truck, and she winced when she pressed his shirt against her head. Egan considered just driving her to the hospital, but the ambulance could arrive soon, and he could hand her off to the medics while staying behind to have a look at her vehicle. Specifically, that window. He wanted to see if the damage had indeed been caused by a bullet, and if so, then he could call out a CSI team.

"Yes, I am making sense," Jordan snarled. "Two of the recipients are already dead, and I think I'm next."

"Recipients?" he questioned.

She looked up at him. "You hadn't heard?"

No. But Egan was 1,000 percent sure he wasn't going to like what Jordan was about to say next.

"Breanna Culver, who got Shanna's liver. Cordell Minter, who got one of her lungs. They're both dead. Murdered." Jordan's last word didn't have much sound. It was mostly breath.

Hell. If that was true…well, Egan didn't want to go there just yet. "It could be a coincidence." Though it would be an eerie one. "You're positive they were murdered?" he challenged.

Jordan's forehead bunched up. "Yes. Their organs were…missing. The organs they got from Shanna."

Egan felt as if someone had punched him. "If that's true, why didn't someone tell me?"

"Because I only made the connection today. I knew the names of the recipients. I got them because, well, I don't know why exactly. Maybe I wanted to know who else was alive because of Shanna. I thought it would give me some peace."

Egan's mind was reeling, but he wanted to tell her that she didn't deserve peace. Neither of them did. "You're positive about those two people? Positive they were murdered and their organs taken?"

She nodded and motioned to her head. "And now this. Someone shot me."

No way could he just accept all of this just yet. "Your injury could have been a prank gone wrong. Or a hunter. It could have even been caused by a rock going through the window. A rock that maybe a passing truck kicked up from the road."

Her expression let him know she wasn't buying any of this. "What about the break-in at my house?"

He was clueless about that, too, but then he hadn't kept up with Jordan.

"I was supposed to be home," she continued. "But I'd left only about five minutes before to go into San Antonio to meet one of my old criminal informants. I wanted to ask him about the other two deaths. Anyway, while I was gone, someone broke in and set fire to the place."

Again, that didn't mean anyone was trying to murder her—though the "coincidences" were stacking up.

"That means there are only three of us left," Jordan added a moment later. "Tori Judd, Irene Adair. And me."

Egan hadn't known the names of the people who'd gotten Shanna's organs. He hadn't wanted to know. But was it possible someone was going after these people. And if so, why?

One name instantly came to mind. Drew Paxton.

The man who'd put a lethal bullet in Shanna. A bullet that Drew had fired during a botched hostage situation that had killed Shanna.

"Drew Paxton is in jail on death row," Egan heard himself mumble.

Jordan made a sound of agreement even though Egan hadn't been talking to her. "And he hasn't had any unusual visitors. You know, the kind of visitors he could have hired to kill people."

Egan was well aware of that because while he hadn't kept tabs on Jordan, he had done just that with Drew. It wasn't a morbid curiosity, either. Shanna had been Drew's parole officer, and the snake had developed a fixation on her. So much so that he'd broken into Shanna's house in San Antonio and taken her hostage.

Jordan had been one of the responding officers. A hostage negotiator. And she'd failed big-time. So had Egan. Because he hadn't been able to save Shanna, and he'd lost the woman he loved.

"I ruled out Drew because all of his calls and correspondence are carefully monitored," Jordan said a moment later. "And that's why I thought you might be doing this. I thought maybe you'd snapped or something."

Egan had come close to doing just that, but even if he had snapped, he wouldn't have gone after the people who'd gotten Shanna's organs. He would have gone after Drew.

And maybe Jordan.

But he hadn't snapped. And wouldn't. However, there were a couple of things that didn't fit here.

"If you thought I'd gone crazy, why were you heading out to the ranch?" Egan asked. "Weren't you afraid I'd gun you down once you got there?" Egan didn't bother to take the sarcasm out of his voice.

"I was going to see your brother, Court. I called dispatch, and they said you were still at work so I thought I could talk to Court alone."

Court was at the ranch all right, and his brother was not only a deputy sheriff, he would have also been more open to having a conversation with Jordan. Court probably didn't have the raw nerves that Egan still had about Shanna's death. Plus, Court and Jordan had been friends once, too.

"Look, I dismissed all of this at first," Jordan continued. "I'm a private investigator these days, and I know how to look at things objectively. Most things anyway," she added in a mumble.

Egan figured that was meant for him. Maybe Jordan hadn't been able to get past the hurt and emotions of Shanna's death, either, and that was why she'd thought Egan might be a killer.

"Have you been keeping an eye on Drew's brother, Kirk?" Egan asked.

Jordan nodded. Then, hesitated. "Well, as much as I can. He's a cattle broker, and he travels a lot. And yeah, he's still riled that his brother is on death row. He could be willing to play into Drew's sick fantasies of making sure every part of Shanna is dead."

Definitely a sick fantasy. And *riled* was putting it mildly for the way Kirk felt about his brother. Kirk thought Egan had provoked Drew into that hostage standoff. Kirk wasn't exactly specific about how Egan had managed to do that, but he blamed Egan for the situation. Maybe Kirk had decided to spread the blame around now and include Jordan. And those other recipients.

Still…

"What's the name and number of the SAPD officer who investigated the break-in and fire at your house?" he asked.

She paused several moments as if she might not tell him. That whole lack-of-trusting-him thing might be playing into this, but Jordan finally handed him her phone. "It's Christian Abrams. He's not the cop I contacted to come out here, but his number is in my recent calls."

It was. In fact, Jordan had called the man three times in the past two hours. And there were six missed calls from Christian to Jordan. It did make Egan wonder, though, why she hadn't phoned this guy after she had gotten injured. Or taken any of those six calls.

While Egan kept watch for the ambulance, he pressed Christian's number, and he answered right away. "Where the hell are you, Jordan?" the cop snarled.

"I'm not Jordan. I'm Egan McCall."

"The sheriff over in McCall Canyon," Christian said after a short pause, and Egan didn't think it was his imagination there was some venom in the man's tone. "Jordan went to you after all. I told her that wasn't a good idea."

Egan skipped right over that and went to the reason he'd wanted to speak to the man. "Is someone trying to kill Jordan?"

Christian certainly didn't jump to answer that. "Is she there with you? Can she hear this?"

The answer to both of those was yes. Egan hadn't put the call on speaker, but the cop's voice was carrying in the truck. Jordan would almost certainly be able to hear him. But that wasn't what Egan said because he didn't want this guy clamming up.

"She can't hear us," Egan lied.

"Good. Because I don't want to alienate her. Jordan needs friends right now. The *right* friends."

Again, judging from the tone, Christian didn't think Egan fell into that category. "Did someone really break into her house and try to kill her?" Egan pressed.

"Yes, but Jordan has this notion—no, it's an obsession now—with connecting anything that's happening to her friend's murder. Did she tell you that she thinks someone is killing organ recipients?"

"She mentioned it."

"Well, I don't think it's true," Christian concluded. "I think Jordan's feeling so overwhelmed with guilt from her friend's death that she's seeing bogeymen who just aren't there."

Jordan's eyes narrowed, and she looked ready to snatch the phone from him, but Egan waved her off.

"You've investigated the two deaths?" Egan asked Christian.

"Yes, and I'm just not seeing what Jordan's seeing. One of the victims was mangled and burned so bad in a car accident that it was hard to tell if she had missing organs or not. The other was dumped in the woods, and animals had ravaged the body."

As gruesome as that was, Egan actually felt some relief. Maybe this wasn't connected to Shanna after all. Or maybe that was just wishful thinking on his part. It sickened him, though, to think that Jordan might be right, that Drew did indeed want any living part of Shanna dead.

"Look, just tell her to come home, and I'll talk this out with her," Christian continued. "Or better yet, tell me where she is, and I'll come and get her. I care for her. A lot. I want to make sure she gets the help she needs."

This time, Jordan did grab the phone, and she hit the end-call button. She opened her mouth, no doubt to try to convince him that she wasn't "obsessed" as Christian had claimed. But the approaching headlights stopped her.

The vehicle wasn't coming from town but rather

from the direction of the ranch. If it was Court or one of the hands, they would stop when they spotted his truck, and Egan would have to explain why Jordan was with him.

Too bad he wasn't sure of the answer himself.

As the headlights got closer, Egan felt his chest tighten. That was because it was a blue truck. Identical to his. And there wasn't another vehicle like it on the ranch. Plus, this vehicle had the same license plate number. Since Egan's plate was legit, this one had to be a fake.

"It's him." Jordan reached for his jeans. No doubt to try to get to her gun. But it was too late.

The bullet crashed through the windshield of Egan's truck.

Chapter Two

Jordan's breath froze. *No, please, no.* This couldn't be happening again.

She heard the hoarse sob tear from her throat, and she took hold of her gun that was in the back waistband of Egan's jeans. She managed to get it, but Egan immediately pushed her down onto the seat. Good thing, too.

Because the next bullet slammed into the seat right where Jordan had been sitting.

If Egan hadn't moved her at that exact moment, she'd be dead. She still might be, and this time the shooter might kill Egan right along with her.

"Hold on," Egan warned her. Keeping low, he started his truck, threw it into Reverse and jammed his foot on the accelerator.

The sudden jolt of motion knocked Jordan against the seat. Hard. Her head hit, too, and the pain jolted through her. Still, feeling the awful pain was better than being shot again, but they weren't out of the woods yet.

A third bullet smacked into the windshield, and

she could have sworn it missed Egan by less than an inch. The bullet went into the headrest next to where he was hunched down.

Jordan lifted her head to get a better look at the vehicle. It was the same truck, all right. And the person inside obviously wanted to have another go at killing her. The guy had the driver's-side window down, and he had a gun sticking out.

"I can't see his face," Jordan said. Because there was a dark tint on the windows. It didn't help, either, that the driver had on the high beams, and they were shining right in her eyes.

"Don't make it easy for him to shoot you," Egan snarled. He shoved her back down, and he kept speeding down the road in Reverse.

Jordan wanted to remind him that she was a PI and former cop. She could return fire. However, at the moment that might not even be true. She was dizzy from the pain, and her hands were shaking. It was possible she couldn't even hit the truck, much less the driver.

There was the sound of tires squealing against the asphalt, and Jordan knew what that meant. "He's coming after us."

Egan didn't confirm that, but since the shots had stopped, it told her that the driver might be the sole person in the truck. If so, it was a gutsy move on his part to go after two armed and trained people. Then again, the guy did have them on the run, and that driver had a lot more control over his vehicle right now than Egan did. It was easier to drive forward than in Reverse, but there was no place for them to turn around on the narrow road.

"Call nine-one-one," Egan ordered. "I want backup. But not the ambulance. Once we're out of this, I'll get you to the hospital."

Seeing a doctor was the least of her concerns right now, and Jordan made the call for backup. The problem wouldn't be getting someone out here because they weren't that far from town. But Egan was literally taking up most of the road, and it would make it hard for the deputies to get in position to help them. Still, she wasn't sure how much longer Egan could keep this up.

Jordan had just finished the call when she felt the jolt. The other truck had slammed into them. Hard. She heard the sound of metal scraping against metal. Unless the second truck had a reinforced bumper, he could be doing as much damage to his vehicle as he was to theirs.

Egan was still low in the seat, using the side mirror to navigate, but he had to adjust so he could better grip the steering wheel when the driver came at them again. If he hadn't done that, they would have gone into the ditch. It hadn't rained recently so it wasn't filled with water, but they'd still probably get stuck. Then, they'd be sitting ducks for the shooter.

The memories came. They always did whenever Jordan had a gun in her hand. That wasn't exactly an asset for a private investigator—to have the memories come at her so fast and strong that it put her on the verge of a panic attack. It was the reason she didn't wear a badge any longer. It was also the reason her life, and her head, were a mess.

If Drew Paxton was behind this, then he was getting a good laugh right now. Not only was he trying to "kill" any living piece of Shanna, he might manage to take out the man Shanna had loved. Of course, Jordan felt as if she had already managed to "take out" Egan. Shanna's death had crushed him.

And Jordan was responsible for that.

Drew had been aiming at Jordan to finish her off when he'd fired that deadly shot. But he hadn't hit his target. Because Shanna had jumped in front of Jordan at the worst possible moment. And now Shanna was dead from a gunshot wound to the head, and Jordan was alive. Egan would never forgive her for that, and she'd never forgive herself.

The memories thankfully moved to the back of her mind when the truck crashed into them. Egan had to fight with the steering wheel again, and it didn't help when the driver rammed into them a fourth time. He would almost certainly continue to do that, too, until he disabled the engine, forcing them to stop. Then, he could try to use his gun on them to finish this.

"Hold on," Egan repeated to her.

Jordan lifted her head again so she could get a glimpse out the windshield, but the glass was so cracked and webbed that it was hard to see anything. She certainly couldn't tell if the guy was about to hit them again.

But she did hear the squeal of his tires.

Not the other truck's but Egan's. Egan hit the

brakes, and in the same motion, he turned the steering wheel, backing onto what appeared to be a ranch trail. It was gravel, and the rocks pelted the undercarriage. The sound was deafening, like being bombarded with bullets, but it wasn't loud enough to drown out the other driver hitting his brakes, as well.

Now that they were both stopped, Jordan figured either Egan or she would have a shot. Of course, so would the driver of that truck. That was probably why Egan got his window down in a hurry. Before Jordan could even sit up, Egan got off two shots.

Jordan lowered her window, too, and she tried to steady her hand enough to take aim. She didn't get a chance to do that, though.

"What the hell," Egan mumbled.

The other truck's door flew open. Not on the driver's side, either. But the passenger's. Maybe she'd been wrong about the shooter being the only person inside the vehicle.

And then something fell from that opened door.

It was too dark to tell exactly what it was, but Jordan thought maybe it was a person. If it was someone, Jordan figured he or she would get up and start shooting at Egan and her.

But that didn't happen.

The driver of the other truck slammed on the accelerator, leaving the other person behind. Jordan braced herself for the truck to hit them again. It didn't. The driver sped off, heading in the direction of town.

She could practically feel the debate Egan was having with himself as to what to do. He volleyed his attention between the person on the ground and the escaping driver of the other truck.

Egan finally snatched his phone up from the seat, pressed a number and immediately put the call on speaker. No doubt so he could free up his hands in case he needed to use his gun.

"John," he said to the person who answered.

John Clary was one of the deputies who worked for Egan at the McCall Canyon Sheriff's Office. Jordan had known him for years, and she knew he was a good lawman. He had almost certainly brought another deputy with him, too.

"You've got a dark blue truck headed your way," Egan told the deputy. "It's identical to mine, right down to the same license plate, but it's not me. The driver is armed and dangerous. Stop him if you can."

"Will do. Say, are you okay, boss?" John asked.

Egan paused. "I have Jordan Gentry with me."

John obviously knew something had to be seriously wrong for her to be with Egan. And it was. That person on the road wasn't moving. That didn't mean he or she wasn't still dangerous, though. This could be a ploy to get Egan and her out in the open so the person could gun them down.

"Just get to the truck," Egan added to John a moment later. "I don't want whoever's inside escaping."

Neither did Jordan, but there were several ways the shooter could manage to do just that. She'd grown up in McCall Canyon and knew there were plenty of ranch trails between here and town. He could turn onto one of those and hide. Plus, there was even another farm road along the route. If he or she managed to get there ahead of the deputy, then it was just a short drive to the interstate. It would be hard to track him after that because she was betting he would switch out those fake plates.

Part of her didn't mind having some distance between the attacker and her. Especially since Jordan wasn't in much shape to put up a fight. Her shoulder was still bleeding, and her head was throbbing. But she also knew if they didn't catch him now, that he would likely come after her again.

"No matter what happens, I want you to stay put," Egan warned her a split second before he eased the truck out from the trail and back onto the road. "And keep an eye out in case our *friend* returns to shoot at us again."

Jordan was already doing that, but she was also making glances at the person who was still lying on the road. Egan pulled closer, but it was still hard to tell much because he or she was wrapped in a blanket. Of course, the cover could be concealing a weapon.

Had Drew or his brother managed to send would-be killers after them? If so, this could be a hired gun. That was probably why Egan hadn't wanted her out of the truck. But obviously he wasn't going to take that same precaution himself.

He put on his emergency flashers, the red lights knifing through the darkness, and he pulled to a stop directly next to the person. Jordan moved closer to him so she could provide some backup if this turned into a shootout, but there wasn't much she could do to keep him out of the line of fire.

Egan stepped out.

He immediately maneuvered himself so that he was in front of Jordan, protecting her. She knew it wasn't personal, though. Egan was a lawman through and through, and he would now see her as part of the job.

Even if it wasn't a job that he especially wanted.

Jordan moved again, too, so that she could keep watch around them and still see from over his shoulder. With his gun ready, Egan walked closer. There was still no movement, so he used the toe of his boot to nudge the person.

"Is it a dummy?" Jordan asked.

Egan nudged it again and shook his head. "There's blood."

Sweet heaven. That gave Jordan another jolt of adrenaline—along with a really bad thought. Both Egan and she had fired shots into the truck. And they'd done that before the person had been dumped on the road.

Had she shot him or her?

Or had Egan done it?

Jordan forced herself to remember that this could have been the shooter who'd been trying to kill them. He or she might have deserved to die. But like Shanna, the person could have been innocent in all of this, too.

Her lungs started to ache, and that was when she realized she was holding her breath. Her chest muscles were too tight. As if they were squeezing the life out of her. Jordan refused to give in to the memories and the panic. None of that would help Egan right now.

She heard Egan gut out some profanity under his breath as he reached for the blanket. He didn't yank it but rather gave it a gentle tug, touching it only with his fingertips.

The way a cop would touch evidence he didn't want contaminated.

And Jordan soon realized why Egan had done that. The moment he pulled back the blanket, she saw the face of the person who was wrapped inside it.

It was a woman.

And she was dead.

Chapter Three

Egan couldn't push away the sickening feeling of dread. A woman was dead. And he might have been the one to kill her.

"There was no ID on the body," Egan heard Court say from the other end of the line. "We'll try to match her prints so we can figure out who she is."

His brother was at the crime scene with the medical examiner and the CSI team so Court would make sure that everything was done as fast as it could be. Egan had wanted to be there, too, but he also had to make sure Jordan got to the hospital.

And that she was safe.

Ironic, since just an hour ago he hadn't believed she was truly in danger. Well, he sure as heck believed it now. The person in the truck had wanted to kill her. He was certain about that. But the next steps were for Egan to figure out who this dead Jane Doe was and how she fit into what had happened.

Obviously, Jordan wanted to hear all about that, as well. Even though the doctor was stitching up her shoulder, she was leaning closer to Egan. No doubt trying to hear Court's every word. When he finished the call, Egan would give her the condensed version, but first he wanted to try to process it himself.

"Cause of death?" Egan asked Court.

"Two gunshot wounds to the head. No stippling."

Hell.

Stippling happened when particles of gunpowder embedded into the skin. Since it wasn't on the victim, Egan knew she probably hadn't been shot at point-blank range. That meant, she might have still been alive while she was in the truck. *Might.*

Egan dreaded this next question, but he had to know. "Did the victim have any organs missing?"

Court blurted out a single word of bad profanity. "No. Not that I can see. Why would you think that?"

"I'll fill you in when you're back here." No way did Egan want to get into this over the phone, but it was a relief that the woman seemed to be intact. "Were there exit wounds on the body?" Egan asked.

"No. The bullets are still in her."

As grisly as that sounded, that was actually a good thing. "I want ballistics done ASAP," Egan reminded his brother.

Though a reminder really wasn't necessary. Court was already well aware that was one answer they had to have right away.

"I'll get it," Court assured him. "You do know, though, that even if the shot came from your gun, or Jordan's, this was an accident? From everything you told me, both of you were aiming at the driver, who was shooting at you. You didn't even know there was a passenger in the vehicle."

Yeah, he knew that in his head. But his gut was having a lot of trouble with it. If the woman had died from his bullet, then the bottom line was that he'd been the one to kill her.

"Also, I've made some calls about the truck the gunman was driving," Egan continued a moment later. "It had to be custom since the windshield was bullet resistant and the front end had been reinforced. We might get lucky and find out who ordered a vehicle like that."

"I can help you with that when I get back to the office," Court answered. "Might not be for a while, though, since we want to process Jordan's vehicle, too. How is she, by the way?" Court asked after a pause.

She had a lot less blood on her than when Egan had first seen her, but she had that stark look in her eyes. The one that told him she was dealing with a serious adrenaline crash and was maybe in shock.

"Jordan's, well, Jordan," Egan settled for saying. Stubborn and driven. Not necessarily a good combination.

"She really should be in the hospital," Dr. Lucy Madison said to Egan the moment he was finished with his call.

Dr. Madison had been working at McCall Canyon Hospital since Egan was a boy. She knew her stuff. And she was right. Jordan should be in the hospital, but when she'd repeatedly refused, Egan had brought her to the sheriff's office instead and called Dr. Madison to come and check her out.

"I'd rather not be at the hospital with a killer on the loose," Jordan grumbled.

It wasn't her first grumble about that, either, and Egan could definitely see her side of it. Jordan was a former cop and hadn't been able to stop the attack, and this thug could just come walking into the hospital to finish what he'd started. At least Egan could control who came in and out of the sheriff's office, and the gunman would have to be plenty stupid to come into a building with cops.

"Will she be okay?" Egan asked Dr. Madison. It wasn't a general kind of question, though. He needed to know how soon he could move her to a safe location so he could get on with this investigation.

"I think she'll be all right," the doc answered. "I'd still like to run some tests, but if it's absolutely necessary for her to be here, it can wait."

"It's necessary," Jordan assured her.

Dr. Madison made a suit-yourself sound and gathered up her things. "I'll call in a script for some pain meds, but something tells me you won't be taking them."

Jordan looked at her. "I won't be." And there wasn't a shred of doubt in her voice.

The doctor sighed. "Well, just take some over-the-counter stuff if it gets too bad. You'll have a doozy of a headache for a day or two."

Egan figured from the way Jordan kept wincing that it'd gone well past the *doozy* stage. Still, he didn't press it. But he would when the doctor was finally out of his office.

"I will need my immunosuppressant meds, though," Jordan told the doctor. "They're at my place in San Antonio, but I haven't had my dose today."

"Immunosuppressant?" Egan asked.

Jordan dodged his gaze. "For the kidney transplant." She gave the name of the drugs to the doctor.

Dr. Madison nodded. "I'll get you a new script. Will she be here for the next hour or so?" she asked Egan. "Because if so, I can have the pharmacy deliver it to her. Jordan really shouldn't miss taking it even for a day. It could cause her body to reject the donor kidney."

Egan wasn't sure he'd wanted to know that. It was always hard to think of Jordan having part of Shanna inside her. If that part died, it'd be a little like losing Shanna all over again. That probably didn't make sense to most people, which was why Egan kept it to himself.

"Jordan will be here for a while," Egan assured the doctor. Just how long "a while" was, though, he wouldn't know until he'd learned more about what was going on.

"Tell me about the other two living recipients," Egan said to Jordan once the doctor had left.

Jordan had already given him the names—Tori Judd and Irene Adair—and while Egan had been making some calls, he'd done internet searches on them, but he hadn't pulled up much. Irene Adair didn't even have a driver's license so there was no

DMV photo on her. He had gotten a look at a photo of Tori, but Egan didn't know if she was a match to the dead woman or not.

Jordan drew in a deep breath and moved from the corner of his desk where she'd been sitting to the chair across from him. "I have computer files on both of them, but I honestly don't know if one of them is the dead woman. There was too much blood for me to get a good look at her face."

Ditto. But what he had been able to see would be etched in his mind forever. So would some of the details that were eating away at him. "I'm not sure our attacker had enough time to wrap her in a blanket before he dumped her out of the truck."

"Yes." Jordan said it so quickly that she'd probably given it some thought. But then she lifted her shoulder. "Unless she'd already had the blanket draped around her." She winced again. Hesitated. "Did the woman have a missing heart or pancreas?"

"No."

Egan saw the same relief in her eyes that he'd felt when Court had told him that. Like him, the relief didn't last long.

"It's possible the gunman had the woman on the seat next to him," Jordan said, "and he pushed her out only after she'd been shot."

Egan had considered that, too. That was why they needed to find the driver of that truck so he could shed some light on this.

"How long before we have ballistics?" she asked.

Egan nearly told her there was no "we" in this investigation, but there was. Whether he liked it or not, and he didn't, Jordan and he were in this together.

"As soon as the ME can get the bullet out of the Jane Doe, Court can do the comparison with our guns."

Egan had gone ahead and sent both his and Jordan's weapons to the lab. Still, it might be tomorrow before they heard anything. It might be that long as well before they got an ID on the woman. It'd be hell waiting, but it wouldn't be downtime.

"I've already called Kirk," Egan continued. "He didn't answer, but I left a message for him to get in here for questioning."

"He won't like that," she said under her breath.

No. But then Kirk didn't care much for anything Egan did. Kirk apparently wasn't objective enough to figure out the only person to blame for Shanna's murder was Drew himself.

"Kirk is obviously a suspect," Egan went on, "but I have to wonder why he'd wait nearly two years before doing something like this."

Jordan gave a frustrated sigh. "Maybe it's just now sinking in that his brother is going to die on death row. Or Drew could consider this a loose end he wants tied up before he gets that lethal injection. He lost his appeal."

True. But there'd be other appeals. Ones that would take a long time. The average inmate in Texas spent over ten years on death row. It didn't matter that there'd been eyewitnesses to what Drew had done. It didn't matter that the man wrecked plenty of lives. He would still survive years longer than Shanna. Justice definitely wasn't a substitute for the havoc that had played out that day.

"I also need to know if there's someone else you've crossed paths with," Egan went on. "Someone you ticked off enough to do something like this. Because what happened tonight might not even be related to the two dead recipients."

Jordan didn't argue with that verbally, but she did shake her head. "I'm not seeing anyone."

He waited for her to add more. When she didn't, Egan went with his next question. "How about the cop, Christian Abrams? He said he cared about you *a lot*."

Her mouth tightened. "He thinks I'm crazy. I'm not."

Egan was beginning to believe that. "Could something have happened between you two to make him want you dead?"

"No." But then she huffed. "We worked together when I was still on the force. Now I do death penalty case reviews for a watchdog group called The Right Verdict. They want to make sure people haven't been wrongly convicted, and Christian is still my main contact at SAPD. He and I have had a disagreement or two about whether or not someone incarcerated actually got a fair shake at justice. But other than that, nothing."

That didn't seem like much of a red flag to turn a cop into a killer. Still, it was worth checking out. Egan pushed a notepad and pen across the desk toward her. "Give me the names of the cases where you disagreed."

The surprise flashed through her eyes. "You don't really believe Christian could have done this?"

"I won't know until I've checked him out." He tipped his head to the notepad. "Names, dates, anything else you have."

Jordan hesitated a moment and then wrote down a website address and password. "That will get you into my online storage account. The first file will be everything about the organ recipients. The next two will be the case files I'm working on for my job, the ones where Christian and I didn't see eye to eye."

Good. He put the note with the info in his pocket so he could go through that while he was setting up a safe house for Jordan. He was about to broach that subject with her, but Jordan spoke before he could say anything.

"One of the calls you made while I was being stitched up was to Alma Lawton. She's the woman who'd had an affair with your father, Warren."

Obviously, Jordan had been keeping tabs on him. Of course, that wouldn't have been hard to do since his father's affair had made the newspapers. It had come to light after Warren had been shot and nearly killed. His father had led a double life for over thirty years, and his lover, Alma, had been a suspect. Initially so had her and Warren's son, Raleigh. Egan's half brother. But both had since been cleared.

"Alma has an alibi for tonight," Egan explained. "And the rangers are monitoring her bank accounts.

If she'd withdrawn any money for a hired gun, we would have known about it."

"But if you called her, you must have thought she could possibly be involved in this," Jordan pointed out.

Egan shrugged. "Just ruling her out. That's why I'll check into Christian, the living recipients and the cases you're reviewing for your job."

She looked up and their eyes connected. For just a moment he saw the fear and pain—something she quickly tried to rein in. He saw something else, too. Jordan, the woman. She was attractive. Always had been. And she'd always had a thing for him since way back in high school.

That "thing" she had for him was apparently still there.

Egan figured that was because Jordan and he had been each other's first lovers. That sort of thing created weird bonds between people. But the bond hadn't kept Jordan in McCall Canyon. She'd always wanted to be a big-city cop and had left Egan behind. It had hurt at the time, but they'd both moved on. And Egan had eventually met Shanna and fallen in love with her.

During the time he'd been with Shanna, Egan hadn't felt the old attraction for Jordan. But he darn sure felt it now. Felt it and shoved it aside as fast as he could. It wasn't hard to do because of the voice he heard in the squad room. Apparently, it was a voice Jordan recognized, too, because she pulled back her shoulders and slowly got to her feet.

Their visitor was Leeroy Sullivan, Shanna's father.

As Egan usually did when it came to Leeroy, he gathered his breath and got ready for battle. Leeroy would never just pay him a casual visit, and since it was well past normal duty hours, something must be wrong. Of course, often the only thing that was wrong was that Leeroy was drunk and wanted to vent. However, Egan didn't see any signs of drunkenness tonight.

Simply put, Leeroy had not aged well. He was in his early fifties, but looked ten years older than that. And he'd let himself go, too. Once he'd been a big college football star and careful about keeping in shape. All of that had gone by the wayside, though, when he'd lost his only child. Shanna had been the center of his life.

"Egan," Leeroy greeted. It wasn't friendly. Never was when it came to Leeroy. He blamed Egan for Shanna's dying. But judging from the glare he shot Jordan, she had top dibs in the blame department.

"I heard you were here," Leeroy said to her. He spared a glance at the bruise on her head.

"How'd you hear that?" Egan asked.

"My wife was in the ER with a stomach bug, and I heard the nurses talking about Doc Madison having to come over here and stitch up Jordan. The gossip is that someone attacked her." Leeroy didn't sound choked up about that.

"Someone did," Jordan said, but she had to clear her throat and repeat it to give it some sound. Obviously, she didn't like dealing with Shanna's father any more than Egan did. "The person shot at Egan, too."

Definitely not choked up about that, either. Leeroy's scowl stayed in place.

Since Egan wasn't in the mood for getting into a scowling match with Leeroy, Egan just laid it all out there. "If you were hoping Jordan and I would be killed, you didn't get your wish."

Leeroy didn't jump to deny that was indeed his wish. And it might be.

"I came to tell Jordan that I don't want any more visits from her cop friend," Leeroy finally said. "In fact, I don't want anything to do with her or anyone else who considers her a friend."

Leeroy let his scowl linger a bit on Egan, probably because he likely thought that friendship label applied to him simply because he was standing next to Jordan.

Jordan shook her head. "What cop visited you?" she asked Leeroy.

"Christian Abrams."

Egan looked at her to see if she'd known about that, but she obviously hadn't. He definitely didn't like the way the cop's name had come up twice now.

"What did Christian want?" she pressed.

"To tell me some cockamamie story about the folks that got Shanna's organs, that somebody was killing them off. He didn't believe it. Neither do I. But he said he was worried about you going off the deep end over it. I told him I didn't give a rat whether you went crazy or not."

Later Egan would find out why Christian would make a visit like that to Shanna's father, but for now, he wanted to address the pure venom he'd just heard in Leeroy's voice.

"You hate Jordan that much," Egan commented.

"I hate you just as much." Leeroy's face was tight with anger, but he seemed to be blinking back tears, too. "If it hadn't been for you two, my baby would be alive. You two let her get killed." His attention slashed back to Jordan. "Shanna took a shot that was meant for you. That bullet should have gone into you."

"A bullet did go into Jordan," Egan reminded the man. Even though it did feel strange defending Jordan. Still, she wasn't defending herself. "It damaged both of her kidneys, remember?"

"I remember," Leeroy spat out. "But Jordan got the easy bullet. My baby took the one that should have killed Jordan instead. And she died. My baby died. Jordan lived because she got a part of Shanna. So did those other people, and it's not right."

Egan latched right on to that. "Are you saying the recipients should have died, too?"

He didn't say it with actual words, but his expression confirmed it. Leeroy's feelings weren't much of a surprise to Egan. That didn't mean hearing it didn't sting, though. It did. Because Leeroy was right. Still, that much hurt and anger was a red flag to a lawman.

"I gotta ask," Egan said to him. "Where were you tonight?"

The jolt of surprise seemed to make Leeroy's muscles even tighter. "Oh, no. You're not going to try to pin this on me."

"It was a simple question," Egan pointed out.

"Usually it's simple to answer for someone who isn't hiding anything."

If looks could have killed, Leeroy would have ended Egan's life right there. "Like I said, I was at the ER with my wife. If you don't believe me, just ask the nurses."

Oh, he would. But Egan wouldn't like doing it. Plain and simple, he felt guilty when it came to Leeroy. He hadn't protected Shanna, and part of Egan would always believe that he deserved every bit of hatred and venom that Leeroy sent his way.

"Tell that cop friend to stay away from me," Leeroy growled to Jordan before he turned and stormed out.

"I'll call Christian," she said, taking out her phone.

She wasn't scowling exactly, but Egan knew from her tone that this wouldn't be a pleasant conversation. However, it was one he wanted to hear. He didn't get to do that because his own phone rang, and Egan knew he had to take the call when he saw Court's name on the screen.

"No ID yet on the Jane Doe," Court volunteered the moment Egan answered. "But when the ME and his crew were moving the body, something fell out of the blanket. I bagged it, but I thought you might want to see it before I send it to the crime lab."

"Why? What is it?"

Egan thought he heard his brother mumble some curse words. "It's a note," Court finally said. "It's not good, Egan. And it's addressed to Jordan and you."

Chapter Four

Jordan had no trouble hearing what Court had just said to Egan, and it caused everything inside her to go still. For a couple of seconds anyway. Then the new wave of panic came. And pain. But the pain was because she'd bunched up her forehead, the motion pulling at the stitches.

It was a reminder she didn't need of just how close she'd come to dying tonight. The note was perhaps going to be another of those unnecessary prompts.

Since the note was addressed to Egan and her, that meant the attack and the woman's death weren't just some fluke, that they did indeed have something to do with them. Of course, she hadn't actually believed that it was a sick coincidence, but she'd held on to the hope like a lifeline.

Well, that lifeline was gone now.

And Jordan just sat there, trying to gather what little of her composure she had left so she could listen to the rest of what Court had to say. Judging from Egan's grimace and his muttered profanity, he was trying to do the same thing.

"The note's handwritten," Court went on. "It's scrawled as if the person wrote it in a hurry. It says, 'Want to put an end to the killings? Meet me. I'll be calling you soon.' And there's no signature."

That last part definitely wasn't a surprise. No way would the person who'd written that note want them to know who he or she was. Because if they did know, Egan could make an arrest for attempted murder. Maybe even murder. But the jury was still out on who'd killed that woman who'd been dumped from the truck.

"I'll be calling you soon," Court repeated. "You think this could be a situation where this clown is going to demand payment so the killings will stop?"

"Maybe." Though Egan didn't sound especially hopeful about that.

Neither was Jordan, but it was sadly the best-case scenario here. If the person could be paid off, then the motive was simply money. Not that she had money, but Egan did, and plenty of people knew that. Still, this didn't feel like something that simple. It would be a lot harder for them to stop this guy if the motive was revenge because their attacker might not be satisfied until Egan and she were dead.

She stood and started walking, just to give herself something to do with the slam of fresh adrenaline she got. Egan's office wasn't that big so she soon ended up in front of the bookcase and filing cabinet, where there were framed pictures of his family.

And Shanna, of course.

Every detail of Shanna's features was etched in

Jordan's memory, but it was even more painful seeing that face. That smile. Jordan went back to the chair so the photos would be out of sight and hopefully out of mind. For a couple of seconds anyway. She needed to regain her footing, and she didn't stand a chance of doing that if she was looking at Shanna's face.

"Are you okay?" Court pressed when neither of them said anything.

"Fine," Egan snapped, but all three of them knew that wasn't the truth. "Have the handwriting on the note analyzed. Also check the paper for prints or trace."

"I will," Court assured him. "But I think this makes it pretty clear that Jordan and you are the targets. Please tell me you won't go to a meeting with this snake if he or she actually calls."

A muscle flickered in Egan's jaw. "If there is a call, I'll see what he wants and take things from there."

Judging from Court's huff, he didn't like that answer, but Jordan felt the same way as Egan. If a meeting truly would put a stop to the killings, then she would go for it. Well, if she could figure out a way for Egan and her to come out of it alive.

"It's late, and I'm sure you're both exhausted. Are you taking Jordan to the ranch?" Court asked a moment later.

There was more of that muscle flickering from Egan. "Maybe. But if that's where we go, it would be just for tonight."

Jordan was shaking her head before he even finished, and she got to her feet. "I don't want to go there," she protested.

Egan didn't even acknowledge that. He just kept talking to his brother. "Call me the minute you get anything back from the ME, CSIs or the lab. Are there any safety measures you want me to take for Rayna?"

"Rayna and I have already worked that out." And Court proceeded to tell Egan about some hands standing guard and an armed security system.

Jordan knew that Rayna was a local horse trainer who was also engaged to Court. That likely meant the woman had already moved to the ranch, and Jordan figured she could use that to win the argument she was about to have with Egan. An argument that started the moment he finished the call with Court.

"I don't want to go to the McCall Ranch," she repeated. "Your family will be there. Your father, your sister and apparently Rayna, too. My being there could put them in danger. Not to mention that none of them will want me there after what happened to Shanna."

"No, my family won't be there. Court and Rayna have their own place on the back of the property. My sister, Rachel, lives with her soon-to-be husband in a house near town. And my dad has been staying at his fishing cabin down by the river."

Even though she wasn't ready to give up her argument, that did give her a new reason for alarm. That was because the fishing cabin was a good mile from the main ranch house.

"Is it safe for your father to be there?" she asked.

"I mean since someone tried to kill him just two months ago."

Egan lifted his shoulder. "Some people ignore the danger and hope that it doesn't come back to bite them."

"You mean me."

"Yeah," he readily admitted. "Just because you didn't die with Shanna doesn't mean you have to choose to die now."

Surprised, Jordan pulled back her shoulders. Egan didn't usually bring up Shanna's name around her. Nor did he usually show any kind of concern for her. Of course, maybe the concern was because of the danger she might have brought to his doorstep.

"You blame me for what happened tonight?" she came out and asked.

"No," he snapped, but it certainly sounded as if he meant yes. "It was beyond risky, though, for you to investigate those other deaths on your own. You should have turned all of this over to the cops before things got this far."

She heard the words and was certain that they were true, but there was another angle to this. "You didn't believe me when I told you about the other deaths. You thought I'd gone off the deep end."

And maybe he still did think that, but Egan managed to give her a flat stare. "You really want whoever's behind this to get his hands on you?"

"No. Of course not." It put an icy chill through her just thinking about it. This person had likely killed three people, and she didn't want her or anyone else to be his next victim. "The same goes for you, though. We need a safe house, not your family's ranch."

"That's probably true, but it's nearly midnight and too late to come up with an alternative."

She tipped her head toward the back of the building. "How about the break room? There used to be a shower and a sofa back there."

The last time she'd seen it, it had definitely qualified as bare-bones. Nothing more than a flop room for cops pulling double shifts. Still, it beat going back outside. She didn't want to run from a killer, but Jordan wasn't sure she could face him head-on right now.

Egan stared at her, and she saw the fatigue and weariness in not only his eyes but in every part of his body. He probably needed to crash for at least a nap anyway. Still, she doubted either of them would get much sleep no matter where they were.

He took out his phone again, and he fired off a text. "I'll have one of the hands bring us a change of clothes and some toiletries. Some dinner, too." He motioned for her to follow him.

And that was when Jordan realized she had actually won the argument with Egan. Too bad it didn't exactly feel like a win. Every part of her was on edge, and apparently it was the same for Egan because when the front door opened, he reached for his gun. So did Ian Meade, the deputy who was at his desk in the squad room. But their visitor wasn't the killer. Or if it was, he was wearing a white lab coat.

Jordan didn't recognize him, but Egan and Ian

must have because they both huffed and reholstered their weapons.

"It's okay," Egan said to her, and he blew out a quick breath. "That's Billy Watson. He works at the pharmacy."

Billy nodded and volleyed uneasy glances at all three of them. "Uh, Dr. Madison asked me to bring over these meds." Billy handed Egan the small white bag, and he in turn gave it to Jordan.

Jordan thanked him, but Billy didn't hang around. He got out of there, fast, probably because he'd figured there must be some potential trouble for Egan and Ian to have drawn so fast.

Egan took a laptop from one of the desks and got her moving again toward the break room, but this time it was Ian who stopped them. He gave Egan a thick file. "You said you wanted to go through that," Ian commented. "I can do it for you. I mean, you need to get some rest."

Jordan didn't know what was in that file, but Egan didn't take Ian up on his offer. He simply told the deputy to come and get him if there was any hint of a problem, and he led Jordan to the break room.

Yes, it was as bare-bones as she had remembered with a kitchenette, sofa and chair. The attached bathroom wasn't much bigger than a storage closet. Egan put the file and laptop on a small table next to the chair.

"You can take the couch," she said when he took several blankets and pillows from one of the lockers.

"I'm not the one who got shot tonight." He motioned to the bag that the medic had brought and dropped the bedding on the sofa. "Take your meds and get some rest." Egan immediately poured himself a cup of coffee, took it to the chair and opened the file.

"If you're drinking coffee, you must not be planning on getting any sleep," she pointed out.

He made a sound of agreement and started thumbing through the papers in the file. Since he obviously wasn't in a chatting mood, Jordan grabbed a bottle of water so she could take the pills, but instead of heading straight to the sofa, she walked in Egan's direction to get a look at what had captured his attention.

And her stomach went to her knees.

Because the first thing she saw was a picture of a dead woman. Even though it was impossible to tell the woman's identity from the photo alone, the name was beneath the grisly image.

Breanna Culver.

The woman who'd gotten Shanna's liver. Receiving that organ had saved Breanna's life, but she certainly wasn't alive in the photo. The shot had been taken after the horrific car wreck that had killed her.

Egan looked up at her, and while he didn't look especially pleased about her looming over him, he didn't close the file or tell her to move away.

"When the doctor was examining you, I texted Ian to print out everything on the other two dead women," Egan explained.

Yes, but there seemed to be more in that file than

just that. When he moved aside another page, she saw the police report on Shanna's murder.

Jordan had read it, of course. Actually, she could probably tell him word for word everything that was in it. But she couldn't figure out why Egan was looking at it now. Certainly, he didn't want all those painful memories brought to the surface at a time like this. Maybe, though, the memories were always with him.

They were always with her.

"I have to look at all the angles," he said. "What happened tonight and what happened to those other two women might be linked to Shanna. Or someone could just want it to appear as if it is."

She thought about that a moment. "You're talking about Christian now."

He didn't need to confirm that, but since they were on the subject of the possibly dirty cop, she opened up the laptop and made her way to the online files.

"I don't like that Christian went to visit Leeroy," Egan added a moment later.

Neither did Jordan, and she'd considered calling Christian about that. But it could wait. The numbing medication was wearing off from where she'd had her stitches, and the wound was starting to throb. Best if she had a clear head when she confronted Christian. And it would indeed be a confrontation since he had no right to go to Leeroy with any of this.

She opened the computer files where she'd had some crossover with Christian and passed the laptop to Egan. "Like I said, I do death penalty reviews. Just to make sure corners weren't cut, etc. And those are the two cases I flagged. Both were arrests that Christian made."

Egan immediately began to read through them. "What made you suspicious about them?"

Jordan hoped this didn't make her sound foolish. "Gut feeling. Christian was the only officer on scene for both arrests. Both of the prisoners claimed he set them up. I know, a lot of people in prison insist that happened," she added. "But this just felt like something I should look at a little closer."

Egan lifted his head and made eye contact with her. "And Christian knows about these *closer looks*?"

She nodded. "I think he'd like for me to back off, but that, of course, only makes me want to dig deeper."

Egan made another of those sounds of agreement and went back to reading the file. The reading, though, came to an abrupt halt, and she saw him go stiff. "Christian was supposed to be one of the officers on scene the night Shanna was murdered."

Yes, that was in her notes. "He said something personal came up, and he asked another officer to fill in for him." She paused. "Christian knew Shanna, of course, because she was a parole officer in San Antonio, but I think that's the only connection between them."

If there was something else, Jordan hadn't been able to find it. And she'd looked—hard.

Egan continued to stare up at her, and she saw the concerns and questions in his eyes. At least that was what was there. But it changed a little when his attention dropped to her mouth. He frowned as if disgusted with himself.

"Go ahead and get some sleep," he insisted. He set the file that Ian had given him aside. "I'll get to work on finding a safe house for you. The marshals can take over protective custody until we figure out what's going on."

He was putting some distance between them. That was a good thing, Jordan reminded herself, even if it suddenly made her feel worse than she already did. It made her ache for the closeness that Egan and she had once had.

She moved away from him, going to the sofa. No way would she get any sleep tonight, but it was obvious that Egan wanted the space between them to happen right now. However, Jordan had barely managed to get settled on the makeshift bed when the sound of Egan's phone ringing cut through the room. Since it could be an update on the case, she immediately sat back up.

"It's Court," Egan relayed to her when he looked at the screen. He dragged in a deep breath. The kind of breath people took when they were bracing themselves for bad news. He answered the call and put it on speaker.

"Still no sign of the shooter," Court said the moment he was on the line. "But we did find out more about the body." Court hesitated. "The ME took pictures, but I'm not sure this is something you should see. Jordan, either."

That got her attention, and she came off the sofa so she could go back across the room to Egan.

Egan ground out some profanity. "I've seen pictures of dead bodies before." His voice was edged with sarcasm.

"Not this dead body," Court practically whispered.

"Just send it," Egan insisted. "And tell me what the heck this is all about."

Court certainly didn't jump into an explanation. "There was…damage to the body. Damage not caused by the bullet." He hesitated again. Then groaned. "I think we're dealing with a very sick serial killer."

Chapter Five

Egan kept his eyes closed and pretended to be asleep when he heard Jordan get up from the sofa and go into the bathroom. A moment later, he heard her turn on the shower. He'd already taken one about an hour earlier, but it hadn't helped soothe his knotted muscles as he'd hoped it would.

Of course, nothing was going to soothe him right now.

Over the past six hours or so, he'd managed a few catnaps while sprawled out in the chair, but it hadn't been anywhere near a peaceful sleep. He'd had the nightmares again. Those images of Shanna being shot, and dying. But now he had a new image to add to the hellish mix.

The photo from the medical examiner that Court had sent him.

His brother had warned him that it was something he shouldn't see, but Egan hadn't exactly had a choice about that. He was the sheriff, and he needed every detail of this investigation. And now he had to figure out how to get that specific detail out of his head.

Not only the dead woman. But also the damage that'd been done to her heart.

Court had said they were dealing with a sick serial killer, and after seeing that picture, Egan had to agree with him. Well, unless someone was trying to trick them into believing they were dealing with a madman. If that was indeed what was happening, it was going to take some concrete evidence to start unraveling all of this.

They still didn't have a positive ID on the dead woman yet, but Egan thought she might be Tori Judd, the woman who received Shanna's heart. Her heart had still been there in the woman's body, but she'd been stabbed multiple times. The stab wounds were injuries that the medical examiner had thought might be postmortem. So, if the person responsible wanted them to believe they were dealing with someone vindictive, then he or she was doing a stellar job.

The silver lining in all of this was the other living recipient, Irene Adair, was alive and well. Court had finally managed to track her down while the woman was finishing up a vacation with her boyfriend.

When he heard Jordan turn off the shower, Egan went ahead and got up to start a fresh pot of coffee. He already felt wired, but he stood no chance of making it through the day until he tanked up on more caffeine.

He poured himself a cup as soon as it was ready, but he was still on his first sip when his phone dinged with another call. Something that had been happening most of the night. This time it was Thea Morris, his day-shift deputy.

"Some good news," Thea greeted. "Just got back the report from the lab, and our Jane Doe was killed with a .38-caliber bullet."

Yeah, that was good news, and Egan released the breath he'd been holding. Since both Jordan and he had used .40-caliber ammo, it meant they hadn't killed the woman with friendly fire. That didn't help the woman, of course, but Egan had enough worry and guilt hanging over him without adding this to the mix. He was certain that Jordan did, too.

And speaking of Jordan, she came out of the bathroom, and she was wearing the loaner jeans and blue top that one of the ranch hands had brought over for her. The clothes no doubt belonged to his sister because they weren't a good fit for Jordan. They were snug, practically clinging to her body.

Something that Egan wished he hadn't noticed.

While he was wishing, he would have preferred not to feel the kick from the old attraction. Talk about bad timing. Even if he'd wanted to renew a relationship with Jordan—and he didn't—he definitely didn't need to be reminded of why they'd once been lovers.

She kept her attention on him when she poured herself some coffee, and so that she wouldn't feel the need to come closer to hear his phone conversation, Egan put the call on speaker.

But Jordan came closer anyway. "Is that Thea?" she mouthed.

Since the bathroom was only a few feet away from

where they were standing, it was possible Jordan had already heard his side of the conversation. Just in case she hadn't, Egan filled her in. He filled in Thea, too.

"Jordan's back in the room with me," he told Thea, just so the deputy would know that someone else was listening to their conversation. "The shots that killed the woman didn't come from our guns," he added to Jordan.

He saw the relief go through her eyes and the rest of her. Jordan didn't exactly relax, but her shoulders loosened up a little. "Has there been any progress on confirming the identity of the dead woman?" Jordan asked.

"No. Still no ID," Thea answered. "Court said we were going with the theory that this was Tori Judd, but we're having trouble getting her dental records. Her dentist didn't respond to our calls, but his office should open in a couple of hours."

True. It was nearly seven now, but even after they made the request for the records, it still might take a while for a match to be determined. "How about the check on Tori? Did that turn up anything?"

"Nothing. San Antonio PD sent officers to her house just as you requested, but she wasn't there. She lives alone, and her parents don't know where she is, either."

Probably because the woman was dead. If and when they had that confirmed, then it would be time to start interviewing anyone who might have something to do with this. That meant starting with Kirk and Leeroy. Christian, too, since Egan had plenty of questions about the cop's possible involvement in this.

Whatever *this* was.

It was hard to swallow that someone might be trying to make sure no part of Shanna lived on. But that might be exactly what was happening here. If so, then Kirk and/or Leeroy had to be at the top of his suspect list. Kirk because this might be a way of getting revenge for his murdering brother, and Leeroy because he was well past the grieving-father stage.

"Kirk Paxton should be coming in for questioning in about an hour," Thea went on. "I doubt you got much sleep last night so you want one of the other deputies or me to do the interview?"

It was tempting to hand that off, but Egan really wanted to see Kirk's face when he asked him about the dead woman. And asked him if he had an alibi. "No. I'll do it. How about the search of Kirk's place?"

That was something else that Egan had also requested in the wee hours of the morning. Not just for Kirk but for Leeroy, too. He wanted their houses checked for any signs of that custom truck or the murder weapon.

"The searches should be starting soon," Thea answered. "We're using reserve deputies for that." She paused, and he heard the clicks of her computer keyboard. "I got the visitors' log from the warden at the prison where Drew's incarcerated a couple of minutes before I called you, but nothing stands out. In the past month, he saw Kirk once and his lawyer twice.

He didn't answer any of his fan mail. Yeah, he gets fan mail," Thea said in a grumble.

Egan knew about that, too, but anytime it came up, it ate away at him. Drew had murdered an innocent woman and nearly killed a second one, and there were sick idiots out there who worshipped him for that. He'd gotten more than a dozen marriage proposals.

"I asked the warden to go back another two months for the visitors' records," Thea continued. "I know you've been keeping up with it, but it might be worth another look."

It was, especially since they had so little to go on right now.

"Thanks," Egan told his deputy. "I'll be working from back here a while longer. Fewer windows."

Though it hadn't been necessary to add that last part. Thea and Jordan were well aware that the gunman who'd attacked them was still at large, and Egan's office was just off the squad room, where Jordan could be an easier target for a sniper.

"I understand. I'll let you know when the marshal arrives," Thea added before she ended the call.

"The marshal?" Jordan immediately asked.

"I put in that safe house request. There's a place near here, and a marshal's checking it out now."

Jordan nodded and sipped her coffee, but Egan noticed that wasn't exactly a happy look she was sporting. "You don't think the safe house is a good idea?" But he didn't wait for her to answer. "Surely, you don't want to spend another night in here with me."

It was a simple comment, definitely nothing sexual, but it didn't get a simple response. Jordan's gaze came to his, and he saw the heat again. Maybe because of the whole spending-the-night-together thing. They hadn't done that in years, but the last time had been when they were still lovers. And he darn sure hadn't slept in a chair back then. He'd been in bed with her.

The memories came. Of Jordan and him. And even though they weren't memories he especially wanted, they were better than the nightmarish ones he'd been having of Shanna.

"Yes," she muttered as if she knew exactly what he was thinking. "I think it's just a knee-jerk reaction on our parts. It's something to think about other than the fact someone tried to kill us."

Maybe she was right. Of course, the attraction had been around long before the attack, but it was best not to bring up that reminder.

"As for the safe house, yes, I think it's a good idea," she said. She paused. "You said the marshals will be guarding me."

He frowned. "You have a problem with that?"

"Maybe. Because of Christian. He has a lot of friends who are marshals. I just wondered if the one checking out the safe house is someone you can trust."

Egan had thought he could, but now he wasn't so sure. "I don't personally know the guy," he admitted. "Do you have someone in mind you'd rather me use for this?"

"No," she readily admitted. Then, she huffed. "I would say private security is the way to go, but I just don't know where the threat is coming from. If it's from Christian…"

She didn't finish that. No need. Because a well-connected cop would have friends in personal security, as well. Hell. He didn't want to hand over Jordan to someone with connections to a killer, but then he also didn't want to keep doing bodyguard duty. It was bringing back too much of the past. Still, he might not have a choice. In the short term anyway. But he might be able to call in enough reserve deputies to arrange a protection detail.

"Court managed to track down Irene Adair," Egan explained to her. "She's alive," he quickly added when he saw the renewed alarm in Jordan's eyes. "Her boyfriend's an Austin cop, and he said he'd keep an eye on her."

"Good." She took a deep breath and repeated that.

"How are your stitches?" he asked, motioning toward her shoulder. Even though she was wearing a shirt, he could still see the edge of the bandage on the front of her neck.

"It hurts," she admitted. "I'll take something if it keeps up."

He doubted that. They were both fighting to keep a clear head, which was why they were downing coffee like water. Egan finished off his cup and poured himself another one.

"There's no word yet on the truck that our attacker was driving," he said. Since they were going to be trapped in the break room for a while longer, he figured he might as well get her up to speed on the investigation. "San Antonio PD and the Rangers are helping with that."

"What about the blanket the dead woman was wrapped in? Anything unusual about that?"

Egan had to shake his head. "It was mass produced, but the lab might find some trace evidence on it. Ditto for the note. And no, the clown who wrote it hasn't called yet."

Her fingers tightened around the cup she was holding. "And what will you do when he does?"

"Talk things out with him." He choked back a groan. "Of course, that might not work, but if there is some kind of demand for cash, then I can arrange a drop so we can trap his guy."

She stayed quiet a moment, probably giving that some thought. "That sounds dangerous."

It would be, but Egan wasn't going to put too much energy into working that out right now. "The note could have been placed with the body merely to let us know that the murder was connected to us. Maybe it was even meant to scare us."

"It worked," she admitted. "I'm scared." That grip on the cup got even tighter until her knuckles were white.

Egan touched her fingers to let her know to relax, but he quickly realized that touching Jordan under any circumstances just wasn't a good idea. That little brush of his skin on hers was enough to send the coil of heat through him again, and that was why he stepped back.

His phone rang, giving him a welcome reprieve.

At least it was welcome until he glanced at the screen and didn't recognize the number. His heartbeat kicked up a notch, and he put the call on speaker and hit the app to record it just in case this was from the would-be killer.

It wasn't.

"I'm Detective Martinez from San Antonio PD," the caller said when Egan answered and identified himself. "My lieutenant said you wanted us to keep you updated on Tori Judd."

"I did. Did you find her?"

"No. There's still no sign of her, and she hasn't checked in with her parents or the law office where she works. We're at her house right now, though. Her folks had a spare key, and they came over to let us in so we could have a look around." He paused. "And we might have found something."

Egan wanted to curse because he was betting that something wasn't good. Rather than speculate about how bad it could be, he just waited for the detective to continue.

"There doesn't seem to be signs of a struggle in her house," Martinez explained. "No busted locks or indications of forced entry, but there was a letter in the trash can next to her desk. That's why I'm calling. The letter mentions you, Sheriff McCall."

"I've never met Tori." That didn't mean she didn't know who he was, though. It was possible Tori had found out about Shanna, and if so, the newspaper articles about her murder had mentioned Egan. "Did Tori write the letter?"

"No. The return address says it's from the Gift of Life Foundation."

Jordan pulled in her breath. "That's a group for organ recipients. They can write letters to the families of the donors to thank them, and the families can write back through the Gift of Life. That way, the names and addresses of the donors' families and the recipients are kept secret."

"Well, it doesn't appear the person who wrote this letter kept his name a secret. It seems to be a reply to Tori's letter to thank him for the heart she got. It's short, only a couple of lines, but the language is pretty raw," Martinez added. "You want me to read it to you or would you rather I send you a photo of it?"

"Read it but leave out the language. I can fill in the blanks."

"All right. Here goes. 'Don't send me another letter to go on and on about how thankful you are for getting something you shouldn't have. I don't even want you alive when my precious girl is dead. As far as I'm concerned, you helped kill her. You, Jordan Gentry and Egan McCall.' The person who wrote the letter signed it Leeroy Sullivan. Does that name mean anything to you?"

Egan cursed, probably using some of the words that Martinez had omitted. "Yeah, and I'll get him in for questioning ASAP. But just in case the letter is a fake, I want it processed for prints."

"Sure. Will do."

"You said the letter was in the trash?" Egan pressed.

"Yes. It was a little hard to read because it had a

couple of cuts and gashes on the paper. You know, like maybe somebody had stabbed it with a knife."

Jordan made a soft sound. A quick intake of breath. And she looked pale again. Without letting go of his phone, he took hold of her arm and had her sit back down on the sofa.

"There's no knife nearby, though," the detective went on. "And she didn't report the letter to the cops even though it does sound threatening to me."

It did to Egan, as well. He didn't know Tori, but it was possible the woman ripped up the letter if it'd upset her. That was about the best angle Egan could come up with for this. The other angle was that Leeroy had found her address and gone there to take out his rage on an innocent woman who just happened to have his daughter's heart.

"If Tori turns up or if we find anything else, I'll give you a call," Martinez assured him before he ended the call.

Egan turned off the recorder function and was about to call Leeroy, but there was a knock at the door. A moment later, Thea opened it and stuck her head inside.

"There's someone here to see you," she said. But Thea wasn't looking at Egan. Her attention was on Jordan. "He's a cop. And he says he's got proof of who's trying to kill you."

Chapter Six

"A cop," Jordan repeated under her breath. She was about to ask his name, but it wasn't necessary because she heard the too-familiar voice in the squad room when he called out for her.

Christian.

Great. She wasn't anywhere near the right frame of mind to see him, but he certainly knew how to get her attention. *He says he's got proof of who's trying to kill you.* And maybe he did. But getting that so-called proof wouldn't be a pleasant experience. Maybe not a safe one, either.

Of course, Christian wasn't the only one who seemed unsafe at the moment. After hearing about the ripped-up letter in Tori's house, Leeroy was certainly a suspect. Then again, he'd never made his anger a secret, and perhaps someone had planted the letter to frame him. Maybe someone like Kirk or Christian.

"Jordan, you need to see me now," Christian demanded. "It's important." He sounded close. And he was. That was because he'd obviously followed Thea down the hall to the break room.

Thea stepped in front of Christian, blocking him from entering, and Egan moved in front of Jordan. Obviously, he considered Christian a threat because Egan put his hand over his gun.

Since Christian was a head taller than Thea, he had no trouble seeing Egan and her. He also made a sweeping glance around the break room, his gaze lingering for a moment on the covers on the sofa and then on her hair that was still damp from her shower. His expression changed just enough to let her know that he was filling in the blanks. However, he wasn't filling them in correctly because he seemed to believe that Egan and she had had sex.

"I wondered where you'd stayed the night," Christian grumbled, and he shifted back to Egan. "I guess you no longer believe the sheriff is trying to kill you if you spent the night with him."

No, she didn't think Egan was a would-be killer, but Christian's tone troubled her. It sounded as if he was mocking her for believing it in the first place.

"I guess you no longer believe that I made up the threat," she fired back. "After all, you told Deputy Morris that you had proof of who was trying to kill me."

"That's proof I'll want to see," Egan insisted.

Christian certainly didn't jump to agree with Egan's demand, and he looked as if he was having a debate with himself about that. However, he must have known if he truly did have evidence that he would have to share it with Egan. After all, the attack had not only happened in Egan's jurisdiction, but he'd also nearly been killed by the gunman.

"Fine," Christian spat out like profanity. "Let's go to your office where we can talk."

Now it was Egan's turn to hesitate, and he finally shook his head. "We'll use one of the interview rooms. No windows," he added to her under his breath.

Jordan watched Christian to see if he was unhappy about that, but he didn't have a reaction. He merely followed them into the hall. The other deputy, Ian, was there, and he had his hand over his holstered gun as if he expected some kind of trouble.

"You want me to stay with you?" Thea asked Egan. "To take notes or something?" What the deputy was probably asking was if her boss wanted some backup. It was a good offer because it was possible there was just as much threat inside the building as there was from a potential sniper at the window.

Egan shook his head. "Go ahead and call Court, though, and see if he has any updates. Also press to get those dental records."

Thea nodded and cast another uneasy glance at Christian before she went back in the direction of the squad room.

"Dental records," Christian repeated. "You're trying to confirm that Tori Judd is the dead woman."

Egan ignored that comment, probably because he didn't want to share any info about the case with Christian. "What evidence do you have?"

That tightened Christian's jaw a little. "We're on

the same side, Sheriff. I want Jordan to be safe just as much as you do."

She hoped that was true, but Egan certainly didn't look as if he believed it. He huffed and stared at Christian, obviously waiting for the cop to tell them what he'd learned.

Christian finally huffed, too, and took out a piece of paper from his pocket. If it was indeed evidence, it wasn't much because there was only a name written on the paper.

Leon Brunson.

Jordan repeated the name a couple of times, but it didn't mean anything to her. "Who is he?" she asked.

"A criminal informant. A good one, too. After I found out about the truck used in last night's attack, I started asking around."

Egan didn't ask how Christian had heard about the truck. He'd learned about it through police channels. "And?" Egan prompted when Christian didn't continue.

"Leon Brunson knew about a chop shop. One that also does custom builds from stolen auto parts. He said he was at the shop earlier in the week, and he saw a blue truck that the owners had just finished building. Don't bother calling about it," Christian added to Egan when he took out his phone. "The shop is no longer there. When I started asking questions, it picked up and moved."

Now Egan cursed. "Then, you shouldn't have been asking questions until I'd had a chance to check it out."

Christian's eyes narrowed. "Don't tell me how to do my job. I've been a cop just as long as you have, and I've had a lot of experience dealing with things like this. I knew I had a very narrow window of time to get any info from the shop."

"A window of time that you could have told me about," Egan argued.

Christian's glare only got worse. "Those men wouldn't have talked to some cowboy cop from a hick town."

Egan stared at him. "Apparently, they didn't talk to you, either, if they closed up shop."

Bingo. That really didn't help Christian's stare. "Do you want to hear what I learned from Leon or not?"

"I'm all ears." And there was plenty of sarcasm in Egan's voice.

"Leon said he was there when the buyer picked up the truck," Christian answered once he got his jaw unclenched. "He gave me a description of the guy, and it sounded familiar so I showed him two pictures. One of Leeroy Sullivan and the other of Kirk Paxton. He said it was Kirk."

Jordan pulled back her shoulders. "He was certain?"

"Certain enough."

She had no idea what that meant, especially since the info had come from a criminal informant. One Christian had almost certainly paid for the info. And it was also possible that someone else, maybe Leeroy, had perhaps hired the man to lie to Christian so that they in turn would believe that Kirk had been the one responsible for the attack.

"I'll have a Texas Ranger talk to Leon," Egan said, letting Christian know he wasn't just going to take his word for this. "And I'll have my deputy get Kirk in here for questioning." Egan did that by firing off a text to Thea.

"I want to be here when you interview Kirk," Christian insisted.

Egan shook his head. "If I learn anything that falls into your jurisdiction, I'll let you know." He paused for only a few seconds. "And now why don't you tell me your reason for visiting Leeroy Sullivan."

Yes, that was something she wanted to know, as well. "I'd especially like for you to explain why you told Leeroy that you thought I was crazy," Jordan added.

Christian didn't curse exactly, but that was what it looked as if he wanted to do. "Really? Now you're questioning my motive about that?" He grumbled something else under his breath that she didn't catch. "I saw Leeroy because I wanted to find out if he was connected to the deaths of those other two women, Breanna Culver and Cordell Minter. He didn't admit to anything, but I believe he could be a loose cannon."

Jordan believed that, too, but it didn't explain the part about Christian claiming she was crazy so she motioned for him to continue.

Christian took in a long breath before he started talking again. "It was obvious that Leeroy doesn't like you or Egan so I thought if I fed him something he wanted to hear, that he would open up. I wanted to make him believe we were of a like mind, and that in turn would get him to trust me. It didn't work, by the way. He just kept spouting his hatred for you two and his grief over losing his daughter." He paused. "I believe Leeroy could be a very dangerous man."

Again, Jordan thought that, too, but what they needed was something more than talk and a shredded letter.

"It wasn't your place to visit a person of interest in what could be three murders," Egan said to Christian. His tone had warning written all over it. "Why have you taken such a strong interest in this case?"

Christian kept his stare on Egan for a moment before he turned to Jordan. "You know why," he said to her. "I care for you. Maybe more than care," he added in a frustrated-sounding grumble. "And I know you don't feel the same, but that doesn't change how things are for me."

Jordan wasn't exactly shocked about Christian's feelings, but she hadn't expected him to spell them out like that. Especially not in front of Egan.

Egan looked at her, no doubt to see her reaction. She shook her head and aimed her answer at Christian. "I don't want you to have feelings for me. And I need you to back off of this investigation."

Christian looked as if she'd slapped him. "You're in danger, Jordan. I'm trying to stop someone from killing you."

"I'm well aware of that, but you're not helping me right now. I need you to do as Egan said and back off."

Christian sighed, put his hands on his hips and volleyed a few glances at both Egan and her. "Fine. But I'm a hundred percent sure you'll regret this."

Egan moved in front of her again. No doubt because that sounded like a threat. But Christian didn't add anything else. He gave them both a final glance and walked out. Jordan wished that meant she was seeing the last of him, but she wondered if Christian would indeed stop interfering in the investigation.

"You knew he was in love with you?" Egan asked. He stepped into the doorway and watched the man leave.

"Yes." But then Jordan had to shake her head. "I know that he claims to care for me."

That sent Egan's gaze shifting to her. "You think it's all an act?"

"I just don't know," she admitted. "We've spent a lot of time together going over those old cases. He's always been, well, attentive. And he's asked me out a few times. I wasn't interested," she added.

Egan opened his mouth as if to ask a question, but he seemed to change his mind about what he was going to say. Maybe he didn't want to hear her admit the reason she hadn't dated Christian was because of him. Because she still had feelings for Egan. It wasn't especially something Jordan wanted to admit to him, either, but she was afraid it was true.

"I've always had an uneasy feeling about Christian," she added. And it was the truth.

"Because of those case files." Egan made a sound of frustration, snatched up the piece of paper with Leon's name on it and headed back toward the break room.

Jordan followed him, and once he was there, he immediately picked up his laptop and opened the death penalty files that she had been reviewing for her job.

"You said there were two cases you were suspicious about," Egan reminded her. And those were the two that he pulled up onto the screen.

Egan began to read through them, but there was no need for Jordan to do that. She'd studied them in such depth that the details were all still fresh in her mind.

"As I told you, Christian was the arresting officer in both cases. They happened nearly two years apart, but both involved human trafficking that had resulted in the deaths of several women. One of the victims was just a teenager. Both were big-money operations, and the two men arrested were middlemen."

That obviously got Egan's attention because he looked up at her. "Were the bosses ever caught?"

She had to shake her head. "If they were, they weren't specifically connected to these two cases."

Egan stayed quiet a moment while he continued to read the files. "How were the two middlemen caught?"

"The cops were tipped off, and in both cases the

chain of evidence led directly to the two men who were arrested."

"Men who Christian arrested," he grumbled under his breath.

Obviously, Egan was suspicious. Jordan was, too. But there was something else that stood out about these two cases. "Both men arrested were on parole for other violations, and Shanna was their parole officer."

Egan's head whipped up, their eyes connecting, but he didn't say anything for several long moments. "What's the timing of the men's arrests and Shanna's murder?"

"The first arrest was two years before Shanna's death. The second one happened the same month."

A muscle tightened in Egan's jaw. "It could be a coincidence," he said.

And she prayed that was true. "I've looked for anything to indicate Shanna was murdered because of either of these two men, and I haven't made any connection."

"I'll search, too," Egan assured her. "In the meantime, I think it's a good idea to stay away from Christian."

His gaze locked with hers again, and even though Jordan had no intention of arguing about what he was saying, it seemed as if Egan was waiting for her to do just that. Or at least he was waiting for something anyway. And then it hit her. This could be about the attraction again. It definitely wasn't a good time for it while they were discussing Shanna and possible motives for not only her murder but also the attack against them.

Egan looked disgusted with himself, and Jordan figured he was about to put some distance between them. However, before he could move, his phone rang, and she saw Thea's name on the screen. Since he'd asked the deputy to get him any updates on the case, Egan answered it right away, and he put the call on speaker.

"I just got a call from one of the reserve deputies," Thea immediately said. "Dakota Tillman."

Jordan knew Dakota. He'd once worked full-time for Egan but was taking a break to finish his criminal justice degree.

"They're at Kirk's place now, and they need one of us to get out there." Thea paused. "They found something."

Chapter Seven

Egan figured whatever Dakota and the other reserve deputy had found, it had to be important, so he just waited for Thea to continue. He didn't have to wait long.

"Dakota found a .38 Smith & Wesson in the bottom of Kirk's dresser drawer," Thea explained. "It was wrapped in plastic and hidden under several layers of clothes. Dakota said he was pretty sure it had been recently fired, and there appear to be traces of blood on it."

Jordan obviously realized the importance of that because she pulled in a hard breath. Their still yet-to-be-identified Jane Doe had been killed with a .38.

"What did Kirk have to say about this?" Egan asked. Because he wanted to know how the man was going to try to explain the hidden gun.

"Kirk isn't at the house," Thea went on. "He's actually on his way here, but his live-in housekeeper is there, and she's putting up a fuss about the deputies taking the weapon."

"We have a search warrant," Egan reminded her,

though he was sure it wasn't necessary. Thea knew that, and the deputies had almost certainly shown the housekeeper the warrant when they entered the house.

"Yes, but she ran into the backyard with it, and she's threatening to throw it in the pool. She said that Kirk told her that the cops were trying to frame him and that she believes they planted the gun."

Well, hell. Jordan looked as if she wanted to curse the same words that Egan had just belted out.

"Call Court and tell him to go to the scene to assist you," Egan instructed. "I want the housekeeper arrested and that .38 taken to the lab ASAP." He would have preferred to go there himself, but it was too risky to take Jordan. Too risky to leave her at the station, as well.

"Kirk is on his way here," Jordan repeated when Egan had finished his call with Thea.

Yes, because Egan had wanted to question him about the chop shop allegation that Christian had made, but now he could ask Kirk about the gun, too. But he understood the concern he heard in Jordan's voice. Kirk was a hothead under normal circumstances, and his housekeeper had likely told him about the reserve deputies and the gun. That meant Kirk was going to be even more unpleasant than usual.

"You can wait here or in my office when I question him," Egan said.

She nodded, but that wasn't a look of agreement in her eyes. "If Kirk truly did try to kill us, I'd like to hear what he has to say. I won't compromise the interview," she quickly added. "I just want to listen."

Her nerves were already right there at the surface, and Egan knew that it wouldn't help her to hear what would almost certainly be another Kirk tirade, but he couldn't refuse. Because she was right. If Kirk was the one who was after them, then she might be able to pick up on something when Egan questioned him.

Egan's phone rang again, and he braced himself in case it was one of the reserve deputies calling to tell him that things had escalated in a bad way at Kirk's house. But it wasn't. However, the name that popped up on a screen was a familiar one. Harlan McKinney, the marshal who was setting up the safe house for Jordan. It certainly wasn't something Egan had forgotten about, but with everything else going on, he'd put it on the back burner.

"Sheriff McCall," Harlan greeted the moment Egan answered. Since this was likely about Jordan, he put the call on speaker. "I have a problem. I believe the location of the safe house might have been compromised."

That brought back the knot in Egan's stomach. "What happened?"

"Nothing yet, but it's possible someone hacked into the computer system. There's been some sort of irregular activity, and even though I don't know for sure, someone might have been able to get access to info on the safe house we were setting up for Jordan Gentry."

Egan heard the hitch in Jordan's breath and saw

the renewed fear in her eyes. "Who did this?" Her voice barely had any sound, but the marshal must have heard her anyway because he answered.

"I'm guessing you're Miss Gentry?" the marshal asked, and he didn't continue until Jordan had confirmed that she was. "I don't know who could have done the hacking, but trust me, if there's been a breach, I'll find out who's responsible. In the meantime, I don't want you anywhere near that safe house."

Egan didn't want her there, either, but that left him with a huge problem. He needed a place to take her where the would-be killer couldn't get to her.

"I can put in another request for a second safe house," McKinney went on, "but I'd rather not do that until I'm sure the problem has been fixed."

"I understand," Egan answered. "I'll make my own arrangements for Jordan." Though at the moment he wasn't sure what those would be.

"Just be careful," the marshal warned him. "If someone can hack our system, they can probably hack yours, too." And with that stomach-knotting reminder, he ended the call.

"I don't think Christian has hacking skills," Jordan immediately said. "What about Kirk or Leeroy?"

Egan had to shake his head. "If they're good at that sort of thing, they haven't spread that news around. But it's possible one of them hired a hacker. Christian could have done that, too."

A thin weary breath left her mouth. "In other words, this doesn't rule out any of our suspects."

No, and the not knowing was clearly taking a toll

on Jordan. Of course, the lack of sleep wasn't helping, either. It would have been too much for most people to handle, but he wasn't even sure that Jordan was in good health. And speaking of health, Jordan no longer looked steady.

"Are you okay?" he asked. "Do you need your meds?"

"It's not time for my next dose," she assured him.

"What about pain meds? Those stitches and your head are probably hurting."

"I'm fine."

She wasn't *fine*. Far from it, and he only hoped her stark expression was from the head injury and that it wasn't some symptom caused by the transplant. Egan took hold of her arm, intending to have her sit down on the sofa. But at the exact moment he touched her, Jordan looked up at him.

Definitely not good.

Because just like that, the old attraction returned, and now it was mixed with the other feelings he was having for her. The need to do his job and protect her.

"Yes," she said. "I'm sorry about this."

He knew exactly what she meant, but Egan didn't confirm it. Not with words anyway. However, he did do something pretty darn stupid. With his hand still clutching her wrist, he pulled her closer until she was in his arms.

She made another sound. Not a weary sigh this time. This was more of relief, and she seemed to melt against him. Worse, Egan felt himself melt a little, too. The memories came flooding back. Memories of the times she'd been his lover, and even though he tried to push those images away, he failed. The heat just washed over him until he thought about doing something stupid.

Like kissing her.

Even after all these years Egan thought he could remember the taste of her. The way she would feel if he pressed his mouth to hers.

"You'd regret it," he heard her whisper.

True. And Jordan would regret it as well, because they didn't just have memories of the attraction. There were those of Shanna's murder, and they would no doubt come flooding back if he opened this particular door with Jordan.

She was the one who moved away from him, stepping back until they were no longer touching. The corner of her mouth lifted into a smile. "At least we're not at each other's throats. That's progress."

No. It wasn't. Because it was easier for him to deal with the anger than with the grief. Or the heat. Thankfully, though, Egan didn't have to face either at the moment because he heard a familiar voice coming from the squad room.

Kirk.

Good. Even though he wasn't looking forward to dealing with the man, it would get his mind back on business. Besides, Kirk could maybe give them the answers they needed to blow this investigation wide open.

Egan gathered his breath and made his way to the squad room. As expected, Thea was there, and she was frisking the man. Something that obviously didn't please Kirk, but Egan didn't care. He didn't want an armed suspect in the building.

Like the other times that Egan had seen Kirk, he was dressed like a cowboy. A rich one. Which he was. As a cattle broker, Kirk made plenty of money, and from what Egan had heard, he spent plenty of it, too. He had a reputation for womanizing and throwing expensive parties. Oh, and hiring lawyers to help overturn his brother's conviction.

Ian had gotten up from his desk, and he seemed to be standing guard while Thea patted down Kirk. Good. With three lawmen and a former cop in the building, maybe Kirk would think twice before starting any trouble.

Kirk looked past her, his attention on Egan. "I just got off the phone with my housekeeper."

"I hope you told her to surrender that gun," Egan growled.

"I did, but you know that's a plant. It's not mine. One of your deputies put that gun in my house."

"I know no such thing. But the lab should be able to tell us something. For instance, if your prints are on the .38 and if the blood on it belongs to a woman who was murdered. A woman we've yet to identify."

"And if it is her blood, it proves nothing. The gun was planted."

Maybe. But Egan wasn't going to give him the benefit of the doubt just yet. He motioned for Kirk to follow him to the interview room, but the man didn't budge even when Thea moved away from him.

"My lawyer's on the way," Kirk snapped. "You're not starting an interrogation until she gets here."

Great. He'd lawyered up. Of course, that was probably a smart move, considering the gun found at his house, but it meant Egan was going to have to hold off on getting those answers.

Or not.

"I know what you're trying to do," Kirk continued, shifting his attention to Jordan. "You're trying to set me up to protect your cop friend."

"Christian?" she asked. And it was definitely a question. Jordan shook her head. "Why would I protect him?"

"Because you're best pals. Probably lovers, too. All of this is starting to get messy, and you don't want him behind bars."

She huffed, folded her arms over her chest. "What do you think Christian has done that would require me to cover for him by framing you?"

Kirk opened his mouth as if to answer, but Egan lifted his hand to stop him. While he wanted to hear what Kirk had to say about that, he needed to do something first. Egan read the man his rights. Since part of that included the mention of his attorney, Egan thought it might be a reminder for Kirk to shut up. But no. Kirk just kept on talking.

"I figure Christian's a dirty cop, just like you were. And like you are now." Kirk aimed a glare at Egan.

"I'll bite. How am I dirty?" Egan asked. "Because you can't possibly think I did anything to put your brother behind bars."

"No, but this is about the vendetta that Jordan and you are carrying on. You don't want me around because you think I might get someone to hear the truth—that Drew wasn't mentally stable the night he pulled the trigger. He should be in a hospital, not on death row."

"A jury didn't see it that way," Jordan pointed out. "I didn't see it that way, either."

"Yeah, you were a dirty cop who likely set him up. I figure you wanted Shanna out of the way so you could be with your lover-boy here, and you and Christian used my brother to take Shanna out of the picture."

The anger roared through Egan, and it took every ounce of willpower not to punch the guy. He reminded himself that Kirk almost certainly wanted him to throw a punch because it would then in turn compromise the investigation.

"Of course, your plan didn't work," Kirk continued. "Because Egan and you still aren't together. Maybe his guilty conscience got the best of him and he figured out you're bad news."

"Shanna was my friend," Jordan said, her words barely louder than a whisper. "I wouldn't have knowingly put her in the path of a killer."

Unlike Egan, she didn't seem to be having trouble with the anger that Kirk had just provoked. But her eyes shimmered as she fought back tears. Kirk certainly wasn't on the verge of tears, though. The man had a smug look on his face because he was well aware that he'd just hit a very raw nerve with Jordan.

Egan considered returning verbal fire by reminding Kirk that he had just spelled out his motive for why he would want Jordan and him dead. But it was best to keep that until the lawyer was present, and then Egan could fully question him about it.

Thea's phone dinged with a text message, and the moment she read it, she looked at Egan. "The deputies got the gun from the housekeeper. They're arresting her for obstruction of justice and sending the gun to the lab."

Good on both counts, but the news only made Kirk's eyes narrow even more. Then he cursed. "Leeroy," he ground out "He came to my house last night, and he could have planted the gun then."

Interesting. "Now you're saying it's Leeroy who was behind the attacks. Just a few seconds ago, you were blaming Jordan and me. It seems as if you're having trouble making up your mind."

Kirk made a sound of raw frustration. "I didn't say that Leeroy was a saint. He hates me because of my brother."

"And yet he paid you a visit," Egan pointed out.

Kirk suddenly got quiet, and for several moments Egan thought that maybe this would be the end of their little chat, but then Kirk shook his head. "He's never done that before, and that's why I should have known something was up. He said he wanted to talk to me about the women who'd been killed. The ones who got Shanna's organs."

Jordan and Egan exchanged a glance, and even though she didn't say anything, Egan knew that had caught her attention as much as it had his. Still, Egan didn't want to question him about it because it could be argued that Egan had continued an interrogation after Kirk had lawyered up.

"Leeroy must have planted the gun when he came to my house," Kirk added a moment later. "He asked to use the bathroom, and he could have done it then. It's definitely not mine. I don't own a .38."

"He doesn't have one registered to his name," Thea explained. "I checked."

Yeah, but that didn't mean Kirk hadn't bought it illegally. Of course, it was just as possible that Leeroy had indeed set him up. And if so, then Egan was going to have to untangle this mess to get to the truth.

"Why would Leeroy do something like this now?" Jordan asked Kirk, but she immediately waved off the question. Probably because she, too, remembered that asking questions wasn't a good idea without Kirk's lawyer present.

Kirk ignored her waving-off gesture, though, because he turned to her. However, he didn't jump into an answer. Instead, he glanced out the window when a car pulled to a stop in front of the building and a woman stepped out. "Maybe because of her." He tipped his head toward their visitor, who was now making her way to the door. "That's my lawyer, and Leeroy probably heard about it."

Of all the things that Egan had thought Kirk might say, that wasn't one of them. And this was something he could most certainly ask and not violate any protocols of an interrogation. "Who's your lawyer?"

Kirk gave them a blank look as if the answer were obvious. But he was giving that blank look to Jordan. "I thought you knew."

Jordan shook her head. "Knew what?"

The corner of Kirk's mouth lifted into a slight smile. Not a good smile, either. And he turned toward the woman who walked in. It wasn't someone Egan knew personally, but he certainly recognized her from the photos.

The same woman who'd received Shanna's heart.

Tori Judd.

Chapter Eight

Jordan heard the small gasp of surprise that she made, but the feelings inside her were far from small. The first thing she felt was relief.

The woman hadn't been murdered after all.

But the questions soon followed the relief. Yes, Tori was alive, but then who was their Jane Doe?

"Tori Judd?" Egan questioned.

The lawyer nodded, confirming that. Though Jordan hadn't needed confirmation. Tori looked exactly like her DMV photo. The same long auburn hair and intense blue eyes.

"We've been looking for you," Egan said to the woman. "Because we thought you were dead."

"Yes. I just heard about that on the drive over." She touched her fingers to her forehead. "I've been dealing with a migraine for the past two days so I turned off my phone and took enough meds to knock me out. I didn't see all the calls until I was on the way over here. I got in touch with my parents to let them know I was okay, but I figured I could wait and tell you in person."

Jordan glanced at Egan to see if he was buying this, but she couldn't tell. She certainly had her doubts. "You weren't at your house," Jordan told her.

"No," Tori answered at the same moment that Kirk said, "She was staying at my place."

Neither Tori nor Kirk added anything to that, but after seeing the look they gave each other, Jordan was even more confused. It was the sort of look that passed between lovers.

"You two are together," Egan grumbled. And Jordan heard the skepticism and disgust in his voice. "You do know that Kirk is trying to get Shanna's killer released from jail."

Tori nodded again. "I doubt this will make sense to you. Or you," she added to Jordan. "I know from everything I learned that you both loved Shanna, but Kirk isn't responsible for her death. He's just trying to be a good brother."

Egan mumbled some profanity. "There's a difference of opinion about that, but let's agree to disagree on that specific point. But there's something you can't dispute. Someone murdered a woman who looks like you. What do you know about that?"

"Nothing," Tori said without hesitation. "But from what Kirk told me, you believe he committed the crime. He didn't. He was at his house with me."

"While you were *knocked out* on pain meds," Egan fired back. He didn't need to spell out that she was either lying about the migraine or there was no way she could have known if Kirk had murdered the woman or not.

But who the heck was the woman?

"When the San Antonio cops searched your house, they found a letter," Jordan said. "One from the Gift of Life Foundation."

"It was shredded," Egan added.

Until Egan had said that last part, Tori had had no reaction. But she had a reaction now. Her eyes widened, and she no longer looked as confident or as steady as she had when she'd arrived.

"That letter upset me a lot so I ripped it up." Her voice was a little shaky, too. "Leeroy seemed, well, crazy, and I was afraid of him."

"That's why she's been staying with me," Kirk volunteered.

Strange since Kirk might have been the one who was following her. Of course, it was just as likely that it was Leeroy.

"Now you can see why I was so concerned when Leeroy showed up at my place," Kirk went on. "I thought he was there to find Tori, but he never even brought up her name."

Egan stayed quiet a moment as if processing that, and he turned back to Tori. "You do know that two recipients of Shanna's organs are dead?"

She nodded. "I figured that out after I got the letter from Leeroy." She tightened her grip on her purse. "Someone wants to kill me, don't they?"

"I believe someone does. Jordan, too." Egan motioned to the bandage on Jordan's head. "The person nearly succeeded with Jordan. My advice would be for you to go into protective custody."

A burst of air left Kirk's mouth. A laugh, sort of, but it wasn't from humor. "Why should Tori trust you to keep her safe?"

Egan gave him a look that could have frozen the desert, and he tapped his badge. "But I didn't say *my* protective custody. She can call the rangers or marshals."

"You really think that's necessary?" Kirk asked.

Egan lifted his shoulder. "Two other organ recipients are dead. So is another woman who's connected to this in some way. And someone tried to kill Jordan. I think that's a good indication that Tori might be in danger."

"But you're not positive the attack and those deaths actually had anything to do with Shanna," Kirk argued.

"No, but common sense tells me Tori should be taking precautions."

"I will," the lawyer assured him, interrupting whatever else it was that Kirk had been about to say.

At least Tori seemed to be understanding the seriousness of all of this. Well, maybe. It was just as possible that she was so mixed up with Kirk that he'd been able to convince her that she wasn't in any real danger.

"What about the other recipient, Irene Adair?" Tori asked.

"She's alive, as far as we know," Jordan answered.

"So, is Kirk free to go?" Tori asked after a crisp nod.

"No." And Egan didn't hesitate for even a second.

"In addition to the gun and the murdered woman, I need to ask him about a chop shop in San Antonio. I have a witness who identified him as being there."

Kirk lifted his shoulder. "The mechanic who comes to my house to service all my vehicles lives in San Antonio. But if he's got a connection to a chop shop, this is the first I'm hearing about it. Who's the witness?"

"Someone credible," Egan growled.

That could be an out-and-out lie, but at the moment, Jordan was going to accept it as truth. Apparently, so was Egan. Or at least he was going to let Kirk believe he believed it.

Kirk clearly didn't accept it, though. His mouth tightened. "I'm guessing this is just another thing you'll try to use to railroad me. Well, it won't work. I haven't done anything illegal."

Again, that could be a lie, but the bottom line was, the word of a criminal informant alone wasn't enough to hold Kirk. But maybe Egan could get something off the gun.

"Take Kirk and his lawyer to the interview room," Egan instructed Thea, and he waited for her to do that before he made a call to Court.

"I was so sure Tori had been killed," Jordan said while they waited for Court to answer.

"So was I," he assured her.

And the fact that Tori was alive meant the murder and the attack might not be connected to Shanna or Drew after all. Or maybe someone just wanted it to look that way.

"Our Jane Doe isn't Tori Judd," Egan told his brother the moment that Court came on the line. Egan also put the call on speaker.

"Yeah, I just found out and was about to call you. We got an ID on the dead woman, and her name is Lorena Lovett."

The name didn't mean anything to Jordan, and judging from Egan's head shake, he didn't recognize it, either.

"Lorena was a legal assistant at a firm in Austin," Court continued. "No priors. No red flags to indicate she was involved in anything illegal. She was reported missing two days ago, and her fiancé just viewed the body and made a positive ID." He paused. "How'd you know it wasn't Tori?"

"Because she's here at the sheriff's office," Egan answered. "And get this—she's Kirk's lawyer."

Court cursed. "How the hell did that happen?"

"I'm about to find out when I interview them."

"You really think that's a good idea? I mean, because of Shanna. Dealing with Kirk alone is bad enough, but he could use this to dredge up some rough memories for you."

Jordan didn't have to guess how Egan felt about this. The memories were already there, but Court was right. Kirk could use Tori to try to push some of Egan's hot buttons, and since his patience level was probably about as low as it could get, Egan could end up saying something that would hurt this investigation.

"By any chance did Lorena work for the same law firm as Tori?" Jordan asked Court.

"No," he answered. "Tori's law firm is in San Antonio."

That didn't mean the women hadn't known each other, though, or that maybe they'd once worked together, and that might be a critical connection. Perhaps this Lorena had learned something, maybe something about Kirk, and he had her killed for it.

"The gun we got from Kirk's housekeeper is on the way to the lab," Court went on a few seconds later. "It'll be a while before we hear anything on that, and I'm guessing Kirk will say it was planted."

"Yep," Egan verified. "He said it was Leeroy, that he went to Kirk's house last night."

Court made a sound of skepticism, and Jordan felt the same way. There was something unsettling about how all of this was playing out.

"I was about to call to get Leeroy in for questioning," Egan explained.

"I can do that. I'm on my way back now. My advice—why don't you go ahead and get Jordan out of there?"

"There was a problem with the safe house," Egan explained.

"I wasn't going to suggest you take her there anyway. Dad's alone at the ranch. He moved back into the main house."

Since their father, Warren, was a former sheriff, his being alone normally wouldn't have caused that kind of alarm in Court's voice. But Jordan knew that Warren was still recovering from a gunshot wound that he'd gotten several months earlier.

"Isn't your housekeeper, Ruby, with him?" Jordan asked. Ruby had been working for the McCalls for so long that she was practically family. And even though she was in her sixties now, Jordan knew the woman could handle a firearm.

"No. Dad insisted she take some time off."

Court didn't mention his mother, but Jordan knew that the woman was in a mental hospital. She'd had a breakdown after learning about her husband's long-time affair with Alma Lawton. But even though their parents and sister weren't at the ranch, that left one other person.

"What about your wife, Rayna?" she pressed.

"She's with Rachel, and I'll have her stay there until things settle down. If you don't want to stay at the main house with Dad, you can go to the guest-house. No one's using it now, and it has a security system."

She knew exactly what guesthouse he meant because Egan had taken her there a couple of times when they'd still been together. It wasn't ideal, but it was probably safer than a hotel.

Thea came back into the squad room, and she gave Egan a thumbs-up to indicate she had Kirk and Tori in the interview room.

"If Jordan and you go to the ranch, it'd solve two problems," Court pressed. "Dad would have someone close by to keep an eye on him. But it would also get Jordan out of the squad room and away from our suspects. I figure she's already had enough of all of them."

Jordan had indeed had *enough*, and she did want

to make sure Warren was okay, but if they stayed at the sheriff's office, she might be able to learn something from the interviews. Though the chances were slim. Tori probably wasn't going to let Kirk say anything stupid or incriminating. Leeroy might let his temper get the best of him and blurt out something, but even that was a long shot.

"You're sure you want to tackle questioning both Kirk and Leeroy?" Egan asked his brother.

"Definitely. This wouldn't be nearly as hard for me to do as it would be for you. And while I'm talking to our suspects," Court went on, "Jordan and you can work on following up with the lab on the gun and trying to figure out how Lorena Lovett fits into all of this."

Egan still wasn't jumping to agree to that. But then he looked at her, and she saw his expression change. That was probably because she made the mistake of touching the bandage on her shoulder. Yes, the stitches were hurting, and she hadn't wanted to take any pain meds because it would have clouded her mind. No way could she risk that now. Still, she was in pain, and there was no way to hide that from Egan.

"How far out are you?" Egan asked Court.

"Only about fifteen minutes. Go ahead and leave. I'll be there soon enough."

Egan ended the call, but even after everything Court had just said, there was still some hesitation in Egan's eyes.

"I could follow you to the ranch," Ian volunteered. "After you're there, I could come back here if there are enough hands to help you guard the house and the rest of the grounds."

The McCall Ranch was huge, which meant it would be next to impossible to keep watch of every part of it. Egan was no doubt considering that, but after one look at her again, he nodded and then turned to Thea.

"Call one of the reserve deputies to fill in here for a while," Egan said to Thea. "If they're all tied up, ask Griff to come in."

Griff was Thea's brother, Texas Ranger Griff Morris. He would also soon be marrying Egan's sister. Better yet, he'd once been a deputy in McCall Canyon so he'd know how to handle their suspects. If Egan wanted him to handle them, that was. Apparently, he did because he motioned toward the break room.

"Get your things, and we can leave now," Egan instructed her.

Jordan nodded and headed to the break room. The interview room door was closed, but she could hear Tori and Kirk having what appeared to be a heated conversation. Jordan couldn't hear specifically what they were saying, but Tori sounded agitated. She considered putting her ear to the door, but since that would be a violation of attorney-client privilege, Jordan walked away. If Kirk was charged with something, then she didn't want to be the reason he was set free.

By the time Jordan had gotten her things and made it back to the squad room, Egan was already at the front door, and he had the cruiser keys in his hand.

"Move fast," he told her.

She did, and when they were both in the cruiser, that was when she spotted Ian in the vehicle parked directly behind them. The moment Egan pulled out, so did the deputy.

"If you're going to the ranch because of me—" she started, but Jordan didn't get a chance to finish.

"It's not just you. My dad's been getting death threats."

She pulled in a quick breath. "Because of me?"

He quickly shook his head. "We're not sure who's sending them, but he's been getting them for a couple of months now. Ever since his shooting. The threats keep getting worse with each new one he gets."

Jordan was relieved that this wasn't on her shoulders, but it couldn't be pleasant for the McCalls for this to be happening. They were a family of cowboy cops, and it probably ate away at Egan that he hadn't been able to protect his father. Warren had nearly died from his gunshot wound, and apparently someone might try again to kill him.

"My dad takes too many chances," Egan went on. He took the turn off Main Street and onto the rural road that led to the ranch. "It's almost as if he's trying to draw out the person behind the threats. Maybe so he can put an end to them. That's why Court wanted someone to be with him."

Jordan understood that need for the threats to end, and if she thought that calling out her attacker would work, then she would do it. At least then Egan might not be in danger.

"I think Kirk and Tori were arguing in the interview room," she told him.

That caused Egan to give her a long glance. "Something's not right between those two. I hope Kirk hasn't been able to convince Tori to kill the other recipients as some kind of sick revenge for his brother."

Jordan hoped that, too, but even if Tori didn't know anything about the murder plot, she could still be in danger.

"Maybe we can find something you can use to arrest Kirk," Jordan threw out there. "If Christian's CI can identify Kirk in a lineup, will that be enough for you to make an arrest?"

Egan shook his head while he continued to keep watch around them. "Just because Kirk was at the chop shop, it doesn't mean he had them build that custom truck. What I need is someone who saw Kirk with a truck like that. Maybe someone like his housekeeper."

True. But since she'd tried to keep the gun from the reserve deputies, the woman seemed very loyal to Kirk. Loyal enough to lie about a truck that was a key part of a murder investigation.

"The reserve deputies arrested the housekeeper," Egan went on, "so Court can question her, too." He added a low groan at the end of that. Probably because he was frustrated about all of these interrogation duties landing on his brother.

"I'm sorry you have to babysit me," she mumbled.

Something flashed through his eyes. Possibly anger. But Egan's attention didn't stay on her for long.

That was because his phone dinged, the sound shooting through the cruiser, and when he took it from his pocket, Jordan saw his father's name on the screen. Egan immediately hit the answer button and put it on speaker.

"We have a problem," Warren McCall said the moment he was on the line. "One of the hands just spotted an armed intruder coming over the fence."

Chapter Nine

Egan felt the slam of adrenaline and fear. This was what Court and he had been worried about.

But now he had another worry. Jordan was with him, and while everything inside him was yelling for him to get to the ranch, he could be taking her right into the middle of another attack.

"Don't even think about driving me back to the sheriff's office," she insisted. "Your father could be in danger, and you need to get there ASAP."

It wasn't a surprise that Jordan wanted him to hurry to the ranch. No way would she expect him to put her safety ahead of his father's.

And Egan didn't intend to do that.

He wanted them both safe, but that might not happen if he did indeed turn around. That would mean either heading back to the sheriff's office while Ian proceeded to the ranch. That would leave Jordan and him open for an ambush. Plus, it would leave his father more vulnerable. Ian was a deputy, but Egan might need even more backup if this intruder went after Warren.

If this guy was after him, that was.

It was entirely possible that this person was after Jordan and him. Even though Egan had told only Ian, Thea and Court that he was going to the ranch, that didn't mean the person after them hadn't anticipated what might happen. This could be a would-be killer getting himself into position to make sure Jordan and he didn't survive another attack.

Egan didn't have time to debate this with himself. "I'll be at the ranch in about five minutes," he told his father, and after he ended the call, he handed Jordan his phone. "Call Ian and tell him what's going on. Court, too." He hit the accelerator and continued toward the ranch.

Jordan made the calls while she kept watch around them. She also threw open the glove compartment. "I want a gun just in case."

He hated the idea of her having to be in a gunfight, but there wasn't much about this situation that he liked. He reached over, his arm brushing against hers. Her muscles were already tense and knotted, something he completely understood. Egan took out the Glock that he kept as a reserve weapon and handed it to her.

"Thanks," she muttered just as his phone rang again with another call. It was his father's name on the screen again.

"Put it on speaker," Egan instructed. He wanted to hear what his dad had to say, but he also needed to keep his attention on the road. After all, the intruder could really be just a trap for another attack.

"Art lost sight of the armed man," his father immediately said.

Art Stovall was one of the top hands at the ranch and wouldn't hesitate to protect Warren. "Where did Art last see him?" Egan asked.

"The west fence near the guesthouse."

That caused Egan's chest to tighten. The guesthouse had come up during his conversation with Court. It might be just a coincidence that the intruder had gone there, but it was entirely possible that Kirk and/or Tori had heard him mention it. Even if they had, though, there probably hadn't been enough time to send someone to the ranch. Still, maybe they'd had the thug waiting nearby.

"I'm taking the final turn to the ranch now," Egan told his dad. "Stay inside and stay down."

His father made a sound to indicate that wasn't going to happen. And it wouldn't. Once a lawman, always a lawman, and there was no way his dad would just stand by and be attacked.

"I have Jordan with me," Egan added. "So when we get to the front of the house, open the door for us."

"Will do," his father assured him.

Egan motioned for Jordan to press the end-call button, and he used the remote to open the large cattle gate that stretched across the ranch road. The gate would stop someone from getting to them by vehicle, but it obviously hadn't stopped someone from coming across the fence. Egan closed it behind them as soon as Ian and they had made it through.

There were acres of pastures on each side of the

road, and the ground was flat enough that it would have made it impossible for someone to hide there. It was a different story, though, when they made it to the house. The place sprawled out, and there were plenty of trees and shrubs in addition to several trucks and outbuildings. An intruder would find plenty of places to hide if he'd made it this far.

Another ranch hand, Bennie Jensen, was on the side of the house near one of the trucks. He had a rifle, which meant he'd been alerted that there was a problem. Egan wanted the hand as backup, but he didn't want him out in the open like that.

"Take cover in the barn," Egan called out to Bennie the moment he came to a stop in front of the house and opened the cruiser door. Bennie could still keep watch from there. Well, hopefully he could. No matter where he was, there'd be blind spots.

Bennie moved, hurrying to the barn, and Egan intended to hurry as well when he got Jordan from the cruiser to the house. As he'd instructed his father, the front door opened.

"Don't come out on the porch," Egan warned his dad. "Stay back."

As soon as his father had done that, Egan drew his gun and motioned for Jordan to crawl across the seat and get out on his side of the vehicle. He waited until both Ian and she had their feet on the ground before he took hold of her arm to help her get up the eight steps that led up to the porch. They got up the first two when Egan heard a sound he didn't want to hear.

A gunshot.

This one blasted through the air and slammed into the steps right where they were.

Egan got another jolt of the adrenaline, and even though he had his gun ready, he didn't know where to shoot to return fire. Plus, his first priority had to be to make sure Ian, his father and Jordan were out of the line of fire.

"Dad, get down!" Egan shouted.

Egan hooked his arm around Jordan's waist and dragged her off the steps and into the yard. It was a risk because they could still be in the path of any other bullets, but it was even riskier to try to make it to the front door. They'd be easy targets while on the steps.

They landed, hard, in the middle of some shrubs, and Egan tried not to react to the sound of pain that Jordan made. It was possible, though, that she'd been hurt in the fall. Or maybe she'd even been shot. He didn't see any blood, but he couldn't take the time to check and make sure she was okay.

That was because another bullet came at them.

This one smashed into the stone step and sent a spray of debris through the air. Egan automatically pushed Jordan all the way to the ground and covered her body with his as best he could.

"You see the shooter?" Ian called out. The deputy had scrambled beneath the cruiser. Not an ideal position, but then the bullets hadn't gone in his direction.

Egan glanced around, trying to pinpoint the direction of the two shots. They had come from straight ahead. Not from the pasture, though. He thought these shots had come from the heavily treed area on the other side of the road past the cattle gate. If so, it meant the shooter was using a long-range rifle. However, it also meant something else.

They likely had two gunmen targeting them.

Art had said he'd seen the intruder near the guest-house. That was at the back of the main house. The guy probably wouldn't have been able to get past Bennie's or Warren's watchful eyes to make it to the front of the property. The second shooter could have already been in place by the time Jordan and he arrived at the ranch. The guy probably hadn't shot at them sooner because he would have known that the cruiser would be bullet resistant.

Egan passed Jordan his phone. "Text Ian and Dad. Tell them there could be a second gunman. Bennie needs to know that, too."

She gave a shaky nod and took his phone. That was when Egan got a better look at her. And this time he saw what he didn't want to see. Blood. The stitches on her shoulder had obviously come out, probably in the fall, and she was bleeding again. He didn't have time, though, to do anything about that because another shot came.

The third bullet was even closer than the other two had been, which told them that the shooter was adjusting his aim. He might just be able to hit them the next time. And that meant Egan had to do something now.

"Stay put," he told Jordan.

He was about to move, but she caught onto his arm. "You're not going out there," she insisted.

"I have to. I can pull the cruiser in front of you and use it to block the shots."

She was shaking her head harder with each word he said. "You could also be killed. Whoever's doing this will gun you down."

Maybe. But he was about to tell her the same could happen if they stayed put. At least this way he might be able to save her from being shot. It could save Ian and his father, too, since his dad would almost certainly try to return fire. In fact, he was probably already going after his rifle. Egan would have welcomed that if it hadn't meant his dad would have to come out in the open to try to stop this.

Egan gave Jordan another warning to stay down, but whether or not she would was anyone's guess. As a former cop, it was likely hard for her not to give him some kind of backup. Still, his efforts would be all for nothing if this snake managed to kill both of them.

More shots came. All of them coming way too close to the shrubs where Jordan and he were. When there was finally a lull, Egan took a deep breath and launched himself toward the cruiser. It wasn't far. Only about four yards, but it felt like miles.

Suddenly, there was no more lull in the shooting. The bullets came, smacking into the ground around him as he made a dive for the side of the cruiser. The fall hurt like the devil, but at least he was finally out of the line of fire.

Or not.

The next shot that came was from a different angle. Not on the side of the house where the barn and Bennie were. This one had come from the other side closer to Ian. Egan threw open the cruiser door just as another bullet smacked into it.

Egan looked around, trying to pinpoint this second gunman, and he saw the guy peering around the corner of the house. Since he was positive this wasn't one of the hands, Egan sent a shot his way. So did Ian. And when the guy ducked back behind cover, that gave Egan his chance to scramble into the cruiser.

The moment he was behind the wheel, Egan started the engine and pulled it in front of Jordan. At least now she was semiprotected since the porch steps would block any shots coming from the second gunman. However, that didn't mean the danger was over. The gunman in the trees must have gotten riled at Egan moving the cruiser because the shots started to come nonstop. But they were no longer going at Jordan and him.

These were going into the house.

That was when Egan saw his father in the doorway.

"Get down!" Egan shouted out to him.

Warren did drop to the floor, but Egan wasn't sure if he'd done that because of his order or if because he'd been shot.

Enough of this. With the cruiser door still open, Egan turned in the direction of the second gunman, and the moment the guy leaned out from cover, Egan fired. Not once but twice. And he put two bullets in the man's chest. He dropped, too, but Egan hoped the guy wasn't dead, just out of commission. He wanted this clown alive so he could tell them who'd put him up to doing this.

More shots cracked through the air, and it took Egan a moment to realize they weren't all coming from the first gunman. These were coming from the barn area, and for several heart-stopping moments, he thought there might be a third attacker in all of this.

But it was only Bennie.

The ranch hand had a rifle and was returning fire, his barrage of shots going in the direction of the first gunman. Since Egan didn't have a rifle, he couldn't help with that, but he could do more to protect Jordan now that the second gunman was down. He pulled even closer to her, moved to the passenger's seat and motioned for her to get in the cruiser.

She didn't waste a second doing that, and Jordan immediately took aim at the downed gunman by the side of the house. Good. With her keeping an eye on him, it freed up Egan to figure out what to do about the first shooter. He didn't want to go after him in the cruiser since it would mean taking Jordan closer to the gunfire. Too many things could go wrong with that.

Bennie continued to shoot, causing the gunman to shift his fire toward the hand. Egan hoped like the devil that Bennie got down because this guy wasn't stopping. He was either reloading very quickly or he'd brought multiple weapons with him and was trading out as soon as one was out of ammo.

There were more shots, and these caused Egan to curse. Something his father likely wanted to do as well since he was standing again and firing at the thug who was trying to kill them. Just as Egan feared, that caused the thug to turn his shots on Warren.

Hell.

Egan watched as the bullet sliced across his father's arm. It wasn't a deadly shot, but the next one could easily be. That didn't cause his father to get down, though. He kept pulling the trigger. So did Bennie.

Until finally the shooting stopped.

Egan couldn't tell if one of them had managed to take out the first gunman, but as the seconds crawled by with the silence, he figured the guy was either dead or making a run for it. He didn't mind the first possibility, but he didn't want this snake getting away. He wanted him to answer for what he'd just done.

While he kept watch around them, Egan sent Court a text to warn him that he might cross paths with this would-be killer and to have him get an ambulance out to the ranch for their dad. He was about to call Ian to tell him to head to the end of the ranch road so he could try to spot the gunman, but the movement from the corner of his eye stopped him.

"The gunman's alive," Jordan said on a rise of breath.

The gunman lifted himself up just enough, and he fired a shot right at them.

Chapter Ten

Jordan tried to keep her breathing level. She also tried not to wince in pain, but it hurt when the medic restitched her shoulder. She figured it was going to hurt a lot more when the numbing spray wore off, but that was minor in the grand scheme of things.

She'd killed a man today.

Since she'd once been a cop, Jordan had always known that doing something like that was a possibility, but still it caused her to feel raw and bruised. It didn't matter that the man she'd killed was trying to murder them. She had shot him to keep Egan, Ian, Warren, Bennie and herself alive, but it would take a while for her to feel like she'd done the right thing. Especially since a dead man couldn't give them answers.

Neither could his partner, who was still at large.

Ian had gone after him. So had Court. But they'd both come up empty. Whoever had fired the shots from those trees was long gone. Of course, that didn't mean he or she wouldn't be back to have another attempt at killing them.

The medic finished, moving to the side so he could

gather up his things, and she was finally able to see Egan. He was pacing in the foyer while talking on his phone. Even though she was in the adjacent family room, she couldn't hear what he was saying. However, she could tell from his body language that he was agitated.

She turned to the other side of the room when a second medic was finishing up with Warren. He, too, was getting stitches. The bullet had grazed him, but there was an angry-looking gash on his arm. It wasn't life-threatening, but since he hadn't fully recovered from his other attack, this might set him back.

Court was next to his father, but when he saw her looking at them, he stepped away and went to her once the medic had left. "I would ask if you're okay, but I know you're not. You need a drink, meds or something?"

Jordan hadn't meant for it to happen, but at the exact moment Court was asking his question, her gaze drifted to Egan. And Court noticed, too, because the corner of his mouth lifted for a second.

"Yeah, my big brother might be a temporary fix for what you're feeling," he mumbled. Then, he sighed and scrubbed his hand over his face. "Not sure that he'd let himself get too close to you, though."

No. He wouldn't. In fact, Egan was probably cursing himself for feeling so protective of her. Those protective feelings could lead to something more. Something that he definitely wouldn't want. Jordan tried to lie to herself and say she didn't want it, either. But it was just that. A lie.

She did want Egan.

And she wasn't certain it was solely because of the spent adrenaline and tangled nerves. It had felt good earlier when he'd taken her into his arms, and she figured it would feel just as good or better now.

Jordan turned back to Court, forcing her thoughts off Egan. It wasn't the time for them, and besides, they had plenty more to discuss. Jordan started with the easy subject first.

"How's your father?" she asked.

"Not as tough as he's trying to appear to be." Court glanced back at Warren. "He's shaken up. Riled, too, that the other gunman got away."

Jordan felt the same way. Here, they'd nearly been killed again, and they still weren't any closer to figuring out who was behind this. "We won't be staying here, will we?"

Court didn't hesitate. "No. Some of the windows have been shot out, and that might have compromised the security system. Plus, we know now that a sniper can take shots at the house. I'm taking Dad to Rachel and Griff's place in town. Egan and you will go back to the sheriff's office for a little while. Just until I can finish up the interviews with Kirk and Leeroy."

With everything else going on, Jordan had forgotten about the interviews, and they were more important now than ever. Of course, she didn't expect either of the men to confess to hiring those gunmen or killing anyone, but they might slip and say something incriminating.

"Where will Egan and I go after the sheriff's office?" she pressed.

"Egan's working that out now." Court blew out a weary breath. "There's a lot that has to be worked out. We need an ID on the dead guy to see if that leads us to the person behind this. Also, a CSI team needs to process the whole area around the house and in those trees. The shooters might have left some kind of evidence behind."

That would be a good break if they had indeed done that, but Jordan wasn't counting on it. If the shooters had been pros, then they would likely have been careful about that sort of thing.

Egan finished his call and walked into the family room, glancing first at his father before making his way to her. His expression wasn't exactly pleasant, but it got even worse when he looked at the fresh bandage.

"Sorry about that," he grumbled. "I did that to you when I pushed you off the step."

"Yes, so I wouldn't be shot. Thank you. I'd rather have the stitches than a bullet in me."

That caused Court to smile a little, but when Egan saw his brother's expression, Court's smile faded, and he went back across the room to his father. When Egan's attention came back to her, their gazes connected, and she saw the stripped-down emotions there that were no doubt mirrored in her own eyes.

Since he looked ready to berate himself about allowing this attack to happen, Jordan decided to stop it with a question. An important one. "How are Ian and Bennie?" she asked. She got to her feet and tried to look a lot stronger than she felt.

"Neither was hurt."

That was good, but she figured both men would be having nightmares about this for a long time. Especially Bennie. Ian was a cop and had been trained for situations like this, but Bennie probably hadn't expected his ranch hand duties to include a shootout with hired guns.

"I'll go ahead and take Dad to Griff's," Court called out to them. "I'm guessing Jordan, Ian and you will be leaving shortly?"

Egan nodded. "After Ian finishes checking the cruisers to make sure there was no damage."

So, maybe not long at all. Jordan knew it wasn't safe to stay put, but they could also be attacked again on the road.

"I'm pretty sure I know the answer to this," Egan said, "but do you want me to take you to the hospital? The medic took care of those stitches, but—"

"No hospital. There's no reason for me to see a doctor." She hoped.

He gave her a suit-yourself nod and mumbled a "be safe" to Court and his father when they went out of the house and to the cruiser.

"Will they be okay?" Jordan asked. She followed him to the window where he watched his brother and father drive away.

Egan nodded. "Several of the hands are following them into town. Everyone will be on the lookout for that gunman who got away."

And maybe the gunman was done for the day so that Warren could get to safety. The man had been through enough. Of course, Egan and she fell into that "enough" category, too.

"This means we might end up staying in the break room again at the sheriff's office," he added a moment later.

She'd suspected as much, and while it was far from ideal, at least there'd be immediate backup around if something went wrong. It also meant, though, that Egan and she would be sharing close quarters again and therefore wouldn't get much sleep. But the close quarters wouldn't just fuel the lack of sleep. It wouldn't help the attraction, either.

Jordan looked at him, knowing it was a mistake. Because there was no way she could conceal the worry, the pain or anything else. They had just survived a horrible ordeal, and the danger might not even be over.

Egan gave a heavy sigh, reached out and pulled her into his arms. The relief was instant. With just that simple gesture, it felt as if he took some of the weariness from her body. It might have stayed as simple as relief, too, if Egan hadn't looked down at her. He growled out some profanity, but she didn't have to ask why he'd done that. That was because she saw the kiss coming before it happened.

She even felt it.

The memories of his other kisses were still plenty clear enough, but she still got a jolt when his mouth touched hers. And the heat roared through her. Jordan felt herself moving right into that kiss and closer to him. Until his chest was against her breasts. He deepened the kiss, but the sound he made wasn't one of pleasure. Egan was already regretting that he was doing this, but like her, he wasn't able to stop.

"Damn you," he whispered against her mouth.

That would have caused most women to move back, but she was positive he wasn't cursing her but rather himself. His frustration came out in the kiss, too. Almost an angry kiss. In fact, coming from any other man that was exactly what it would have been, but this was Egan. The attraction cut through anger and everything else.

For those few scalding seconds, Jordan forgot all about the attack, their past and the danger. Heck, she forgot how to think or breathe. She could only stand there and let the kiss rage on. It wasn't Egan or her who ended it. It was the sound of his phone. That must have jolted him back to reality because he finally pulled away from her.

When he took out his phone, she saw Thea's name on the screen. Since this could be important, he answered it right away and put it on speaker.

"Sorry to bother you," Thea said, "but Leeroy's yammering on about having waited around here long enough. You want me to reschedule the interview?"

"Are Tori and Kirk still there?" he asked. His breathing was still a little rushed just as hers was.

"Yes, but they're whining, too. I can reschedule them, as well."

Egan's forehead bunched up while he obviously

gave that some thought. "Court will be there soon. He can talk to Tori and Kirk. Reschedule Leeroy, but put him on the phone first. I want to ask him a question."

"You're sure you're up to that after just getting shot at?" Thea pressed.

"No, I'm not sure, but put him on the phone anyway." Egan glanced out at Ian again and then motioned for her to move to the center of the room with him. Away from the windows. A reminder that the gunman could return at any moment.

A few seconds crawled by, but Leeroy finally came onto the line. "You'd better have a damn good reason for keeping me waiting," Leeroy immediately snapped. Maybe the man hadn't heard about the attack at the ranch, but it was just as likely that he didn't care. He hated Egan and her, and he wouldn't cut them any slack simply because someone had tried to kill them.

Egan didn't even respond to that. "Tell me why you visited Kirk," Egan demanded.

"You asked me that last night. Am I gonna have to explain every move I make to you now?"

"You do when you might have committed a crime." Egan huffed. "Look, my patience meter is at zero right now so either answer the question, or I'll have Thea arrest you. Why did you go to Kirk's house?"

It was hard to miss the profanity that Leeroy spat out. "Because I'm going to file a wrongful death suit against Jordan and you, and I thought I could count on Kirk as an ally."

Egan pulled back his shoulders. "A lawsuit?"

"Yeah because the two of you are partly responsible for Shanna's murder. I want both of you to pay for that."

Jordan could only sigh. Leeroy was clearly hurting over losing a child, and he apparently thought her killer's conviction wasn't enough justice. It wasn't. But nothing the man could do was going to bring Shanna back.

"So, let me get this straight," Egan said. "You thought Kirk would help you with a lawsuit. Why exactly would he do that?"

"Because he doesn't think you two did all you could to help or stop his brother. I agree."

Of course, Kirk and Leeroy would believe that, but judging from Egan's disgusted expression, he wasn't buying this. After all, Kirk had thought Leeroy was there to find Tori. It was possible that Leeroy had concocted the story about a possible lawsuit to cover for the fact that he was indeed looking for Tori.

"Are you sure you didn't go to Kirk's house to plant a gun?" Egan snapped. "A gun that maybe you used to kill a woman?"

"No way in hell," Leeroy practically shouted. "Is that what the weasel Kirk said I did?"

Apparently, Leeroy wasn't feeling so good now about his possible alliance with the brother of his daughter's killer.

"I'm saying it," Egan clarified, and he sounded very much like the formidable sheriff that he was. "The timing of your visit is suspicious. You show up at Kirk's house and only an hour later, my deputies find a gun there."

"A gun they must have planted." Leeroy grumbled something else she didn't catch. "Was it really used to kill that woman?"

"I don't know. It's at the lab now for testing. Is there a chance your prints or DNA will be on it?" Egan demanded.

"None. Well, unless someone stole a gun from my place and planted it at Kirk's. What kind of gun was it?"

"What kind of guns do you own?" Egan fired back. "And remember, I can check to see if you're lying."

"There's no reason for me to lie about that. I own a couple of hunting rifles, a shotgun and two handguns. One is a Glock 43, and the other is a .38 Smith & Wesson."

Bingo. The gun found at Kirk's was a .38 Smith & Wesson, and the dead woman had been killed with a .38. But why would Leeroy have killed her? The woman wasn't even one of Shanna's organ recipients.

Maybe it had been a case of mistaken identity. If Leeroy had been targeting Tori, he could have accidentally kidnapped Lorena by mistake. But if he had planned something like that, why would he have used his own gun? Maybe he'd simply messed up and then tried to cover his tracks by planting the gun at Kirk's.

"How much longer am I going to have to wait around here for you to show up?" Leeroy snarled.

"Maybe a long time. I'm not sure when I'll be in my office." Egan had probably told Leeroy that since

he didn't want him to know that they would be traveling there soon. If Leeroy was behind the attacks,
then it was best not to let him know their plans so he
could send that sniper after them again.

"You expect me to just keep waiting for you?"
Leeroy howled. "I've wasted enough time with your
witch-hunt accusations."

"Yes, you're going to wait. My advice? Call a lawyer because you're going to need one if that gun in
question turns out to be yours."

Egan didn't give Leeroy a chance to argue with
that—something the man would have almost certainly done. Egan just ended the call.

"You think Leeroy will try to leave?" she asked.

"I hope so because then Thea can arrest him.
That'll get him off the streets while we try to work
out if he's behind the attacks."

True. But just because Leeroy was behind bars, it
wouldn't mean the sniper couldn't come after them
again. If Leeroy had hired the gunmen, then he could
hire others even if he happened to be in jail.

"Ian's ready," Egan told her, and he looked at her
as if he wanted to say more. Maybe remind her to be
careful when she went outside. If so, it was unnecessary. Jordan knew they were still in danger.

They started toward the front door when Egan's
phone rang, and she saw Court's name on the screen.
Egan answered it right away, and as he'd done with
his other calls, he put it on speaker.

"Please tell me the gunman didn't go after you," Egan immediately said to his brother.

"No. But it looks as if he went after someone." Court paused, then cursed. "We have another dead body."

Chapter Eleven

Egan still had enough adrenaline left over from the attack, but hearing his brother's words gave him a jolt of even more. Jordan must have felt the same thing because the color drained from her face, and she dropped down into the chair next to her.

"Who was killed?" Egan asked Court.

"I can't tell yet. But it's a woman, and she was obviously murdered. It's pretty…messy."

So, there'd been blood and lots of it.

"The victim is a woman, and it appears she was killed at point-blank range with gunshot wounds to the head—just like our other victim. The body was on the road not far before the turn into town," Court added.

That was fairly close to where Lorena's body had been dumped. That meant the escaped sniper could have tossed her out there after he'd fled from the ranch. Or maybe there was a third hired thug who'd done the job.

One thing was certain, Egan knew that Leeroy or Kirk hadn't personally dumped the body because they'd been at the sheriff's office not only during the attack but in the time following it. If either of them had left the building, Thea would have told him about it.

That left Christian. The cop certainly hadn't been under Thea's watchful eye so he could have been the actual sniper. As a cop, he certainly would have had the firearm skill to pull off an attack like that.

"Could the body be Irene Adair?" Jordan's voice was so hoarse that Egan had to repeat the question to Court.

"Possibly. She's the woman who got one of Shanna's organs, right?"

"Yeah," Egan verified. "I don't have a picture of her, but her file is on my work computer. There's contact info in there for her and her family."

"I'll check," Court assured him. "I'm waiting with the body until the medical examiner, CSIs and a reserve deputy arrive. They were on their way out to you, but I think they need to process this scene first since it's closed down the road."

Egan agreed. It wasn't pleasant having a dead guy on the ranch, but the body on the road might give them more clues about the attacks than a hired gun would. Of course, he wanted answers from both bodies and both scenes. Maybe, just maybe, he'd get them, too.

"Is Dad with you?" Egan asked.

"No. The hands are dropping him off now at Griff's. They'll head back here to wait with me once they're done with that."

Good. Even though Court didn't seem to be the target of this sick piece of work who was behind these attacks, Egan didn't want his brother out there alone where he could be an easy target. Besides, their attacker could use Court to try to get to Jordan and him.

"I'm thinking it's not a good idea for you to have Jordan out on the road right now," Court added.

Egan was thinking the same thing. The body could have been left there as a way to draw them out into the open. As the sheriff, he wanted to see the crime scene firsthand, but that would be way too risky. Of course, there wasn't exactly a safe place for him to take Jordan to make sure the sniper didn't get to her again.

"You can use my place," Court said, no doubt knowing what was on Egan's mind. "Or the guesthouse or the fishing cabin."

Court's house and the cabin were at the back of the property. The guesthouse was much closer, which would cut down on the risk of Jordan being outside any longer than necessary. Still, there was a problem. Jordan and he had been lovers there, and he was sure every room would bring back memories. One look at Jordan, and he knew she'd be remembering the same thing. That was better, though, than having her stay in the main house with the shot-up windows.

"The guesthouse," Egan finally answered. "Once we're there, I'll have some of the hands help guard the place so I can send Ian back to work."

"You can keep him there if you want," Court suggested.

It was tempting, but the sheriff's office was already short of help because of the first murder investigation and the attacks. Now, with a second murder, a dead gunman and missing sniper, Court would need all the help he could get. No way could Egan justify tying up a deputy—even if that was what he wanted to do.

Twice now someone had come close to killing Jordan. Too close. And even though the hands were good with weapons, they weren't cops. Plus, the ranch was a big place, and it would be fairly easy for someone to sneak in on foot. The dead gunman outside the house was proof of that. Despite all of that, Egan was running out of options, and the guesthouse was the safest solution right now.

"Is it okay if I call Thea right now and have her reschedule Kirk's and Leeroy's interviews?" Court asked.

"Yes, do that." With everything going on, it was possible that Thea could end up manning the office alone, and Egan didn't want her there by herself with not one but two of their suspects. "Also have Thea remind Tori that she could be in danger and that she needs to be careful when she leaves."

"I will. And I'll call you once the medical examiner and reserve deputy are here to take over the crime scene," Court added. "It's possible the dead woman has an ID on her. She has a wallet sticking out of her pocket, but I don't want to touch it until the CSIs have had a look at it."

"If it's Irene, she'll have a scar on her belly from the transplant surgery," Jordan said, getting to her feet.

"I can't see her stomach. She's wearing jeans, but she has a lot of stab wounds on her torso."

Again, like their other victim. It ate away at him that this monster was doing this to innocent women. It was obviously having the same effect on Jordan because she shuddered and closed her eyes for a moment.

Even though Egan knew he should keep his hands off her, it was hard to do with that fear in her eyes. Not just fear for herself, either, but because this snake might include him and others in the killings. Egan slipped his arm around her, pulled her to him and brushed a kiss on the top of her head. It wasn't nearly as intimate as the other kiss had been, but it still reminded him that every time he got close to her like this, he was playing with fire.

And losing focus.

The first one might land them in bed, but the second one could get them killed, and that was why he eased back from her.

"We should go to the guesthouse," he said. He grabbed his laptop and the bag of supplies he'd gathered, and he got Jordan moving toward the door.

There were signs of the attack all around them. His father's blood in the doorway. The bits and pieces of wood that the bullets had torn from the door frame. There was broken glass on the porch. Of course, the worst sign was the dead gunman, and Jordan gave the guy more than a lingering glance when Egan was getting her into the back seat of the cruiser.

"You did what you had to do," Egan assured her.

He knew the assurance wouldn't mean much, but he had no idea what else to say. He'd killed someone once in the line of duty, and it wasn't something you forget. Jordan would carry this with her for the rest of her life, and she was already carrying too much baggage from Shanna's death. Now she was probably blaming herself for the two dead women, too. Egan got confirmation of that when he saw the tears shimmering in her eyes.

It was blurring more of those boundaries between them, but Egan still slipped his arm around her. As she'd done in the house, Jordan settled against him, reminding him of just how stupid that kiss had been. Because everything no longer felt like old times between them. It felt just as it had years ago when they'd first felt the attraction for each other.

Yeah, definitely a distraction.

Thankfully, it was a very short drive to the guesthouse. In fact, they could have easily walked if this had been a normal situation. It wasn't. But Egan used the couple of minutes to fill Ian in on the plan for him to return to the sheriff's office. Egan also texted Art, their ranch hand, to let him know that there would need to be someone watching not only the guesthouse but also the road that led to the ranch. Egan didn't want any surprise visitors, though if the sniper returned, he likely wouldn't use the road but would rather sneak onto the grounds.

When Ian pulled to a stop directly in front of the guesthouse, Egan got out first so he could unlock the front door and have a look around. It didn't take long since it was basically a living room-kitchen combo area, a bedroom and bathroom. Once he was certain that no one was lurking inside, he went back to the cruiser to hurry Jordan inside. He didn't waste any time locking the door and setting the security system.

"The windows are wired, too," he let her know. He hoped that would cause some of the tension to leave her face. It didn't, though.

Jordan stood in the living room and glanced around before her attention came back to him. She didn't say anything, but he figured she had noticed that the place hadn't changed that much since they'd last been here. His mom had had it redecorated a little with some fresh paint and a new sofa, but that was it. Once she went into the bedroom, she would see that it was the same, too.

"There should be bottled water in the fridge if you're thirsty," Egan explained. "There's also soup and stuff in the pantry, but I can have someone bring us in something to eat. There's plenty of food in the main house."

"Thanks. Maybe later I'll be hungry."

Egan wasn't counting on that. Her stomach was probably turning the same way his was. Still, she would have to eat something soon.

He went to the window to check and see if Ian had already driven away. He had. But Egan also saw two hands drive up in a truck. Maybe they wouldn't have to stand guard for long, but he wanted them there at least until the deputies showed up with the medical examiner and the CSIs. Considering they were just now getting to the other body, though, that might be at least several hours.

"Maybe you should try to get some rest," Egan added.

She nodded, scrubbed her hands along the sides of her jeans. In addition to the fatigue and weariness, Jordan's nerves were showing. Maybe because of the leftover adrenaline from the attack. Or maybe just because of him. Egan was certainly feeling some nerves, too.

Jordan started for the sofa, but before she even made it there, her phone rang. She huffed when she looked at the screen and then showed him the name of the caller.

Christian.

"I can talk to him if you like," Egan offered.

"Thanks, but I can do it." She pressed the answer button, put it on speaker and then laid her phone on the coffee table as she sank down onto the sofa.

"Jordan, are you okay?" Christian immediately asked. "I just heard about the attack at the ranch."

"Who told you?" Jordan fired back.

He didn't jump to answer that, maybe because Jordan's tone had been so sharp. "A fellow cop. He has a friend in the medical examiner's office. Did you really have to kill a gunman?"

"Yes. What did your cop friend tell you about that?" Again, her tone wasn't exactly friendly.

That was probably why Christian muttered some profanity. "I can tell that Egan's turned you against me."

Blowing out a heavy breath, Jordan groaned and

leaned the back of her head against the sofa. "Was there a reason you're calling? Because I'm tired, and I don't want to have another argument with you."

"Yes, there's a reason," Christian practically growled. "The criminal informant who told me about Kirk being at the chop shop is missing. He was supposed to meet me so I could pay him for some information he'd given me, but he didn't show. That's definitely not like him. When money's involved, he doesn't miss our meetings."

"You think someone silenced him?" Egan asked.

Judging from the huff Christian made, he hadn't known the call was on speaker and that Egan was listening. "Yes, that's exactly what I think, and this is on your shoulders. You should have found and arrested the person responsible for these attacks. If you'd done your job, Jordan wouldn't be in danger and my CI wouldn't be missing."

Egan agreed, but he hadn't failed at finding the person from lack of trying. And he would continue to try. "Let me know if your CI turns up," Egan insisted.

Since that definitely sounded like a goodbye, Egan expected Christian to end the call. He didn't.

"I think someone's been following me," Christian said after a short pause. "I just want to make sure it's not one of your deputies."

"It's not." Now it was Egan's turn to pause. He wasn't sure that Christian was telling the truth, but if he was innocent, then it was entirely possible that the killer had the cop in his sights.

"Then I'll have to watch my back," Christian grumbled, and he ended the call.

Jordan immediately looked up at Egan. "Christian could have said that to make himself seem innocent."

Egan nodded. "And that's why I want to keep digging in the cold cases you've been researching." He brought his laptop to her. "If you could access the file, I can work on that while you get some rest."

Jordan shook her head but then winced a little when her shoulder moved, as well. She was no doubt still in pain from the fresh stitches. "We can work on them together."

Since Egan knew the pain would only get worse, he went to the medicine cabinet in the bathroom and came back with some over-the-counter stuff. "It won't make you drowsy," he reminded her, and he gave her a bottle of water so she could take two of the pills.

"Thanks." She didn't look at him when he sat next to her. And Egan knew why. Even with the interference from the pain, the leftover heat from that kiss was still zinging between them, and it was best not to tempt fate by kissing again.

She opened the files and went to the two cases that she had already pointed out to him when they'd been at the sheriff's office. Egan moved the computer to his lap so he could have a closer look. Not at the files themselves. But rather at Jordan's notes.

"You've been suspicious of Christian for a couple of weeks now," he pointed out.

"Yes. I keep going back to the theory that he could have been, or still could be, running a human traf-

ficking ring." She paused. "Since Shanna was the parole officer for both men associated with this case, I
wonder if one of them mentioned something to her
about that."

"You mean something that would have incrimi-
nated Christian as their boss," Egan finished for her.

She nodded, and now she looked at him. But it
wasn't heat and attraction he saw in her eyes now.
It was a boatload of concern. "If so, Christian could
have wanted to silence her by setting up Drew Paxton to murder her."

Egan had already reached that same conclusion,
but it still felt like a punch to the gut to hear it spelled
out for him. Drew had been the one to pull the trigger and put a bullet in Shanna, but if Christian had
provoked him in some way to do that, then Christian
was equally guilty of her murder.

But that was a big *if.*

Leeroy and Kirk might not have had anything to
do with Shanna's murder, but either of them could be
behind these attacks. What they needed was an ID
on the gunman Jordan had killed, and they might be
able to link him to one of the suspects. Right now,
that seemed their best shot at solving this.

Egan took out his phone to see if there was a CSI
available to come to the ranch, but his phone dinged
before he could make the call, and it was Court's
name that popped up on the screen.

"Is everything okay?" Egan asked the moment he
answered.

"More or less. I'm still at the crime scene with the

dead woman. The CSIs just arrived, and I had them check the wallet first. No driver's license, but there's a photo ID. It's Irene Adair."

Jordan's arm was right against his so he felt her go stiff. Of course, they'd been expecting this, but there was no way to prepare for hearing that another of Shanna's recipients had been murdered.

"Of course, I'll get her next of kin to confirm it, but the woman matches her photo, and it's a legit ID from where she works."

Egan didn't doubt this was indeed Irene. But he still didn't know if her murder was actually connected to Shanna or if someone just wanted to make it look that way.

"Any chance you can spare one of the CSIs?" Egan asked. "I'd like them to take a look at the dead guy here at the ranch."

"There are three here, and I'll send out one of them. I'll see if Griff can spare someone from the rangers, too."

Egan thanked him, ended the call and then turned to Jordan to see how she was handling this. Not well. Her eyes had watered, the tears threatening, and her bottom lip was trembling.

"This has to end," she whispered. Jordan was still fighting the tears, but it was a battle she was losing.

Egan wasn't immune to those tears, either. Seeing her like this caused his chest to tighten until it felt as if someone had latched on to his heart and was squeezing hard. He had no idea what to do to make this better. But he apparently had a bad way of trying to fix it.

He kissed her.

He felt her go stiff, probably because she was stunned that he was doing this. Egan was stunned, too. Kissing Jordan was the last thing that should be on his mind, but he didn't stop. In fact, he made things worse by pulling her to him. She not only landed in his arms. Jordan also slid her hands around the back of his neck.

She made a sound of pleasure. Something soft and silky. Something that loosened up the muscles in his chest, but it tightened other parts of him. Specifically, that stupid part of him behind the zipper of his jeans. The kiss was reminding him of the times when they'd been lovers, and it was starting to feel more like foreplay than just a simple kiss. Of course, nothing stayed simple when it came to Jordan and him.

Egan was mindful of her injury and tried not to hurt her, but he deepened the kiss. And the taste of her slammed through him. It was a familiar taste, one that stirred not just the old memories but also the heat and the attraction that was quickly racing out of control.

That still didn't stop him.

He kept kissing her. And Jordan certainly wasn't doing anything to stop it or even slow it down. She lowered her hand from his neck, sliding her palm down his back until she reached the waist of his jeans. This was the problem with them being past lovers. It was the next step of foreplay for her to go after his zipper. And for him to go after hers. But Egan couldn't risk having sex with her now. Even if that was exactly what his body wanted him to do.

He pulled back from her at the exact moment that she pulled away from him. For a moment he thought that was a timely coincidence, but then he felt her take out her phone from her pocket.

"I had it set on vibrate," she said. "And I have a call."

Egan was actually thankful for the interruption. At least he was thankful until he saw the screen.

Unknown Caller.

Hell, this couldn't be good.

Jordan looked at him, silently asking him what to do. "Answer it," he said. "But put it on speaker."

She gave a shaky nod and did as he said. It didn't take long for the caller to start talking. "Jordan," he growled.

At least Egan thought the caller was male. It was hard to tell because he seemed to be speaking through some sort of voice scrambler.

"Who is this?" Egan demanded.

Again, it didn't take long for the guy to respond. "I'm the person who'll kill Jordan, and there's nothing you can do to stop me."

Chapter Twelve

I'm the person who'll kill Jordan.

Jordan had no trouble hearing what the caller had just said. No trouble believing that was his intention, either. And it sent a chill straight through her. Egan had a different reaction, though. He cursed and snatched the phone from her.

"Who the hell is this?" Egan snapped.

"Oh, you want my name? Sorry, but you can't have that." And it sounded as if the caller laughed. "If you want to catch me, you'll have to do your job. I'm not going to make this easy for you."

This could be someone playing a hoax, but she didn't think so. No. This was the real deal. The man behind the attacks and murders along with being the person who'd left that note with Lorena Lovett.

"What do you want?" Jordan asked. She was glad that her voice sounded a lot stronger than she felt.

"First of all, don't bother to trace this call. It's a burner cell. No way to find me with a trace. And now that we've got that out of the way, here's what I want you to do. Meet with me. Just you and me. You can't bring Egan with you. Then you and I will have a little chat."

"You mean a chat where you'll try to kill me," Jordan said.

The caller certainly didn't jump to deny that. "You have to admit you've been living on borrowed time. Drew Paxton's bullet hit you in the side and damaged both your kidneys so badly that you needed a transplant. If it weren't for Shanna, you'd be dead by now."

That sounded like something Leeroy would say. Of course, the person could want them to think that Shanna's father was responsible.

"You want to put an end to the attacks and the killings?" the caller went on. "You want to save Egan?"

"You know I do." She didn't even have to think about that.

"But saving me isn't what you have in mind," Egan said to the caller. "You want to use me to get to Jordan. I have something different in mind. I want you to stop these games and turn yourself in to the cops."

He laughed again. "Dream on, cowboy. That's not going to happen. But you and I can put an end to things if you'll just have that chat with me. I'll tell you all about why I've done these things."

"Dream on," Egan repeated like venom. "Because Jordan's not meeting with you."

"Too bad because that means someone else will die."

There was another sound. Not laughter this time, but Jordan couldn't tell what it was since it was filtered through the scrambler. However, it sounded as if someone was with the caller.

Oh, mercy.

The fear slid through her again, and she prayed this snake didn't have another soon-to-be victim with him.

"Haven't you killed enough?" Jordan pleaded with him. "Please, just let this end."

"I've told you the only way it can end. By meeting with me. But I can tell that's not going to happen. That's okay. But just remember—you could have stopped this, and you didn't."

Even though the scrambler was still on, Jordan was certain of the next sound.

A scream.

The kind of scream a person made when they were in severe pain. Terrified. Or being murdered.

"Stop, please!" Jordan shouted into the phone.

But she was talking to the air because the caller had already hung up.

Jordan immediately turned to Egan, hoping that he could stop whatever was happening. She knew that wasn't possible, though. They didn't even know where the caller was.

"The scream could have been fake," he reminded her, and he took out his own phone.

Jordan so wanted to latch on to that and believe it. And it very well could be true. The caller obviously wanted to draw her out into the open so he could kill her, and an easy way to do that was to make her think someone was being hurt, or worse, because of her.

"Text Thea and give her the caller's number," Egan

instructed. "It's a long shot, but he might have lied about it being a burner."

True, and while Jordan sent that text, Egan made a call. Not to Court or one of the other deputies. Instead, he pressed Leeroy's number, and the man answered on the first ring.

"What do you want now, Egan?" Leeroy barked.

"Where are you?" Egan snapped right back.

"I'm about to head home. If you're calling to have me come back in for questioning, don't bother. Thea already set me up with another appointment for tomorrow morning."

If Leeroy had been the one to make that scrambled call, he certainly wasn't showing any signs of it. He sounded as angry and ornery as he usually was. Of course, that could be an act. He could have put away the burner cell and scrambler to answer the call from Egan.

"Don't be late for your interview tomorrow," Egan warned the man.

He ended the call and immediately went to one of their other suspects. Christian. Unlike Leeroy, however, he didn't answer.

"I can call Christian's office at San Antonio PD," Jordan offered.

She waited for Egan to nod in agreement before she searched through her contacts and found the number for Detective Marvin Daniels, Christian's partner. And he did answer almost right away.

"This is Jordan Gentry," she greeted. "I'm trying to get in touch with Christian—"

"So am I," Marvin interrupted. "What the hell is going on with him?"

That certainly wasn't the response she'd expected. "What do you mean?"

"He just called me and said someone tried to kill him."

Jordan tamped down the slam of emotions and tried to see both sides of this. Yes, someone could have attacked Christian, but it was possible this was part of the ruse to make him look innocent.

"How long ago did Christian call you?" Jordan asked.

"Five minutes or so. Maybe a little longer. Why?"

If it was longer, then that would have been when Egan was still on the phone with the scrambled caller. And that meant it couldn't have been Christian. Of course, that didn't mean he couldn't have hired someone to make that call.

"Jordan?" Marvin pressed when she didn't say anything.

"I'm not sure what's going on," she answered. "Do you have any idea if Christian is all right?"

"I don't know. I'm on the way to the hospital now."

"Hospital?" Jordan repeated on a rise of breath. If this was a ruse, then Christian was making it look very real.

"Yeah. He's driving himself there, so I don't know how bad he's hurt. You want me to have him get in touch with you when he can?"

"No. That's all right. But if you could text me and let me know his condition, I'd appreciate it."

"Will do," Marvin agreed before he hung up.

She looked at Egan again to see his reaction to what they'd just heard about Christian, but he had already moved on to calling their third and final suspect, Kirk. While Egan was waiting for him to answer, however, he got another call from Thea, and he immediately answered it.

"I'm pretty sure I know the answer to this, but I have to ask. By any chance did you leave your truck on Smith Road by the Welcome to McCall Canyon sign?" Thea asked.

"No. It's still in the repair shop."

"That's what I figured. Well, there's a truck identical to yours back there. I'm thinking it's the one used in the attack since the windshield is shot up. And guess who found it?"

"Kirk?"

"Leeroy," Thea answered. "He says he spotted it a couple of minutes ago when he was driving home."

That was possible since Smith Road led to his place. Still, it seemed a huge coincidence that one of their suspects would be the one to find it. Unless someone had set it up so that Leeroy would be the one who stumbled on it. Plus, it sounded as if the truck hadn't exactly been hidden away.

"Please tell me that Leeroy didn't touch the vehicle," Egan said.

"He claims he didn't. Griff and I are on our way there now to check it out, and I told Leeroy to get back in his own truck and wait for us," Thea went on. "He said he would, but he claims that there's blood on the outside of the door."

"The killer threw the dead woman out of the truck," Egan reminded her. "And she'd been shot and stabbed so it could have gotten there then."

"Yeah," Thea agreed. Then, she paused. "But Leeroy is insisting this blood isn't from the other attack. He's saying this is *fresh*."

FRESH BLOOD.

That was *not* what Egan wanted to hear. Especially coming on the heels of the phone call from a thug claiming that he would kill someone else if Jordan didn't meet with him. This might not even be connected to that call, but Jordan would almost certainly think it was.

"Call me when you get to the truck," Egan insisted. "And if the connection's good enough, make it a video call so I can see what's going on."

"Will do," Thea assured him before she hung up.

Even though it would likely be only a few minutes before Thea and Griff got there, he wanted to use that short amount of time to try to calm that look on Jordan's face. And this time, he wouldn't kiss her to do that.

"Leeroy could be wrong. It might not be fresh blood," he reminded her. "And even if it is, he might have been the one who planted it there."

She nodded, but the agreement didn't quite make it to her eyes. "I need to figure out a way to stop this."

Since she looked ready to panic—or agree to the

meeting that the killer wanted—Egan took her by the shoulders. "Someone could have set all of this up just to draw you out."

"But Irene—"

"She could have been dead long before the thug called you and asked you to meet him."

Jordan still didn't look convinced so Egan pulled her into his arms. No kiss. But he did hold her. It wasn't much, but then there wasn't a lot he could do to help her until he caught the piece of dirt who was behind all of this.

His phone rang, and Egan answered it right away when he saw Thea's name on the screen.

"We're pulling up to the truck now," Thea said the moment she was on the line. Just as they'd agreed, it was a video call with audio so he could see Thea. "Leeroy's sitting in his own vehicle just like I told him to do."

Good. That was something at least. If they found any prints or DNA from Leeroy, Egan didn't want the man claiming that it had gotten there just now because he'd touched something.

"Leeroy's getting out of his truck," Thea went on, "but I'll have Griff deal with him while I take a closer look."

Thea turned the phone in the direction of the truck as she approached it, and Jordan stood right next to him, watching and listening to everything. The truck was indeed identical to his, including the license plates, which were obviously a fake duplicate. It wouldn't have been especially hard for someone to create a bogus tag, but it did let Egan know that this person had gone to a lot of trouble to make everyone believe that he'd been the one behind the murder.

But why?

Egan could only guess about that, but it might have been so that he would be blamed for Lorena's, and Jordan's, murders. For that to happen, though, there would have had to be a witness. There hadn't been. But since the attack had happened on a road, maybe the killer had been planning for any contingency.

Thea continued to move closer to the truck, and in the background Egan could hear Leeroy arguing with Griff. He didn't catch every word that Leeroy was saying, but the gist was that Leeroy was worried about being blamed for this. Of course, that could be all hot air since maybe he was indeed responsible.

"There's the blood," Thea said, aiming her phone camera at the driver's-side door. There was certainly something there. And it looked like blood spatter. The kind of spatter that could result from a gunshot wound or high-velocity spatter from an impact wound.

"I don't want to touch the door handle," Thea said. "There might be prints or DNA on it."

Egan was about to agree with her, but then he heard Thea mumble some profanity. "There's a body on the floor by the passenger's seat."

Jordan gasped and touched her fingers to her mouth. She hadn't exactly looked steady before Thea's second call, but now it was worse.

"Is it Tori?" Jordan asked.

"No. It's a man. And I think he's alive. Griff, call

an ambulance," Thea shouted, and while she was still holding her phone, she hurried to the passenger's door and threw it open. There was indeed a man on the floor, and he was in between the seat and the dash. His hands were tied, and he had a gag around his mouth. But Egan had no trouble recognizing him.

It was Kirk.

And he was alive. He was moaning.

"Kirk," Jordan muttered under her breath. She didn't say more, but Egan figured she was thinking the same thing he was—that Kirk was no longer a suspect. Well, maybe he was. Kirk could have set this up.

Or not.

"He's been shot," Thea said. And that had Egan rethinking his theory that Kirk could have done this to himself. It seemed an extreme way to make them believe he was innocent.

Thea set her phone down on the seat, and while it wasn't a perfect angle, Egan could still see the man. There was blood on Kirk's shoulder and chest, but the moment Thea untied the gag from his mouth, he opened his eyes. His face was tight, his forehead bunched up, and he was still moaning in pain.

"The ambulance will be here in a few minutes," Griff called out.

Good. Because Egan didn't want Kirk dying before he had a chance to answer a whole lot of questions. Egan went ahead with the first question on his list.

"Who did this to you?" Egan asked.

Kirk moaned again and shook his head. "A big guy.

He was hiding in the back seat of my car, and I didn't see him until it was too late." Kirk glanced around. "Where am I? How did I get here?"

Egan wanted to curse. Either Kirk had been unconscious after he was shot or else he was going to claim that he was. Too bad because that meant the man couldn't give them critical details.

"Was Tori with you when you were shot?" Jordan asked.

"No. She left in her own car." Kirk shook his head, and his eyelids fluttered down, threatening to close. If the man was faking this, he was doing a good job because he definitely looked in pain and as if he were fighting to remain conscious.

"Did the shooter say anything to you before he shot you?" Egan pressed.

"No." Kirk didn't hesitate with that answer, but he did pause right afterward. "I think he was just a hired gun."

Probably, but it didn't explain why the guy would have moved Kirk from his car to the truck. Obviously, the person behind this had wanted the truck to be found, but did that mean the plan had been to leave Kirk alive? Egan just didn't know, and he might not have the answer to that until Kirk got to the hospital. If his injury was life-threatening, then maybe the hired gun had figured he would just bleed out.

But why hadn't he just made sure that Kirk was dead?

"I think I know who set the thug on me," Kirk said. His voice was even weaker now. "I think it was Tori."

Of all the things that Egan had thought Kirk might say, that wasn't one of them. "Tori?" Egan and Jordan questioned at the same time. It was Egan who continued, "Why would she have hired someone to kill you?"

Kirk mumbled something that Egan didn't catch and then he winced in pain. "Because Tori found out that I knew about her."

Egan would have definitely pressed for more info about that, but Kirk's head dropped to the side, landing against the dash, and his eyes closed. Thea immediately pressed her fingers to the man's neck.

"He's still alive, but he needs to get to the hospital," Thea said, urgency in her voice. In the background, Egan could hear a welcome sound. The sirens from the ambulance.

"Go with him in the ambulance," Egan instructed Thea. "If he regains consciousness, ask him about Tori."

"I will, but Kirk's lost a lot of blood. You think maybe he was just talking out of his head?"

Egan didn't know, but he would do everything to find out. "Just let me know whatever Kirk says," Egan instructed.

He ended the call, turning to Jordan to see if she had any idea about this, but she shook her head. *"Because Tori found out that I knew about her,"* she repeated. "What would Kirk have learned?"

But she didn't wait for him to answer. Jordan went to the laptop and accessed the files from her storage cloud. "I had info on the transplant recipients, but I don't think anything is in here that would give us a clue."

Neither did he. Because if there had been something, Jordan would have already connected the dots. Still, she scanned through the details she'd saved. However, Egan's thoughts went in a different direction.

"We both thought it was strange that Tori would be Kirk's lawyer," Egan said, thinking out loud. "But what if Tori also knew Drew?"

Jordan immediately looked at him. "I didn't even look for a connection like that."

There would have been no reason for her to do that. She'd been researching the organ recipients to find out who might want all of them dead, but Drew didn't seem to be a viable suspect since he'd had no way to arrange for hired guns. Because he was on death row, all of his visits and correspondence were carefully monitored.

Jordan exited the storage files and instead did an internet search on Tori. "There's not a lot," she said. "She's only been a lawyer…" She stopped. "When she was still in law school, she interned at the law firm that defended Drew."

That caused a bad feeling to snake up his spine. "You have the number for that firm?" he asked, taking out his phone again.

Egan pressed in the number as Jordan rattled it off, and it took him several minutes to work his way through to someone who might know anything about Tori. He was eventually connected to the head of personnel for the law firm, Stanley Clark. He put the call on speaker so that Jordan would be able to hear it.

"I'm Sheriff Egan McCall," he greeted the man, "and I need info on one of your former interns, Tori Judd. It's important. She could be in danger." Egan wouldn't mention that she might have had part in shooting in a man.

"Danger," Stanley repeated. "Does this have anything to do with her heart transplant?"

So, the man knew her. That was a good start. "Maybe indirectly."

"That's a shame. She was really sick when she worked here, and I'd hoped the heart transplant would give her a chance at life. Did her body reject the heart or something?"

"I'm not sure." Yeah, it was a lie, but this guy might clam up if he realized this was a murder investigation. "By any chance, did Tori work on the Drew Paxton murder trial?"

Silence. For a long time. And that silence was a red flag for Egan. "It's important," Egan repeated. "I believe she's been getting threats."

"No. She didn't work on his murder trial, but she did on his previous narcotics conviction."

That was the conviction that had put Drew on parole with Shanna as his parole officer. "Tori worked directly with Drew on the trial?" Egan pressed.

Stanley sighed. "Yes. Everybody warned Tori to keep her distance from that man, but she didn't listen. Maybe because that was about the time she was getting so sick."

Or maybe Tori had a thing for bad boys. And Drew was the ultimate bad boy.

"Anyway," Stanley went on, "I don't believe anything inappropriate went on between them, but a lot of people thought Tori had allowed herself to get too close to him. It didn't matter, though, because after the transplant, she went to work for another law firm." Stanley paused. "Is Drew Paxton the one who's threatening her?"

"Possibly. Do you know anything about that?"

"Nothing concrete, but I got the feeling that he'd developed a fixation on her, and I thought the man was bad news. I was right because I've heard he's in jail again for murder."

"He is." And Egan hated that just talking about the snake brought all the bad memories back to the surface. "Do you have any idea if Tori stayed in touch with Drew after his drug conviction?"

"There were rumors that she saw him, but like I said, she went to work for another firm, and I lost contact with her after that."

Too bad that had happened because Egan needed to know just how close Tori had gotten to Drew and if it was connected to everything that was going on right now.

"If you remember anything else about Tori, please let me know," Egan told Stanley.

Egan ended the call and immediately pressed in Tori's number again. No answer. However, he did leave her a message to contact him ASAP. When his phone buzzed with an incoming message, Egan thought maybe she was calling him, but it was Court.

"Griff just filled me in on what happened with Kirk," Court said when Egan answered. "You want me to go to the hospital?"

It was tempting because Court was good at interrogation, but Egan needed him to man the office and work the murder investigation. And if Kirk didn't make it, they'd have another murder to try to solve.

"No. Stay put," Egan answered. "I just found out that Tori knew Drew, so Jordan and I will be working on that."

"She what?" Court added some ripe curse words to go with that.

Surprise had been Egan's reaction, too, and it wasn't a good thing that Tori hadn't volunteered that info. A connection to Drew meant she could also be connected to the attacks and killings, and that was probably the reason she hadn't volunteered that to him.

"If you need any help with the Tori angle, let me know," Court went on. "In the meantime, the reason I called was to let you know that a pair of CSIs are on the ranch, and they're examining the dead guy. No ID on him, but they'll take his prints and run those ASAP."

"Thanks." The sooner they knew who the guy was, the sooner they could use him to try to link him to one of their suspects. Of course, their suspect list was changing. Egan was adding Tori as a person of interest, and Kirk had dropped to the bottom. If Kirk had merely wanted to give himself an injury so that he looked innocent, he wouldn't have taken things that far. Well, unless something had gone seriously wrong with whatever he'd planned.

When he finished his call with Court, he saw that Jordan was already doing a computer search on Tori. Good. Maybe she'd find something they could use.

Egan tried a different angle. He sent a text to the warden at the prison where Drew was incarcerated and asked if Tori had ever visited Drew or written him a letter. Even if there was no record of the letter, it didn't mean the two hadn't stayed in touch that way. Letters could often get past security by having a lawyer deliver them.

He debated calling Drew's lawyer, but the guy probably wasn't going to admit that he'd broken prison rules by bringing in letters from the outside. Still, it was worth a try. Anything was at this point. Well, anything other than Jordan surrendering herself to this killer.

Egan was about to use the computer to look up a number for Drew's attorney, but his phone rang again before he could do that. It wasn't Court this time. It was Thea, and he hoped she had good news.

"We just got to the hospital, and they took Kirk into surgery," Thea said the moment Egan answered.

Well, at least he was still alive. "Any idea if he'll survive?"

"Not yet. The doctor didn't talk to me, but Kirk did. He woke up a couple of times while we were still in the ambulance."

That grabbed Egan's attention. Jordan's, too, because she stood and went closer to him. "What did he say?" Egan asked.

"I'm not sure it makes sense. Kirk was drifting in and out of consciousness so take this with a grain of salt. But Kirk mumbled that Drew found out something. Something important, he insisted. He said that Drew learned that Shanna was *the one*."

Jordan obviously heard that because she shook her head. "The one?" she repeated.

"A match," Thea clarified. "According to Kirk, Drew knew that Tori would be a match to get Shanna's heart. And that's why Drew killed Shanna."

Chapter Thirteen

Jordan heard every word Thea said, but it was hard for her to process it. For two years she'd believed the events of that fateful night had played out because of Drew's obsession with Shanna.

But had it all been a lie?

Judging from Egan's bunched-up forehead and stark expression, he was having trouble with it, too.

"Remember, Kirk might not have known what he was saying," Thea added. "Or he could have just made it up."

True, but what reasons would Kirk have had to lie about something like this? The only possibility that came to mind was that this lie was part of some semi-botched attempt to make them believe he wasn't responsible for all the murders and attempted murders.

"Griff took Leeroy to the sheriff's office to get his statement about finding the truck," Thea went on. "But once he's done with that, he can go to the prison to talk to Drew. Or I could go," Thea continued when Egan didn't say anything. "I just don't think it's

a good idea for you to try to talk to him right now."
She paused. "Are you okay?"

Egan cleared his throat, and Jordan could see that
he was trying to steel himself up. "Have Griff go out
and talk to Drew," Egan finally answered. What he
didn't do was address Thea's question if he was okay.
He clearly wasn't.

Even if what Kirk had said was a lie, it was bringing back all the memories and grief for Egan. For
Jordan, too. And this time the grief was worse. Something that she hadn't thought possible. But it was
heartbreaking to think that Shanna might not have
been killed by a madman after all. She might have
been murdered because she could be an organ donor
for Tori.

"I want you to stay at the hospital and keep watch,"
Egan added to Thea several moments later. "If someone did try to kill Kirk, they might come back and
try to finish the job."

Oh, mercy.

With everything else going on, Jordan hadn't even
considered that. But it was a possibility. And if the
person succeeded in finishing off Kirk, that might
prevent them from ever learning the truth. She seriously doubted they were going to get the truth from
Drew.

Egan ended the call with Thea and then glanced
around as if trying to figure out what to do. Finally,
he groaned. Then cursed.

Jordan doubted he would want her to do this, but
she slipped her arm around him anyway. He didn't

push her away. Nor did he relax any. She still felt his rock-hard muscles.

Egan looked down at her, their eyes meeting, and Jordan got another jolt of that bone-deep pain they were both feeling. At least Egan didn't seem to be blaming her for that pain.

But she was still blaming herself.

Even if Drew had orchestrated the hostage situation with the ultimate goal of killing Shanna, Jordan should have still been able to stop him. If that was what Egan was feeling, though, he certainly didn't show it. In fact, he brushed a kiss on her mouth, causing her own muscles to tense. Then relax. He stared at her as if trying to decide if he wanted to kiss her again, but he obviously decided against that because he stepped away from her.

He scrubbed his hand over his face and groaned softly. "Focus," he grumbled under his breath, and when his attention came back to her again, he did seem all business. "How the hell would Drew have found out that Shanna was a donor, much less a match?" he asked.

She lifted her shoulder. "Maybe Drew saw it on her driver's license. Or hacked into the DMV database." Of course, it would have required him to do more than that. "He must have gotten into Shanna's medical records, too, for him to find out."

"But that would have only told him her blood type, right? Is there more to it than that?"

"There is. It's called cross-match typing, where they mix together blood from the donor and possible recipient. If the recipient's cells attack the donor cells, then the transplant will fail."

Egan huffed. "So, why would Drew have believed that Shanna was a match in the first place?"

Jordan had to think about that a few seconds. "Maybe because of Shanna's blood type. She was B-positive, which meant the recipients had to be either B or AB. I was AB," she added under her breath. "Only a small percentage of the population has that particular type."

And that meant she'd gotten very lucky to even have a donor. Of course, maybe Drew had created that "luck" by trying to get Tori a heart. He probably had no idea that Jordan would be a match for an organ transplant, too.

"If we can find Tori's blood type," she went on, "I'm betting it'll be B or AB." Well, it would if Kirk was telling the truth.

Egan made a sound of agreement. "Drew's target could have been Shanna all along. That's why he shot her in the head with a low-caliber gun." But he seemed to be talking more to himself than her. "He knew the shot probably wouldn't kill her immediately. That way, she'd linger on, and there'd be time to harvest her organs."

The relief came flooding through her. For a couple of seconds anyway. Maybe she hadn't been to blame for Shanna's death, but it certainly didn't feel like a victory. Because Shanna was still dead, and this was all just a theory. To prove it, they'd need a lot more information.

"I'll try to find out Tori's blood type," she offered. "I can use my phone to search for that if you need to use the laptop."

"I do. I want to read through the files that San Antonio PD collected on Drew for the murder trial. It's possible they included his internet searches."

Yes, and that way they could tell if Drew had been looking for ways to save Tori. And speaking of Tori, Egan tried one more time to call her, but it had the same results. No answer, and the call went to voice mail.

On another huff, Egan sank down on the sofa and got to work. So did Jordan, but she'd managed to search for only about five minutes when her phone rang. Jordan's heart nearly stopped when she saw *Unknown Caller* on the screen.

"This could be from the killer," she said to Egan.

He took out his own phone to record the call, and once he'd done that, he motioned for her to answer it. Jordan hit the answer button and pulled in her breath, waiting.

"It's me," the caller said. The voice wasn't filtered through a scrambler this time, and it was someone she recognized.

Christian.

Jordan didn't especially want to have to deal with Christian now, but she did want to know if he'd indeed gone to the hospital. She took his call and put it on speaker for Egan.

"Why are you using an unknown number?" she asked.

"I thought it'd be smart to go with a burner cell

in case someone's trying to track my location. You know, someone like you who wants to kill me. Why do you want me dead?" Christian snapped.

She hadn't thought anything he could say would surprise her, but that did it. "Why would you think that?"

"Because the thug who tried to kill me said you'd hired him."

The chill that ran through her was ice-cold. Not because there was any hint that it was true but because someone was trying to set her up. Well, maybe. Or Christian could be doing like Kirk might have and grasping at straws to make himself look innocent.

With a scowl on his face, Egan dropped down next to her. "Who's the thug? And then tell me everything he said to you."

Christian cursed. "We didn't exchange names or introduce ourselves. The guy stepped out from the side of the building when I was going to my car. He said, 'This is for Jordan,' and he pulled the trigger."

Jordan nearly gasped. "He shot you?"

"Damn right, he did. He clipped me in the shoulder before I drew my gun. I shot at him, and he ran."

"And you didn't go after him?" There was a lot of skepticism in Egan's voice and question.

"No. Because I was bleeding and needed to get to the hospital. But now that I'm stitched up, I'll look for him."

That didn't make sense. "Why didn't you call someone from San Antonio PD to find him?" Jordan pressed. "The guy will be long gone by now."

"He'll be back. And that brings me to my original question. Why would you want me dead?"

"I don't, and I certainly didn't hire someone to kill you. Why would I?" she tossed right back at him.

"I've been giving that some thought, and I think you might be trying to cover up something. Maybe something in one of those files you're reviewing for The Right Verdict. You couldn't just destroy the file because that would make them suspicious. So, maybe you're trying to set me up."

Jordan forced herself not to lash out, but that riled her. She hadn't been a dirty cop, and she wasn't dirty now. However, Christian could be.

"Your injury must not have been serious," she said, "if they didn't keep you in the hospital."

Christian cursed again. "I figured you'd tried to put all of this back on me. Just own up to whatever it is you're doing so this stops."

"I was about to ask you to do that same thing," Egan snarled. He ignored Christian's profanity-laced protest and kept on talking. "Someone just tried to kill Kirk Paxton, and he's not walking out of the ER with his injuries."

"Did Kirk say who hurt him?" Christian asked.

"Well, it wasn't some thug claiming that Jordan hired him. Not that we know of anyway. But whoever did it, it was probably the same person who called Jordan just minutes before that happened. He wanted Jordan to meet him so the killings would stop. You know anything about that?"

"No. I was too busy getting shot." Christian didn't rein in his sarcasm, but he did pause. "Did Kirk say anything?"

Egan's eyes narrowed with suspicion, and she knew why. That question sounded more than just a fishing expedition. Christian seemed concerned, or something.

"Kirk said a lot of things," Egan threw out there. "That's why I tried to call you earlier. I wanted to question you about some things he said."

Christian stayed quiet several moments. "If Kirk brought up my name, then he's a liar. Or else his attacker wanted to set me up...hell. I gotta go. I just spotted the guy who tried to kill me."

Jordan called out to Christian so that he wouldn't hang up. She wanted to tell him to call for backup. But he'd already ended the call.

Egan didn't waste any time calling San Antonio PD to let them know they might have an officer in danger. *Might.* Still, it was too big of a risk not to have someone at least try to help Christian.

Since she was feeling a little wobbly and her head was hurting, Jordan went back to the sofa. "Leeroy's the only one of our suspects who hasn't been hurt," she said. "And Tori."

Egan made such a quick sound of agreement that it meant it was something he'd already considered, and he sank down next to her to continue working on the laptop. "That doesn't mean either of them are innocent."

She nodded. "Leeroy or Tori could have intended to kill Christian, Kirk and me, and they could have simply failed." And that meant whoever was behind this would only keep coming back until the job was done.

Jordan didn't voice that last part aloud, but Egan must have picked up on it because he slid his arm around her and kissed her again. Like the other one, it was just a simple brush of his lips, and it landed on her forehead. She wasn't even certain he'd been aware he'd done it because his attention stayed on the computer screen.

"We'll have to wait for Drew's files to be emailed to me," he explained. "But the request is in. Any luck finding Tori's blood type?"

"No. Sorry." She lifted her phone to get back to doing that, but Egan took hold of her hand. At first, she didn't know why he had done that, but then Jordan realized she was trembling.

He frowned, maybe at the trembling. Maybe because he wasn't so pleased that he was touching her again. "You want to try to take that nap now?" he asked.

Jordan didn't even have to think how to answer that. "No. I wouldn't be able to sleep. Besides, I need to work on getting that information about Tori."

Egan stared at her, maybe trying to come up with some argument that would cause her to give in. But there was no good argument for that. Or at least that was what Jordan thought.

Until Egan kissed her again.

This time it wasn't some mindless peck on the forehead. It was a real kiss, and she immediately felt the heat and sensations that went along with it. Of course, she always felt that way whenever Egan got close. He was obviously doing this to comfort her, though, and she figured he would stop after only a few seconds.

He didn't.

The kiss continued, and he slipped his arm around her, pulling her closer to him. More heat came. More of that fire that'd been simmering between them since they were teenagers, but this particular fire was already flaming much too hot.

Jordan eased back, meeting his gaze. She expected to see some doubts there. But there were none. There was only a moment of silence before Egan pulled her back to him and kissed her again.

EGAN WAS ABOUT 90 percent certain that this was a mistake, but he held on to the remaining 10 percent as if it were a lifeline. Even if this was wrong and something he would almost certainly regret, it was what he needed.

And what Jordan needed, too.

She proved that when the sound of pleasure purred in her throat, and she kissed him right back. He hadn't needed anything to up the ante on this and make it feel like foreplay, but that did it.

He forced himself to think of the logistics of this. There was a CSI crew on the grounds, plenty of ranch hands, too, and any one of them might come to the door at any second. If that happened, the foreplay would end, and Jordan and he would have another chance to think this through. But he figured if that decision was left to either of them, stopping and re-thinking just wasn't in the cards.

He put his phone on the coffee table to free up his hands. Jordan had the same idea, though, because she put aside her phone as well before she hooked her arm around the back of his neck. She pulled him down lower so that the kiss raged on, and she didn't leave things at that. Her other hand went to his chest, and she started to undo the buttons on his shirt.

The memories came. Not of the past two years but of when they'd been lovers. When they'd been very good at what they were doing right now. And his body reacted, all right. Egan got rock hard, and there was a sudden urgency to take this up a notch.

So he did.

He lowered his head to her neck so he could kiss her there, and he went after her buttons, as well. Once he had a few of them open, Egan dropped the kisses lower. To the tops of her breasts. He'd remembered that Jordan liked to be kissed there, and since she reacted with one of those sounds of pleasure, apparently she still did.

The breast kisses put some urgency in her, too, because she started to fight with his shirt. She managed to get it off him, and Jordan must have also remembered where he liked to be kissed because her mouth went to his bare chest. Egan hadn't needed anything else to fire him up, but that did it.

She went lower to his stomach. Another sensitive spot for him. Too sensitive. And he knew if she kept this up that this was all going to end much too fast. That was why he took hold of her, easing her back up so he could take off her top.

Oh, man.

He'd forgotten just what an amazing body she had, but he was sure as heck remembering it now. Remembering even more when he took off her bra, and her breasts spilled into his hands. This time when he pulled her back against him, he had the pleasure of feeling her bare skin against his.

He kissed her mouth again and got her moving toward the bedroom. Thankfully, it was only a few feet away, but even that short distance was enough time for the flames to rise even higher. Yeah, this was wrong, but Egan suddenly wanted her more than his next breath.

And speaking of breaths, Jordan pretty much took his away when she slid her hand over the front of his jeans. Touching him. Reminding him that it had moved from the "want" stage to the "need," and what he needed was Jordan.

He stripped off her top, all the while backing her toward the bed. Still kissing and touching, they fell into a heap on the soft mattress. All in all, the alignment was darn good considering he landed on top of her, and he went after the zipper on her jeans. Egan succeeded with the zipper, but when he went to slide the jeans off her hips, he felt something he didn't want to feel.

Jordan went stiff.

Egan immediately stopped and looked down at her. Her face was flushed with arousal, her breath gusting from her mouth.

"The scar," she said.

This crazy need for her had obviously dulled his mind because it took Egan a couple of seconds to figure out what she meant. She had a scar from her kidney surgery, and it was clearly visible now that he had her partly naked. She'd figured that the scar would remind him of Shanna.

And it did.

But it wasn't a reminder that cooled down his body enough to stop this. He hoped Jordan would feel the same since he was aching to have her.

With Jordan staring at him, Egan waited. Not long, though. She muttered a single word of profanity, slipped her hand around his neck again and pulled him back to a long, deep kiss. Egan was sure he would have felt some relief if she hadn't slid her hand into the waist of his jeans. No relief. Just a higher notch for the heat and need.

Egan did something about her jeans. It wasn't easy with her kissing him, but he finally managed to get them off her. Her panties, too. And he got another jolt of just how beautiful she was. He managed a single kiss on her stomach before Jordan flipped him onto his back so she could rid him of his jeans.

Years ago, they'd had sex in this very room. This very bed. Neither of them had known what they were doing then. It hadn't mattered, though. The only thing that had mattered was satisfying that hunger for each other. Just like now.

Egan took a condom from his wallet before she peeled off his jeans and boxers, but Jordan played a little dirty. She kissed him as she made her way up his body. Egan was already primed and ready, and that didn't help. However, it did feel darn good.

They switched positions again, and he tried to be mindful of her injury. Jordan wanted no part of gentleness, though, because she took hold of his hips and pulled him to her. Until he was deep inside her.

Exactly where he wanted to be.

Egan stilled for a moment just to give her body time to adjust to him. Like the hot, melting kisses, it didn't last, either. The need took over, and he began to move inside her. Jordan moved, too, meeting him thrust for thrust.

Yes, he remembered this, too. The way they'd always fit together. And the fit was just as good now. Maybe too good. Because it didn't last. He felt Jordan's climax ripple through her. Through him, as well. Even though he tried to hang on as long as he could, he knew he couldn't. Egan pushed into her one last time, and he let himself go with her.

Chapter Fourteen

Jordan was afraid to even breathe for fear that Egan would move off her. She wanted to hang on to this close contact with him for as long as possible. Especially since they might not ever be together like this again.

The thought of that twisted away at her, but she had to be realistic. Egan might never be able to forgive her or get past what had happened to Shanna. In fact, he could already be regretting this.

Or not.

He lifted his head, looking down at her, and he kissed her. That certainly didn't seem like something a man with regrets might do. He pushed her hair from her face, continuing to stare at her before he groaned. Now the regrets would come. Except they didn't. He kissed her again, rolled off her and then headed for the bathroom.

"I've got work to do," he added in a grumble.

That was true, but she still wasn't convinced that Egan would use work as a way of distancing himself from her.

She sat up, watching him as he went into the bathroom, and she got a great look at his backside. She wasn't sure how the man managed to look good from all angles, but he did.

Since she didn't want to be sitting around stark naked when Egan returned, Jordan forced herself to get up, and she started to gather her clothes. They were scattered all over the floor so it took her a couple of moments to do it, and she was still dressing when Egan came out of the bathroom. He was still butt naked, which gave her a good look at the front of him.

Yes, definitely great from all angles.

The corner of his mouth lifted as if he'd known what she was thinking, and he began to pick up his clothes. However, he didn't start dressing until he went to her and kissed her again.

"Just in case you're having doubts about this," he drawled.

Well, she certainly didn't have doubts with that chrome-melting kiss, but Jordan figured the postorgasmic glow would wear off soon for both of them. Then reality would put things in perspective. They had a killer after them, too many suspects, few answers and, as Egan had already pointed out, they had work to do.

Egan continued to dress as he made his way back into the living room, and he cursed when he got to his phone on the coffee table. "I have a missed call from Court," he grumbled.

Jordan groaned. She hadn't heard it ring, which was probably the best argument for them not to have landed in bed. Now she only hoped that Court hadn't been in some kind of immediate danger that would have required Egan's help. If he had, then there was no way Egan or she would forgive themselves for that.

Egan put the call on speaker as soon as Court answered. "Are you okay?" Court immediately asked. "I was worried when you didn't answer."

"I'm fine." Egan's jaw was so tight she was surprised he could speak. "What about you?"

"Better than I was about fifteen minutes ago. We got some good news for a change."

Jordan released the breath she'd been holding and went closer to Egan so she could hear Court better.

"The dead guy at the ranch is Donald Brawley," Court continued a moment later. "His prints were in the system because he has two priors. One was an arrest that happened at a chop shop, and it was owned by the same guy who built the custom truck where Kirk was found."

She doubted that was a coincidence, and judging from the sound Egan made, he didn't believe it was one, either.

"But the chop shop arrest is just for starters," Court went on. "Donald is on Leeroy's payroll. He's been working as a ranch hand for him for the past two years."

Jordan's first reaction was relief because they finally had a solid connection that Egan could use to make an arrest. But it didn't take her long to look at this from a different angle. If Leeroy was going to do a murder for hire, then he probably wouldn't have used someone with such a strong link back to him. That was probably why Egan groaned and scrubbed his hand over his face.

"I've already requested financials on Donald," Court explained. "But I'm figuring this was a cash transaction."

"Yeah, but maybe Leeroy got stupid and sloppy and withdrew a large amount of cash in the past forty-eight hours."

"We can only hope. In the meantime I'll have Dakota go out to Leeroy's place and question the other hands there. Dakota'll be able to do that as soon as he finishes with the CSIs at the ranch."

Jordan hadn't even known the reserve deputy was nearby, but it made sense. With a sniper still at large, the CSIs would have wanted police protection while they processed the scene.

"Is Leeroy still there at the station?" Egan asked.

"No. He left a couple of minutes ago after Griff took his statement."

Too bad because if Leeroy had still been in the building, Court could have detained him while they searched for more evidence surrounding his dead employee.

"I can get Leeroy back in here if you want," Court offered.

Egan stayed quiet a moment as if giving that some thought. "Not yet. I'd rather not alert him that we've got an ID on the dead guy. His other ranch hands might clam up and not talk to Dakota if they find out their boss could be a murder suspect."

True. Maybe one of them saw or heard something that they would spill to a deputy.

Egan ended the call, looked up at her, and that was when she saw the regret over what they'd done. At least she thought that was what she was seeing, but Egan shook his head. "We're distractions for each other," he said.

Yes, they were, and he was talking about the missed phone call now. It hadn't been time sensitive, but it could have easily been.

Jordan was about to make the offer to shut herself up in the bedroom. That way, they could work in separate parts of the house. That wouldn't stop her from thinking about him, of course, since in Egan's case, out of sight would not be out of mind. Still, it might help them focus. However, his phone rang before she could even get a chance to suggest it.

"Dakota," Egan said, glancing at the screen.

Since Court had just mentioned the deputy, she thought maybe Dakota was calling to verify that he could indeed go out to Leeroy's, but the way Egan's forehead bunched up, something could be wrong. Since he hadn't put the call on speaker, she went closer, hoping to find out what'd happened.

"What the hell does she want?" Egan snapped.

That question definitely caused Jordan's concern to spike. So did Egan's response several moments later after he listened to whatever it was Dakota said. "They're sure?" Egan asked. A few seconds passed before he groaned and added. "No. I'll talk to her.

But I want you to come to the guesthouse to stay with Jordan while I do that."

Egan ended the call, looked at her, and Jordan was certain he was about to tell her something she didn't want to hear. "Is it Tori? Is she here at the ranch?"

He nodded. "She's at the cattle gate, and she told the hands guarding it that she needs to see me, that it's important. She says she'll only talk to me in person. The hands frisked her, and she's not armed. But it appears she has been injured. There are possible stun gun marks on her neck."

Since a stun gun left distinctive marks, it wouldn't have been hard for someone to recognize what they were. But that didn't mean Tori had been attacked. She could have put the marks there herself as some sort of ruse to draw them out into the open.

And it was working.

Well, it was unless she could talk Egan out of going out there.

"This could be a trap," she reminded him. "The sniper could be nearby."

He gave another nod. "I'll stay in the cruiser, and I won't let her anywhere near you."

Jordan shook her head. "It's you that I'm worried about."

"I'll be fine," he assured her, but the heavy sigh that left his mouth suggested otherwise. "We have to get to the bottom of this, and Tori might have the answers we need."

She couldn't argue with the part about Tori having answers, but whether the woman would actually give them to Egan was anyone's guess. Still, she couldn't fault him for wanting to try this.

It wouldn't take the deputy long to get there. Only minutes. And while they waited, Egan finished buttoning his shirt, adjusted his holster and slid on his Stetson.

When she heard the cruiser pull to a stop in front of the guesthouse, she thought maybe Egan would just walk out. He didn't. He hooked his arm around her waist, pulled her to him and kissed her. It wasn't one of the long, smoldering ones that had led them to bed, but it was a reminder that he was indeed an incredible distraction.

And she was falling in love with him all over again.

Jordan kept that to herself. The timing for spilling news like that couldn't be worse. Plus, Dakota knocked on the door.

"It's me," Dakota called out to them.

Egan disconnected the security system so he could let in the deputy. Dakota was wearing a Kevlar vest, which meant he'd been well aware that the sniper could return. Hopefully, the CSIs were wearing the same kind of protective gear.

"Any signs of trouble?" Egan asked him.

"No. Well, other than Tori. But everything else is going okay. The medical examiner just arrived with his crew."

Egan made a sound of approval, and he gave Jordan one last look. "Reset the alarm after I leave." He rattled off the code to her. "I won't be long."

She hoped that was true, and while she was hoping, Jordan added that Egan would stay safe. If the sniper had managed to shoot into the main house before, he could do it again, and this time they might not get so lucky.

As Egan had reminded her to do, Jordan reset the security system and went to the window to watch him drive away in the cruiser. From where she was standing, she couldn't see the cattle gate or even the road that led to it, but Dakota would have had line of sight of it from the main house.

"Did the hands check Tori's car trunk to make sure no one was with her?" she asked.

"Yeah." He walked to the window and stood next to her. "You think I should call Court for backup?"

Obviously, Dakota was as uneasy about this as she was, but she had to shake her head about calling Court. If Egan had wanted that, he would have already made sure Dakota called him. But Egan had likely figured that his brother already had his hands full without doing backup. Plus, Dakota was there if something went wrong.

Since it wasn't a good idea for her to stay at the window, Jordan went back to the sofa so she could start searching through her files again. She knew she was on edge, but she didn't know just how much until she gasped when the sound of her phone ringing shot through the room.

She hoped it might be Egan's name on the screen and that he was calling to tell her that he was nixing this plan to talk to Tori. But it wasn't Egan. It was coming from an unknown caller again. Since this was probably Christian, she debated if she wanted to talk to him or not. Her nerves were already right at the surface, and a conversation with him likely wouldn't help that. Still, he might be calling about something important so she hit the answer button.

"Jordan," the caller said. Not Christian. Or if it was, he was using a scrambler to disguise himself. This was the same voice of the person who'd called earlier.

The killer.

"What do you want?" Jordan snapped.

The man laughed. "Ready for some fun?" he taunted.

Before she could even respond to that, Jordan heard something she didn't want to hear. The security alarm went off.

Someone was breaking into the house.

From his rearview mirror, Egan kept watch of the guesthouse until it was out of sight. He hadn't wanted to leave Jordan, but he had to do something to put an end to the danger. Those hired thugs had already come way too close to killing her, and he couldn't risk another attack.

Not that Tori would for certain be able to help him with that.

Still, he had to try.

Egan drove past the main house, glancing at the CSIs who were still at work. It was nearly six pm, past what some would consider normal duty hours. However, the CSIs would stay until the job was done.

The body was still there, but since the medical examiner's van was indeed already in place, it meant they'd be moving it soon. That didn't exactly mean things would return to normal. However, it was a start.

He soon spotted the silver car on the other side of the cattle gate. The hands had wisely kept the gate closed, which meant Tori couldn't have driven onto the property even if that was what she'd intended to do. She didn't look ready to do that, though. She was leaning against the driver's door, and she had one hand pressed to her neck. Her other hand was on her forehead.

Tori looked up, her attention zooming straight toward him as he drove closer. Egan stopped, but as he'd told Jordan, he didn't get out. Instead, he backed up and angled the cruiser so that the driver's side would be facing Tori. He drew his gun, holding it on his lap in case he needed it, and he lowered the window just enough for her to see him.

"You have to help me," Tori said. She went toward him, stumbling several times, before she caught on to the wrought iron rods that made up the gate. "Someone tried to kill me."

"Welcome to the club," he grumbled.

She flinched as if he had struck her. "You're a cop. People probably try to kill you all the time, but this is a first for me. You need to let me in. You need to put me in protective custody."

Egan had to admit that Tori did look as if someone had attacked her. Her hair was a tangled mess, and her blouse sleeve had been torn. There were also what appeared to be bruises and scrapes on her knees.

"What happened?" Egan asked her.

She glanced around, obviously trying to make sure they weren't about to be attacked. Of course, Tori could be faking that glance, and that was why Egan kept watch, too.

"When I was leaving the sheriff's office, someone was hiding in my car. I didn't see the person until it was too late, and he used a stun gun on me." Tori turned to show him the marks on her neck.

"Interesting. That's almost identical to what Kirk said happened to him," Egan commented.

Tory's eyes widened, and a quick burst of breath left her mouth. "Kirk was hurt, too?"

Egan studied her to see if she was truly surprised, but he couldn't tell. "He's at the hospital now."

He wouldn't mention that Kirk might not make it. If Tori was genuinely shocked, hearing that might make her hysterical, and he might not get any information from her.

"Did the same person attack both of us?" she asked.

Egan lifted his shoulder. "I'm still trying to work that out. Did you get a good look at the person who used the stun gun on you?"

"No. He was wearing a ski mask. It happened so fast, and then he clubbed me on the head. I didn't black out, but I couldn't move. I could hear, though."

Again, that was similar to what'd happened to Kirk except Kirk had then been shot. "Did the man say anything or threaten you?"

"Not that I can recall. Like I said, it happened fast. But I think he was about to shoot me when he heard someone." She touched her fingers to her head as if she was trying to recall something. "I think the guy got spooked. Maybe because Kirk called out to him?" She looked at Egan again. "Was Kirk there, or did I imagine he was?"

"I have no idea." But it was possible that it was indeed Kirk if he was the person behind this. Maybe he'd set it all up, and then one of his hired thugs had turned on him.

But why would Kirk have wanted to hurt Tori?

They'd seemed pretty chummy when they'd been at his office, and Tori had mentioned she'd been staying at Kirk's house. Maybe Kirk hadn't intended for things to go this far. Still, there was something about this that didn't make sense.

"If you honestly thought your life was in danger, why come here?" Egan asked her. "Why not go back to the sheriff's office or the hospital?"

"Once I could move, I knew I had to get out of there. I was afraid the guy with the stun gun would come back to finish me off. So, I started driving, and I ended up here."

Egan was even more skeptical now. "How'd you know this was the McCall Ranch and that I'd be here?"

"I'd looked it up when I first thought someone

might be trying to kill me." She paused, her mouth trembling. "I thought maybe you were the one who wanted me dead."

Jordan had thought that, too. At first. She didn't feel that way now, and that was because of their… well, relationship. If that was indeed what they had. One thing was for certain, he no longer felt the same about Jordan as he had two days ago, and he could partly blame the sex for that. Sex had a way of ripping down barriers. And clouding his mind.

Like now.

Tori was clearly still a suspect. Maybe she'd been a victim or she could be just playing the part. Either way, it was obvious he wasn't going to get what he needed from her.

"Wait here," Egan told Tori, "and I'll have a couple of the hands follow you back into town. I want you to go to the hospital so your injuries can be checked."

And that way, Egan could get a report back from the doctor so he could figure out if her injuries were self-induced.

"I don't want to wait here," she protested. Her grip tightened on the gate. "It's dangerous. I want to go with you."

No way would that happen, but he had a sickening feeling that Tori might be trying to stall him. And there was only one reason she would do something like that.

Hell.

Egan glanced back at the medical examiner's van and the other two cars that the CSIs had almost certainly used to get onto the ranch. "Did either of you search those vehicles?" he asked the hands.

The hands both shook their heads, causing Egan to curse. Tori called out for him to stop, but he ignored her. He turned the cruiser around as fast as he could, hit the accelerator and sped toward the guesthouse.

He kept watch in his rearview mirror to make sure that Tori didn't try to get past the gate or attack one of the hands. She didn't. She appeared to be cursing at him when she hurried back to her car and got inside. Egan slowed just enough to make sure she wasn't going to ram into the gate, but instead she drove out in as much of a hurry as Egan was.

His pulse was pounding by the time he braked to a stop on the side of the guesthouse behind Dakota's cruiser. He got his weapon ready, stepped out and immediately heard something.

The security alarm.

It was clanging, which meant something or someone had triggered one of the sensors. He figured it was too much to hope that Jordan or Dakota had accidently set it off.

And then he saw something else from the corner of his eye that confirmed that this wasn't a false alarm.

He saw the man climbing through the bedroom window.

Egan took aim and fired. But it was too late. The man was inside the house.

Chapter Fifteen

Jordan had gotten her gun the moment she heard the security alarm go off, but the alarm was also masking other sounds that she needed to hear.

Like the specific location of the intruder.

Dakota readied his gun, too, and they both fired gazes around the guest cottage, looking for any signs of what was going on. Nothing. Well, nothing until the thick blast from someone firing a shot outside.

That caused her heart to jump to her throat, and she hurried to the security keypad so she could turn off the alarm. That was when she heard the sound of hurried footsteps coming from the bedroom. The door was open, and she pivoted in that direction.

But it was too late.

A man was already there. Someone whom she didn't recognize, and he had his gun aimed. Not at her but rather at Dakota.

The thug pulled the trigger before either Dakota or she could, and the shot slammed into the deputy's chest. Dakota made a sharp sound of pain and dropped to the floor.

Jordan knew the bulletproof vest had probably stopped it from being a fatal shot, but it had obviously knocked the breath out of him. The next one could kill him if she didn't do something to prevent it from happening. Since the gunman was also wearing Kevlar, it meant she had to go for a head shot.

Jordan was about to fire, but the man lunged at her. There were only a few feet of space between them, and that was gone within a split second when he crashed into her and knocked her gun from her hand. They both went to the floor with the back of her head slamming against the door. It hit so hard that the pain shot through her, and her vision blurred. Not good. Because she needed to be able to see her attacker to try to stop him.

Her attacker obviously had no trouble seeing her, though. He bashed his elbow right into her chin, causing her head to slam against the door again. This time, it was more than just blurry vision. She saw the dark spots and knew that she was about to lose consciousness.

"Jordan?" someone called out.

Egan. He was close. Right outside from the sound of it, and it made her wonder if he'd been the one to fire the shot she'd heard. Of course, it could have been this goon shooting at Egan, and if so, she prayed he was all right. Dakota, too. The deputy was alive, but he was clutching his chest and moaning in pain.

The man hit her again with his elbow when she tried to reach back for the doorknob. This blow was the hardest yet, and she was surprised that it hadn't broken her jaw. It only added to the god-awful pain she was already feeling.

She fought to stay alert. And tried to fight the thug, too, but he outweighed her by a good fifty pounds. Jordan latched on to him with the only weapon she had. She sank her teeth into his hand and bit down with every ounce of energy she could muster.

The thug howled in pain and punched her again. That stopped her, temporarily, but she would have gone back for a second assault if he hadn't caught on to her hair. He grabbed a huge handful, and he dragged her to her feet.

He put the gun to her head just as Egan threw open the door.

"Watch out!" Jordan tried to warn him.

But it was already too late. The thug turned his gun in Egan's direction. And he fired. Thankfully, Egan jumped out of the way in the nick of time, and he landed on the ground just to the side of the door.

Since the thug's gun was right against her ear, the shot, and the one that followed, was deafening. The sound roared through her head and made the pain even worse. But she tried to push the fear and pain aside so she could help Egan. That was hard to do, though, because her attacker had her in a choke hold.

Egan glanced around the corner of the door and lifted his gun. He cursed, though, probably because he realized he didn't have a clean shot. Her attacker was using her as a human shield. Plus, if Egan leaned out too far, he would make an easy target, and this time the thug might not miss.

She could hear Dakota groaning. The deputy was still on the floor, still trying to catch his breath. But if he managed that, he might be able to pick up his gun that had fallen to the floor and use it to stop the man before someone got killed.

"Did Tori send you?" she managed to ask the man.

Jordan didn't expect him to answer, and he didn't. That didn't mean Tori was innocent, and the timing of her visit was certainly suspicious. The woman could have used her arrival as a distraction so that her hired gun could break into the house. The goon might not have tried something like that if Egan had been inside. And Jordan was certain that Egan was cursing himself about that.

"I've already called for backup," Egan told the man. "Let Jordan go."

"Not a chance. She's coming with me." And with the choke hold even tighter now, he started backing up toward the rear door that was just off the kitchen.

Maybe the man had someone out there waiting to help him. Or he could have a vehicle he could use to escape with her. Yes, the hands had been keeping watch, but that didn't mean someone couldn't have gotten past them.

Egan continued to make glances around the door. No doubt looking for an opening so he could shoot. Jordan doubted the hired gun was going to allow such an opening, so she looked around for anything she could use to help fight him off. There was a wooden block with knives on the kitchen counter, but they were out of her reach. The only other thing was a coffee cup.

So, that was what Jordan grabbed.

She figured she had only a few seconds at most, so the moment she had it in her grip, she threw her weight against the man. In the same motion, she raised the cup and bashed it against the side of his head.

He cursed her and immediately tried to jostle her back into his choke hold. Jordan dropped down, sliding right out of his grasp. She didn't take the time to get her footing. She just started running toward the front door, and the moment she reached it, she went out and ducked to the side as Egan had done.

Egan was crouched down with a tight grip on his gun, but he used his left hand to sling her behind him. So that he was in front and protecting her. Jordan didn't want his protection, though, if it meant he was going to take a bullet for her.

And the bullet came, all right.

It bashed into the door frame, tearing off a chunk of the wood. The second one did even more damage.

"Keep watch behind us," Egan told her.

That sent her pulse skyrocketing. Of course, she'd known this thug might not have come alone, but she didn't want Egan and her to be ambushed.

Egan took out his backup weapon from the sliding holster in his jeans and handed it to her. Good. At least now she had a way to try to defend them. Thankfully, though, there didn't seem to be anyone else around them, though she could see the CSIs peering around the side of the main house. They'd no doubt heard the shots and were looking to see if they could help.

Jordan motioned for them to stay back, and she turned, ready to help Egan with the hired gun. But the shots stopped. Egan cursed again, and since she couldn't see into the guesthouse, she wasn't sure what had caused his reaction. Or why his muscles suddenly went even stiffer than they already were.

"Backup plan," the thug growled. And he laughed.

She risked peering around the jamb then, and her stomach went to her knees. That was because Dakota was no longer on the floor. Just as the thug had done to her, he now had Dakota in front of him.

"You'll be coming with me," the thug said, looking directly at Jordan. "Or else Deputy Cowboy gets a bullet to the head."

FROM THE MOMENT that Egan had seen the gunman and the situation in the guesthouse, he'd known it could come down to this. He'd just hoped, though, that he could stop the snake before anyone got hurt.

But someone was already hurt.

Dakota had a chest injury probably from a bullet that this jerk had fired into his bulletproof vest. Jordan's face was bruised and bleeding, and she was clearly in pain. Enough pain that forced Egan to rein in his temper. If he didn't, he was going to rush inside and tear that idiot gunman limb from limb. He couldn't risk doing that because he could be shot.

That would leave Dakota and Jordan even more vulnerable than they already were.

And they were already plenty vulnerable enough.

He didn't even know what they were up against. If his theory was right about the gunman getting onto the ranch in the ME's van, then he could have brought several hired thugs with him. Maybe the person behind this had come as well, with the plan to finish them all off.

Egan glanced behind him at the CSIs. They weren't armed, so hopefully they'd stay behind cover. Maybe Court would arrive soon, too. Egan had texted him right before he'd unlocked the guesthouse door. But even if Court did get there in record time, he didn't want his brother walking into the middle of what could easily turn out to be a gunfight.

"Well?" the thug snarled. "Are you just gonna cower there and let the deputy die?"

The question and the attitude were no doubt meant to draw Jordan out. And it just might work, too. That was why Egan stayed in front of her. He considered asking her to use her former hostage-negotiating skills, but he didn't want her to engage in conversation with his moron. Jordan was almost certainly thinking about her last hostage situation. One where Shanna had been killed. This thug would play on that grief and use it to try to kill her.

"If you shoot the deputy," Egan tossed back at him, "you'll lose your human shield, and I'll blow your brains out. You're sure you're ready to die for your boss?"

Egan glanced around the doorjamb and saw that the guy's jaw had turned to iron. Good. Egan wanted to keep pushing at any hot button he could find.

"Did your boss pay you enough to die?" Egan added. He adjusted his stance in case he had to fire. No way could he surrender or give in to this guy's demands. Because Egan was certain the thug's orders were to kill Jordan and him. Then he'd kill Dakota so there wouldn't be any witnesses.

"I can match whatever your boss is paying you," Egan went on. "And give you a sweet deal to cut down on your jail time."

The last part was an out-and-out lie. Even if he could have, he wouldn't have made that kind of deal and let a killer or would-be killer walk. Egan suspected, though, that this guy fell into the killer category. He'd likely been the one to kill at least one of the recipients.

But why?

Egan still didn't have an answer to that.

"Shut up," the man finally snapped. "And get the woman out here right now."

He jammed his gun even harder against Dakota's head, and the deputy winced. Dakota also made direct eye contact with Egan, maybe a way of letting him know that he'd regained enough of his breath to do something to stop this.

"The woman's not going anywhere." Egan made sure there was no doubt whatsoever about that in his tone.

The guy's jaw got even tighter, and he began to fire

some nervous glances around the room. Maybe trying to decide if he should just cut his losses and try to escape with Dakota. But obviously Dakota had a different notion about having that play out. The deputy lifted his left eyebrow, and even though Egan didn't know exactly what he had in mind, he got ready.

Just as Dakota jabbed his elbow into the guy's gut.

Coughing and cursing, the man staggered back. And he pulled the trigger of his gun. Egan wasn't sure where the shot went, but he didn't waste any time. He charged into the guesthouse and tackled the thug before he could get off another shot.

The momentum of his body and speed sent both the thug and him crashing against the fridge. Egan managed to hold on to his gun, but so did the thug. He tried to bring it up so he could shoot Egan, but he put a stop to that by head-butting the idiot. He'd have a helluva headache later, but it'd be worth it because the impact knocked the guy against the fridge again.

This time, Egan disarmed him. And he punched him.

"That's payback for what you did to Jordan and Dakota," Egan growled. "I need some plastic cuffs," he added to Dakota.

While Dakota was getting those from his pocket, Egan turned the thug, shoving him face-first against the fridge. He wasn't easy with him when he put on the cuffs, but then this idiot hadn't been easy with Jordan or Dakota.

Once he had him restrained, Egan put him belly-down on the floor, the best position to make sure he didn't try to escape. Egan wanted him alive. And talking. He wanted to know the name of the person who'd hired him to create this hellish nightmare.

But the nightmare wasn't over.

Egan's heart slammed against his chest when he looked in the doorway to check on Jordan.

Damn.

She wasn't alone. There was a man wearing a ski mask directly behind her. And he'd taken her hostage.

Chapter Sixteen

Jordan couldn't breathe. The man holding her was choking her as he moved back from the door with her. But she didn't need her breath to silently curse herself for getting into a position like this. She should have been paying closer attention to her surroundings, but instead she'd been focused on keeping her gun aimed at the thug whom Egan was arresting. She hadn't wanted him to try to fight his way out this situation and hurt Egan or Dakota in the process.

Now she was paying for her lapse in judgment.

Unfortunately, though, Egan and Dakota might have to pay, too.

Both of them immediately took cover, which meant they were out of the line of fire, but she doubted that would last. Egan probably wouldn't just stand by while she was in danger. But she wished he would. Jordan wished that he would stay put and save himself and his deputy. Because if he came out after her, he'd be an easy target for this snake who had her.

Unlike the hired gun who'd shot Dakota, this one didn't say anything to Egan. He just started dragging her toward Egan's cruiser. It wasn't far, only a couple of yards away, which meant it wouldn't take him long to get her there and inside.

His choke hold was so tight that Jordan wasn't even sure she could speak loud enough for the goon to hear her, but she tried anyway. "How did you get on the ranch?"

In the grand scheme of things, it wasn't important for her to know the answer, but she wanted to hear him speak so she could try to recognize his voice. If he was a stranger, just another hired gun, maybe then she could try to bargain with him by offering to pay him more than his boss was paying him. That hadn't worked with the goon inside the house, but she had to try.

"He came in the ME's van," she heard Egan say. He was no longer in the kitchen but rather to the side of the doorway. "He knew the van would be coming to the ranch, and he used it to sneak onto the grounds."

The man certainly didn't deny that.

Egan stepped out even farther into the doorway, and she prayed if this man turned his gun on him that Egan would at least get down.

"Take me instead of Jordan," Egan bargained. Jordan shook her head to nix that. Or rather she tried. But the man held on, and he didn't stop until he had her right next to the cruiser.

"You think it's smart to start driving off with Jordan?" Egan continued. With a firm grip on his gun, he came out into the yard. "She's a former cop. She'll fight you. And if you wreck, it could kill both of you."

For the first time since the man had taken her, she felt some hesitation. He didn't reach for the door. He stood there a moment staring at Egan.

"Get behind the wheel," the man said. Like the phone calls, it wasn't a normal voice. He was using some kind of scrambler. Maybe a small one hidden beneath the ski mask.

"No," Jordan managed to say. She definitely didn't want Egan coming with them because it would be a death sentence. But her "no" didn't do a thing to stop him.

"Drop your gun on the ground," the man ordered.

Now it was Egan's turn to hesitate, and she knew why. She had his backup gun. Or rather she'd had it before this thug had knocked it from her hand and taken her captive. Now, if Egan surrendered his primary, he wouldn't have a weapon that he could use to fight back.

Egan's hesitation didn't last long, and her heart sank when he tossed his gun on the ground and started for the cruiser. She braced herself in case the goon tried to kill him, but he didn't. With her neck still in his tight grip, he stepped back so that Egan could open the door, and he got behind the wheel. The man then shoved her into the back seat and followed right behind her. He didn't waste any time putting the gun back to her head.

"Drive," he told Egan.

Dakota came to the door of the guesthouse, and

the deputy looked ready to come after them, but Egan waved him off and started the engine. Even though Jordan didn't want to be at the mercy of this snake, she also didn't want the deputy hurt or killed. If Dakota tried to get to them, that would almost certainly happen.

Egan's phone rang. Perhaps it was Court or one of the hands or CSIs trying to figure out what was going on, but Egan didn't answer it.

"Where to?" Egan asked as he put on his seat belt.

He met her gaze in the rearview mirror, and it wasn't hard to tell what he was thinking. Egan was blaming himself for this. But it wasn't his fault. Nor was it hers. Jordan put the blame for this solely on the shoulders of the man who now had them at gunpoint.

Since she'd been a cop, she knew how plenty of situations like these played out. If their captor could manage to get them to a secondary location, it would be easier for him to kill them. Probably the only reason he hadn't done that at the guesthouse was because he wouldn't have had an escape. This way he did, which meant he probably intended to kill them as soon as he had them off the ranch.

"Just drive," the man snarled. "When you get to the gate, make sure your hands back off or they'll die. Then get the gate open."

Egan had a remote to do that, but maybe the man didn't know that. A remote would just get them off the ranch faster, and maybe Egan could claim he needed to get out of the vehicle to open it. Of course, he wouldn't use that opportunity to get away, but maybe he could at least get himself out of the line of fire. That might give Court time to arrive so he could help them put a stop to this.

When Egan started driving, Jordan looked back at the CSIs. They were armed now, maybe with weapons they'd gotten from the house. But like the ranch hands, they were unable to do anything for fear their captor would kill them. Or rather one of them anyway. Jordan figured she was the expendable one now, and it sickened her to think that she might die and not even know the reason why.

The person under the ski mask could be another hired gun. One working for Leeroy or even Kirk if his thugs had indeed gone rogue. Or the man's boss could be Tori, who was working on behalf of Drew. She couldn't rule out their other suspect, either—Christian.

"Why are you doing this?" she asked.

He didn't answer, of course. He just kept the gun on her while he watched every move that Egan made. She felt his hand tense, though, when Egan approached the gate. That was probably because of the two armed hands there.

"Call them," the man said to Egan. "Tell them to stand down."

Egan took out his phone and did that, and she watched as the hands hesitantly lowered their guns and stepped back off the road and away from the gate. Egan looked at her again in the mirror, and it seemed as if he was trying to tell her something. Exactly what, though, she didn't know, but Jordan tried to brace herself for whatever it was he was about to do.

She didn't have to wait long.

Without warning, Egan slammed his foot on the accelerator, crashing the cruiser into the iron gate.

EGAN HAD KNOWN the crash was a huge risk, but everything he did at this point would be. But the biggest risk of all would have been to allow this thug to get Jordan and him off the ranch. This way, he at least had some backup if he managed to get her out of the cruiser.

That was a big *if*, though.

Egan was wearing his seat belt, and when he'd made the call to the hands, he'd turned off the airbag so that it wouldn't punch him in the face. But Jordan and the thug holding her weren't strapped in so they went flying into the back of the seat. Exactly what Egan had wanted. Now he only had to hope and pray that Jordan didn't get hurt worse than she already was.

The man cursed, the words still filtered through the scrambler, and he regained his balance a little sooner than Egan had wanted. He also managed to hang on to his gun. Still, Egan came over the seat after him. He needed to pin the guy long enough for Jordan to escape.

"Get out of here," Egan shouted to her. "Run!" And he launched himself at the man.

Egan tackled him, trying to pin him to the seat, but he didn't manage to do that before the idiot pulled the trigger. The shot blasted through the cruiser, and

Egan prayed the sound of pain that Jordan made was because it hurt her ears and not because she'd been shot. He couldn't check on her, though, because Egan was suddenly in the fight for their lives.

The man bashed his gun so hard against Egan's head that he was certain he'd have a concussion. Still, that didn't stop him. Egan swung his fist and managed to connect with the guy's jaw. His head flopped back, but he managed to get off another shot.

Worse, Jordan was still in the cruiser.

Egan wanted to shout at her again to get out, but she started hitting the thug on the head. It wasn't doing much to deter him, though, because he fired a third time, and he latched on to Jordan, dragging her against him. He was going to use her as a human shield again if Egan didn't do something to stop it.

From the corner of his eye, Egan saw the hands move closer. They both had their guns aimed, but there was no way they had a clean shot because Jordan was between the hands and the thug.

Jordan kept clawing at the man, and everything seemed to go still when she ripped the ski mask off his face. Egan had expected to be staring down at another hired gun. But he wasn't.

It was Christian.

Jordan gasped and then froze for a split second. It was just enough time for Christian to grab her again and put the gun to her head.

"I won't miss at point-blank range," Christian growled, and he used his left hand to yank the voice scrambler pressed to his throat.

No, Christian wouldn't miss, and the look in the man's eyes told Egan everything he needed to know. Christian was going to kill them.

And Egan knew why.

"You're a dirty cop," Egan snapped. "And you were afraid Jordan would uncover the evidence in those files she had."

Christian certainly didn't deny it. "Get behind the wheel again, and you'd better pray you didn't damage the cruiser so much that you can't drive it. If you did, I start putting bullets in Jordan. The shots won't be fatal, but she'll be in so much pain that she'll wish she was dead."

It wasn't a bluff. Christian would do it, and Egan wasn't sure he could watch another woman he cared about be gunned down right in front of him. He fought to keep the flashbacks at bay, but it was hard to do.

Hell. He could lose Jordan.

"Drive!" Christian shouted.

Egan didn't have a choice. He climbed back over the seat and hoped he got another chance to stop this piece of dirt from doing any more harm.

Thankfully, the cruiser engine was still running, but Egan didn't know if the engine had been damaged or not. He might not make it far, and he'd almost certainly meet Court along the way. He had to make sure his brother didn't get hurt while trying to save them. His first priority, though, was to get Jordan out of this. She was no doubt Christian's primary target. The only reason the cop wanted Egan dead was probably because he knew Jordan had talked to him about what she'd uncovered in those files.

Too bad that Egan hadn't let someone else know. That way, if Christian did manage to murder them and get away, then his brother and Griff could go after him. Egan wasn't even sure the hands had gotten a good enough look at Christian's face to ID him.

This time, Egan used the remote to open the gate, and he kept watch of Christian and Jordan while he waited for it to slide open. Christian would be ready if Egan tried to crash the vehicle again so he couldn't do that. However, he could watch for some kind of opening for him to stop this.

"You killed all those people to cover up what you did," Jordan said. Her voice was trembling, but she managed to glare at the man.

"I did what I had to do," Christian mumbled.

"No, you did that to save yourself from the death penalty," she fired back. "People died, and two men are on death row because of you."

"Those men deserved it. They weren't angels. They were just as deep in the operation as I was."

The *operation* in this case was human trafficking. And yeah, there'd been deaths associated with both cases.

"I'm guessing the men on death row didn't know you'd honchoed both the human trafficking and their arrests," Egan commented.

He watched Christian's expression in the mirror and was pleased when he saw the raw anger in the cop's eyes. Maybe he could goad Christian into turning his gun on him instead of Jordan.

When the gate was finally open, Egan drove through it and onto the road that would take him to the highway. He spotted Court's truck, making his way toward them, and he knew he didn't have much time.

"I'm guessing Leeroy and Kirk didn't have anything to do with this," Egan continued. "But you're working for Tori, right? She's the one who put all of this together. She's definitely got more brains than you do."

No way did Egan believe that, but it got the reaction he wanted. Another flash of anger went through Christian's eyes.

"I'm the one holding Jordan," Christian practically yelled. "I'm the one cleaning up my own mess. That bimbo lawyer didn't have anything to do with this. In fact, if I hadn't gotten the wrong woman, she'd be dead by now."

So, Lorena's death had been a mistake. That wouldn't bring much comfort to her grieving family, and Christian didn't seem the least bit concerned that he'd murdered a woman who'd had no part in this.

Egan rarely put the cold-blooded-killer label on anyone, but it fit Christian to a T. Worse, he was a cop, and he'd used his badge to help him commit these crimes.

"You're the one who left that note with Lorena's body?" Egan asked.

"Of course!" Christian snapped. "But that doesn't matter now. None of that matters."

Court stopped his truck at the turn from the highway to the ranch road, and Egan knew his brother was preparing to fight back. That meant Egan had to do something now. He just prayed that the *something* he was about to do was right.

When he was only about ten yards from Court, Egan jerked the steering wheel to the right and sent the cruiser straight into the ditch. It was like hitting a brick wall, and this time Egan wasn't wearing his seat belt. He slammed into the steering wheel, the pain shooting through him, but he ignored it and barreled over the seat again.

Christian was ready for him.

But Egan was ready, too.

Christian had turned the gun on him, but Egan crashed right into him before the man could pull the trigger. Egan grabbed hold of Christian's right wrist, pinning his shooting hand and the gun against the window. But Christian didn't exactly surrender. The cop used his left fist to punch Egan.

Jordan fought, too. She latched on to Christian's arm to try to stop him from hitting Egan again, but the rage and adrenaline fueled Christian so that he could easily throw her off. Jordan landed hard against the cruiser door, and Egan figured that would only add more injuries to the ones Christian had already given her.

The thought of that gave Egan his own surge of rage and adrenaline. Egan couldn't pry the man's grip off his gun, and he managed to get his own hand in a position to bash the weapon against Christian's head. Christian cursed him and kept fighting, but Egan continued to hit him with the gun. Egan had so much anger in him that he hoped he bashed his brains out.

The cruiser door flew open, and Egan got a glimpse of Court. His brother had his weapon raised, but like the hands he didn't have a clean shot. Egan tried to do something about that.

While Egan continued to hit Christian, he also tried to push Jordan out of the cruiser. She wouldn't budge, though, and she managed to land some hard blows to the side of Christian's face.

Until Christian pulled the trigger.

The fear slammed into Egan as hard as the adrenaline had, and he pinpointed all of that into one last effort to stop this snake. Egan rammed the gun not against Christian's head but to his throat.

Finally.

Christian made a garbled sound as he fought for his breath, and he relaxed his grip on the gun just enough for Egan to take hold of it. He immediately pointed it at Christian.

"Please move so I can kill you," Egan warned him. And it wasn't a bluff. More than anything he wanted this man to pay for what he'd done.

Well, almost more than anything.

He needed Jordan to be okay, but Egan was almost afraid to look at her. When he did, his stomach went into a knot. There was blood on her face, and she looked as if she'd been beaten to a pulp. But she was alive, thank God, and it didn't appear that Christian had managed to shoot her.

"Go to Court," Egan told her, though he wasn't sure how he managed to speak. It felt as if his throat had clamped shut.

She gave a shaky nod and started to move. But Christian moved, too.

He whipped out a knife from his pocket.

Egan saw the light glint off the shiny metal blade, and he fired at him, the bullet slamming into Christian.

But the damage had already been done.

In that exact second that Egan's bullet was killing him, Christian plunged the knife into Jordan.

Chapter Seventeen

This was a repeat of the nightmare.

Just like the night Shanna had died, Egan could do nothing but pray and pace across the hospital waiting room. Maybe, just maybe, this would have a different outcome.

The images kept replaying in his head. Of Christian jabbing his knife into Jordan. Images of the blood and the color draining from Jordan's face. There'd been no color in Christian's, either, because Egan's shot had killed him, but now the same thing might happen to Jordan.

"You want me to pace for you for a while so you can get some rest?" Court asked him.

Egan appreciated his brother's concern and even Court's half attempt to lighten things up, but no way could he sit down. If he stopped, he might explode. Too bad he didn't have Christian there in front of him so he had a way to burn off some of this dangerous energy coiled inside him.

Court's phone buzzed, something it'd been doing a lot since they'd arrived at the hospital nearly a half hour earlier. Egan suspected Court was getting updates on the case. Updates that Egan wanted to hear, but first he needed to make sure Jordan was okay, and that wasn't happening.

When they'd arrived, the nurses had immediately whisked Jordan away and had stopped Egan when he tried to follow. He'd argued with them, but then the doctor had come out and said he might need to prep Jordan for surgery. Even that hadn't worked until the doctor had reminded him that the knife wound was in the same area as Jordan's only kidney.

If the kidney was damaged, Jordan might die.

That had finally stopped Egan from trying to follow Jordan, but he was wishing it hadn't. There were things he wanted to say to Jordan, and he might not get a chance to do that.

"Tori's all right," Court relayed when he finished his latest call. "But the marshals are going to put her in protective custody for a while just in case Christian has another hired thug out there somewhere."

That was a good precaution to take, though Egan figured any hired thug would be long gone now that his boss had been killed. There'd be no reason for someone to hang around and risk arrest when there were multiple murder charges involved.

"Thea's questioning Christian's gunman who you caught at the guesthouse, and she's been sending me text updates," Court went on. "The guy's name is Steve Bartow, and he's talking. He says he wants a plea deal."

"He's not getting one," Egan growled.

Delores Fossen

211

Court made a sound of agreement. "He claims he didn't kill anyone, that the murders are all on Christian."

He might be saying that to save his own skin, but it didn't matter. Accessory to murder carried the same penalty as murder. "I want him charged with all the deaths and the attacks. If he gives us anything that will tie up any remaining loose ends, I'll consider asking the DA to take the death penalty off the table."

"You think there are any loose ends?" Court asked.

"Not really. I believe Christian might have even been the sniper who attacked the ranch," Egan added. "As a cop, he certainly had the training to do something like that." And he would have known how to evade an arrest.

It sickened Egan to think that Christian could have been following their every move through legal police channels. That was probably how he'd managed to get to those other women.

Court got another text. "It's from Thea," he said after he read whatever was on the screen. "The talking hired thug said it was Christian who attacked Kirk. Apparently, Christian did that because he thought Kirk and Tori were on to him."

If they were, neither Tori nor Kirk had brought that to Egan. Of course, there'd been a lot of accusations and bogus info thanks to Christian. Maybe he'd let something slip, and Tori and Kirk had figured out he was up to no good. Egan certainly wished he'd figured it out sooner. If he had, Jordan might not have gotten hurt.

The ER doors slid open, and because Egan was still on edge, he automatically put his hand over his gun. And he kept it there when he saw Leeroy come in. Leeroy looked around the room and made a bee-line toward Egan when he spotted him.

"I don't have time for your smart mouth and venom," Egan snapped. He expected that to set Leeroy off and have the man launch into a tirade.

He didn't. In fact, Leeroy nodded. "It's all over town that the dirty cop was killing the folks who got Shanna's organs. Is it true?"

"Yeah. He did it so he could murder Jordan to silence her." Just saying that twisted away at him, and it felt as if someone had put his heart in a vise and was squeezing hard. "The other donors were just decoys he used to cover up his real motive."

Leeroy shook his head and muttered something under his breath that Egan didn't catch. "You know I was against Shanna donating her organs, but I never wanted this. I never wanted anyone else to die."

The man sounded genuine, and Egan decided to take him at his word. "Then, you need to back off. Jordan could have a long recovery ahead of her, and she'll need some peace and quiet." He refused to think the worst, that this could end the same way for her as it had for Shanna.

Leeroy nodded. "I won't give her any trouble. Nor Tori." He paused. "I guess you could say this is a truce."

Since they'd been at each other's throats for two years, Egan was suspicious. "Why the change of heart?"

Leeroy stayed quiet a moment. "It was all these people dying and getting hurt. I guess it finally hit me square in the face that I'll never get Shanna back. But I don't wish anyone else any harm. Not even you. I hope Jordan recovers and you two have a happy life together." He tipped his Stetson in a farewell greeting and walked away.

A happy life together?

Egan silently repeated those words to himself, wondering if it was even possible.

"You think hell just froze over?" Court asked.

No. This was more like a mini-miracle. One that Egan would take. He had enough craziness in his life and was glad to have Leeroy out of the mix.

Egan checked his watch again, and he was certain that time had stopped. So had his stash of patience, and he headed in the direction of the examining room where he'd seen the nurses take Jordan. Thankfully, Court didn't even try to stop him. Not that he could have anyway. Because Egan had to know what was going on.

He tried to prepare himself for what he would see. Maybe Jordan would be bleeding. Dying. And there was blood, all right. That was the first thing he noticed when he opened the door. Her blood-soaked shirt was on the table. She was still wearing a bra, but it was bloody, too.

But she wasn't dying, thank God.

In fact, she was sitting up while the nurse stitched up her side. Dr. Madison was there, and she immediately went to him as if to show him right back out. Egan held his ground.

"I have to know how Jordan is," he said with way too much emotion in his voice. He needed to stay calm because Jordan had already had a megadose of fear and emotion today.

"I'm fine," Jordan insisted, and she reached out her hand to him, causing the nurse to scold her for moving. "The knife didn't hit anything vital."

Egan snapped toward the doctor to make sure that was true, and he released the breath he'd been holding when Dr. Madison nodded.

"She was very lucky. Another inch higher, and... well, she wouldn't be sitting up right now."

An inch. That squeezed at his heart even more. That was how close he'd come to losing her.

When Jordan held out her hand again, he went to her. Egan wanted to pull her into his arms and kiss her. He wanted to hold her and make sure she was okay, but he didn't want to interfere with the stitches. Especially when he got a better look at the wound. It was an angry-looking gash on her rib cage.

"It looks worse than it is," Jordan assured him, and she gave his hand a gentle squeeze.

A nick would have looked bad enough for him right now, especially considering the bruises on her face. He lightly touched the one on her cheekbone, and he felt another jolt of rage for Christian. The idiot had done this to her, and death was too easy of a punishment for him.

"Again, it looks worse than it is," Jordan said when

he touched the bruise on her chin. "How about you? Please tell me yours are worse than they look."

Egan had no idea what she meant until he glanced at himself in the mirror above the sink. Yeah, he was a mess. His lip was busted, and he had plenty of bruises. Again, thanks to Christian.

"He refused medical treatment," the nurse said. Her name was Mildred Jenkins, and Egan had known her his entire life. What he hadn't known was that she was a tattletale.

"I'm okay," he assured Jordan, and that wasn't a lie. Now that he knew her injuries weren't life-threatening, that knot in his stomach had eased up considerably.

"How's Dakota?" Jordan asked.

"Court checked on him shortly after we got here. He's got a cracked rib and a fist-sized bruise on his chest, but he'll be fine."

"And Kirk?"

The news wasn't so good on that front. "He made it through surgery. I'm sure he'll be glad to hear that I no longer consider him a suspect."

"Yes," Jordan said, her voice cracking a little. There it was. More of that emotion that she probably didn't need, but it would be with them for a while. Maybe not a lifetime, though.

"In hindsight, the pieces all fit," Egan continued. "Christian orchestrated the murders to cover up his crimes, and he hired some thugs to help him." In this case, thugs whom he hoped to use to implicate others—like Leeroy.

But it hadn't worked.

"His hired thug is talking, by the way," Egan added.

"Good. I don't want any doubts in anyone's mind that Christian was a killer."

No. No doubts. And they didn't have to worry about his trying to launch another attack because he was dead.

"The cases of the men who Christian put in jail will have to be reviewed." Jordan made it sound as if she'd get straight to work on that. She probably would, too. Even after everything she'd been through, she'd want justice for those whom Christian had set up.

Mildred finally finished with the stitches, stepped back and looked Egan straight in the eyes. "When you kiss her, be careful, or you'll pop her stitches and bust open your lip again."

Egan frowned. "Why are you so sure I'm going to kiss her?" He was going to do that, but he'd wondered how Mildred had figured it out.

Mildred gave him an isn't-it-obvious look, patted his arm and walked out.

"I'll see about getting you some pain meds," Dr. Madison added. "And then you can take her home."

Egan had been so sure they'd be keeping Jordan overnight, so this was a gift. It meant she really was okay. Well, physically anyway. He didn't like that troubled look in Jordan's eyes, and that was why he did kiss her as soon as Dr. Madison was out of the room. He kept it gentle.

But Jordan didn't.

She slipped her arm around his waist, pulled him closer and made the kiss much longer and hotter than it should have been. It worked, though, because when she finally stopped the kiss the troubled look was gone, and she was smiling.

"I need to tell you some things," she said before he could speak. Ironic, since he was about to say that he needed to tell her some things, too.

"You saved my life," Jordan went on, "and I'm very thankful for that."

"I wouldn't have needed to save your life if I hadn't left to go talk to Tori. That's when the thug broke into the guesthouse, and he wouldn't have done that had I been there."

"You're wrong. He would have still gotten in, and he would have shot you just as he did Dakota. Except you would have had worse than a cracked rib because you weren't wearing Kevlar."

"I could have maybe stopped the guy from shooting," Egan argued.

He didn't get far with that argument, though, because she kissed him again. And again, it was way too hot. He was pretty sure he busted his lip open again, but he didn't care. He had Jordan in his arms, right where he wanted her.

"Now, on to the next thing I have to tell you," she said. "This is going to make you very uneasy, but I have to say it. I'm in love with you. I've been in love with you for most of my life, and I didn't realize it until today when I almost lost you." She stared at him. "Now you can panic."

Egan was feeling a lot of things, but panic sure as heck wasn't one of them. The knot in his stomach finally eased up. So did the tightness in his chest. And he felt something he hadn't felt in a long time.

Happiness.

Yep, that was what he was feeling, all right.

She kept staring at him as if trying to steel herself up for him to reject her. No way was that going to happen, so he gently pulled her back to him. "You love me?"

Jordan nodded.

"Good. Because I'm in love with you, too, and I don't want to go through another minute of it without letting you know."

She smiled again, and this one was dazzling. Jordan was obviously feeling a little happiness as well because it was all over her face. She caught on to the front of his shirt, wadding it up in her hand as she pulled him down for another kiss. It was hot enough to violate a lot of hospital rules, and Egan couldn't wait until she'd healed enough to haul her off to his bed.

"So, what are you doing for the rest of your life?" Jordan asked with her mouth still against his.

"Spending it with you, of course." And he went back to her for another kiss.

* * * * *

SIX MINUTES
TO MIDNIGHT

ELLE JAMES

I'd like to dedicate this book to the military working dogs, who are such an important addition to our fighting forces. They are loyal, smart and dedicated to doing what they do best. Friends of mine adopted a retired military working dog, which gave me the idea to include him in this book. Agar, thanks for your service!

Chapter One

"Four days and a wakeup," Trace McGuire, T-Mac to his friends, said as he sat across the table in the chow hall on Camp Lemonnier. They'd returned from their last mission in Niger with news they were scheduled to redeploy back to the States.

He glanced around the table at his friends. When they were deployed, they spent practically every waking hour together. In the past, being stateside was about the same. They'd go to work, train, get briefed, work out and then go back to their apartments. Most of the time, they'd end up at one of the team members' places to watch football, cook out or just lounge around and shoot the crap with each other. They were like family and never seemed to get tired of each other's company.

T-Mac suspected all that was about to change. All of his closest SEAL buddies had women in their lives now. All except him. Suddenly, going back to Virginia wasn't quite as appealing as it had been in the past. T-Mac sighed and drank his lukewarm coffee.

"I can't wait to see Reese." Diesel tapped a finger against the rim of his coffee cup. "I promised to take her on a real date when I get back to civilization."

"What? You're not going to take her swinging through the jungle, communing with the gorillas?" Buck teased.

Petty Officer Dalton Samuel Landon, otherwise known as Diesel, shook his head. "Nope. Been there, done that. I think I'll take her to a restaurant where we don't have to forage for food. Then maybe we'll go out to a nightclub." He tipped his head to the side. "I wonder if she likes to dance."

"You mean you don't know?" Big Jake Schuler, the tallest man on the team, rolled his eyes. "I would have thought that in the time you two spent traipsing along the Congo River, you would know everything there was to know about each other."

Diesel frowned. "I know what's important. She's not fragile, she can climb a tree when she needs to, she doesn't fall apart when someone's shooting at her and she can kiss like nobody's business." Diesel shrugged. "In fact, I'm looking forward to learning more. She's amazing. How many female bodyguards do you know?"

Big Jake held up his hands in surrender. "You got me there. None."

"I can't wait to see Angela." Corpsman Graham "Buck" Buckner, the team medic, smiled. "She's interviewing for positions around Little Creek."

"With her doctor credentials, and the work she did with Doctors Without Borders, she's sure to get on pretty quickly," Big Jake said. "If not one of the military hospitals, there are lots of civilian hospitals and clinics in the area."

Buck nodded. "I can't believe after all these years, she'd want to be close to me." He smiled. "I'm one lucky guy."

"Yeah, and maybe she'll talk you into going back to

school to finish your medical degree." Built solid like a tank, Percy Taylor had the tenacity of a pit bull, thus his nickname, Pitbull. He gave Buck a chin lift. "You'd make a good doc."

"What?" Buck spread his arms wide. "And give up all this?"

T-Mac chuckled. "I know. It's hard to believe anyone would want to stop being on call at all hours of the day and night, deploying to some of the worst hellholes on the planet and not getting back to see your family for months on end. Who would want to give up all that?"

"Hey, are we getting cynical in our old age?" Harmon Payne clapped a hand on T-Mac's back. "We're the ones who are going to suffer. We all have women to come home to now."

"All except T-Mac," Buck pointed out. "Maybe we should fix him up with someone? You think one of our women knows someone who could put up with his being a computer nerd and all?"

T-Mac shook his head. "I don't need help getting a date, thank you very much."

"I'll bet Reese has met some pretty hot chicks in the DC area through her work as a bodyguard," Diesel said. "Or maybe she still has some connections in the mixed-martial-arts community. One of those women are bound to be able to stand toe-to-toe with our guy."

"Seriously." T-Mac pushed to his feet. "I don't need a woman in my life. You all know how hard our lives are without relationships. I'm surprised all you self-confirmed bachelors broke the cardinal rule."

Pitbull stabbed the mystery meat on his tray with his fork and held it in the air, inspecting it with a frown. "What cardinal rule?"

T-Mac pounded his fist on the table. "Don't get into a permanent relationship as long as you're a full-time SEAL."

"Nope." Harm's eyes narrowed and his lips twisted. "I don't remember that line in the BUD/S training manual."

"Before we came to Africa," T-Mac reminded them, "we were drinking beer and talking about how we didn't have wives and kids—"

"Ha!" Pitbull held up a finger. "We were drinking beer. That's where we got off track."

Swallowing his irritation, T-Mac continued. "We all agreed that relationships were doomed to failure as long as we were doing the jobs we do. No woman will be satisfied being on a part-time status, what with us shipping out as often as we do to fight some battle nobody else wants."

"Then I found Marly," Pitbull said. "She can stand on her own two feet. And we get along pretty well." He smiled, his rugged face softening. "She's even getting me to like flying in crop dusters. And she's found a charter company in Virginia that wants her to pilot for them. She won't be waiting around for me to come home. Hell, we'll be lucky to be home at the same time."

"Exactly," T-Mac said. "And how's that going to work for you? You won't see each other."

Pitbull frowned. "We'll find time." His frown turned upside down. "And when we do…yup." He nodded. "We'll find time. I'm not ready to give up on her, and I don't think she'll give up on me."

"The point you're missing, T-Mac, is that we found women who can stand on their own," Harm said. "They don't need us any more than we need them. We *want* to be together. And that makes all the difference."

"Uh-huh." T-Mac knew they wouldn't listen. His five friends were so besotted by their women, they couldn't see past the rose-colored glasses to reality. He might as well save his breath.

"Guys." Buck stared around the table at everyone but T-Mac and lowered his voice to a conspiratorial whisper. "We've got to get T-Mac laid. He's strung way too tight. He's likely to blow a gasket soon."

"What's the use?" T-Mac pushed to his feet. "We're headed home in four days. Let's not screw anything up between now and then."

"What could possibly go wrong?" Buck asked with a grin and then ducked as everyone else threw their napkins and food at him.

Pitbull snorted. "Thanks for jinxing us, dirtbag."

"You guys can hang around talking about your women you'll rarely see. I'm going for a run." T-Mac walked out of the chow hall to the laughter of his friends.

"Gotta get him a girl," Buck said.

As T-Mac rounded the corner of one of the stacks of shipping containers that had been outfitted to become sleeping quarters, a hard object landed at his feet.

He jumped back, his heart racing, his first thought *Grenade!* Then a hair missile barreled toward him, all four legs moving like a blur.

T-Mac braced himself for impact.

The black-faced, sable German shepherd skidded to a stop, pushing up a cloud of dust in the process. He grabbed the object in his teeth and raced back the way he'd come.

"Agar, heel!" a female voice commanded.

The animal stopped immediately at the female soldier's side, dropped the hard rubber object on the ground and stared up at the woman as if eagerly awaiting the next command.

"Good dog." She patted him on the head and then glanced up. "Sorry. I didn't know you were there until after I'd thrown his KONG." Her hand continued to stroke the dog's head.

T-Mac stared at the woman, who was wearing camouflage pants, boots and a desert-tan T-shirt. Her hair was pulled back in a bun that had long since lost its shape. Coppery red strands danced in the breeze. She returned his stare with a direct green-eyed gaze. "If you're afraid of Agar, I'll hold him while you pass." She cocked an auburn eyebrow.

"What?" T-Mac shook his head. "I'm not afraid of the dog. Just startled."

"Then don't let us keep you." She snapped the lead on the dog's collar and straightened.

Curiosity made T-Mac ask, "You're new at Camp Lemonnier?"

She shrugged. "I've been here a week, if you consider that new."

He laughed. "I do. And I just got back to camp, or I'm sure I'd have seen you." There weren't too many good-looking redheaded females in the world, much less in Djibouti. "Hi, I'm Petty Officer Trace McGuire. My friends call me T-Mac." He took a step forward, slowly so as not to alert the dog, and held out his hand.

She clasped it in a firm grip. "Specialist Kinsley Anderson." She glanced down at the dog. "And this is Sergeant Agar."

T-Mac dropped to one knee in front of the German shepherd and held out his hand.

Agar placed a paw in his palm.

With a chuckle, T-Mac shook the dog's paw and then stood. "He's very well trained. What's his mission?"

"Bomb sniffing."

"Bomb sniffing?" T-Mac glanced again at the woman. He hadn't really thought about females on the front line. But with the army graduating females from Ranger School, it was a natural progression.

"Well, I hope you don't have to put that skill to use anytime soon."

Her eyes narrowed and she lifted her chin. "We came here to do a job. I'm not afraid."

Having seen his share of action and lost members of his team to gunfire and explosions, T-Mac didn't wish any of it on anyone. But a person had to live through the horrors of war to truly understand how terrible it was. He couldn't begin to explain it to the shiny new specialist who'd probably never been shot at or stood next to a man who'd been blown away by an IED.

And he had no business chatting up a female soldier when fraternization was strictly forbidden on deployment. Especially since it could lead to nothing and he and his team would be shipping out in four sleeps and a wakeup. "Well, it was nice to meet you."

"Same," she said, then grabbed the KONG and took off with Agar in the opposite direction.

As T-Mac continued on toward his quarters, he couldn't help sighing. He'd never considered dating a redhead, but something about Specialist Anderson made him reconsider. Perhaps it was the way her coppery hair seemed out of control, or the light dusting of freckles across her nose and cheeks. Or maybe it was the way she absently, or automatically, stroked the dog's head, showing it affection without having to think about it. Either way, she was off-limits and he was leaving. Once again he reminded himself, *Don't get involved.*

KINSLEY HURRIED PAST the navy guy. She'd spent the past two hours working with Agar, keeping his skills fresh and helping him burn off energy. Now it was her turn.

Though she'd been in the country for a week, she and Agar had been tasked only with inspecting vehicles entering Camp Lemonnier. Thankfully, they hadn't found any carrying explosives. Training sessions were a must, or Agar might forget what he was looking for and Kinsley might not pick up on the behavior Agar displayed when he sensed he'd found something.

Meanwhile, her male counterpart had gone out on missions with the Special Operations Forces into more hostile environments, working ahead of the teams to clear their routes of IEDs.

Kinsley had signed on as a dog handler because she loved dogs and because she wanted to make a difference for her country and her brothers in arms.

Her heart contracted as she thought about one in particular. Cody, her best friend from high school, had been killed in Iraq when he'd stepped on a mine.

Kinsley wanted to keep other young military men and women from the same fate.

On her first deployment, she'd hoped to land in Afghanistan or Iraq. Instead she'd landed in Djibouti, a fairly stable environment but also a jumping-off point to other more volatile areas. She hoped that her being female wouldn't keep them from mobilizing her to support missions outside the safety of the camp's borders.

Kinsley reached her quarters, filled a bowl full of water for Agar and stripped out of her uniform pants and boots. While Agar greedily slurped the entire contents of the bowl, Kinsley slipped on her army-issue PT shorts and running shoes and switched her desert-tan T-shirt for her army PT shirt. After strapping her flourescent belt around her waist and pulling her hair back into a ponytail, she planted a black army ball cap on her head and stepped out the door, leash in hand.

She moved smartly, walking past the rows of shipping-container quarters and other buildings, working her way through the complex toward the open field designated for PT.

She passed the motor pool and offices set aside for contractors who were providing additional support and building projects for the camp.

A silver-haired man stood at the corner of one of the buildings, smoking a cigarette. He wore khaki slacks and a polo shirt, incongruous with the multitude of uniforms from all branches of the military.

As she approached, he smiled. "Good afternoon," he said.

Not wanting to be rude, Kinsley slowed, though she'd rather speed by without engaging. "Hello."

He stepped in front of her. "You're new to the camp?"

"Yes, sir." She frowned, her gaze running over his civilian clothing. "I'm sorry, I don't think we've met." She held out her hand. "Specialist Anderson."

"William Toland." He reached out and shook her hand. "No, we haven't met. I'd remember a woman and her dog."

Kinsley's hand automatically dropped to Agar's head. "Sergeant Agar is a Military Working Dog."

"I assumed he was." The man reached out as if to pet the dog.

Agar's lips pulled back in a snarl and he growled low in his chest.

Toland snatched back his hand. "Not very friendly?"

Kinsley stepped between Agar and Toland. "He wasn't trained to be friendly. He's trained to sniff out explosives, not to be petted by strangers."

"Handy skill to have in a war." Toland stepped back. "And message received."

Kinsley nodded toward the construction crane at the far end of the camp. "Are you working with the contractors to build the new water towers?"

"I am," Toland responded. "But please, don't let me keep you from your exercise. I'm sure Sergeant Agar needs a good run to keep him in shape, too." He waved his hand as if granting her passage.

All in all, Kinsley was irritated by the man's arrogance in stepping in front of her in the first place. And even more convinced Agar was right to growl at the man. She'd learned to trust her dog's judgment of character.

Toland hadn't said or done anything too far out of the ordinary. Even so, Kinsley couldn't put her finger on it, but she wasn't sure she trusted the man. After all, why did a man stop a lone female soldier just to talk? Didn't the contractors get the same briefing as the military personnel?

Don't fraternize. Period.

As soon as she cleared the buildings, she shook off the prickly feeling at the back of her neck and quickened her pace into a slow, steady jog, with Agar easily keeping up at her side.

Running had never been a joy, but she did it to stay in shape for the semiannual fitness test and to be able to keep up with the physical demands of the job. She had to be in shape to walk long miles carrying a heavy ruck-sack. She might also be required to run into and out of bad situations. She expected Agar to be fit; she required nothing less of herself.

She ran along the track circling the containerized living units, staring at the stark desert beyond. She could glimpse a bit of the blue waters of the Gulf of Aden. No matter how hot, she preferred running outdoors than in the air-conditioned fitness center on the treadmills set up for residents of the camp. If Agar had to run in the heat, then she would do no less. The peace of the desert, with the wind off the water and the salty tang in the air, lulled her into a trance, nearly clearing her thoughts of the man Agar had come close to slamming into earlier.

Kinsley had to admit McGuire had appeal, unlike William Toland, who was perhaps old enough to be her father. Knowing McGuire was a SEAL made her all the more curious about the man. Anyone who had gone through BUD/S training had to be not only physically fit, but also mentally equipped to handle the most extreme environments and situations.

Based on the man's broad shoulders pulling tautly at his uniform, he was fit. But she wasn't sure about his mental fitness. For a long moment, he'd stared at her before actually opening his mouth. Perhaps he'd been hit once too often in the head and had suffered a brain injury.

At least that's what Kinsley told herself. She preferred to come up with reasons she should stay away from the man rather than reasons to fall under his spell. She hadn't joined the army to get married. And fraternization at Camp Lemonnier was strictly forbidden.

Footsteps sounded behind her, disturbing her not-so-peaceful escape.

She tightened her hold on Agar's lead and moved to the outside of the dirt path, making room for the other runner.

Instead of passing her, the runner slowed to match her pace.

She frowned over at him, ready to tell him to move on, when she noticed it was him… Petty Officer McGuire, the navy SEAL who had been occupying entirely too many of her thoughts since she'd run into him minutes before.

"Mind if I join you?" he asked with a grin.

She shrugged and kept moving. "Can't stop you."

"All you have to say is *shove off*, and I'll leave you alone," he said. "Sometimes it's nice to have a running buddy to fill the time."

"I actually have one," she said, and tipped her head toward Agar.

As if he could understand, Agar glanced up at her, his tongue lolling to the side.

"I see." With a twist of his lips, McGuire gave a curt nod. "Then I'll leave you two to your workout." And he picked up his pace, leaving Kinsley behind.

For a moment, Agar strained at the leash, wanting to keep up with the jogger ahead.

Kinsley gave him a sharp command. "Heel."

The German shepherd immediately fell in step with her, looking up at Kinsley and back to McGuire as if to tell her he could easily catch the man.

"I suppose I was rude," Kinsley admitted to Agar.

Agar looked up at her words, his mouth open, tongue hanging out the side. He appeared to be smiling, when in fact he was only trying to keep cool in the incredible heat.

"It's just as well. He has red hair. I make it a point not to get involved with men while I'm deployed. But even if we weren't deployed, I couldn't date the man. He has red hair. Our babies would all be doomed to red hair." She shuddered. "I wouldn't wish all of my children to that lot in life. Not if I have a choice."

Her gaze followed the SEAL as he ran to one corner of the huge field, turned and kept running, his powerful thighs pushing him forward with ease.

Kinsley's heart beat faster and her breathing became more labored as she watched the man's tight buttocks and well-defined legs. If she were into gingers, he'd be the one to catch. Thank goodness she wasn't.

Nevertheless, she slowed to a fast walk, letting McGuire widen the gap between them. She didn't want to risk running into him again at the end of her run. The man had *complication* written all over him.

When she arrived back at her quarters, she found a note stuck to the door.

Meeting at command center ASAP.

Kinsley had never received a message like that. Her pulse kicked up a notch, but she focused on staying calm. For all she knew, someone might have lodged a complaint about her exercising Agar too close to the living quarters. Or they were switching her to night shift.

She refused to get excited and dare to think she might be sent on an actual mission.

Chapter Two

T-Mac had just stepped out of the shower facility when Big Jake found him.

"Meeting in the command center, now," Big Jake said.

"Give me two minutes to get dressed." T-Mac hurried in his flip-flops toward his quarters, threw on his uniform, hat and boots and ran out the door, buttoning his jacket as he went. He jogged all the way to the command center and stepped inside the air-conditioned containerized office unit.

Inside, his team sat around a long, narrow table. Navy Commander Trevor Ward stood at the head of the table, his gaze on T-Mac as he entered. "Now that we're all here, let's get this party started."

T-Mac remained standing near the door, his curiosity piqued, his adrenaline pumping. He preferred missions to boredom any day.

"We're all ready to mobilize back to the States—" the commander held up his hand "—and as far as everyone is concerned, we will still be leaving in four days. However, we just received intel on a trade deal going down tonight on the border of Somalia."

The team waited quietly for Commander Ward to continue.

"You might ask what we have to do with trade in this

area. But here's the deal. Someone from around here has been funneling shipments of weapons from around Camp Lemonnier to the Al-Shabaab terrorists in Somalia. Intel intercepted a text communication from a burner cell phone nearby. Apparently, there will be handoff of a shipment conducted tonight in one of the abandoned, shelled-out villages on the other side of the border between Djibouti and Somalia." He nodded to his assistant, who clicked the keys on a laptop.

A map of the Horn of Africa blinked up on the whiteboard behind the commander.

Commander Ward turned to point at the location marked with a red dot. "The mission is simple. We go in, capture the traitors involved and return them to camp."

"All in a night's work," Harm said. "What's the catch?"

"Previous attempts by army rangers to recon this village were met with explosives."

"As in mortars and rocket-propelled grenades?" Buck asked.

The commander's lips pressed into a thin line. "Not so easy. IEDs and land mines. That's why we'll have two additional members on our team."

As if on cue, the door behind T-Mac opened and a German shepherd entered, followed by Specialist Kinsley Anderson, still dressed in her PT uniform of shorts, a T-shirt and running shoes.

The woman glanced around the room full of men and lifted her chin. "I'm sorry I'm late. I got here as soon as I received word of the meeting."

"No worries," the commander said. He waved his hand toward her. "Team, meet Specialist Anderson and Sergeant Agar. They will be with us on this mission tonight."

All eyes turned to the only female in the room.

T-Mac's pulse quickened. He'd never been on a mission with a female. Would having a woman in the mix change the dynamics of his team? Not that he was superstitious, but would the others be worried that a woman would jinx their mission?

He glanced around the room at the others' gazes. For the most part, they appeared more curious than apprehensive.

"Anyone have any issues?" the commander asked.

Specialist Anderson's chin rose another notch, her gaze sweeping the room full of men, challenging them with just that one look.

Big Jake shrugged. "I'd be glad to have a dog ahead of us. I've seen what one can do. They're pretty amazing."

"Same," Buck said. "Rather sniff out the bombs than step on one."

The rest of the men voiced agreement.

"Then get ready, you leave in—" Commander Ward glanced down at his watch "—one hour."

T-Mac followed Anderson out of the building. "Do you need help getting ready?" he asked.

"I think I can figure it out," she said, stepping out smartly and moving toward the containerized living quarters.

Falling in step beside her, T-Mac hustled to keep up. "Is this your first mission outside the wire?" he asked.

She tensed and frowned. "I know my job, and I know what to carry and wear into combat. You don't have to coddle me because I'm female."

He held up his hands. "Oh, believe me, I wouldn't dare do that." Then he ruined it with a chuckle. "I'd help out the new guy, male or female. I like to come back with all the people we left with intact."

Her shoulders relaxed. "Sorry. I shouldn't be so defensive."

"I'm sure you have a right to be."

She lifted her shoulders and let them drop. "I get tired of people underestimating my abilities just because I'm a woman."

"I've seen you two in action. I have complete confidence in you and Agar."

The dog lifted his head at the sound of his name and then looked forward again, trotting alongside his handler.

"Well, you don't have to worry about us. We can handle our job. We'll keep you and your team safe from explosives."

"And we'll do our best to keep you and Agar safe from loose bullets."

She shot him a hint of a smile. "Thanks." By then, they were standing in front of her quarters. Specialist Anderson frowned. "I didn't ask where we should meet."

T-Mac's lips twisted. "We'll be loading up in helicopters. If you like, I can swing by and we can walk over together."

Her frown cleared. "Thanks. I'd appreciate that."

"My pleasure," he said, and left her at her door to hurry toward his own quarters, where he'd gear up for the mission ahead.

In the back of his mind, he couldn't help but worry about the addition to their team. The SEALs trained together. They hadn't trained with a dog handler working out in front of them. Specialist Anderson and Agar might know what they were doing when it came to sniffing out bombs, but they had no experience in hostile environments.

When T-Mac entered the containerized quarters he shared with Harm, his roommate glanced up from assembling his M4A1 rifle with the SOPMOD upgrade. "Hey, T-Mac."

"Harm." T-Mac pulled a hard plastic case out from under his bunk, extracted his rifle and pulled it apart piece by piece. He'd cleaned it after his last mission and had assembled and disassembled it a number of times since. Handling his weapon was second nature.

"Saw you walked the dog handler back to her quarters," Harm said.

"Yeah." T-Mac stiffened. "So?"

Without looking up from what he was doing, Harm continued. "You know we were just kidding about fixing you up with a female, right?"

T-Mac snorted. "No. I fully expect you guys to bombard me with women."

Harm gave a twisted grin. "You're right. But we'd wait until we got back to the States. What with how touchy folks are about not fraternizing while deployed."

With a frown, T-Mac shook his head. "If this is about Specialist Anderson, forget it. I only offered to help her get ready for the mission. She hasn't actually been on one before."

Harm's head shot up. "Never?"

His chest tightening, T-Mac pressed his lips together. "Everyone has to have a first time."

His roommate frowned. "I'd rather it wasn't with us."

"Would you rather she went out with some teenaged infantry soldiers who are barely out of boot camp?"

Harm sighed. "I suppose not. But I don't like the idea of babysitting when we have a mission to accomplish."

T-Mac pulled the bolt from his weapon, inspected it and shot it back home, reassembling the weapon in record time. "I'd almost rather take my chances with the mines and IEDs than risk losing her and the dog."

"Not me," Harm said. "Remember what happened to Roadrunner when he got too far ahead of the rest of us on that extraction mission in Afghanistan?"

T-Mac's stomach clenched at the memory.

Roadrunner had been point man when he'd stepped on a land mine. Thankfully for Roadrunner, he'd died instantly. The team had been left to pick up the pieces, physically and mentally.

"Hopefully Anderson and Agar know their stuff," T-Mac muttered.

"Yeah. But they're all about sniffing out explosives. We have to worry about the snipers. A lot of money goes into training dogs and handlers."

"And SEALs," T-Mac reminded him.

Harm nodded. "That's a given. I'd like to make it back to the States in four days. Talia will be waiting at my apartment. I let her use it for a place to stay while she's house hunting."

T-Mac shot a glance toward his teammate. "I thought you two were a thing?"

"We are. But I want her to be sure. Moving from Africa back to the States is a big deal. And dating a SEAL won't make it much easier." Harm lifted a shoulder and let it fall. "I don't want to pressure her. She needs time to make up her own mind and be comfortable with herself."

"Before she commits to you?"

"Yeah." Harm grinned. "You know our lives aren't

easy even for us. I want her to know how it is and what she can expect before we tie the knot."

"What happened to being confirmed bachelors? I thought we were a team. And now you all have women." T-Mac shook his head. "I don't get it."

Harm chuckled, pulled his steel-plated vest out of his go bag and laid it out on his bunk. "You'll get it when you find the woman who makes you reconsider everything you ever thought to be true."

"Now you're starting to sound sappy. I'm not sure I want to find a woman who makes me go soft." T-Mac strapped a scabbard around his calf and stuck his Ka-Bar knife into it. "Next thing you know, you'll be second-guessing yourself on the battlefield."

"Never." Harm shrugged into his vest and secured several empty magazines into the straps. "Let's quit flapping our gums and go meet up with your cute dog handler."

"She's not *my* dog handler."

"No?" Harm gave him a side-eye glance and raised one eyebrow. "Sure looked like it to the rest of us."

"She's not my dog handler," T-Mac insisted, his tone hard, his lips tight.

"Whatever you say." Harm grabbed his helmet and stepped out of the box. "But between the two of you redheads, you'd make some really cute redheaded babies."

"She's not my redhead," T-Mac said through clenched teeth as he snagged his helmet and followed Harm. "And we're not having babies."

"Who's having babies?" Buck fell in step behind Harm and T-Mac. "If T-Mac is planning on marrying the dog handler, they can start their own ginger basketball team. Or hockey team. Or whatever team they want. They'd all be gingers."

"We're not getting married. She's not my dog handler, and I'd appreciate it if you wouldn't say anything around her about babies and basketball teams." T-Mac picked up the pace, hoping that by walking faster, his teammates wouldn't have the time nor desire to poke fun at him.

Pitbull and Big Jake stepped out of the quarters they shared.

"What's this about babies and basketball teams?" Pitbull asked. "Is T-Mac marrying his dog handler?"

T-Mac threw his hand in the air. "She's not my dog handler."

Big Jake chuckled. "I think he protests too much. I swear I saw something between the two of them."

"You can't see something that wasn't there." T-Mac sighed. "I get it. This is all part of razzing me because I choose to stay a bachelor and have my pick of women out there while you losers commit to being with one woman for the rest of your lives. I think I have the better deal."

"What deal?" Diesel jogged to catch up to the team. "What did I miss?"

"T-Mac's met his match," Buck said.

T-Mac gritted his teeth. "I didn't."

"His dog handler?" Diesel guessed.

"She's not my dog handler." T-Mac might as well have been talking to a wall.

"Oh, he's going to fall hard," Diesel said. "She's got attitude and a dog. A killer combination. What's not to love about that?"

"I'm not in love. She's not my handler, and I don't even think the dog likes me." He glanced toward the container where Specialist Anderson was staying and debated walking past and letting her find her own way to where the helicopters were parked. But he'd promised to walk with her. He slowed, hoping the rest of the team would walk on without questioning why he was stopping.

But he knew them better than that. They weren't stupid and they would figure it out pretty quickly.

"Look, guys, could you be serious for once?" He turned and raised his hand to knock on the door.

All five of his friends came to a complete stop.

T-Mac groaned as the door opened.

Agar came out first and immediately sniffed T-Mac's crotch.

A rumble of chuckles sounded behind T-Mac.

"I guess the dog likes you after all," Buck muttered.

More chuckles sounded.

Heat rose up T-Mac's neck into his cheeks as he glanced up at Specialist Anderson. "Don't listen to anything these yahoos say. They're all full of… Well, they're full of it, anyway."

KINSLEY TORE HER gaze away from the SEAL standing in front of her looking all hot and incredibly sexy in his combat gear. Beyond Petty Officer McGuire stood five of the other men who'd been in the command center minutes before. She stepped out of the doorway, looped the strap of her rifle over her shoulder and double-wrapped the dog's lead around her hand. "What am I not supposed to listen to them about?"

"Tell her, T-Mac," one of them encouraged.

"We don't have time for games," McGuire said. "We have a mission to accomplish before we head home."

"You're heading home?" Kinsley asked.

"Four days and a wakeup," the tallest of the group answered.

"Where's home?" Kinsley fell in step with them as they wove their way through the temporary buildings to the landing strip where planes and helicopters parked.

"Little Creek, Virginia," McGuire answered.

"What about you?" one of the guys asked. "Where is your home base?"

"San Antonio, Texas, was my last PCS assignment," Kinsley said.

"That's where they train Military Working Dogs, isn't it?" McGuire asked. "They have a facility at Lackland Air Force Base. Is that where you and Agar received your training?"

She nodded. "I spent the past year in training."

"T-Mac says this is your first assignment since training."

Again, Kinsley nodded. "That's true. Agar was the best in his class. He could find trace amounts of explosives that none of our own detection equipment could pick up." She patted the dog's head. "He's good at what he does. If there are IEDs or land mines, he'll prove himself tonight."

As they reached the helicopters, more SEALs gathered. Ammunition was dispensed. Then it came time for them to load into the helicopters.

Kinsley started for one of the choppers away from McGuire and his group.

The navy commander who'd briefed them caught up to her. "You're riding in the other bird. Stick with T-Mac. He'll make sure you're safe."

"I can take care of myself," Kinsley insisted.

"I understand," the commander said. "But the team isn't used to working with a dog and its handler. It's for their safety as well as yours."

Kinsley couldn't argue with that. Apparently, she was to have a handler. "Yes, sir."

The commander escorted her back to the other helicopter where McGuire, or T-Mac, as his team nicknamed him, stood, waiting his turn to climb aboard.

"T-Mac," the commander called out.

The SEAL turned when he saw who was with his superior.

"I have an assignment for you," Commander Ward said.

"Yes, sir," T-Mac replied.

"You're to keep up with Specialist Anderson and Sergeant Agar. Bring them back safely."

T-Mac's eyes narrowed. "Sir?"

Kinsley stiffened.

The SEAL didn't look too excited.

"You heard me," the commander said. "Take care of them out there. You don't know what you'll be up against."

"Yes, sir." T-Mac nodded.

When the others in the helicopter chuckled, T-Mac shot a glare their way.

With the odd feeling she wasn't in on the joke, Kinsley stepped up to the chopper.

"Has Agar been in a helicopter?" T-Mac asked.

Kinsley nodded. "Not only has he been up, he's been hoisted in and out on a cable multiple times. He's calm throughout."

"Good." T-Mac offered her a hand up.

Ignoring the hand, Kinsley motioned for Agar to go first. Then she stepped up into the chopper and found a seat between the tallest guy and one who was stout with a barrel chest. She settled between them and buckled her safety harness, keeping Agar close at her feet.

"I'm Jake," said the tall man. "They call me Big Jake."

Kinsley shook hands with the man. "Nice to meet you, Big Jake."

"I'm Pitbull." The barrel-chested guy stuck out his hand. "Here, you'll need these." He handed her a headset.

She removed her helmet and settled the headset over her ears. Immediately, she could hear static and the pilot and copilot performing a communications check with the passengers.

She watched and listened as each of the SEALs answered, and she committed their names to memory.

"Diesel."

"Pitbull."

"Buck."

"Big Jake."

"Harm."

"T-Mac."

Her heart skipped several beats when T-Mac spoke. He sat in the seat opposite, his gaze on her. When no one else spoke, he winked and touched his finger to his own microphone.

Kinsley realized she'd forgotten to say her name. With heat rising up in her cheeks, she spoke into the mic. "Anderson and Agar."

T-Mac grinned.

A moment later, the helicopter lifted off the ground, swung out over the Gulf of Aden and then turned south, back over the Horn of Africa.

The sun had sunk low on the horizon, bathing the land in a bright orange glow.

If they hadn't been headed into a potentially hostile environment, Kinsley would have enjoyed the view, the sunset and the warm wind blowing in her face. But this was her first real combat assignment. She wasn't scared, but she was anxious to do well.

She sat back in her seat, forcing herself to be calm. Agar needed her full focus. He sensed her every mood and emotion. He needed to know she was in full control of herself as well as him. They'd trained to save lives by finding dangers lurking beneath the surface or behind walls.

For the duration of the flight, she concentrated on reducing her heart rate, breathing deeply and going over everything she'd learned in the intensive training she'd been through with Agar. Dogs weren't deployed unless they were ready. And dog handlers didn't last long in training if they weren't capable, consistent and calm. She'd excelled along with Agar.

All of her training had been for more than inspecting vehicles entering through the post gates.

Agar nudged her foot with his nose and looked up at her.

Kinsley rubbed the dog's snout and scratched him behind his ears.

He laid his head on her lap, as if sensing her unrest.

When Kinsley glanced up again, it was to stare across the darkening fuselage at the SEAL seated across from her. Though she resented feeling like she had to be babysat, she was glad she had someone with more combat experience watching her back.

All too soon, the helicopter touched down. The second one landed beside it.

Kinsley removed the helicopter headset, slipped her helmet on and latched the buckle beneath her chin. She exited the aircraft and stood to the side with Agar while all twelve SEALs alighted, checked their gear and waited for the signal to move out.

T-Mac approached her and handed her a small electronic device. "You'll need these earpieces to hear the team as we move through the village. You'll have to keep them up-to-date while they're looking for our traitor."

Kinsley fitted the device in her ear and spoke. "Testing."

Big Jake took charge, giving directions, performing one last communication check on their radio headsets.

After everyone checked in, Big Jake gathered them in a circle. "The village should be another four clicks to the east. We need to get in, clear the rubble of any enemy combatants and wait for the handoff. Any questions?"

Big Jake nodded toward Kinsley. "Take it, dog soldier."

Kinsley's heartbeat quickened. This was it. She and Agar had a job to do, lives to save and explosives to find.

She tugged on Agar's lead, sending him in the direction Big Jake indicated. She allowed the dog to run out at the extent of the retractable lead and walked behind him. She carried her rifle in her right hand, the lead in her left.

T-Mac fell in step beside her, his specialized M4A1 at the ready position.

Darkness had settled over the landscape with a blanket of stars lighting their way.

Agar zigzagged back and forth in front of her, his

nose to the ground, tail wagging, moving swiftly enough that Kinsley had to hustle to keep up.

One kilometer passed without incident. Then two. As they neared their target, Kinsley slowed Agar, encouraging him to take his time. The team had chosen to approach the abandoned village from the west, establish a defensive position and wait for the party to start. The handoff was supposed to take place at midnight. That gave them a few hours to get in place and hunker down.

From what some of her more experienced counterparts had reported, sometimes it took hours to navigate a quarter-mile stretch. If their adversary considered the location to be worth the effort to defend or sabotage, they could have rigged it with land mines or trip wires hooked to detonators.

Glad for T-Mac's protection, she led the SEALs toward the crumbled buildings at the edge of the little village.

As they neared the closest of what was left of a mud-and-stick hut, Agar stopped, sniffed and lay down on the ground.

Kinsley's pulse quickened. "He found something."

She marked the spot with a flag and bent to scratch Agar behind the ears, then gave him the command to continue his search. Within a few feet he lay down again.

Marking the new spot, Kinsley worked with Agar, moving a few feet at time, ever closer to the village, at what felt like an excruciatingly slow pace.

"I don't like it," T-Mac said. "If they have a sniper waiting in one of those buildings, they can easily pick us off."

"Unless they figure the explosives will alert them to

anyone coming in from this direction," Big Jake said into Kinsley's ear.

She ignored the chatter and continued until she and Agar had identified a clear path to the village through what appeared to be a short field of submerged mines.

Once inside the crumbled walls of the village, Agar moved from structure to structure, sniffing without lying down.

Kinsley didn't let her guard down for a moment. After encountering the mines, she wouldn't put it past whoever set them to have more hidden treasures to keep unwanted visitors out.

She had Agar enter huts along the way, clear them and move on, aiming toward the center of the village and the road that led through the middle.

All the while, T-Mac remained at her side, his weapon ready, hand on the trigger.

As Agar neared the building on the edge of the road, he slowed. His hackles rose on the back of his neck and he uttered a low and dangerous growl.

Kinsley dropped to a squat in the shadow of the nearest building.

T-Mac followed her movement and knelt on one knee at her side. "What's the growl mean?"

"Someone's nearby," Kinsley whispered.

T-Mac held up a hand where the others could see his command to stop.

Kinsley didn't dare look back. All her focus was on Agar and what was in front of the dog.

"We'll take it from here." T-Mac rose and started forward.

Kinsley caught his arm before he could move past her. "But what if there are more explosives?"

"You're not going any farther." T-Mac glanced down at her. "Bring Agar back."

Kinsley didn't like being relegated to the rear. She'd come this far; she wanted to complete her work.

Before she could bring Agar back, the dog turned and entered a building, his growls increasing in volume and intensity.

Kinsley hurried after him.

"Wait," T-Mac called after her.

She had to know Agar was all right. As she ran forward, she pulled her flashlight from her pocket. When she turned into the doorway of the building, she flipped on the switch and shone the light, filtered with a red lens, into the room.

Agar stood with his feet planted and his lips pulled back in a wicked snarl.

As she panned the light around to see what Agar was growling at, a man's face appeared in the glow…a face she knew.

Kinsley gasped but didn't have time to react when the man lifted his rifle and fired point-blank into her chest.

The bullet hit with enough force to knock her backward through the door. She landed flat on her back and lay stunned.

Before she could catch her breath, the world erupted in gunfire around her.

Agar flew out of the building and landed on his side.

"No!" Kinsley screamed silently, though nothing would come from her lungs. She rolled to her side and tried to rise.

Agar yelped, the kind of sound only emitted when an animal was hurt.

Pushing past her own breathlessness and the pain in

her chest, Kinsley crawled toward the dog, her heart in her throat, her need to reach Agar foremost in her mind.

Then an explosion went off in the building in front of her, shooting mud, rock and shrapnel in all directions.

Kinsley felt the force of the blast against her eardrums. Her body was peppered with rock and shrapnel like so many pellets from a shotgun shell. Dust billowed outward, choking the air, blinding Kinsley before she could reach Agar.

A sharp pain ripped through her side; still she staggered to her feet, crying out, "Agar!"

A high-pitched whistling sound screamed through the air.

"Incoming!" T-Mac yelled. Then he hit her from behind, sending her flying through the air to land hard on the packed dirt.

T-Mac landed on top of her, knocking the air from her lungs yet again. At the same time, another explosion rocked the ground she lay against.

Her ears rang, and for a moment she couldn't breathe or move. Dust and debris rained down on them. A darkness so deep closed in on her, threatening to pull her under.

"Agar." She reached out her hand, patting the ground, unable to move or crawl forward. Then her fingers touched fur. A sob rose in her throat as her vision faded and the ringing in her ears became a roar. She couldn't pass out. Agar needed her.

The next thing she knew, she was being lifted into the air. She struggled to get free. "No."

"Be still, Kinsley." T-Mac's voice sounded in her ear. "I'll get you out of here."

"No," she croaked, choking on dust. "Can't leave—"

Gunfire sounded all around.

"I have to get you out of here," T-Mac insisted. "You've been hit."

"Can't leave." She fought him, pounding her fists against his chest.

Big Jake appeared beside her. "Get her out of here."

T-Mac fought to retain his hold on her. "She refuses to go."

"Agar." Kinsley pushed against T-Mac's chest.

"He was hit," T-Mac said.

She swung her legs out of T-Mac's grasp and dropped to the ground. "Not leaving without him." Her knees buckled and she would have crumpled into a heap if T-Mac hadn't been holding on to her.

Again he scooped her up into his arms. "You can't stay here."

"I'll get the dog." Big Jake ran into the swirling dust and reappeared a moment later, carrying Agar.

"Oh, God," Kinsley sobbed. "Agar." Tears streamed from her eyes. "Let me help him."

"Not until we're out of here." T-Mac ran through the village, back the way they'd come. He passed his team as they moved in the opposite direction.

Over T-Mac's shoulder, Kinsley watched for Big Jake. The big man appeared out of the cloud of dust, still holding Agar.

Then, as they cleared the edge of the village, Big Jake staggered and fell to his knees, his arms hitting the ground first, cushioning Agar's landing.

"Stop!" Kinsley screamed. "Big Jake's down."

"I can't stop," T-Mac said. "I can only carry one person at a time."

Behind Big Jake, another one of the SEALs appeared, looped Big Jake's arm over his shoulder and half carried the big man down the path between the flags Kinsley had planted to identify the buried land mines.

Agar remained on the ground…left behind.

"Let me down," Kinsley begged. "Please." She didn't dare struggle, afraid that if she did, she'd make T-Mac stumble and veer into one of the mines. Her strength waned, and a warm wet stickiness spread across her right arm and leg.

"Please, you can't leave Agar. He's my partner. He trusted me." Her voice faded to a whisper as tears trickled down her face and darkness threatened to block out the stars shining above.

The crackle of gunfire and the boom of explosions seemed to be coming from farther and farther away.

Kinsley must have passed out. When she came to, T-Mac was laying her on the floor of a helicopter. When she tried to sit up, her body refused to cooperate. All she could lift was her head, and only for a moment before it dropped to the hard metal floor. "Agar," she said on a sigh.

"Buck, do what you can," T-Mac said. "She's bleeding in several places."

"Don't worry about me," she said. "Please, go find Agar."

No one seemed to be listening as they pulled off her helmet, unbuckled her protective vest and applied pressure to her wounds.

"Shh, you're going to be all right." T-Mac leaned over her, brushing her hair from her face, while someone else ripped her uniform jacket away from her leg.

The rumble of rotor blades sounded and the helicopter lifted from the ground.

As they rose into the air, Kinsley reached out a hand. "Agar."

T-Mac took her hand. "We'll take care of you."

"But who will take care of Agar?" she whispered.

And then the sounds of the rotor blades faded, and the world went black.

Chapter Three

T-Mac stayed with Specialist Anderson from the moment he carried her out of the village until they wheeled her into the medical facility at Camp Lemonnier. At that point, the medical team on standby grabbed him and made him take a gurney as well.

"You're bleeding," one of the medics said.

"I don't care. I promised to take care of Anderson." He pushed to his feet and slipped in something wet on the floor.

The medic grabbed his arm and steadied him. "She's in good hands. And you can't go back with her."

"But it was my responsibility to take care of her." And he'd failed. Miserably.

The physician on call appeared in front of T-Mac, a frown furrowing his brow. "You might not care about your own injuries, but you're putting everyone else in this facility in danger with the amount of blood you're getting on the floor. Take a seat, SEAL."

At the command in the doctor's voice, T-Mac sat on the gurney.

The medics stripped him of his body armor and uniform jacket and cut away the leg of his trousers.

In minutes the doctor had fished out the shrapnel, stitched the wound and applied a bandage.

The medics cleaned up the blood from the floor and set his gear on a chair beside the examination table.

T-Mac pushed to a sitting position and reached for his boots. Once he had his feet in them, he slid off the table to stand on the floor. He swayed slightly.

The medic was there, helping him stay upright. "Hey, you're going to rip a stitch if you're not careful."

"I want to see Specialist Anderson."

"They're taking care of her now." The young medic, who couldn't be more than nineteen years old, released his arm. "I'll go check on her and let you know how it's going." He helped him out of the room and nodded toward the front of the building. "In the meantime, you can take a seat in the lobby. I'll bring your gear."

Gritting his teeth, T-Mac turned away as another gurney entered the building with Big Jake on it.

His face was pale, but his eyes were open. He grabbed T-Mac's arm as he passed. "How's the dog soldier?"

"They're working on her now." T-Mac scanned his friend. "Where were you hit?"

"Took a bullet in the buttocks." Big Jake laughed and grimaced. "Only hurts when I laugh, or move, or hell, anything. I'll be glad when they get it out."

T-Mac stood back, his gaze going to the medics pushing the gurney. "Take care of my friend."

"We've got this. You might want to take a seat while you're waiting," the medic who'd helped him said. "You lost a little bit of blood yourself."

T-Mac made his way to the lobby. The window looking out was still dark.

As promised, the medic delivered his gear, setting it on the floor beside a chair.

Wearing his torn pants, the air-conditioned air cool on his exposed leg, T-Mac paced the short distance between chairs. He prayed the female dog handler and Big Jake would be all right. Part of him wanted to be back in the bombed-out village, wreaking havoc on those who'd hurt his team.

Seeing Anderson blown back out of the building by the power of a point-blank attack made his gut clench. He'd tried to grab her arm before she went in, but she'd been too fast, worried about her dog. He should have known she'd do something like that and thought ahead. She was his responsibility. Even if the commander hadn't tagged him with the job, he would have taken it anyway.

As he stared at his body armor and helmet, he wondered if the rest of his team was still fighting or if they'd brought the little village under control.

The whole mission had felt as if it had been a fiasco from the very beginning...as if they had been led into the chute like lambs to slaughter.

Unfortunately, Specialist Anderson had been first up. She'd taken a bullet to her armor-plated chest. Thankfully, she'd worn her protective gear, or she'd be dead. As it was, the mortar having landed near them had taken its toll. If she didn't die of a punctured or collapsed lung from the blunt force of being fired on at close range, she might die from the multiple shrapnel wounds across her arms and legs. Or suffer from traumatic brain injury.

He didn't feel the stitches pinching since the doctor had given him a local anesthetic, but he felt ridiculous in his one-legged pants.

All the while he sat in the lobby, his teammates could be facing the fight of their lives, and he wasn't there to help.

An hour passed, and the medic came out. "Your friend, Petty Officer Schuler, is going to be okay. He should be out shortly."

Minutes later, Big Jake limped out into the lobby, wearing what T-Mac assumed were borrowed gym shorts and his T-shirt.

A medic carried his body armor and helmet, as well as his shirt and the remainder of his pants. "I can help you get back to your quarters when the shift changes in an hour," he promised. He glanced over his shoulder. "I have to get back in there."

"Wait." T-Mac took a step forward. "What's the status of Specialist Anderson?"

The medic shook his head. "They removed all the shrapnel, but she's still unconscious. They were waiting to see if she'd come out of it on her own, but she got kind of combative, so they sedated her. The doctor thinks she might have a concussion. We've called for transport to get her to the next level of care. They'll either take her to Ramstein in Germany or back to the States."

T-Mac's chest tightened. "How soon?"

"As soon as we can scramble a crew and medical staff to fly out on a C-130." The medic turned. "Now, if you'll excuse me, I need to get back." He disappeared before T-Mac could ask any more questions.

Big Jake laid a hand on T-Mac's shoulder. "I'm sorry about your dog handler."

For every time T-Mac had corrected his teammates, he knew he'd been lying to himself. He didn't know Kinsley Anderson well, nor did he have any ties to her, other than having been assigned to protect her. Still, he had felt she was his dog handler and that he was responsible for seeing to her safety.

The door to the medical facility burst open behind T-Mac and Big Jake. Buck, Harm, Diesel and Pitbull pushed through, covered in dust and smelling of gunpowder.

"Thank God you're both okay." Buck clapped a hand to T-Mac's back.

"We didn't know what had happened to you when you took off," Pitbull said.

Diesel nodded toward their pant legs and grinned. "New fashion statement in uniform trousers?" Then his smile faded. "You're okay?"

Big Jake snorted. "Other than a stitch here and there, we'll survive."

"What about T-Mac's dog handler?" Harm asked.

T-Mac's jaw tightened. "They're going to ship her out to the next level of medical support." He turned to Harm. "What about Agar? What happened to the dog?" T-Mac knew the first thing Kinsley would want to know was if her dog made it out alive.

Harm shook his head. "We got him onto the helicopter and carried him to the camp veterinarian. I can't tell you whether he'll make it. He was nonresponsive when we delivered him, but I think he still had a heartbeat."

When Kinsley recovered enough to ask, she'd receive yet another blow if the dog didn't make it. T-Mac wanted to know more about Agar's condition, but he wasn't leaving the medical facility until the army specialist did.

"You might as well get some rest," Big Jake said. "You can't do anything for her now."

"I know. But I'm staying," he said.

Big Jake nodded. "You know it wasn't your fault she was hurt."

T-Mac's fists knotted, but he didn't say anything.

Big Jake touched his arm. "You couldn't have known the dog would dart into that building, or that someone was there waiting to shoot her."

"That's right," Buck stated. "She's lucky she had on her body armor, or she wouldn't be alive—"

Pitbull elbowed Buck in the ribs. "She's going to be okay. The docs will take good care of her. And when they get her to a real hospital, they'll make sure she gets even better care."

T-Mac knew all that, but he wouldn't feel better about any of it until he saw the dog handler standing in front of him, giving him attitude.

"If you two are up to it, the CO wants a debrief," Harm said. "He's out for blood. The way we see it, we were set up, plain and simple."

"Did you find the guy who shot Specialist Anderson?" T-Mac asked.

Harm's lips thinned. "We thought we'd find pieces of him after the explosion, but he got away. There was a back door to that hut."

Anger seared through T-Mac's veins. "He got away?"

"Yeah," Buck said. "And the only guy they left behind was in no condition to give us any answers."

"He was dead," Pitbull said.

"Shot in the back," Diesel finished.

"Not only were they waiting for us," Harm said, "but they had their escape plan in place before we got there."

Buck's eyes narrowed. "Someone tipped them off about what time we left. We got there well before the arranged trade deadline."

"Any others hurt besides the three of us and Agar?" T-Mac asked.

"No," Pitbull said. "When the dust settled, they were gone in a couple of pickup trucks. We would have gone after them, but we figured the dog needed medical attention."

"What exactly happened to the dog handler?" Harm wanted to know.

"She was shot in the chest by whomever was in that hut."

"That'll give her nightmares." Diesel shook his head. "Seeing the face of the man who shot you would leave an indelible image in your mind."

T-Mac snorted. "She was more concerned about Agar being hurt than the fact she'd nearly been killed."

"I hope they make it." Big Jake gently rubbed a hand over his backside. "The whole mission was a disaster."

T-Mac ran a hand through his hair. "Absolutely. Tell the commander what I told you. I'll be here, if he wants to hear it from me in person."

"Will do." Big Jake limped out of the facility with the others on their way to the debrief.

T-Mac paced the lobby again, his frustration growing with each step. He hoped he could be around when Kinsley came to. He wanted to let her know how sorry he was for not keeping her and Agar safe.

Just when T-Mac was ready to ignore the rules and march back to Kinsley's bed, the medic returned.

"She's still out of it," he said. "But you can come back and sit with her."

KINSLEY HOVERED BETWEEN the dark and the light. Every time she felt as if she were surfacing from a deep, black well, she stretched out her hand only to slip back into it. No matter how hard she climbed and scraped her hands on the hard stone walls, she couldn't seem to get to the top. Her fingers grew chilled from the coldness of the stones.

And then warmth wrapped around her hand.

She quit fighting to climb and lay back, basking in the warmth radiating from her hand up her arm and throughout her body.

A deep voice came to her through the black abyss.

"Kinsley, wake up and tell me I'm wrong."

That voice made her want to wake, but that well she'd been clawing her way out of wouldn't let her go.

"Kinsley, you're going to be okay. You just need to wake up and give me all kinds of grief for not taking care of you."

Who was talking to her? And what was he talking about? She tried to open her eyes but she didn't have the strength. So, she lay listening to the warm, deep tones, letting them wash over her, fill her, hold her up when she couldn't stay afloat in the bottomless well. The voice permeated her insides while a strong hand cupped hers, providing heat when she felt so very cold.

Images and sensations swirled in an endless cyclone, refusing to coalesce into anything she could recognize. Faces, dust, fur, sounds, blinding flashes, all spinning inside, making her dizzy, forcing her back into that well, away from the light.

"Kinsley, sweetheart, you're going to be all right. Open your eyes. You'll see. I should have been the one entering that building. You and Agar wouldn't have been hurt if I'd gone first. You have to be okay. Agar is going to need you."

Agar? The word was odd, yet familiar. Still, she couldn't remember why. Nothing made sense. The only anchor keeping her from drowning in the whirlpool threatening to take her under was the voice in the darkness urging her toward the light.

As the black abyss pulled her under, she tightened her hold on the big hand.

MINUTES, HOURS or days later—Kinsley couldn't tell—she blinked her eyes open and stared at the top of an auburn head lying on the sheet beside her. She wasn't in her apartment back in San Antonio. Then she remembered—she'd deployed. Her brow furrowed. To where? She thought hard, the truth just out of her grasp.

She was in the army. They'd sent her on a long flight to...

Nothing.

Frustration made her want to hit something. But when she tried to clench her fist, she couldn't. Someone was holding her hand.

Again, she stared at the head on the sheet beside her. Perhaps the man who owned the head was also the one holding her hand.

But why?

The astringent scent of disinfectant assailed her nostrils. Her gaze moved from the stranger's head to the walls around her. Once again, she realized she wasn't in an apartment, and based on the unusual bed, the bright overhead lights and the monitor tracking her heartbeat, she had to be in some kind of hospital.

Had she been hurt? Kinsley took inventory of her body. Twinges of pain answered for her. Stinging on the surface of her arms and legs let her know she had cuts and abrasions. Her chest felt bruised, and breathing deeply made it slightly worse.

But who was the man with his head on her bed? And what was she forgetting that was so important? Something tugged at her mind, something she should remember, but couldn't.

"Psst," she said.

The man remained facedown on the sheet.

"Hey." When she spoke, her voice sounded like a frog's croak.

The head stirred and lifted. Blue eyes opened, and ginger brows knitted together. "Kinsley?" the man said.

"Yes, that's me." She frowned. "But who are you?"

He sat up straight in the chair beside her bed and pushed a hand through his hair. "I'm T-Mac. Don't you remember me?"

Her frown deepened, making her head hurt. "If I remembered, would I be asking?"

He chuckled. "You still have your bite. We met yesterday, near your quarters."

"Quarters?" She looked around. "These aren't my quarters."

His brows pinched together again. "No. You're in the Djibouti medical facility."

"Why am I here?" she asked.

"You were injured in a skirmish in Somalia."

"Skirmish?" she asked, feeling like she was missing a chunk of her memory. And it was scaring her. "What day is it?"

He told her the date. "You were shot and involved in an explosion."

She gasped, her heartbeat fluttering uncontrollably.

"What was I doing in Somalia?" The green line on the monitor jumped erratically.

The auburn-haired man pushed to his feet. "Let me get the doctor."

"I'm okay," she said. "I'm okay," she repeated, as if to remind herself. "I just can't remember any of that."

He didn't listen, leaving the room in a hurry.

Kinsley lifted her head. A sharp pain slashed through her forehead. She lay back, closed her eyes and let it abate before she opened her eyes again.

By then T-Mac had returned with a man in a white coat. He introduced himself as her doctor. She couldn't commit his name to her memory with the pain throbbing in her head.

He shone a light into her eyes. "Do you remember what happened to you?"

She tried to shake her head, remembering too late that it caused pain. Kinsley winced. "No." Her heart beat fast and her hands shook as she pressed her fingertips to her temple. "I can't remember what day it is."

"Do you know who the president of the United States is?" the doctor asked.

She thought, but couldn't come up with a name. "No."

"What about where you were born?" he persisted.

The more she tried to remember, the worse her head hurt. "I can't remember." A tear slipped from the corner of her eye to run down her cheek.

The doctor patted her hand. "Don't be too alarmed. You had a concussion. Temporary memory loss can be a side effect."

"Will it come back?" Kinsley asked. "Will I remember where I'm from and who the president is?"

He smiled down at her. "You should. Give yourself

time to recover. We're trying to get a transport to send you back to a higher-level medical-care facility, but we can't seem to find a C-130 we can tap into for the next couple days. You might be stuck with us."

"I'm fine," she said, and pushed up on her elbows. "I need to get back to work." She shook her head. "If only I could remember what work I do."

The doctor touched her shoulder. "Don't strain your brain. The memories will return, given time."

She lay back on the bed, her gaze following the doctor as he left her room. Kinsley wanted to call him back, to make him give her some pill or potion to force her memories to return. Not knowing things was confusing and frightening.

Her gaze shifted to T-Mac. "Why are you here?"

He smiled. "I wanted to make sure you were going to be okay."

"I'm okay. You don't have to be here. I'm sure you have more important things to do."

"Do you mind if I stay? I'm not on duty or anything. After being here all night, I feel invested in your well-being."

She shrugged. "Suit yourself. I'm probably going to go back to sleep. Maybe when I wake up again, I'll remember what I've forgotten." She laughed, the sound catching on a sob. "I don't even know what I've forgotten."

He lifted her hand and gave it a light squeeze. "I'd fill you in, but I barely know you."

"Then you're no help." She closed her eyes but didn't try to pull her hand free. Holding on to T-Mac was the lifeline she needed at that moment. If that made her weak…so be it. Until she got her memories back, she felt as though she'd been set adrift on an ocean, far from shore.

"What exactly happened?" she asked.

His eyes narrowed as if he were assessing her.

She waved her free hand. "I'm a soldier. Don't pull your punches. Give it to me." Then her eyes widened and a smile lifted her lips. "I'm a soldier."

T-Mac smiled. "See? Your memory's already coming back." He nodded. "We entered a village with the intention of getting there ahead of people coming to make a weapons handoff. We ran into resistance. You were shot in the chest. The team was overwhelmed by incoming grenades and mortars, and we backed out to regroup. Fortunately, you were wearing body armor, or the outcome could have been very different."

"That's it?" She studied T-Mac. He wasn't telling her everything. "What else?"

"Agar was injured."

That name. She should know that name. She didn't want to say it, but she couldn't remember who Agar was.

T-Mac's gaze pinned hers, his lips pressing together for a moment. "Your dog."

As if a floodgate had been unleashed, images and memories poured over Kinsley, all revolving around Agar, his training, her training as a dog handler and the heat of summer in San Antonio, Texas. She tried to breathe, but her lungs were constricted, the air refusing to enter or leave. "Agar," she mouthed. Her hand squeezed his tightly.

"He's with the veterinarian. I haven't been there yet to check his status."

Kinsley pushed to a sitting position. Her head spun and pain knifed through her temple. "Have to see him."

T-Mac pressed a hand to her shoulder. "You're not going anywhere until the doc clears you to move."

"I'm going." She shoved his hand away and swung her legs over the side of the bed. That's when she noticed she was only wearing a hospital gown and not much else. "Where are my clothes?"

"They cut away the trousers and shirt to get to your shrapnel wounds."

"Great. I don't suppose I can walk across the camp in this gown?" She glanced down at the flimsy hospital dress and back up at T-Mac.

"I'll bring a change of clothes for you."

"Thanks." Her brows rose.

"Oh, you mean now?" He grinned. "I should say, I'll get your clothing when the doctor releases you to go back to your quarters."

"I'm leaving." She scooted her bottom to the edge of the mattress. "With or without clothes."

"Specialist Anderson, you haven't been released from my care." The doctor chose that moment to return to her room. "Until that time, you're under my command. You leave, and I'll have to report you as AWOL."

Kinsley frowned. "I need to see my dog."

"You can see your dog when I release you. I want to keep you one more night. If everything looks good in the morning, I'll sign your release orders." The doctor shone his penlight into her eyes, listened to her heartbeat and then left her alone again with T-Mac.

"I'll check on Agar and let you know how he's doing," T-Mac said.

Kinsley wanted to see for herself, but she couldn't risk her career by disobeying orders. "Okay. But could you go now?"

T-Mac chuckled, the rich tone warming her in the air-conditioned room. "Going." He performed an about-face and marched to the door, where he turned back. "Don't go anywhere. I'll be back in a few minutes."

"You might want to shower before you return." She wrinkled her nose. "You smell."

He leaned close and inhaled. "You're no bed of roses either, Specialist." He moved out of range of her swinging arm and winked.

She watched him leave in his torn pants and dirty uniform jacket. Even with dried blood smeared across his leg, he was handsome.

Kinsley crossed her arms over her chest, every nerve in her body urging her to jump out of bed and race after him, to go to the vet's office. Agar had to be okay. He was more than just a working dog to her. He was her only friend.

The image of T-Mac's head lying on the bed beside her returned. He'd been by her side throughout the night when he didn't have to be. Why had he stayed for a relative stranger?

Now that T-Mac was gone, Kinsley felt alone and overwhelmed. At least she had part of her memory back.

Agar. She could remember every detail of her dog and the training they'd gone through to make him the best explosives-sniffing dog he could be.

But no amount of training made either one of them bulletproof.

Kinsley prayed Agar would be okay. And she hoped T-Mac would hurry back. Not only for news on her dog, but because she already missed holding his hand.

Chapter Four

T-Mac hurried to his quarters and grabbed a clean uniform and his shaving kit. After a quick trip to the shower unit, he felt almost human. His leg stung where his stitches were, but he'd get over it soon enough. The injury wouldn't keep him from a mission, and it sure as hell wouldn't keep him from checking on Kinsley.

On his way back to the medical facility, he swung through the chow hall and snagged a couple of sandwiches and pieces of lemon pound cake. He had them wrapped in cellophane and tucked them in the large pockets of his jacket.

Next stop was the camp veterinarian. When he entered, he found Harm talking to the vet with Agar sitting at his feet.

"It's the darnedest thing," the vet was saying. "One minute he was unconscious, the next he was up and moving around as if nothing had happened. I watched him through the night, but he seems to have suffered no lasting damage from the explosion." The vet handed over the lead to Harm. "He's been fed and has had plenty of water for now. You might test his abilities before he returns to duty. And he could use some exercise. He's been cooped up in a crate until now."

"Will do," Harm said, and handed the lead to T-Mac. "I'm sure your dog handler would like to see her dog."

T-Mac grinned. "I'm sure she would." He reached down to scratch Agar behind the ears. "I'll take him out for a run first." He nodded toward the vet. "Thanks."

"My pleasure. He's a well-behaved animal."

He had to be. Military Working Dogs were selected based on physical ability, temperament and intelligence. Agar had all that going for him, plus a rigorous training program of which Specialist Anderson had been a major part.

T-Mac and Agar followed Harm out of the veterinarian's building.

Harm stopped and faced T-Mac. "How's your dog handler?"

T-Mac smiled. "She's awake and talking." His smile faded.

Harm's brow creased. "But?"

"She's suffering some temporary amnesia."

"Not good."

"No kidding. The doctor thinks she'll get most of her memory back."

"Do you think she saw the man who shot her?"

He shrugged. "It was dark. Even if she did see him, there's no guarantee she'll remember."

"That's too bad."

"It's too bad he got away." T-Mac clenched his fists. That man had fired with all intentions of killing Kinsley. She would be dead had her body armor not protected her.

"The CO wants to see you when you get a chance." Harm held up his hand. "He was satisfied with what we told him, so he said no hurry."

"Good." He wanted to get back to Kinsley as soon

as he exercised Agar. "I'll stop by later, after she goes to sleep."

"I'll let him know."

"Did he say anything about the mission?"

"He was hot." Harm bent to smooth his hand over Agar's head and then glanced up at T-Mac. "Someone around here tipped off our quarry. They were ready for us."

"The only people who knew where we were going were our team and the helicopter pilots."

"The commander has the intel folks interviewing the crews and maintenance people," Harm said. "I'll let you know if they learn anything."

"Thanks." T-Mac glanced toward the containerized living units. "Big Jake doing okay?"

"He's sore, but he'll live. The commander wanted him to sit out the next mission, but Big Jake laughed and told him he might as well go. Sitting wasn't an option."

T-Mac chuckled.

"What about you?" Harm pointed to his leg.

"Just a flesh wound. I'm in if they go after the people who did this to us."

"We're all in. You think your dog handler will join us?"

"God, I hope not." He hated to think of Kinsley back in the line of fire. She might not be so lucky next time. "The doc said they're trying to get a transport to carry her to the next level of care. But now that she's awake and coherent, they might change their minds."

"Awake and coherent is a good sign," Harm said. "I can see you're anxious to get back to her. Don't let me hold you up."

"Thanks for checking on Agar." T-Mac left Harm and

half walked, half jogged around the camp, giving Agar the exercise he needed. From what he could tell, the dog had completely recovered. At one point, while they were passing the motor pool, Agar growled low in his chest.

With a quick glance around, T-Mac couldn't identify what set off the dog. He'd seen Agar's behavior when he found explosives. He hadn't growled, just lain down beside the find. The only other time he'd seen the dog growl had been before he'd gone into the building with the rebel who'd shot Kinsley.

After he'd walked Agar for fifteen minutes, he headed for the medical facility and strolled through the door as if he owned the place. Bravado might get him past the guy manning the front desk.

"Excuse me," a voice called out behind T-Mac.

He slowed, pulling Agar up on a short leash. "Yes?"

"I'm pretty sure animals aren't allowed in the facility." The young man stood.

"This isn't just an animal. This is Sergeant Agar. He outranks you. You might show him a little more respect."

"You're kidding, right?" The young man's brow twisted.

"Sergeant Agar is on his way to see his handler, Specialist Anderson."

"Oh." The young man sat back in his seat, a worried frown still pulling at his brow. "I guess that's okay, then."

"Right." T-Mac marched past him to the room where he'd left Kinsley. When he entered, he did a double take. The bed was empty. He walked back out and went to the next room only to turn around and come back.

Agar tugged at his lead.

T-Mac released him and he ran for the door to the adjoining bathroom and sniffed at the gap beneath.

The door opened and Kinsley stepped out, holding the back of her gown together behind her. When she saw Agar, she let go and dropped to her knees to hug the German shepherd.

He nuzzled her, licked her face and wagged his tail.

"Thank God you're okay," she whispered, tears running down her face. She ran her hands over his body and legs. "Did you get hurt?" She checked him over thoroughly, blinking back her tears. When she was done, she looked up at T-Mac. "Thank you for bringing him."

T-Mac smiled. "I think he missed you."

"Even if he didn't, I missed him." She hugged the dog's neck.

A twinge of envy rippled through T-Mac. He found himself wishing he was the dog, being lavished with all the attention and hugs. But the smile on Kinsley's face made T-Mac's day brighter. "Now that you have Agar, I suppose you don't need me anymore."

Her eyes widened and she straightened. "You can stay, if you like. Though it's horribly boring being stuck in bed all day. I don't know why the doctor doesn't let me go. I feel fine. And Agar needs to be exercised. I have to know, the next time we're out, that he'll be able to sniff out explosives."

"I walked him before we came into the facility. And tomorrow should be soon enough to test his skills," T-Mac assured her. "In the meantime, do you want me to take him back to my quarters?"

Her eyes widened and her hold on Agar tightened. "He sleeps in my room, with me."

He leaned close and dropped his voice to a whisper. "I bet if Agar's really quiet no one will notice if he stays."

Kinsley pushed to her feet and walked to the bed.

Agar followed, his body pressed against her legs.

Kinsley slipped beneath the sheets and lay back.

Agar paced around the bed, lifting his nose to sniff at Kinsley. Then he leaped up onto the foot of the bed.

Kinsley laughed and moved over.

Agar stretched out beside her and rested his snout on her arm.

The image of the two of them lying against the white sheets made T-Mac's heart swell. For a fleeting moment, he wished he was Agar, and that he'd put that happy smile on Kinsley's face.

She closed her eyes and sighed. "I guess I can stay another night as long as Agar's with me."

T-Mac cleared his throat. "Since you don't need me, I'll go."

Kinsley's eyes flew open. "Do you have to?"

He shrugged. "No. My buddies are covering for me with my commander."

She held out her hand. "I think they gave me a sedative. Could you stay until I go to sleep?" Her lips twisted. "You don't have to if you don't want to."

He chuckled. "Playing second fiddle to a dog isn't quite a compliment, but I'll take it."

T-Mac pulled the chair close and gathered her hand in his, reveling at how small it was in his, yet how strong and supple her fingers were.

Agar leaned his long snout over Kinsley's body, sniffed T-Mac's hand once and then laid his head back on Kinsley's other side, seemingly satisfied T-Mac wouldn't harm the dog handler.

For a long moment, she said nothing. T-Mac assumed she was sleeping.

"Don't tell anyone," Kinsley whispered, her eyes closed, her breathing slow and steady.

T-Mac stroked the back of her hand. "Tell anyone what?"

"That the tough-as-nails army soldier needed to hold a navy SEAL's hand."

"I could find another poor soul to hold your hand, if you like." His fingers tightened around hers. "Maybe even an army puke," he offered, but he really didn't want to relinquish his hold.

"No need to disturb anyone else." She lay for a while with her eyes closed.

T-Mac studied her face. Freshly washed, free of any makeup, she had that girl-next-door appeal, with a sprinkling of freckles across her nose and cheeks.

T-Mac had the sudden urge to kiss those freckles.

"Why did you want to be a SEAL?" Kinsley's voice yanked T-Mac back to reality.

He barely knew this woman. They were deployed. Fraternization could get them both kicked out of the military, or hit with an Article 15, which would put a black mark on their records and keep them from getting promoted.

"I joined the navy because I didn't want to be a farmer," he said. "My father owns a farm in Nebraska. I grew up running tractors and combines through the summer. He inherited the farm from his father, who inherited it from his father."

"Was your father disappointed when you didn't want to take over the farm?"

T-Mac shrugged. "Not really. I think when he was

a teenager, he had dreams of traveling the world and doing something else with his life. But his father had a heart attack and he stayed to take care of the crops and his mother. And he never left."

"Any siblings?" she asked.

"A younger sister." He grinned. "And she's all about the farming. She's in college now, studying agriculture and researching all kinds of things that will help improve crops and yield. My father is so proud of her."

"And he's not proud of you?" Kinsley asked.

T-Mac nodded. "He is. I'm doing what he would have wanted to do. Whenever I can, I send pictures of some of the places I've been. I think he lives vicariously through me. One of these days, I hope to take him and my mother to Europe on vacation. I want them to see Italy, Greece, Spain and France. My father is a big history buff. He'd love it."

Kinsley smiled, her eyes open, the green color seeming deeper. "Sounds like you had a good childhood. You must love your folks a lot."

He nodded. "I miss them, but I also love what I'm doing." T-Mac tilted his head. "What about you? What made you join the army?"

Her lips twisted. "I didn't feel like I had a lot of choices. My mother didn't have the money to send me to college. I joined the army to build a better life for myself. When I get out, I plan on going to college."

"What do you want to study?"

"I don't know yet. I might go into nursing. But for now, I love working with the dogs. Agar in particular."

As if he knew she was talking about him, Agar rested his head over her belly.

Kinsley stroked the dog's neck. "Working with Agar

has taught me more about life and living than all twenty-something years of my life."

"How so?"

"I grew up with a single mother. She worked two jobs to keep a roof over my head and food on the table. I didn't see her enough."

"Sounds like you were pretty much on your own."

"I was, from about ten on. I didn't have many close friends in school because I didn't join any extracurricular activities. I couldn't. I had to ride the bus home. Walking wasn't an option. Between home and high school were some pretty sketchy neighborhoods. So I went home on the bus and locked the doors. I guess you could say I was pretty introverted. Handling Agar taught me patience with others and helped bring me out of my shell."

"How did you get in with the dogs?" T-Mac asked.

"I was working on a detail near the canine unit at Fort Hood, Texas. I asked how I could get into the program. My first sergeant helped me apply, and here I am." She laughed. "My first real mission and I blew it."

"You didn't blow it." T-Mac squeezed her hand. "Someone tried to blow you away."

She touched a hand to her chest. "Feels like it."

"Bruised?"

"Just sore." Her eyebrows dipped. "But not too sore I can't go back to work."

"I'm sure you let the doctor know."

"Damn right I did." Her chin tilted upward. "Agar and I have work to do…lives to save."

"Yes, you do." Though he didn't like the idea of Kinsley and Agar going out on point again. "About last night… Did you see the face of the man who shot you?"

Kinsley closed her eyes and scrunched her face. After a minute, she shook her head. "I can't remember even going out with the team. How did we get where we were going?"

T-Mac shook his head. "By helicopter."

Her eyes narrowed. "That's right. You walked me to the helicopter pad."

"Just me?" he prompted.

Kinsley sighed. "That's all I remember. Everything else is a blank." She looked up at him with her pretty green eyes. "Why can't I remember? I feel like I'm forgetting something important."

"Like someone shooting you point-blank in the chest?" T-Mac snorted. "That's something you might want to forget. Or maybe it's your mind's way of protecting you." He brought her hand up to his mouth and pressed a kiss to the back of her knuckles. "Don't let it worry you. When you're ready, you'll remember." He kissed her hand again before he even realized what he was doing.

Her gaze went from her hand to his face. "Why did you do that?"

Heat rose up his neck into his cheeks. "I don't know. I'm sorry. I shouldn't have." He laid her hand on the sheet. "Maybe I should go."

"No." She reached out and snagged his fingers with hers. "Please, don't go. Unless you have to." Her cheeks flushed. "I didn't say I didn't like it."

"Yeah, well, I shouldn't have done it anyway. I don't know why, but it just felt right." He held out his hand. "I'm sorry. It won't happen again."

An awkward silence ensued. One in which T-Mac couldn't look Kinsley in the eyes.

Finally, she squeezed his hand and let go. "I've kept you here long enough. I plan on sleeping until tomorrow and then initiating my escape plan."

T-Mac chuckled. "I'm sure Agar will be a big help in your endeavors." He stepped away from the bed and looked around. "If Agar is staying with you tonight, we need to see to his comfort as well as yours. I'll be right back."

He turned away, kicking himself for kissing the woman's hand. What if a nurse or doctor had walked in? He was taking advantage of the woman when she was at her most vulnerable. And worse, his actions could have been construed as fraternization, which could not only get him in trouble, but Kinsley as well.

T-Mac searched through the cabinet in the room. He found a bedpan and some kind of sterile bowl. He pulled the bowl off a shelf, filled it with water from the sink in the adjoining bathroom and set it on the floor.

Agar leaped down from the bed, trotted over to the bowl of water and licked it dry.

T-Mac chuckled. "Hey, boy, you must have been really thirsty."

"I swear that dog is part camel." Kinsley laughed. "I keep expecting him to grow a hump from all the water he consumes."

Squatting next to the dog, T-Mac rubbed the animal behind the ears. "You're lucky to have Agar."

"I know," Kinsley said, her voice low. "I'm sick that I almost lost him."

T-Mac glanced up to catch Kinsley staring at him. Not the dog. His pulse pushed blood through his veins at an alarming speed. He didn't know what was wrong with him, but if he didn't leave soon, he'd do more than just kiss the woman's hand. And he couldn't let that happen. "I'm sorry, but I have to go."

She nodded. "I know. You can't babysit the dog handler forever."

He turned to leave.

"T-Mac." Kinsley's voice stopped him from making good his escape.

He made the mistake of turning back.

Kinsley lay against the sheets looking small and vulnerable.

"Yes?" T-Mac kept his distance, while clenching his fists to keep from reaching out to take her into his arms.

"You're an amazing man. Thank you for rescuing me."

"Don't mention it," he said, and left the room.

Chapter Five

The nurses and the doctor who visited Kinsley throughout the rest of the day and into the night didn't seem at all put out by Agar's presence. Kinsley suspected T-Mac had something to do with their casual acceptance. And for that she was grateful.

Having Agar with her helped her make it through the nightmares that woke her several times in a single hour.

At one point, she woke up calling out T-Mac's name. When she realized what she'd done, she looked around quickly, hoping no one else had heard. Once she ascertained she was well and truly alone, she was able to relax. At the same time, she missed having the navy SEAL there in her room, holding her hand. And, if she were honest with herself, she wanted him to kiss her again. But not on her hand.

The sun and Agar's soft whining woke Kinsley the next morning. She rolled out of the narrow bed and landed on her bare feet. The cool tile flooring against her toes and the draft through the back of her gown made her shiver.

Agar danced beside her, ready to go outside for his morning run.

"Sorry, boy, we have to get permission from the doctor."

"Speak of the devil…" The doctor entered the room. "And here I am." He chuckled at his own joke and then got serious. "Headache?" The doctor pulled a penlight from his breast pocket.

"No, sir."

He shone the light into her eyes. "Dizziness?"

"No, sir."

"How are those ribs?" He patted his hand on the bed. "Hop up and let me look you over."

"The ribs are mildly sore, but livable." She scooted her bottom onto the edge of the bed and swung her legs up.

"Lie down on the bed," the doctor ordered.

After a nurse joined them in the room, the doc lifted her gown to inspect the bruising on her ribs, pushing here and there until he was satisfied nothing was broken.

Kinsley bit down hard on her tongue to keep from crying out a couple of times. It hurt, but she refused to be put on profile until the bruising went away. She wanted to get back out and make sure no one triggered an unexpected explosion and lost lives or limbs. She and Agar had a job to do, and by God, they were going to do it.

"As much as I'd like to keep you and have someone for my staff to work on, I can't find enough wrong with you."

Kinsley sat up, grinning. "Really?"

"The nurse will give you discharge instructions."

"So, I can return to duty?"

The doctor held up a single finger. "Light duty for a day, to make sure you don't have any residual effects of the explosion or gunshot."

"Thank you." Kinsley was so relieved she wanted to cry.

Agar's tail pounded the floor beside the bed.

"I'm really releasing you to get this hairy beast out of my facility." The doctor brushed a dog hair from his white coat. "Now, get out of here before I change my mind."

"I will." Kinsley hopped off the bed, grabbed Agar's lead and made for the door.

"Eh-hem." The doctor cleared his throat. "Aren't you forgetting something?"

The cool tile beneath her feet and the draft on her backside made a rush of heat climb up her cheeks. Her heart sank. "I don't suppose I can borrow some scrubs or something?"

"As a matter of fact, I have what you need." The nurse reentered the room carrying a stack of clothing. "A handsome navy SEAL delivered these this morning for you. He apologized about the size but said he didn't have access to your room to get your own things." She grinned.

Kinsley took the shorts, T-shirt and socks from the woman. "These will do."

"Let me know if you need any help," she offered.

"Thank you."

Once the doctor and nurse left the room, Kinsley stripped out of the gown and pulled the T-shirt over her head. The hem fell down around her knees. Undaunted, she slipped into the shorts and dragged them up over her hips. They were too big, but she was able to tighten the string at the waist to keep them from falling off.

The heels of the socks came halfway up her ankles, but they were fine to get her to her quarters. She found her boots in the corner and pulled them on. Feeling like an orphan in hand-me-downs, she grabbed Agar's leash and headed out of the medical facility and across the compound to the containerized living units.

Agar trotted alongside her, his steps light, tail wagging. Thankfully, he seemed to have no ill effects from his own brush with death.

As she walked past the motor pool, a man in an army uniform smiled and waved in her direction.

Kinsley nodded and waved back.

Another man stood on the front bumper of one of the big trucks, leaning over the open engine. He raised his head for moment but didn't acknowledge her. Instead, his gaze followed her.

Agar growled.

"I agree. He wasn't very friendly," Kinsley whispered, and walked faster until she moved out of sight of the motor pool.

As she passed by the command center, the navy commander who'd called for the mission that had almost gotten her killed stepped out of the building. "Ah, Specialist Anderson. I'm glad to see you up and about." His gaze swept over her outfit.

Kinsley lifted her chin. "I was just released from the medical facility. I'm on my way to my quarters to change into a uniform."

The commander's brow dipped. "Should you return to work so soon?"

"I'm on light duty for a day, then I'm back to regular duty." She motioned for Agar to sit. "I wanted to let you know I'm ready and able to perform my mission, should you need me."

"Good to know. I might have something coming up soon. I'll keep you in mind."

"Thank you, sir," she said.

"Can I interest you in some fabulous food from our neighborhood chow hall?" He waved his hand toward the dining facility. "I'm headed there now."

"No, thank you, sir," Kinsley said. "I need to change and exercise Agar."

"Don't overdo it," the commander said.

"Yes, sir." Kinsley hurried along, determined to reach her quarters before she encountered anyone else. She didn't like being out of uniform in the oversize shirt and shorts, looking goofy in a pair of combat boots. She'd seen worse while she'd been there, but she held herself to a higher standard. And she was grateful for the clothing to get across the compound. She couldn't imagine traipsing across Camp Lemonnier in nothing but boots and a hospital gown.

Thankfully, she didn't encounter anyone else on her way to her quarters. Her skin crawled with a strange feeling someone was watching her. She flung open the door.

Agar stepped inside.

Then Kinsley slipped into the shipping container, closed the door behind her and stood for a moment, listening for footsteps outside.

The crunch of gravel sent a shiver along her spine.

Agar pressed his nose to the door crack and sniffed. Then he sniffed again, his hackles rising.

Kinsley knew she should look outside and see who was there, but she couldn't bring herself to do it.

Then, as quickly as Agar's hackles rose, they fell back in place and he trotted over to her bed and lay down.

"What was all that about?" Kinsley asked.

When the dog looked up at her from his lounging position on the floor, he cocked his head to one side.

"You're hopeless." Kinsley yanked off the T-shirt that smelled amazingly like T-Mac. She pressed it to her nose, inhaled his scent and tossed the shirt on the bed.

The shorts were next.

Wanting to prove she was up to working again, Kinsley changed into a clean uniform, brushed her hair and pulled it back into a tight bun at the nape of her neck. Sore around the stitches on her leg and achy around the ribs, she didn't slow down, but called for Agar. She snatched up his lead, his KONG and the training aid she used with the trace scent of explosives inside.

Agar leaped to his feet as soon as he saw the dog toy. He loved chewing on the KONG and would do almost anything she asked just to get to play with it for a few seconds.

Feeling a little more like normal, if somewhat beaten up, Kinsley left her quarters and walked out to the camp trash containers. With the sun rising high in the sky, barely a breeze to stir the air and the sun's heating the earth and the trash, the smell was barely tolerable and perfect to help disguise the training aid.

Kinsley tied Agar to a post and then ducked between trash bins to hide the toy.

When she returned, Agar's ears perked. She gave him the signal to find the explosives and let him out to the end of his lead.

Within minutes, he found the aid. Kinsley's heart swelled and she praised the dog for his find. She rewarded him by throwing his KONG and letting him run to fetch it. Repeating the exercise several more times, she was satisfied Agar hadn't lost his touch. She took him for a long walk around the perimeter of the camp, hoping to stretch the kinks out of her body and work thoughts of a certain navy SEAL out of her mind.

She'd have to return his clothes soon, and the thought warmed her all the way to her core. Which scared the crap out of her. She did *not* need to get involved with a navy guy. Nothing could come of it. They were both committed to their military careers.

Besides, nothing could happen while they were deployed together. And when they returned stateside, he'd end up in some navy base on the East or West Coast and she'd be at an army post, probably in the middle of the country, like Texas or Oklahoma. They might as well be on different continents.

The sooner she got the man out of her head, the better. But the more she walked, the more she thought about Petty Officer Trace McGuire. The man with the strong hands and big heart, who'd rescued her when she'd been knocked down and stayed by her side in recovery.

AFTER A TERRIBLE sleepless night, T-Mac left his bed early and went for a run around Camp Lemonnier. Then he hit the weight room for forty brutal minutes pumping iron. And he still couldn't get Kinsley out of his head.

He'd purposely resisted going straight to the medical facility and checking on her. But the longer he stayed away, the more he wanted to go. He showered, put on a fresh uniform and stepped out of his quarters. Despite his effort to stay away, his feet carried him to the medical facility. The closer he got, the faster he walked until he burst through the door.

He didn't stop to say anything to the guy at the desk, but kept walking straight to Specialist Anderson's room.

About to barge in, he stopped himself short and forced calm into his fist as he knocked.

When no one answered, he knocked again. Was she asleep?

When no one answered the second time, he pushed open the door and marched in.

The bed was freshly made and completely empty.

Damn! Where had she gone?

"Specialist Anderson was discharged first thing this morning," a voice said behind him.

He turned to face the nurse who'd checked on Kinsley the day before.

"Is she well enough?"

The woman smiled. "She was. The doctor signed her release papers. She practically ran out the door with her dog. Oh, by the way, thank you for bringing the clothes. I think she would have walked out of here in her boots and the hospital gown if she hadn't had them to change into."

A smile tugged at the corners of T-Mac's mouth. "I'm sure she was happy to be free."

The nurse's lips twisted. "It's not like we're a prison in here."

He chuckled. "No. And thank you for taking such good care of us."

She nodded. "Not many guys have the patience or desire to sit in a hospital room for hours on end. She's lucky to have you."

T-Mac didn't try to correct the woman. Kinsley didn't have him. He'd just done the right thing to take care of a fallen comrade. Nothing more.

"Thanks again," he said, and turned to leave.

"Do you want us to check your stitches?" the nurse asked. "We don't often get shrapnel wounds here. Most people come in with colds, allergies or the occasional broken bone from playing volleyball or football."

"No, thank you. You all did a good job. It's healing nicely," he said as he turned to leave. He didn't want to stand around and chitchat. He wanted to find Kinsley and see for himself that she was well enough to be back on her feet.

His first stop was her quarters. Once again, he knocked. No one answered.

When he raised his hand to knock again, someone spoke behind him.

"T-Mac, there you are. I've been looking all over for you."

T-Mac turned to find Harm standing behind him. The SEAL wore his desert-camouflage uniform and a floppy boonie hat instead of his Kevlar helmet.

"What's up?" T-Mac asked.

"The CO wants us in the command center for a briefing in fifteen minutes. I'm headed there now."

His fists tightening, T-Mac sighed. So much for finding Kinsley. He'd have to wait until after the briefing.

T-Mac fell in step beside Harm.

"How's your dog handler this morning?" Harm kicked a pebble in front of them.

"The doc released her." He didn't tell him that he wanted to see her and had yet to find her. Harm didn't need to know how the dog handler had him tied in knots. He'd get a big kick out of it and razz him even more than he already did.

"Glad to hear it," Harm said. "When will she be able to return to duty?"

"Tomorrow." Too soon, by T-Mac's standards.

"What about the dog?"

"Agar spent the night with her at the medical facility. He seemed to be no worse for the wear."

"Good to hear. We might need them on the next mission."

"We've done just fine on most missions without a bomb-sniffing dog."

"What? You don't want Anderson and Agar in the heat of things with us?"

"Not really."

Harm grinned. "You really like her, don't you?"

"I didn't say that," he grumbled. "I just think she's a distraction we can ill afford."

"There's probably a little truth in that statement." Harm glanced toward the command center. "You were quick to load her up and get her out of there without looking back."

"My point exactly." T-Mac stopped in front of the building. "Don't you dare tell her I said that. She'd skin me alive if she knew I didn't want her on a mission."

"Too late," a female voice said behind him. "So, you don't want me on a mission?"

T-Mac balled his fists, dragged in a deep breath and turned to do damage control with Kinsley.

"Look, Kin—Specialist Anderson, I didn't say you weren't good at your job. I'm just saying that we're used to working as a combat team. The night before last was the first time we've integrated a dog team in a mission. And, well, you know what happened. It wasn't a raging success."

"And that was my fault?" she asked.

"If you hadn't been there…" T-Mac started.

Harm cleared his throat. "You might reconsider going there, buddy."

Kinsley held up a hand. "No, let him go. I want to know how deep he'll dig his own grave."

Anger rose up inside T-Mac, and he plowed right into waters he knew would be over his head in the next few words out of his mouth. "If you hadn't been there, one of us would have breached that building in a way we've been taught that doesn't involve walking through the door as if we expect a big hug and a hallelujah."

Her eyes narrowed. "And you think that's what I was doing?"

Harm crossed his arms over his chest and shook his head. "Told you to think before you opened your mouth." He held up his hands. "Now you're on your own. I'll see you two inside." Harm bailed on T-Mac and entered the command center.

"So, you think I don't know what I'm doing?" Kinsley asked.

"I think you're more concerned about your dog than your own life."

"Maybe you're right. I care about Agar." Her chin lifted even higher. "At least I care about someone."

"I'm sure you and Agar are good at sniffing out IEDs and land mines, but clearing buildings might not be the right fit for you."

Kinsley's face grew redder and redder. "It's a good thing you're not my boss, or anywhere in my chain of command. Now, if you'll excuse me, I've been summoned for a job. A job you don't think I can do." She spun on her heel and marched into the command center without looking back.

Once again, T-Mac could kick himself for opening his big mouth. The woman had a right to be spitting mad at him. He just couldn't see going through what he'd been through two nights ago again.

When Kinsley had been blown out of that hut and lay on the ground like she had, T-Mac's heart had stopped and then turned flips trying to restart and propel him forward to pick up the pieces. What had him all wound up was the possibility that next time, Kinsley might not be as lucky. She might actually be in pieces. And he didn't want to be the one to pick them up.

Chapter Six

Kinsley stood in the command-center war room, too mad to sit. How dare T-Mac tell his teammate he didn't want her on another mission?

Hadn't she and Agar gotten them through a minefield upon entering the abandoned village?

The CO paced at the front of the room, waiting for everyone to enter and take a seat. He raised his brow at Kinsley, who still stood. "Please, take a seat."

"Sir, if you don't mind, I'd prefer to stand," Kinsley said. The only empty seat happened to be beside T-Mac. And she sure as hell wasn't going to sit next to him. Not when he'd impugned her honor and spread doubt about her abilities as a dog handler and soldier.

"Suit yourself," the commander said. He addressed Kinsley and the room full of SEALs. "The mission two nights ago didn't go the way we expected."

Several snorts were emitted by various members of the SEAL team.

Kinsley held her tongue.

"We were lucky to come out with as few casualties as we did," the commander continued. "As it is, having Specialist Anderson join the effort was a welcome addition to the team. Without her, our SEALs might have stepped on and triggered half a dozen or more mines on their way into the village where the arms trading was to take place." He held up a hand. "I know I'm repeating old news, but I want to be clear… We cannot have a repeat of what happened that night."

"Sir, does that mean we're going out again?" Big Jake asked.

"I'm not sure you are," the CO said. "But the rest of the team is going."

Big Jake placed both hands flat on the table. "Sir, I might have taken a hit in the rear, but the rest of me works just fine. I won't be sitting on a mission. And where my guys go, I go."

The CO stared hard at Big Jake. "If you think you're up to it."

"I am, sir," Big Jake said without hesitation.

"Good." He stared around the room again. "What happened two nights ago was an ambush. They knew you were coming and they were waiting for you to enter the village before they attacked."

Kinsley gasped. Having been in the hospital since the incident, and being the only army personnel in a sea of navy SEALs, she hadn't been included in the scuttlebutt. "You think we were set up?"

The commander nodded. "Someone leaked information about the mission. We still don't know who did it, but we suspect it's someone here on Camp Lemonnier."

Kinsley glanced around the table of men, all loyal, career military men who'd risked their lives on many occasions for their country. "You don't think it was anyone in this room, do you?"

"No, not anyone in this room," the commander said.

"I should think not," Kinsley said.

T-Mac's lips twitched, as did others in the room.

"We have a traitor amongst us on Camp Lemonnier. And that traitor is quite possibly connected to the illegal arms trading going on."

"What's being done about it?" Harm asked.

"We've interviewed everyone involved with the helicopters. We don't know for certain, but we don't believe any of them were the culprit." The commander sighed. "And if one of them is, we haven't found the connection yet."

He paused for a moment before continuing.

"But we can't sit back and wait until we find him. We have new intel, and we need to move on it before it becomes useless."

The SEALs all leaned forward in their chairs.

"We have infrared satellite images from two nights ago. When our guys bugged out of that village that night, two trucks left in the opposite direction." The CO stared around the room. "Bottom line is, we know where they went."

"Where?" Kinsley asked.

The commander shook his head. "I can't say. Until we launch a mission, I'm not revealing any specifics about any part of that mission until the choppers are off the ground."

"Radio signals can be intercepted," T-Mac said.

"I didn't say I was going to use radio signals."

Pitbull frowned. "Then how will we know where we're going?"

The commander stared around the room. "I'm going with you. I will have the mission-specific information necessary to carry out the assignment."

"Sir, you haven't trained with the team," Buck pointed out.

"Won't that make the mission higher profile?" Big Jake asked. "If someone is leaking information and learns you're going along for the ride, won't that make the rest of us collateral damage when they're targeting you?"

"First of all," the commander said, "this information is not to go outside this room. No one other than the people here are to know we have intel on a potential location of the attackers from the village the other night. No one outside this room should know what we know. Not the helicopter pilots, the mechanics, anyone in the mess hall or anywhere else."

The commander continued. "Every one of you should be ready to go at a moment's notice. When we take off, you will have only a few minutes to prepare. Can you be ready?"

"Sir, yes, sir!" Kinsley shouted along with the SEAL team.

"Then for now, not a word to anyone." The commander's eyes narrowed. "Not even to each other. We can't risk being overheard. Understood?"

Kinsley stood at attention and shouted, "Sir, yes, sir!" along with the others in the room.

The commander nodded, apparently satisfied. "Then you're all dismissed until further notice."

One by one, the SEALs filed out of the room but without the usual banter.

Kinsley stood in the corner, waiting until the others were gone. Then she and Agar approached the commander. "Sir, do you still plan on using me and Agar in the next mission?"

"Specialist Anderson, I would not have allowed you in the room with the others if I didn't plan on taking you along." He stared hard into her eyes. "Are you up to another mission so soon?"

She nodded. "Yes, sir."

"That's all I need to know. You proved invaluable on the last one. I see no reason to leave you out of the next one."

"Thank you, sir."

"You realize that some of the men might consider you a distraction to the mission."

Her blood pressure rocketed and her jaw tightened. "Did T-Mac say that?"

"Not actually." The commander smiled. "His report to me was that you were fearless." His smile turned into a frown. "Why? Are you and T-Mac at odds? Do you want me to assign a different SEAL to look out for you?"

Fearless? He thought she was fearless? And yet, he didn't want her on a mission.

"I could get Harm or Buck to look out for you," the commander offered.

"No," Kinsley said, her pulse racing. "T-Mac was there for me. I trust him." And she did. She'd bet her life on him. But was she betting his life on her being a part of the mission? Was it right for her to want to go even though she was a distraction to them?

She stiffened her spine and pulled back her shoulders. Based on what had happened on the last mission, and finding all those land mines buried along the path the SEALs were destined to follow, she had to go. Whoever would set those up the way they had could do it again.

Not only did she want to go, she *had* to go. Otherwise, she would be sitting back at Camp Lemonnier, safe and sound, while the SEAL team could be walking into a minefield. They needed her and Agar. She had to be with them. If something happened to them that she and Agar could have helped them avoid, she could never live with herself.

She looked the commander square in the eye. "Sir, I'm ready whenever you are. Just say the word."

He nodded. "That's what I wanted to hear."

"WALK WITH ME," Harm said as they left the command center.

T-Mac would rather have waited for Kinsley, but he didn't want to admit it, so he fell in step beside Harm.

Instead of turning toward their quarters, he headed toward the flight line where the helicopters were parked.

"You know you can't always protect her, don't you?" Harm said.

T-Mac knew it would serve no purpose to pretend he didn't know who Harm was talking about. "Who said I always want to protect her?"

Harm stopped short of the helicopters and stood staring at them. "She's special. I didn't expect her to be so brave about sniffing out land mines."

His lips twitching, T-Mac rolled his eyes. "She doesn't sniff out the mines. Agar does."

"You know what I mean."

"Yeah, I do. You should have seen her go after Agar when he ran into that hut." The image was etched indelibly into T-Mac's mind. "And then watch as she was blown back out by the force of the bullet that hit her vest."

Harm laid a hand on T-Mac's shoulder. "That shook you, didn't it?"

"I've never been more shaken," T-Mac admitted.

"I know what you mean. We anticipate our own deaths and meet that possibility head-on. But when it comes to someone else, we have a more difficult time accepting or even processing it."

T-Mac nodded. "You hit the nail on the head. All I could think about was how to get her out of that place as quickly as possible. I would have felt the same had it been one of my teammates."

Harm snorted. "I know you would rush in to help if one of us was hit, but I think it was more than that with the dog handler."

A frown pulled T-Mac's brow downward. "Don't read more into my actions than what's there."

Harm held up his hands. "Just saying. You don't have to bite my head off."

"You and the others think that just because you have women, I need one, too. I don't need a woman in my life. And Specialist Anderson isn't that woman anyway."

"You don't think so?"

"I wouldn't know," T-Mac said. "We haven't known each other for very long."

"Speaking from my experience," Harm said, "it doesn't take long to fall in love. Sometimes you just know she's the one."

"Like you and Talia?" T-Mac asked.

"Yeah. Like me and Talia." Harm smiled as he stared at the helicopter. He was probably seeing Talia, the petite beauty with the black hair and blue eyes, not the smooth gray hulks of Black Hawk helicopters.

T-Mac shook his head. "How do you know?"

"At first, I didn't recognize it, but the more I was

around her, the more I wanted to be around her. And then when we were apart, all I could do was think about her."

That's not me. T-Mac refused to believe that was what he was feeling about Kinsley. Yeah, he'd seen her around camp. And he'd fantasized about getting to know her better, even how it would be to kiss her. But love?

Oh, hell no.

But, like Harm, he couldn't stop thinking about her and counted the minutes until he could see her again.

What was wrong with him? He did not need a woman in his life, despite what his buddies thought.

He turned away from the choppers. "We should go prepare."

Harm touched T-Mac's arm. "Falling for a woman is not a bad thing."

"I wouldn't know," T-Mac insisted.

"It doesn't make you weaker," Harm continued. "In fact, it makes me stronger, more determined to do the right thing and be a better person. The kind of person Talia would want to be with."

"Well, that certainly isn't me. Not with Kinsley. I told her I didn't want her to be on the next mission."

Harm's eyebrows shot up. "Kinsley?"

"Specialist Anderson," T-Mac corrected.

"That's why she looked mad enough to spit nails." Harm chuckled.

"Yeah." T-Mac started walking again. "She sure as hell doesn't want to be with me now."

"An apology goes a long way to smoothing a woman's feathers," Harm advised.

T-Mac shot a horrified glance his buddy's way. "Apologize? I'm not sorry I told her that. She's one hundred percent a distraction on a mission."

"Maybe for you, since you're into her."

"I'm not into her." He couldn't be. It made no sense.

"No? Then why did you spend the night at her bed-side, holding her hand?" Harm raised an eyebrow. "And don't say you'd have done the same for one of us."

T-Mac opened his mouth to tell Harm that holding Kinsley's hand didn't mean anything, but he knew it would be a big fat lie. So he closed his mouth, sealed his lips in a thin, tight line and stepped out smartly for his quarters.

Harm jogged to catch up. "You can run, buddy, but you can't hide from the truth."

T-Mac came to an abrupt halt.

Harm ran into him.

"Let's get this straight." T-Mac turned and poked a finger into Harm's chest. "I'm not into Kinsley. We're not together. She's just an army puke with a dog. Nothing more. Period. The end."

Harm stared into T-Mac's eyes and then burst into laughter. "Damn, dude, you've got it really bad for the woman."

T-Mac balled his fists and cocked his arms.

The smile left Harm's face and he held up his hands. "Hey, remember me? I'm on *your* side."

Still ready to hit someone, T-Mac kept his fists up.

"All right. I'll stop razzing you." Harm dropped his hands and tipped his head toward the living quarters. "We'd better get ready. Who knows when we'll get the call?" He stepped out.

For a long moment, T-Mac stood with his hands up, jaw clenched and anger simmering. Finally, he let go of the breath he'd been holding and turned to follow his friend.

They were almost to the living units when T-Mac spoke again, as if they hadn't ended the conversation. "It doesn't matter anyway."

"What?" Harm asked.

"Nothing could ever come of something between us."

"Between who?" Harm grinned and jerked his thumb between T-Mac and himself. "You and me? You're right. I'm taken."

"Shut up. You know who I'm talking about."

Harm nodded. "Yeah, but I also know things have a way of working out."

"Like Talia's resort burning down so she's forced to move back to the States to be with you? Or Marly's airplane blowing up so she can move back to the States and be with Pitbull?"

With a frown, Harm kicked at a rock. "When you put it like that, it sounds bad. But maybe there's something to fate."

"I don't wish anything ill on Kinsley or Agar. They've worked hard for what they do. If I was interested in Kinsley—which I'm not—I couldn't ask her to give up her career to follow me around. Nor would I want to give up my career to follow her. So it doesn't matter. Nothing could ever come of a relationship between me and Kinsley."

With a shrug, Harm opened the door to the quarters they shared and held it for T-Mac to enter. "All I know is, you never know."

T-Mac snorted. "Sounds like double-talk to me."

"Maybe. Maybe not. Just wait and see. If she's worth it, you'll find a way."

T-Mac went to work preparing for the next mission, not knowing what it would be, where they would go or how he'd make it through the tough times and keep Kinsley out of the line of fire. One thing he did know, but wouldn't admit to Harm or anyone else, was that Kinsley was definitely worth the trouble. She was brave, loyal and beautiful.

He cleaned his M4A1 rifle and his nine-millimeter handgun. Then he spent time sharpening his Ka-Bar knife and checking his communications equipment. When he was finished, he stood, stretched and asked, "Ready to hit the chow hall?"

Harm nodded. "Give me a minute to lay out my gear."

While Harm set out his body armor, helmet and night-vision goggles, T-Mac did the same.

By the time they finished, T-Mac's belly rumbled.

They left their quarters and walked toward the dining facility.

As T-Mac passed Kinsley's unit, he noticed a package sitting on the ground directly in front of her door. Wrapped in brown paper, it looked like something the postmaster might have delivered. Except the camp postmaster didn't make deliveries.

At that moment, Kinsley opened the door.

Agar started to step out on the ground and stopped. He sniffed the package once and lay down, blocking Kinsley's exit, his tongue hanging out, his gaze seeking her.

Kinsley nearly tripped over the dog, expecting him to exit. When he didn't, she looked past him to the package, her brow furrowing. She hesitated and stepped back into the unit. "Good boy, Agar. Good boy."

T-Mac stared from the dog to the package and back again. "Did you place that package there?" he asked.

Kinsley's gaze locked with T-Mac's, her eyes going wide. "I was going to ask you the same question."

"Don't bother." T-Mac turned to his friend. "Harm, get back to the command center and report a potential bomb located inside the perimeter."

Harm nodded. "On it." He turned and ran back in the direction from which they'd come.

"Is Agar ever wrong?" T-Mac asked.

Kinsley shook her head. "He tests out at one hundred percent, even with trace amounts of explosives in the decoy."

"Can you step around it?" T-Mac asked.

"Probably?"

T-Mac moved closer to the package and held out his arms. "You can lean on my shoulders and I can help you out."

"No," she said.

With a frown, T-Mac dropped his arms. "No, you can't? Or no, you won't?"

"No, I won't leave Agar." Her lips pressed into a straight line.

"Step back—I'm coming to you."

Her eyes widened. "No! You can't. What if it explodes?"

"Then we'll go together." He winked. "Won't that be romantic or something?"

"Are you insane?" She held up her hands. "I'm going inside the unit and closing the door. Let me know when the unexploded-ordnance guys are done." She backed up a step, held the door wide and called to Agar to follow.

Agar rose and entered the unit, trotting past Kinsley.

When Kinsley stepped back and started to close the

door, T-Mac made his move. He took a giant step over the package and fell through the door frame.

"What the—" Kinsley said as he caught her around the waist and took her to the ground with him.

With his foot, T-Mac kicked the door shut behind him and covered Kinsley's body with his own.

He waited for several long minutes, trying to shield Kinsley from the shrapnel sure to pepper their bodies should the package explode.

After three minutes passed, Kinsley stirred beneath him. "T-Mac," she said, her voice barely a whisper.

"Yes?"

"What are you doing?" Kinsley breathed.

"Saving your life."

"Is that what this is?" Her breathing came in short, shallow gasps.

"Of course."

"Sweetheart, you're killing me," she wheezed.

Sweetheart? Had she really called him *sweetheart?* His chest swelled and warmth spread throughout his body from every point of contact with hers. Which was practically everywhere. All that warmth pooled low in his groin. And his body reacted to the heat and he grew hard.

"T-Mac?" Kinsley said.

"Mmm," he murmured.

"I can't breathe," she whispered.

Immediately, he rose up on his elbows, giving her chest the space she needed to take a deep breath and fill her lungs. "Sorry."

"It's okay. I didn't die." She chuckled. "And the package didn't explode."

"No. But we don't know if it will. What if whoever put it there can trigger it to explode at any time?"

"I would think he would have triggered it when I opened the door."

"Maybe, or maybe he's waiting for a bigger crowd. In which case you won't be safe until the ordnance-disposal guys arrive."

"We can't lie here for that long," she said, her voice all practical but still a little breathless.

T-Mac refused to move. He couldn't risk leaving her exposed. "What does it hurt to stay put for a little longer?"

"I don't want you to shield my body with yours. The navy put a lot of training into you."

"And the army put a lot of training into you and Agar. Speaking of which…can you get him to lie down in case the explosives go off? I'd hate for either one of you to be injured."

"Agar, lie down," she commanded.

The dog dropped to his belly beside Kinsley.

She stared up into T-Mac's eyes. "So, does this mean you care?"

T-Mac frowned. "Only because my commander put me in charge of making sure you're okay."

"Really?" She tilted her head. "That's the only reason?"

"Of course."

Her pretty, peach-pink lips twisted. "Your commander tasked you with that responsibility during our last mission," Kinsley pointed out. "We're not on that mission now."

"I take my responsibilities seriously," T-Mac argued, refusing to admit that he probably would have protected her even if his commander hadn't tasked him with the job. Something about Kinsley drew him, and like a moth to the flame, he couldn't resist. And like that moth, he figured he'd eventually be burned in some way or another. Navy SEALs, by the nature of their work, were doomed in the relationship department.

But at that moment, when they faced the possibility of being blown to bits, he stared down into her face, his gaze zeroing in on her pouty lips.

And he couldn't resist.

He leaned down, his mouth hovering over hers. "I take my responsibilities very seriously," he repeated.

"T-Mac?" Kinsley's breath warmed his mouth. "Are you going to kiss me?"

He nodded. "Yup. Do you have a problem with that?"

"Yes," she said, her voice a hot puff of air against his lips. "You're taking too long."

He claimed her mouth in a long, hard kiss that shook him to his very core. She wrapped her arms around his neck, her fingers threading into the hair at the back of his neck and pulling him closer.

When he ran his tongue across the seam of her lips, she opened to him.

He dove in, deepening the kiss, sliding his tongue along hers in a warm, wet caress, one he never wanted to end.

Kinsley wrapped her calf around his and pushed her hips up, making him even harder.

By the time he raised his head, his body was on fire and he couldn't get enough of her.

He rested his forehead against hers and dragged in air. "What the hell just happened?"

Kinsley chuckled and her breath hitched. "You tell me."

T-Mac brushed his lips across hers in a feather-light kiss. He couldn't get over how soft they were, or that she tasted of mint.

Agar crawled forward and laid his head on Kinsley's shoulder.

Laughter bubbled up in T-Mac's chest. Despite the fact there was a bomb outside the container unit, he'd never felt so light. All because he'd kissed Kinsley.

"T-Mac?" Harm's voice called to him from outside the container. "Are you two in there?"

"If we're really quiet, do you think they'll go away?" Kinsley asked.

T-Mac liked that she could joke when the circumstances could go south quickly. "I doubt it."

"Well, damn." She cupped his cheeks between her palms, leaned her head up and pressed a hard kiss to his mouth. "Then you'd better answer."

He drew in a deep breath, every movement reminding him he was lying on top of a female with curves in all the right places. "We're in here," T-Mac called out.

"Hang tight," Harm said. "The EOD guys are going to remove the package. Stay down."

"Will do," T-Mac said, his gaze never moving from Kinsley's.

"I don't like that you're not wearing body armor," she said.

"I'm liking that I'm not. A little too much." His shaft pressed into her pelvis. He shifted his body to ease the pressure.

Kinsley's eyes flared and her hips rose as if seeking to reestablish the connection. Then she dropped her bottom back to the floor. "You should probably move." Her voice sounded as if she'd been running, her chest rising and falling in shallow breaths.

"Sorry, sweetheart," T-Mac said. "I'm not moving until the danger's over."

"I'm not sure where it's most dangerous…outside my door, or in here." She held his gaze.

"Specialist Anderson, are you afraid of me?" he asked, his tone deep, his body humming with a rush of heat.

"No, Petty Officer McGuire." Her gaze shifted from his eyes to his lips. "I'm afraid of me."

Chapter Seven

Lying sandwiched between the hard metal floor of the container unit and the muscular planes of T-Mac's chest, torso, hips and thighs, Kinsley could barely breathe. And it had nothing to do with T-Mac crushing her chest. He'd removed his weight, balancing over her on his arms.

The man stole her breath away by his sheer alpha maleness.

He could have run away from the package of explosives on her doorstep and left her and Agar to whatever happened.

But he hadn't. He'd sacrificed his own safety to protect her.

Kinsley's estimation of the man increased tenfold. Hell, he'd already proven he could rescue her from tight situations.

But when he'd kissed her…

Sweet, sweet heaven. He'd changed everything in just that one meeting of their lips.

Now she couldn't stop thinking about him and really wished he'd kiss her again.

He lowered his head, his gaze shifting from her eyes to her lips. "This could get us in trouble."

"Big trouble," she whispered, her lips tingling in anticipation of his.

"Hang in there, T-Mac. They're moving the package now." Harm's muffled shout reached her through the walls of her quarters.

They had only seconds to live if the explosives detonated. Or seconds to kiss if they didn't.

Kinsley didn't want to die without just one more…

She reached up, her hand circling the back of T-Mac's head, and pulled him down to her mouth.

She'd never felt so empowered and yet vulnerable as she did in that one desperate kiss.

"They're gone!" Harm shouted.

The rattle of the doorknob alerted Kinsley to impending danger. She planted her hands on T-Mac's chest and shoved him over.

He went willingly, springing to his feet just as the door swung open.

"EOD saved the day," Harm said.

T-Mac reached out a hand. Kinsley placed hers in his and let him bring her to her feet to face T-Mac's friend.

"Are you all right?" Harm asked, his gaze slipping over her face and narrowing in on her lips.

She nodded, her cheeks heating. Could he tell she'd just been kissed? Kinsley fought the urge to press her palms to her cheeks and further incriminate herself. No one had seen what had happened between her and T-Mac. No one had to know. She didn't need an Article 15 on her record. She could lose her position as a dog handler.

Command Order number one when deployed was No Fraternization.

And she'd just fraternized.

She shot a glace toward T-Mac. His gaze was on her, making her entire body burn with desire. What was it about this man that made her feel completely out of control?

"What was in the package?" T-Mac asked.

"We won't know until the EOD guys can either dismantle it or blow it up. I suspect they'll blow it up. Either way, they'll let us know."

T-Mac's lips pressed into a thin line and his jaw firmed. "What the hell? We're inside the wire here in Djibouti."

Harm nodded. "Which means we have a traitor among us."

"Someone who doesn't like me," Kinsley added.

"Why?" Harm asked.

"My guess is whoever left the package could be the one who shot Kinsley point-blank." T-Mac's chest tightened. "He's afraid she'll recognize him and blow his cover."

"But I can't remember anything about that incident," Kinsley said.

"He probably knows that," Harm said. "Word gets around camp quickly."

"He probably also knows that your memory could return at any time. He just wants to make sure it doesn't happen before he can get rid of you." T-Mac faced Kinsley. "Until we determine who it is, you're not safe here."

A shiver rippled from the base of Kinsley's neck down her spine. "In that case, we might as well go on another mission. Agar and I will be as safe, if not safer, with your SEAL team."

"True," Harm said.

T-Mac's jaw tightened.

Kinsley almost laughed. The man was torn. He didn't want her on any mission with them, but she could tell he didn't like the idea of her staying behind and being the target of a traitor.

Finally, he sighed. "You're right. In the meantime, I'm hanging out with Specialist Anderson until further notice."

"You know you can't stay in her quarters," Harm reminded him.

"I know, but I sure as hell can camp out on her doorstep."

"I don't need a babysitter," Kinsley insisted.

"No, but you need a bodyguard." T-Mac held up a hand to keep her from saying more. "Just go with this. If this were happening to one of us, we'd do the same."

Harm nodded. "That's true. You always need someone watching your back."

T-Mac winked. "I've got your six. Think about it. If Agar hadn't warned you, what would have happened?"

A chill swept across her skin. She could have been blown to bits.

"Come on." Harm jerked his head toward the command center. "We need to report to the CO. He has to know what just happened."

Agar nudged her hand.

Kinsley rubbed her fingers over the top of his head. "It's okay, boy." Then she snapped on his lead. He couldn't know all of what was happening, but he was unsettled by the number of people in her quarters and Kinsley's physical distress, no matter how she tried to hide it.

T-Mac and Harm marched her to the command center. The other four members of T-Mac's immediate team joined them, asking questions and expressing concern.

Once they reported what had happened to the commander, his face appeared as if set in stone. "We knew we had a possible leak among us, but this takes it to a different level." He nodded toward T-Mac. "You know what you have to do?"

T-Mac nodded. "I'll cover for Specialist Anderson."

"We'll all look out for her and Agar," Harm promised.

"Good." The commander glanced around at the rest of the team. "We all need to be ready and keep our eyes peeled for anything that might lead us to our traitor."

All six SEALs and Kinsley snapped to attention. "Yes, sir!"

The commander touched Kinsley's arm. "Are you good with all this? If not, we can ship you out on the next transport."

"No way," she said, and added, "Sir. I'm in this for the long haul. Whoever is betraying us and our country needs to be brought down. I want to be a part of the takedown. That bastard needs to pay."

The commander grinned. "That's what I like to hear." He clapped his hands together. "Be alert. Be ready."

As they left the command center, Harm asked, "Anyone up for chow?"

"I'm not particularly hungry," Kinsley said.

"Yeah, but you need to fuel up," T-Mac said. "We never know when we'll be called up."

She nodded, knowing he was right. Her stomach was still knotted from the scare of the explosives package and the kiss from the man at her side. She wasn't sure any food would help her stomach relax, but she had to maintain her strength in order to keep up with the SEAL team. Kinsley refused to slow them down in any way.

In the dining facility, she choked down half a sandwich and a few chips and waited while the others finished their meals. By the time they were done, day was turning into evening.

They exited the dining facility and headed toward the living quarters.

Harm, Buck, Diesel, Big Jake and Pitbull peeled off at their quarters, but T-Mac continued beside Kinsley.

"Agar and I are going for a run. You don't have to go with us. We'll be out in the open and safe."

"I need to go for a run, too." He patted his flat abs. "Can't keep up my girlish figure by eating bonbons and sitting around."

"Seriously, I don't want to monopolize your time. Surely whoever left the package won't try anything out in broad—" she caught herself and continued "—out in the open."

"We don't know what he'll try. And if it's all right by you, I'm not taking any chances."

Kinsley sighed. "I don't like taking up all of your time."

"What else do we have to do?" He waved his hand at their surroundings. "It's the typical military deal—hurry up and wait."

"In that case, meet me outside in five minutes."

He planted his feet in the dirt and crossed his arms over his chest. "I'll wait here."

"No, really." Kinsley touched his arm and immediately retracted her hand when sparks seemed to fly off her fingers and up into her chest. "What could happen in five minutes?"

"A lot."

"You can't go with me everywhere, and I can't go with you. Five minutes will be fine." She pointed toward his unit. "Go change into your PT uniform."

"I'm wearing it," he insisted, though he was in his full uniform, boots and all.

Kinsley planted her fists on her hips. "I'm not going anywhere until you change into your shorts. And I'd have to wait for you outside your unit if I followed you. Just do it, and get back. I promise not to get blown up in the meantime."

He stood for a moment longer, staring into her eyes, and then sighed. "Okay, but I want to check your room before you go in."

Kinsley glanced down at her dog. "Agar does a pretty good job of it for me," she reminded him.

"Humor me, will ya?"

She raised her hands. "Okay." Unlocking the door, she pushed it open and released Agar's lead. "But let Agar go first."

T-Mac's lips twisted. "Deal."

She gave Agar the command to search, pointing into the building.

Agar entered, nose to the ground. As small as the unit was, it took only seconds for him to trot back to her side. He displayed no behavioral signs that anything might contain explosives.

She nodded toward T-Mac. "Your turn."

The navy SEAL entered the small box of a room and searched high and low. What he was looking for, Kinsley had no clue.

When he returned to the door, she raised an eyebrow. "Find anything?" she asked, knowing the answer.

His eyes narrowed. "Don't get smart with me, Specialist."

Her eyes widened as she feigned innocence. "Me? Never."

T-Mac's lips curled on the corners and he lowered his voice until only she could hear him. "Don't tempt me to kiss you again."

Her heart fluttered. "Never," she whispered. Although, at that moment, she'd give anything to feel his lips on hers again. But they weren't locked behind a door, away from prying eyes, with the chance of a deadly explosion threatening to take their lives.

"Five minutes," she whispered.

"Close the door behind me," he said, and stepped out of the doorway.

Kinsley entered and closed the door behind her. Then she leaned against it and dragged in a deep breath. The man made her forget to breathe.

Agar nudged her hand, bringing her back to reality and the need to change quickly.

She rushed around the small space, tossing off her jacket and desert-tan T-shirt. She pulled on her army PT shirt, untied her boots and kicked them off. In short order, she switched her uniform trousers for shorts and her boots for running shoes.

A knock sounded as she pulled her hair back into a ponytail.

She grabbed Agar's lead and flung open the door.

T-Mac stood there in a pair of shorts and running shoes, nothing else.

All those muscles on his broad, tanned chest sucked the air right out of her lungs.

"Ready?" he asked.

She nodded mutely, exited her quarters with Agar and locked the door behind her.

They took off at a jog, past the rows of containerized living units and out to the open field.

Though she was in good shape and could run several miles without stopping, Kinsley didn't have the long stride of the much-taller SEAL. But she held her own, aware that T-Mac slowed his pace to match hers.

Agar trotted alongside them, happy to be outdoors.

They didn't talk, but ran in companionable silence for a few laps around the open field. When they approached the living quarters again, Kinsley slowed to a walk, breathing hard. "Any clue as to who might have planted that package?"

T-Mac walked beside her, barely having broken a sweat. "None."

"I wish I could remember anything from that night I was shot."

"Don't worry about it," he said. "The guy will surface. And when he does, we'll get him."

"Hopefully before anyone else is hurt." As they reached her unit, she turned. "I'm going to grab my things and hit the shower facility. You can't follow me inside, so don't argue."

"I'll wait outside. But take Agar with you. I'm sure he could use a shower as well."

Kinsley laughed. "I will. He loves the shower."

T-Mac muttered something low, almost indiscernible, but it sounded like *lucky dog*.

Kinsley chose not to read into the comment she might not have even heard correctly. Leaving her door wide open, she entered her unit, grabbed her toiletries kit, towel and clothes, kicked off her running shoes and slipped on her flip-flops. She was outside again in record time.

T-Mac escorted her to the shower facility and waited outside while she and Agar went in. They had the shower to themselves.

Kinsley shampooed Agar first and rinsed him beneath the spray. Then she washed her hair and body, all the while aware of the man right outside the thin walls of the building. As she stood naked under the cool spray, she thought about what it would feel like to share a shower with the SEAL. The man was all muscular and glorious. Would he be disappointed with her pale, freckled body and soft curves? Or would he touch her all over and light her entire body on fire?

Sweet heaven.

Her core heated. The lukewarm water did nothing to tamp down the flames of desire coursing through her veins. Kinsley had to quit thinking about the man and his soft, firm lips, broad shoulders and narrow hips, or she'd melt into a puddle of goo.

Agar stepped out from beneath the spray and shook.

Kinsley rinsed one last time and shut off the shower.

Running the towel over her skin, she dried off briskly, trying not to take too much time. When she was finished, she dressed, brushed her hair back from her forehead and smoothed the tangles free. Agar would dry quickly in the Djibouti heat.

T-Mac was still there when Kinsley stepped out of the shower facility.

He walked her back to her unit and waited for her

to enter. "Harm is going to stand guard until I can get showered and changed. But I'll be back for the night."

Kinsley frowned. "You can't sleep in my quarters with me. That would be construed as fraternization."

T-Mac shook his head. "I'm sleeping outside."

"No way. You shouldn't have to sacrifice the comfort of your bed for me."

"I don't consider it a sacrifice. You're doing me a favor. I love to sleep under the stars, and an army cot is what I sleep best on."

"No. This is too much. I can go sleep in the office with whoever is pulling charge of quarters duty. You don't have to babysit me through the night."

He touched her arm. "Anyone ever tell you that you argue too much?"

"Only when I'm right," she replied sharply.

"Well, this time, you aren't going to win the argument. Harm will be here until I return. I'm staying the night outside your unit. The end."

She pressed her lips together. The stubborn set of his jaw brooked no further argument. She'd be talking to a brick wall.

Harm trotted up to stand beside T-Mac. "I'm here." He clapped a hand on T-Mac's shoulder and wrinkled his nose. "Whew, buddy, you smell. Go get your shower."

T-Mac grimaced. "Thanks, Harm."

"I heard from the EOD guys. They said the bomb in the package had a pressure detonator. If she'd stepped on that box, it would have exploded."

T-Mac's gaze went to Kinsley, warming her with the concern in his eyes.

"It's a good thing I have Agar," Kinsley said. "He found it before I would have."

"Maybe I should skip the shower." T-Mac's brow lowered.

"Trust me, dude, you need the shower," Harm said.

T-Mac tipped his head toward Kinsley. "Keep an eye on her."

Harm grinned. "Will do."

"I guess I don't have a say in this?" Kinsley asked, though secretly, she was glad to have such great bodyguards.

Harm glanced at T-Mac.

T-Mac gave a quick head dip. "Nope."

Kinsley rolled her eyes. "Fine. Then keep the noise down. Agar's a light sleeper." She stepped into her unit and gave Agar the command to follow. Once they were both inside, she closed the door.

Three days ago, she had thought the assignment in Djibouti was going to be boring. Now, with the current threat to her life and the other threat to her heart… Djibouti was anything but boring.

T-Mac HATED BEING even a minute away from Kinsley. He couldn't be certain whoever had planted the package bomb wouldn't try again, or when.

He made it to his quarters and back to the shower facility in record time. He scrubbed clean and shaved, wishing he had time to get a haircut. But he'd already been gone more than eight minutes.

Back at his quarters, he grabbed a folding cot and returned to Kinsley's building.

Harm leaned against the corner of the unit. When he spotted T-Mac, he straightened. "What took you so long?" Then he chuckled. "Just kidding. Did you even wash behind your ears? That was faster than a shower at BUD/S training."

T-Mac clapped a hand onto Harm's shoulder. "Didn't want you to suffer for too long."

"Suffer? Or you didn't want me to tell your dog handler all your faults?"

"Both," T-Mac said.

Harm moved closer. "Big Jake hobbled by while you were AWOL from your post."

"And?" T-Mac prompted.

His friend glanced around and lowered his voice. "He was at the command center."

T-Mac drew in a breath and let it out slowly. "Are we a go?"

"Soon." He looked over his shoulder at the door to Kinsley's unit. "Are you ready?"

"I am."

Harm tipped his head toward the door. "Are you ready for her?"

"For Specialist Anderson to come along?" T-Mac sighed. "I don't have much choice, do I?" He shrugged. "I guess I am. Any idea when?"

With a shake of his head, Harm squared his shoulders. "Nope. Just be ready."

Which meant no sleep.

Harm left T-Mac alone.

He set up his cot in front of Kinsley's unit. A few people walked by, giving him strange looks, but he ignored them and stretched out with his hands locked behind his head. If he slept, it would be just a catnap, with one eye open. Darkness had settled in on Camp Lemonnier and the stars popped out, a few at a time, soon making enough light that he didn't need a flashlight to see.

The beauty of the night sky, filled with an array of diamond-like stars, made up for the daylight drabness of the desert surroundings.

A soft click sounded behind him.

He turned as the door to Kinsley's unit opened.

Agar trotted out.

Kinsley stood in the crack and gave Agar the command to lie down.

Agar dropped to his belly on the ground beside T-Mac's cot.

Before he could tell Kinsley that he didn't need Agar's protection, she closed the door.

Agar lifted his head beside the cot. T-Mac reached over and smoothed his hand over the dog's back. "She has a mind of her own, doesn't she?"

When T-Mac's hand stopped moving, Agar nuzzled his fingers.

"Needy guy, aren't you?" T-Mac scratched behind Agar's ears and rubbed his back again. He'd rather be running his hands over Kinsley's naked body than over her dog's back, but this was safer.

He must have drifted off, because the next moment, he awakened to the low rumble of Agar's growl.

T-Mac popped to a sitting position, his fist clenched, ready to defend.

A dark figure disengaged from the shadow of one of the container units.

"T-Mac," Harm's voice called to him in a half whisper.

"Yeah."

"It's time."

Chapter Eight

A finger pressed to her lips and a voice sounded in the darkness. "Kinsley, wake up."

Immediately, Kinsley knocked the hand away, and she shot to a sitting position. "What the hell?"

"I knocked lightly, but you didn't answer. I couldn't knock louder without waking others."

She pushed the hair out of her face and stared up at T-Mac. "It's okay. You just startled me."

"You left your door unlocked."

Agar nudged her fingers with his cool, damp nose.

Kinsley smoothed a hand over his head and neck. "I know. With you out there, I wasn't worried someone would break in."

"What if someone slit my throat?"

She yawned and stretched. "Agar wouldn't let that happen." The room seemed smaller with T-Mac in it. "Why did you wake me?" Her eyes widened. "Oh. Is it time?"

He nodded. "Get your gear. Harm's outside. I'll be back in less than five minutes to get you."

She nodded.

He turned toward the door. "Oh, and did you know you snore?"

"No, I do not." She frowned. "Do I?"

He grinned. "You do. And it's cute as hell. Don't let anyone tell you otherwise." He left her sitting on her bunk with her mouth open.

As soon as he shut the door, she was off the bed and dressing in her uniform, body armor loaded with ammunition and a first-aid kit. She pulled on her helmet, grabbed her rifle and snapped Agar's retractable lead onto his collar. By the time she was ready, a soft knock sounded on the door. She opened it to find T-Mac standing on the other side.

Without a word, she stepped out with Agar, closed the door softly behind her and locked it.

They hurried toward the helicopters on the flight line where the rest of the SEAL team had assembled. Already the rotor blades were turning. If someone didn't know they were about to go on a mission before, they knew now.

The SEAL team loaded into the helicopters. Agar jumped in, and T-Mac gave Kinsley a hand up. Even before she had her safety harness buckled, the chopper left the ground and rose into the air.

Kinsley settled back in her seat and willed her pulse to slow. Agar sat between her legs, his chin on her lap. She stroked his fur, calming him as well as herself. The mission seemed to be happening so fast. The silence made it seem all the more dangerous.

She could imagine what it would be like to be one of them on a mission without her and the dog. They probably moved like a well-oiled machine. Each had a position or a part to play, and they did it well. Perhaps T-Mac had been right in concluding she was a distraction. She didn't belong in this group of highly trained fighters.

Sure, she was a good shot and knew basic fighting tactics, but she wasn't like them. They were finely honed weapons in and of themselves.

Then again, the SEALs weren't like Agar. The dog would help to protect them when they couldn't sniff out danger lurking beneath their feet.

She tried not to be so completely aware of T-Mac's thigh pressed against hers. She couldn't move away from him, since they were packed tightly together and Agar gave her no room to shift her legs.

The heat from T-Mac's thigh scorched her own, sending electrical currents through her leg and straight to her core, making her burn with sexy images of him in his PT shorts and bare chest. Her fingers tingled, itching to touch him, to run her hands over his taut muscles and down to… Sweet heaven, how could she even think naughty thoughts of the man when they could be descending into yet another hotbed of enemy activity?

Her mind should be on the task ahead, not the man beside her. She should be planning her and Agar's next moves. But T-Mac was right there beside her, tempting her like no other man ever had.

After half an hour in the air, she'd settled back in her seat and tried to relax, determined to conserve her energy for whatever lay in store for her next. But she was too wound up, thinking about the last time she'd gone out on a mission. Her heart pounded in her chest and her ribs were still sore from the impact of the bullet on her armored vest. At her current pulse rate, she'd be worn out before they landed. She let her hand fall to her side between her and T-Mac.

A moment later, T-Mac's fingers curled around hers, hidden between them from anyone else's view.

His touch at once calmed her and excited her for an entirely different reason. She didn't question it, just drew on his strength.

By the time they landed, she had pulled herself together, ready to face whatever fate had in store for her and Agar.

As soon as the helicopters landed, the SEALs leaped to the ground. Agar was quick to exit, and Kinsley jumped down beside him.

T-Mac was there with a hand on her elbow to steady her until she had her balance.

As soon as they were all on the ground, the helicopters lifted into the air and headed back the way they'd come. The crew would wait within radio distance for the call to extract the team.

Kinsley couldn't help but feel a little stranded as she watched the choppers disappear into the night. She hefted her rifle in one hand and gripped Agar's lead in the other.

"Comm check," Big Jake said.

Kinsley worried that his slight limp would slow him down. But the big guy seemed as determined as the rest to find the people responsible for the attack on them in the last operation that had gone south.

One by one, all six of the SEALs checked in with only their call signs.

Once all of the SEALs had called out their names, T-Mac nudged Kinsley.

"Dog handler and Agar," Kinsley added to the tail end of the comm check. She could hear her voice in the radio and was reassured by the sound. If nothing else, she was connected by radio. If she got separated from the others, she could still connect this way.

"Let's do this," Big Jake said.

T-Mac touched Kinsley's shoulder and nodded in the direction they were heading.

"I'm right next to you," he said into his mic. "We have a lot of ground to cover between us and our target."

Kinsley warmed at his voice coming through the radio in her ear. With T-Mac at her side, she didn't have to worry if she was going the right way. While she concentrated on Agar, T-Mac would make sure they were on track.

Giving Agar the command to search, she followed the dog, moving out quickly. If they wanted to get there in a hurry, Agar had to work his magic without interruption.

As before, the dog sailed past the first mile without stopping.

The second mile, they traversed over rougher terrain, heading into hills with lots of scrub trees and bushes blocking their view ahead.

Agar kept his nose to the ground, working his way back and forth across the path.

Kinsley never let her guard down, constantly watching for any sign from the animal that things weren't all they should be.

"We're getting close to the target coordinates," T-Mac warned. "Slow the dog."

Kinsley pulled back on Agar's lead, checking his progress. The dog immediately returned to her side and looked up at her, his tongue lolling.

She would like to have given him some of the water she carried in her CamelBak thermos, but they didn't have time to stop. Keeping Agar on a shorter lead this time, she sent him forward to sniff for explosives.

"Half a click," T-Mac whispered. "Be on the lookout for guards on the perimeter."

"Roger," Big Jake answered. "You, too."

Ten steps later, Agar lay down.

Kinsley stuck a flag in the ground where he lay and moved on. Five flags later, Agar was moving faster again.

She gave him more of a lead, allowing him to swing wider from center. When he didn't come up with anything, he raced back in the opposite direction, clearing a wider path.

Kinsley understood the need to move slowly, but she also knew the element of surprise could require striking swiftly. The SEALs liked to get in and get the job done.

But she focused on her work with Agar, determined to deliver the team safely to the coordinates. That was her and Agar's primary responsibility. If they didn't accomplish that, what was the purpose of including them on the mission?

T-Mac grabbed her arm and pulled her to the ground. "Tango at two o'clock." He held up his fist for the guys behind him, indicating they should stop in place.

Agar was as far out as his retractable lead would go, still sniffing out bombs and land mines.

Kinsley couldn't call him back without alerting the man pulling guard duty on the perimeter. She tugged the lead.

Instead of coming, as he usually did, he braced his paws in the dirt and strained against his lead.

Kinsley tugged again. Resisting a touch command was not like Agar. The dog always came when he was called or tugged.

"Why is he just standing there?" T-Mac asked.

"Something or someone is out there, not too far from where Agar is standing." Her heart pounding, Kinsley remained in position with one knee on the ground. She aimed her rifle in front of her, ready to take down anyone who tried to attack the team or Agar.

"I'm going forward," T-Mac said.

Kinsley wanted to hold him back, but knew she couldn't. Agar had cleared the path between them, but not beyond. All she could hope was that there were no more land mines or other explosives between Agar and the Tango crouched out of sight beyond.

When T-Mac moved past Agar, Kinsley tugged hard on his lead, calling the dog back to her side.

This time Agar complied, as if he knew he'd done his job and T-Mac would take it from there.

Kinsley held her breath, praying no explosives lay in T-Mac's path. She squatted low to the ground, her hand on Agar's back, her heart pounding an erratic tattoo against her ribs.

T-Mac moved from bush to tree, clinging to the shadows cast by the starlight. Before long, even Kinsley couldn't make him out against the gloom of darkness. The man was like a cat moving through the night after his prey.

A movement beside her made Agar growl low in his chest.

Harm dropped to his knee at her side. "Do you see him?" he asked quietly into her headset.

"No," she responded. "I lost him."

"He's almost to the guy." Harm pointed into the darkness. "Let's hope the guard is asleep."

Kinsley nodded, never taking her gaze from the last place she'd seen T-Mac.

"One down," T-Mac whispered into her headset.

Then a shadow leaped up from a different location and ran away from the team.

"Got a live one on the loose," Harm called out softly.

"Hold your fire. We can't alert the rest of the camp until we can no longer avoid it," Big Jake warned.

"But he's going to alert the others," T-Mac said.

"Not if I can help it." Kinsley unclipped the lead from Agar's collar and gave him the command to take down.

Agar leaped forward and chased after the running man. Within seconds, he hit the man in the back, knocking him to his knees.

The SEAL team closed in.

Kinsley ran to catch up to Agar.

But before she could reach him, a shot rang out.

Shouts sounded ahead and lights flared out of the darkness. Half a dozen pairs of headlights came to life, chasing away the darkness and ruining any night vision they could have hoped for.

"Get down," Big Jake spoke sharply into the headset.

Kinsley didn't have to be told twice. She dropped to her knees, then down to a prone position, her rifle in her hand, aimed at the headlights, waiting for movement.

"Things are about to go sideways," Big Jake said. "Take out who you need to—save a live one to bring back."

Shouts sounded from the camp and gunfire echoed in the sky.

The men moved forward, slipping into the shadows now cast by the many vehicle headlights glowing.

Kinsley eased her way toward Agar and the man whose arm he held between his razor-sharp teeth.

Harm had been there a moment before, dispatching

the man with a clean swipe across the neck with his wicked Ka-Bar knife.

Kinsley shuddered and gave Agar the command to release. Agar shook the dead man once more and then let go of his arm and returned to Kinsley's side.

Harm moved on, leaving Kinsley and Agar alone with the dead man.

As Kinsley moved past the man on the ground, he reached out and grabbed her ankle.

Kinsley screamed and dropped to the ground, kicking at the hand.

Agar leaped to her defense, sinking his teeth into the man's arm.

Kicking wouldn't release the man's grip. She reached down and peeled back the fingers on the hand, finally freeing her ankle.

"Kinsley, are you all right?" T-Mac's voice sounded in her ears.

"I'm okay," she said.

"Where are you?" he demanded.

"I don't know," she admitted. "Not far from where you left me, I think."

All the SEALs had converged on the camp.

"Stay put—I'll find you."

Moments later, T-Mac appeared in front of her.

Kinsley leaped to her feet and fell into his arms.

More headlights flashed from another direction, heading toward the position where Kinsley, Agar and T-Mac stood.

"Come on. We have to get out of here." T-Mac took her hand.

Together they ran around the perimeter, away from the vehicles heading into the camp.

At one point, T-Mac pulled her down to a crouch.

He glanced back in the direction from which they'd come. For a moment, he remained silent. Then he spoke into his headset. "Gang, you need to get out of there. Four trucks loaded with at least ten men each, all armed, are on their way in. You're about to be grossly outnumbered."

"Calling for extraction." Big Jake's voice came over the radio. "Meet at the alternate pickup point, ASAP."

"Where's the alternate pickup point?" Kinsley asked.

"Two kilometers north of our original drop zone."

"Aren't we—"

"South of the camp and our pickup location?" T-Mac grunted. "Yes."

"And aren't those trucks filled with all those reinforcements standing between us and our ride back to Camp Lemonnier?"

"Give the girl a prize." He touched her shoulder. "We'll be okay."

"We have a man down," Harm called out. "We've got him, but we're moving slowly toward the pickup point. Someone cover our backs."

"Gotcha covered," Diesel said. "Go!"

"Getting hot in here," Buck reported. "Heading out. Don't shoot me."

"Those trucks are less than a kilometer away," T-Mac reminded him. "If you're getting out, now would be a good time."

"What about you?" Big Jake asked. "Give me a sitrep, T-Mac."

"We're between a rock and a hard place. Get the injured back to the Lemon. The dog handler and I will stay low until you can send reinforcements back to collect us."

"We're not leaving without you," Big Jake said.

"You can't delay getting that man some medical attention. We'll be all right."

The chatter stilled.

Kinsley held her breath, her heart pounding. "Are we staying?" she asked.

"Looks like it," T-Mac answered. "We can't delay the choppers from getting the men back to Camp Lemonnier."

"Okay." She was with T-Mac. He'd promised to keep her safe. She trusted he would keep that promise. Kinsley sucked in a deep breath and let it out. "What now?"

T-Mac didn't like that he and Kinsley were trapped more or less behind enemy lines. He had to get her safely away from the terrorist camp and hunker down somewhere safe and out of sight until the helicopters could return to pick them up.

His night-vision goggles were useless with all the headlights lighting up the sky. But as long as they weren't pointed directly at them, they could move without being obvious. If their night vision was compromised, so too would the terrorists'.

He checked his compass using a red-lensed flashlight and nodded in the direction they should travel to get away from the commotion. "Let's go."

"Wait." Kinsley touched his arm. "Let Agar go ahead of us."

"We don't have time."

"And we don't have time to be blown up. You saw the mines were set out between one and two kilometers outside the camp. If they set them out on all sides, let Agar find them for us."

"Okay, but we have to move fast. Right now they're probably concerned about the larger group of SEALs. When they're gone, they'll have time to look for others. That would be us. We can't let them see us, or our ducks are cooked."

Kinsley laughed. "Ducks are cooked?"

T-Mac liked the sound of her laughter, even if it was only nerves. "You know what I mean."

"I do, but ducks?" She laughed again but fell in step, moving hunched over.

They crouched as low as possible to the ground to keep from being seen or captured in the light from a moving vehicle.

Agar searched ahead, his nose to the ground, a silent shadow moving back and forth at the end of his lead.

So far, he hadn't found anything, but that didn't mean he wouldn't.

A loud explosion sounded from the other side of the camp. T-Mac's heart plummeted.

"Oh, no," Kinsley said softly.

"One of our guys stepped on a land mine," Buck reported over the radio headset. "He's in a bad way. Really bad."

T-Mac stopped and cursed. He hovered between getting farther away and heading back to help his team. But he had an obligation to protect Kinsley. If he took her with him to help his teammates, she'd be in danger and might either be shot or captured.

"We have to go back," Kinsley said.

Her words brought him back to reality. Even if he

could get past the four truckloads of men entering camp, he couldn't drag Kinsley into the middle of the mayhem.

"We can't go back." His jaw hardened. "My team will return to collect us after they get the injured to safety."

"But Agar could have gotten them out without unnecessary injuries."

"SEAL teams don't usually have the benefit of a Military Working Dog looking out for us. However, we wouldn't have made it as far as we have tonight without you and Agar."

"I wish we could have kept that SEAL from stepping on the explosives."

"We can't second-guess our decisions. Right now we have to lie low and hope we aren't discovered." He kept moving, farther and farther away from the terrorist compound until they could barely see the individual headlights. All they could discern were lights shining out from the camp center.

"How does your team know where to pick you up if you get separated?"

"I'm carrying a GPS tracking device. And when they get close enough, we'll reestablish radio communication with our headsets."

"In the meantime, shouldn't we conserve the battery on these?" She pointed to the device in her ear.

"Yes." He pulled his radio headset off and stuffed it into one of the pockets on his uniform.

Kinsley did the same. "Are we stopping for a few minutes?" she asked.

"We can." T-Mac pulled his night-vision goggles down and glanced around the area, careful not to look directly at the terrorist camp with its bright headlights still burning. He didn't see the green heat signatures of people moving about in the area, and they were far enough away that they couldn't see them. He raised the NVGs and nodded. "Rest for a few minutes."

"Good. Agar needs water." She looped her weapon strap over her shoulder, cupped her hand and squirted water into her palm from the CamelBak water-storage device she wore like a backpack over her body armor.

Agar eagerly lapped up the water and waited while she repeated the process several times until he was satisfied. Then he lay on the ground beside her, seemingly content to rest as long as she was still.

"How long do you think it will take them to come back for us?" she whispered.

"I'm not sure. But it would be good for us to get as far away from the compound as we can before they attempt to bring the helicopter back. Now that the terrorists know we know where they are, they will be moving. And we don't know which direction they will go."

"They could be heading this way?" Kinsley rubbed her hands up and down her arms. "We are south of them, right?"

"Right."

"Wouldn't it be better if someone knew where they were headed?" she asked.

T-Mac didn't like the question, or the direction of her thoughts. "What do you have in mind?"

"If you have a GPS device on you, couldn't you attach it to one of their vehicles? That way we wouldn't have to rely on satellite images to find them again."

"But then our guys would have no way of finding us. And believe me, it's a long way back to Camp Lemonnier on foot."

Kinsley stared at the ground beside Agar and ran her

hand over his head. "It's a shame. These terrorists will probably be gone by morning."

"Military intelligence could pull more satellite photos. They'll find them again."

"You heard the commander. The intel guys said it was lucky they actually found them the first time." She shook her head. "Those bastards could get away again. They'll only go on to hurt more of our military personnel, not to mention the innocent people they terrorize on a daily basis."

"It's too bad we don't have one of the vehicles we saw tonight," Kinsley mused. "We could plant the GPS device and make our way back to Camp Lemonnier on our own."

"To do that, we'd have to steal one of their vehicles," T-Mac said. "It would be insane to try." Then why the hell was he considering trying to steal one of the trucks he'd seen that evening?

But the more he thought about it, the more he liked the idea. He could do it. But would he put Kinsley at too much risk by even attempting such an idiotic feat?

He glanced down at where Kinsley sat beside Agar. "I know you're good at finding land mines and IEDs, but how are you with setting detonators in plastic explosives?"

Chapter Nine

After a quick refresher on detonators and C-4 explosives, Kinsley worked with T-Mac to divvy up what he'd come with into three separate setups.

The camp would still be in a state of disarray, with everyone loading up whatever they deemed valuable in preparation for bugging out. They wouldn't want to stay in one place knowing their location was compromised. After the Navy SEAL attack, they would be expecting even more grief in the way of rockets launched by either UAVs or other military aircraft. If they didn't get out that night, they would be easy targets.

"Since we haven't seen guards out searching for anyone left behind, we can assume they think all of the personnel who participated in the attack are gone for now," T-Mac said. "We have surprise on our side. They will not be expecting anyone else to launch an offensive anytime soon."

Kinsley squared her shoulders, excitement building in her chest. "That's where we come in."

Even in the limited lighting from the stars overhead, she could see the way T-Mac's brow dipped. "Not *we*," he said. "*I* will set the charges in strategic locations."

"Right," she agreed. "While Agar and I hide nearby."

"Exactly." T-Mac continued. "Then, while the Al-Shabaab terrorists are confused by the explosions, I'll see what I can appropriate in the way of a vehicle. You'll need to be ready once I roll out of the camp."

She nodded, wishing she could play a bigger role in the attack. "Agar and I will be ready."

T-Mac pressed a button on the side of his watch. "They should be scrambling out of the camp soon. If we're going, we should leave now and get as close as possible without being seen." He nodded toward Agar. "Will you be able to keep him quiet while I'm setting the charges?"

"Absolutely," she replied, confident in Agar's ability to take command.

"Then let's go." Together, they loaded the detonators into pouches and secured them on his vest. Then they loaded the C-4 into another pouch and secured the pouch to his vest. In order to move quickly, he would leave his rifle with Kinsley and carry only his handgun, Ka-Bar knife and a couple of hand grenades.

Now that they were actually going back to the camp, Kinsley was positive her idea was insane. But no matter how much she wanted to change T-Mac's mind, he was set on his course.

Once he had everything where he could reach it quickly, he stared down at Kinsley. "You can stay here, if you like. I could make it back to you in whatever vehicle I can commandeer, or if that's not possible, I can return on foot and we'll get the hell out of here."

"I'm coming as close as I can get. If you run into difficulties, I can cover for you while you get out."

He shook his head. "I don't know. The more I think

about it, the more I'm convinced you'd be better off staying here."

"I'm not staying. You can't go it completely alone. You might get in okay, but getting back out will be more difficult. They'll be looking for whoever set off the explosions." She touched his arm, ready to do what it took to convince him she was an asset, not a liability. "I'm a pretty decent shot. I qualify expert every time I've been to the range. The least I can do is provide cover for you."

"Being that close to camp puts you at risk."

"I signed up for this gig when I asked to train with the dogs. I knew we'd be on the front line at some point. I'd say this is pretty damn close to the front line." She lifted her chin. "I'm not afraid."

"You might not be afraid for yourself." He cupped her cheek in his palm. "But I'm scared for you." He tipped his head toward the dog. "And Agar."

Her heart warmed at the concern in his voice. She leaned her cheek into his palm. "Don't worry about us. I'll stay low and still. They won't even know I'm there. You just do your thing and create the biggest, loudest distraction you can. I'll be waiting near the road they drove in on. It should be clear of all land mines or they wouldn't have driven in from that direction."

"And you'll have Agar if you get into trouble." He stared down into her face.

T-Mac's eyes were inky pools in the starlight, and Kinsley couldn't read into them. By the way he leaned toward her, she could sense he wanted to say or do more. When he hesitated, she made up his mind for him and leaned up on her toes, pressing her lips to his. "Be careful, will ya? I kind of like kissing you."

He laughed. "You know we could be court-martialed for fraternizing."

She shrugged. "And we might not live to see the dawn of a new day. I'll take my chances." And she kissed him again.

T-Mac gripped her shoulders and pulled her into his embrace, their body armor making it difficult to get closer. "This doesn't end here," he promised.

"I'm banking on that, frogman." She squared her shoulders. "Let's do this."

Though she was scared, adrenaline kicked in and sent her forward. She gave Agar the command to search ahead of them. While he sniffed for explosives in the ground, Kinsley looked at the activity going on in the terrorist camp. They appeared to be loading trucks. Men moved in front of headlights, carrying boxes and other items.

If T-Mac didn't hurry, he might miss the opportunity to tag one of the vehicles and claim one of them for their own.

Kinsley couldn't make Agar move faster. He was doing his job, but apparently between them and the camp there were no land mines. The terrorists must have thought the threats wouldn't come from the south, deeper into Somalia.

Within minutes, they were back in shooting range of the camp.

Kinsley's heart beat faster and her level of fear intensified. She didn't like the idea of T-Mac slipping back into camp to set explosive charges. She couldn't even imagine if he got caught. She prayed it wouldn't happen, that he'd make it in and back out unscathed.

Just outside the camp, close to the road T-Mac was due to escape on, they hunkered low in the brush.

Kinsley sought out T-Mac's hand, having massive second thoughts. "Don't worry about swiping a vehicle. Just get in, plant the GPS and get back out. We'll find our way back to Camp Lemonnier on foot. In fact, let's not do this at all. I'd rather not lose you at this point."

He squeezed her hand and brought it to his lips. "I'll be fine. But thanks for caring." He kissed the backs of her knuckles. "Remember, I'll be driving with the lights out. I'll give three beams of my flashlight in quick succession."

Kinsley smiled. "And I'll return it with a beam from my red-lensed flashlight."

"We might have to repeat the cue a couple of times if I'm off on distance."

"I'll be watching." She sighed and stared up into his eyes. "Hurry back. I'm kinda getting used to having you around, big guy." Kinsley cupped his cheek. "And don't do anything stupid."

"Stupid isn't in the repertoire of a SEAL," he said. "Hang tight. This shouldn't take too long." He kissed her hard on the lips and took off.

Agar strained at the lead, eager to follow, but Kinsley held firm. For the first few minutes, she could follow T-Mac's silhouette moving through the brush and past trees, working his way toward the vehicles and people milling around the camp. Once he reached one of the tents still standing, he disappeared.

Kinsley's heart lodged in her throat and her pulse pounded so hard, she could barely hear herself think.

Minutes ticked by like hours.

If he didn't come out, she and Agar were on their

own to make it back to Camp Lemonnier. But that didn't scare her as badly as the fact that if he didn't make it out, it meant he was either dead or captured and would be tortured by the terrorists.

Kinsley didn't know which would be worse. But she knew one thing… She was falling for the navy SEAL, and she didn't want what she felt for him to end like this.

MAKING IT INTO the camp hadn't been that difficult. The terrorists were in a frenetic hurry to break camp, pack the trucks and get the hell out before their attackers returned with mortars or missiles.

T-Mac hid in the shadow of a tent, studying the layout of the camp, determining where would be the best place to set his charges. To make the biggest bang for his effort, he'd have to take out a couple of the trucks. The pile of empty crates at the north end of the camp would be a good target, drawing attention to the north while T-Mac attempted to take a vehicle and head south, as if one of the terrorists had gotten a jump start on leaving the compound.

Once his decision was made, he went into action, stealing from shadow to shadow. Men in black robes and turbans raced past him, their weapons slung over their shoulders, each carrying something to load into the backs of trucks.

T-Mac slipped up behind one at the back of a lone truck at the north end of the compound, grabbed him from behind and snapped his neck, killing him instantly. He dragged him under the truck, stripped off his turban and robe and dressed in them. He'd have a better chance of mixing in with the bad guys dressed like them.

Then he planted the plastic explosives near the engine

of the vehicle and pressed a detonator into the claylike
material. Lifting a small crate, he ran through the camp
like the others until he arrived at another vehicle on the
northwest side and stood behind another man loading a
box into the back. He handed his crate up to the man in
the back of the truck and turned to leave.

The man in the truck shouted something to him.

T-Mac didn't catch what he said, so he couldn't trans-
late. He pretended he didn't hear and hurried toward
the front of the truck, where he pressed another glob of
plastic explosives into the metal and jammed a detonator into it.

Once he had the two trucks tagged with explosives, he
hurried toward several barrels that he assumed contained
fuel of some sort. As he walked with his hands under the
robe, he pressed another detonator into the C-4. Once he
reached the barrels, he mashed the explosive compound
into the side of one of the barrels that felt full.

A shout from behind made him turn.

Fortunately, the man wasn't shouting at him, but at
another man who'd dropped a container full of boxes of
ammunition, spilling its contents over the ground. Bullets spilled out and rolled across the sand.

A couple of the men ganged up on the one who'd
dropped the box.

While all attention was on them, T-Mac slipped to
the south side of the camp, eyeing two vehicles already
pointed toward Somalia. Men were loading boxes and
weapons into the backs of the trucks. On the one closest to him, a driver sat in the cab, his weapon resting
across his lap.

T-Mac hoped the fireworks would distract all of them

long enough for him to get the truck and get the hell out of camp before anyone knew any better.

He found a position behind the hulk of a vehicle that had flat tires and had been stripped of anything that could be removed, cannibalized or destroyed. Once he was safely in place, he covered his ears, hunkered down and pressed the button to detonate the first charge.

The explosion shook the ground beneath him.

Screams and shouts rose up around him.

From the corner of his hiding place, he watched as half of the men who'd been loading his target truck and the one beside it ran toward the explosion.

Five seconds later, he set off round two.

Again, the explosion made the earth tremble beneath his feet and debris rain down from the sky.

Daring to peek out, T-Mac checked the truck he hoped to steal. The driver had stepped down from the cab, his weapon raised, his gaze darting around, apparently searching for the person setting off the charges. Yet he didn't move away from the vehicle.

T-Mac would have to take the guy down.

He gauged how far he'd have to run out in the open to get to the driver, knowing he could easily do it, especially since he was disguised as one of them.

Gunfire sounded as the terrorists ran to the north end of the compound.

Knowing it was his last chance to create a huge distraction, T-Mac waited a few seconds before detonating the last charge.

Boom! The charge went off. A second later, another, louder bang ripped through the night, sending a tower of flames into the air as the fuel in the barrel ignited.

The truck driver hit the ground and covered his head.

T-Mac made his move. He sprinted across the open space, bent to the man on the ground and slit his throat. With the driver out of the way and the others all concentrating on the north end of camp and the raging fire sending flames a hundred feet into the sky, T-Mac had the chance he'd been hoping for.

He dragged the man beneath the truck, ran to the other vehicle and stashed the GPS tracker in a ripped hole in the driver's seat. Once he had the reason for his visit to the camp in place, he ran back around the front of the truck he hoped to take, leaned into the cab, set it in Neutral and started pushing it toward the perimeter of the camp.

At first, the truck barely moved. But once he got the momentum going, it rolled faster and faster. When he reached the edge of the camp, he jumped into the cab, twisted the key in the ignition and cranked the engine.

A shout sounded beside the driver's door. A man in the black garb of the Al-Shabaab ran alongside the truck, shaking his fist at T-Mac.

T-Mac slowed enough to position the vehicle just right, then shoved the door open fast and hard, hitting the man in the head.

The guy fell to the ground and lay still.

T-Mac didn't wait around to see if he revived. He didn't have time. As soon as the excitement of the explosions waned, the men in the camp would notice one of their vehicles had disappeared and some of their men were down. Someone else might have seen the truck leaving camp and the direction it had gone. T-Mac had to find Kinsley fast and get as far away from the terrorists as they could.

Once outside the camp, he pressed the accelerator to

the floor, sending the truck leaping forward. He couldn't go far at that speed or he'd be forced to use the brakes without knowing if the brake lights would light up.

When he got to within range of where he'd left Kinsley, he pulled out his flashlight and hit the on-off switch three times. He scanned the darkness, praying for a red light blinking back at him.

For the longest moments of his life, he waited. When he didn't see anything, he repeated the three bursts of light.

Damn, had he gone out in the wrong direction? Had she been discovered and captured? Where was she? If he didn't find her soon, he wasn't sure they'd make it out of there undiscovered. He searched the darkness, desperately looking for the silhouette of a woman and a dog, praying they were all right.

Just when he considered turning back, a red dot appeared in the darkness.

Chapter Ten

Kinsley hated waiting, not knowing what was happening. The first twenty minutes were hell, with every possible bad scenario rolling through her mind.

With all the terrorists running around the camp, how could T-Mac get in and do the job without being seen? The operation wasn't like one where they sneaked in while everyone was sleeping. He was going into a stirred-up hornets' nest to stir it up even more.

The more she sat waiting, the more she convinced herself this mission was a very bad idea.

When the first explosion went off, she jumped. She felt an immediate mixture of relief and even more tension.

T-Mac had managed to get in and set at least one charge.

Agar whined softly beside her, but stayed in his prone position, head down, resting. He could be up and running at her command.

The second explosion went off. The corners of Kinsley's lips quirked upward. Two down, one to go.

"Come on, T-Mac," she whispered softly.

At the third explosion, she wanted to cheer, but the

ensuing fireball rising into the air made her heart drop into her belly.

Had something gone wrong? Had T-Mac been caught up in whatever caused the fireball?

Her heart pounded so hard, her pulse beat against her eardrums, making it hard for her to hear.

Men ran around the camp, shouting, their bodies black silhouettes against the bright orange blaze of what Kinsley suspected was burning fuel.

She didn't care how T-Mac got out of the camp as long as he got out alive. If he didn't find a way to commandeer a vehicle, they'd figure out a way to get back to Camp Lemonnier on foot.

He just needed to hurry.

The giant flame held Kinsley's attention, destroying her night vision. She didn't see the truck racing toward her until it was close enough she could hear the engine.

She prayed T-Mac was driving. What had he said? He'd give her three flashes from his flashlight?

Kinsley held her breath, waiting as the dark hulk of the truck grew closer.

Then a bright white light shone out from the cab.

Her pulse sped and she laughed out loud. "It's him, Agar!" she cried.

Agar jumped up, jerking the lead right out of her hand.

Afraid the dog would run out in front of the truck, Kinsley gave him the command to sit.

Agar sat.

Kinsley patted the ground, searching for the lead. When she found it, she looked up again.

The truck was much closer, moving slowly but almost

to where she lay waiting in the brush. Another three flashes of light blinked into the night.

Oh, no.

Kinsley fumbled to unclip her flashlight from her web gear. She was supposed to flash her red-lensed flashlight back to indicate where she was. If she didn't hurry, he'd pass her. Then she'd be left behind. T-Mac couldn't shine his bright beam back toward the camp without alerting the terrorists to their location.

Her hand trembled as she pressed the switch. Nothing happened. Damn. Now wasn't the time for an equipment malfunction.

She slapped the device against her palm and the red light came on. Quickly, she held it up, aiming the red orb at the oncoming truck.

She heard the engine throttle down as if being placed into low gear. It slowed, rolling past her so slowly, she jumped up and ran after it, Agar trotting alongside her.

The screech of an emergency brake sounded, and the truck stopped with a jerk.

T-Mac dropped down from the cab, ran back to her and wrapped her in his arms. "I thought I'd come out of the camp on the wrong road."

"I thought you'd never get here." She laughed and stood on her toes to press a kiss to his lips. "Let's get out of here."

"Good idea." He held the driver's-side door.

Agar leaped up into the cab.

Kinsley climbed in and scooted over.

T-Mac hopped in, shifted into gear and took off as fast as he could without headlights to guide them. Thankfully, the stars shone bright enough to light their way.

With Agar in the passenger seat, Kinsley sat in the

middle, her thigh pressed against T-Mac's, the reassuring strength of him warming her all the way through. She could breathe again.

"GPS?" she quizzed as she removed her helmet.

"Planted," he shot back.

"Thank God." Kinsley settled back in her seat, hesitant to pull off her armored vest so soon. "How far south are we going?"

"Not very." He glanced sideways at her. "We need to find a place to hide and wait for Al-Shabaab to move past, however long that takes."

"Aren't you worried we'll run into more of them coming up from the south to see what the fire is all about?"

"A little. The sooner we find a place to hide, the better."

Kinsley stared out into the darkness, focusing on anything large enough to hide a truck behind. For the first few miles, the land was flat and dry. Only a few bushes and scrubby trees stood out against the desert landscape.

As they traveled farther south, the road turned west. No headlights shone behind them and no one pulled out in front of them to block their escape. Soon, they passed the rubble of a small deserted village.

T-Mac drove past quickly.

Kinsley turned in her seat, looking out behind them. "Why didn't we stop there?"

"That was the first place we could hide. If the terrorists figure out we took one of their vehicles and headed south by the only road in this area, that would be the first place they'd look."

She nodded. "True."

"We should be getting into more hills the farther west we go."

"Can't we pass into Ethiopia? Would it be safer for us to travel back to Camp Lemonnier that way?"

"Al-Shabaab doesn't care about borders, but that's the plan for now. After what I did to them, they'll be hoppin' mad and out for blood."

"Other than the three explosions, which were bad enough, should I ask what you did that was so bad?"

He shook his head. "No. But they are three men fewer."

Kinsley shrugged out of her heavy body-armor vest and laid it on the floorboard. "Here, let me get your helmet."

He lifted his chin, keeping his eyes on the road.

Kinsley unbuckled the chin strap and slid the helmet off his head, without blocking his view of the road in front of him.

She would have offered to help him with his vest, but that would require more effort and he'd need to stop to pull it off. He'd have to wear the heavy plates until they came to a full stop long enough to remove it.

The road grew steeper as they climbed into the hills in northwest Somalia. Soon, they found a turnoff to the north, taking them deeper into rugged terrain, the road turning into more of a path than one used for four-wheeled vehicles.

T-Mac pulled the truck in behind a giant boulder that had fallen from an overhanging cliff. He checked the gas gauge before turning off the engine. "We have three quarters of a tank left. Whatever we do tomorrow, we might have to find more fuel, or find a way to contact my unit for a pickup. But for tonight, we camp here."

Sitting so close to T-Mac for the past two hours, Kinsley had felt a shiver of awareness and anticipation ripple across her skin. Alone in a vehicle with T-Mac was one thing. Alone lying under the stars with the navy SEAL was entirely different.

She gulped back her sudden nerves and blurted, "Let's see what we have in the back." Kinsley started to reach over Agar to open the passenger door.

T-Mac opened his door first. "Come out this way."

Since getting out the other side would be more difficult with Agar in the way, Kinsley followed T-Mac out the driver's side. Before she could step down from the truck, T-Mac grabbed her around the waist and lifted her out to stand on two feet. Agar jumped down behind her and wandered off to sniff at the rocks and brambles.

T-Mac didn't release her immediately, his hands resting on her hips. "You don't know how crazy it made me when I didn't see your red light."

She laughed. "Trust me. Had you been the one waiting the entire time things were blowing up in that camp, you would have gone off the deep end." Kinsley cupped his cheek and stared at him in the starlight. "You don't know how glad I was when I saw those three blinks of your flashlight."

"What took you so long to respond?" He brushed a strand of her hair out of her face.

"Agar and I got excited when he heard the rumble of the truck's engine. He jerked his lead, and I dropped the handle. I had to grab it before he took off after the oncoming truck. At that point, I didn't know if you were the driver, or someone else." She smiled up at him.

"Well, I was pretty happy to see your red lens shining back at me." He touched her cheek with his fingers and kissed her forehead. "I almost turned around and headed back into that mess."

She pressed her hand over his on her face. "Are you crazy? They would have killed you."

"I thought I'd missed you, or gone out of the camp in the wrong direction."

She laughed, the sound shaky in the night. "Need help getting out of your body armor?"

"I can do it myself," he said.

She laughed. "And where would the fun be in that?" She reached for the fasteners, unbuckling them one at a time. When she had them free, she shoved the vest over his shoulders.

He caught it and laid it on the floorboard of the vehicle and then turned to face her, captured her hands in his and lifted them to his lips. "You amaze me."

She shook her head. "I don't know why. You're the one doing all the heavy lifting on this gig."

"You hold your own, no matter the situation. Most females I know would fall apart."

"Then you don't know the right females." She lifted her chin. "I joined the army, not a sorority."

He laughed and took one of her hands in his. "Come on—let's see what they were loading in the back of the truck."

Kinsley liked the sound of his laughter and the way his hand felt wrapped around hers. No, she wasn't a scared little girl needing the protection of a big burly man, but she liked having T-Mac around. And he had a way of making her feel more feminine than she'd felt in a long time. Kinsley knew she was a strong and courageous soldier. Somewhere along the line, she'd had to bury the woman inside in order to fit in in a man's world. T-Mac brought out the desire and longing she thought she'd never feel again.

And he was a navy SEAL and she was an army soldier. In no scenario could they be together for the long haul. Being with him on a dangerous mission in middle-of-nowhere Africa brought it home to her that they might not be in it for the long run. They might not make it to morning. Every minute they were together now was a gift that should not be squandered.

So she reveled in the touch of his hand. They couldn't hold hands on Camp Lemonnier. Someone would see and report them for fraternization. But out in the hills of Somalia, where every day could be their last, no one was watching. No one would know.

Feeling only a little guilty, Kinsley was also titillated and anxious to see what would happen next. Especially since they would be alone all night.

Chapter Eleven

At the back of the vehicle, T-Mac hit the switch on his flashlight and shone it up into the back of the large utility truck. He reluctantly released Kinsley's hand and passed the flashlight to her to hold while he lowered the tailgate.

The back of the truck contained crates and boxes.

T-Mac climbed up into the truck bed and picked through, opening boxes, moving some and setting others to the side.

"These cardboard boxes are full of food and rations marked WHO."

"World Health Organization," Kinsley said. "They must be stealing food and medical supplies destined for refugee camps."

"The wooden crates aren't marked WHO and they weren't destined for refugee camps." His gut knotted as he lifted out a brand new M4A1 rifle and held it up for her to see. "We definitely found the opposite end of the snake, selling illegal arms to the enemy."

Kinsley shone the flashlight away from the boxes for a moment and then back into the bed of the truck. "Holy crap, T-Mac. You need to see this." She pointed to the rear bumper of the truck.

T-Mac dropped down out of the vehicle and stood

beside Kinsley as she pointed the flashlight at a smear of black spray paint half covering numbers and letters stenciled onto the desert-tan paint.

"You've got to be kidding." T-Mac rubbed at the paint covering the numbers. "That's one of ours from the motor pool."

Kinsley nodded. "And those M4 rifles?"

"The armory isn't missing any, that we've heard of, but they're the same style and military grade as what is issued to our soldiers. Plus, they have the bullets to go with them. I saw someone drop a case in the middle of the camp."

"Great. Someone is arming Al-Shabaab with our own weapons." Kinsley rubbed her arms, as if trying to chase away the chilly night air. "I get that people would be able to sell weapons directly to our enemies, but how would Al-Shabaab get their hands on one of our vehicles without us hearing about it?"

"All the more reason for us to get back to Camp Lemonnier...with the evidence."

"Right." Kinsley tilted her head toward the back of the truck. "I don't suppose you found any blankets or immediately edible food in that truck, did you?"

T-Mac shook his head. "Sorry. Only guns, rice and medical supplies on this truck."

Kinsley dug into the pockets on her uniform pants and in her jacket. "Fortunately, I brought some protein bars and some snacks for Agar."

He took one of the protein bars and held it up to the flashlight. "Are you always this prepared?"

"I've learned to be." She reached into another pocket for a ziplock bag of food for Agar. "I know myself and Agar. We work better when we're not hungry."

"Good to know," T-Mac said. "We should get a little sleep before dawn. We might be out here for a day if the terrorists take their time moving from their previous location."

Kinsley glanced around at the rock outcroppings nearby. "I can stay awake and stand guard for the first shift."

"There's not much of the night left."

"You've been driving and did all of the work setting off those charges. I'm sure you're exhausted. You need to recharge."

"I'm fine," T-Mac assured her. "I've gotten by on a lot less sleep. You sleep first."

She frowned. "Only if you wake me in a couple hours so that I can pull guard duty while you get a little rest." She crossed her arms over her chest and raised her brows, waiting.

He sighed. "Okay. But for now you need to find a place to sleep."

"How about in the cab of the truck?" she suggested. "The bench seat is the softest thing around, and if we need to make a quick escape, we don't have to make a dash for it."

"Good thinking." He held the passenger door for her.

"I'll sleep behind the wheel," Kinsley insisted. "That way you can stretch out beside me without any obstructions."

"You mean, if we have to beat a hasty retreat, you'll do the driving?" He grinned and let her get in first.

"If I have to, I will." Kinsley slid across the seat to the driver's side. When he didn't get in, she stared out at him. "What's wrong?"

"Nothing. I just figured Agar needed a warm place

to sleep. He needs some rest, too." He patted the dog's head and then leaned the seat forward, opening up the back seat for a passenger. "He worked hard tonight."

Kinsley smiled at how easily Agar got along with T-Mac. She gave the dog the command to climb up into the vehicle.

Agar leaped up and settled on the floorboard between the driver's and passenger's side.

Kinsley reached back to pat the animal's head.

When T-Mac still hesitated with his hand on the door, Kinsley frowned. "Aren't you getting in?"

"I think I'd be better off standing guard in the open where I can see someone coming."

Kinsley's frown deepened. "Would it make any difference if I said I need you with me?"

His lips turned upward on the corners. "It might."

She shook her head. "Then please, stay."

"For the record, I don't think it's a good idea."

She smiled. "For the record, I agree. But we're out here alone. The only people who will know or care will be us." Kinsley patted the seat beside her. "You need rest, even if you don't sleep."

"I've been sitting for the past couple of hours while driving."

She raised her brow. "Fine. Suit yourself. I'm going to get some sleep so I can take the next shift." She leaned back against the seat and closed her eyes.

T-Mac stood in the open door of the truck, staring at Kinsley, knowing that if he got into the truck, he might not be able to keep his hands to himself.

The woman was sexy without trying. She tipped back her head, exposing the long line of her very pretty, and kissable, neck.

His lips tingled, and he longed to press them to the pulse beating at the base of her throat.

Her lips tipped upward at the corners and she chuckled. "You might as well get in and close the door. It gets cold at night in the desert." The husky tone of her voice made his groin tighten.

Getting into the truck beside Kinsley was a very bad idea when all T-Mac wanted to do was touch her, taste her and kiss her until they both begged for air.

Despite what his head was telling him, T-Mac followed his gut. Or was it his heart? Whatever. He climbed into the truck and sat beside Kinsley.

She tilted her head toward him and opened one eye. "That wasn't so hard, was it?"

"Sweetheart, you have no idea," he murmured.

She closed her eyes and sighed. "Wake me in two hours."

T-Mac forced himself to stare straight ahead. But every time Kinsley shifted, he couldn't help glancing her way.

Her head fell back against the headrest, tipped at an uncomfortable-looking angle.

Before he could think better of it, he found himself saying, "It might be more comfortable lying across the seat."

She gave a weak smile. "Thanks. I've never been very good at sleeping sitting up." Kinsley tipped over and tried to fit herself between the driver's door and T-Mac's thigh.

"Seriously." He snorted. "You can lay your head on my thigh. I promise not to bite."

Kinsley sat up, frowning. "Are you sure? I don't want to make you uncomfortable."

"Oh, babe, I'm way past uncomfortable." He shook his head. "Just use my leg as a pillow."

"But I don't want to make you uncom—" she started again.

"Woman, are you always so argumentative?" He gripped her shoulders and pulled her across his lap. "You can't help but make me crazy, and you don't even have to touch me to accomplish that." He kissed her lips hard and then lifted his head. "I've wanted to do that since we stopped. And I want to do so much more. But this is neither the time nor the place." He sighed and leaned his forehead against hers. "You're an amazing woman, and I want so much more than just a kiss."

Kinsley's eyes widened. "Oh." Then she snuggled into him. "What's stopping you? Because it sure as hell isn't me." She cupped his face between her palms and kissed him. She pulled back until her mouth was only a breath away from his, and then whispered, "It could be a very long night, or far too short. Depends on how you spend it."

T-Mac didn't need more of an invitation than that. "You realize we'll be breaking all the rules?"

"Damn the rules." She kissed him again, this time pushing her tongue past his teeth to slide along the length of his.

T-Mac held her close, his heart pounding against his ribs. After all that had happened and that short amount of time he'd thought he'd lost her…he couldn't hold back. He had to hold her, touch her, bury himself in her.

Her fingers flew across the buttons on his jacket, popping them free of the buttonholes one at a time. When she had his jacket open, she ran her fingers across his chest, the warmth of her hands burning through the fabric of his T-shirt.

He slipped his hand beneath her uniform jacket and smoothed it up her back and down to the base of her spine. "Once we start down this path, I can't guarantee I can stop."

"I don't want you to stop. I want you, Trace McGuire. We might not have tomorrow, but we can make good use of tonight."

"What about not getting involved with a navy guy?"

"Tonight, we're neither army nor navy. We're just two people, alone in the hills."

He chuckled and brushed a kiss across the tip of her nose. "And what happens in the hills stays in the hills?"

Kinsley nodded. "Something like that." She raised her hands to her own uniform jacket and pushed the top button free. "Now, are you going to talk, or are we going to make out?"

He laughed out loud and pulled her into his arms. "I feel like a teen on his first date. All we need is a cheesy song to play and a cop to shine his light into the window."

She smiled. "I can do without the cop with the flashlight, but we can make our own music."

"I like the way you think, Army."

"I like the way you feel, Navy."

He helped her with the rest of her buttons and pushed the jacket over her shoulders.

They became a tangle of hands and clothing in an effort to remove the T-shirts.

All the wiggling on his lap made him even harder and more desperate to be with her.

When she reached behind her back to unclip her bra,

he pushed her hands aside and flicked the hooks loose and then slid the bra from her shoulders and down her arms.

Her small, perky breasts spilled into his hands.

Kinsley inhaled deeply, pressing more firmly into T-Mac's palms. She cupped the backs of his hands and held him there. "You don't know how good that feels."

He chuckled. "Oh, I think I do."

Kinsley shifted her legs until she straddled his hips and slid her center over his growing erection.

"Darlin', it doesn't work that way."

"What?" she asked, her voice breathy, as if she couldn't get enough air past her vocal cords.

"We have too much between us."

Kinsley sighed. "I know. Can we hurry the foreplay along? I'm not a very patient person."

T-Mac set her away from him. In a flurry of awkward movements, bumping into the windows, doors and each other, they got naked and spread their clothing out on the seat.

By then, T-Mac was breathing hard, his body on fire from touching hers so many times in the process of undressing.

"Uh, this could be a bad time to ask," Kinsley started, "but I don't suppose you brought protection?" She laughed nervously. "I mean, it's not like you think about things like that when you're gearing up. I wouldn't expect you to have anything like that. I know I didn't think to pack it."

T-Mac sealed her mouth with a kiss. "Knowing you were on this mission, I packed extra first-aid supplies and even tossed in some protection. Don't ask me why. My gut instinct has never steered me wrong."

"Hear, hear for your gut." She kissed him hard and once again straddled his hips, skimming her already wet entrance over his rock-hard staff. "So, where is it?"

"You were serious about skipping the foreplay," he said.

"Damn right. Life's short—you have go for what you want… Be in the moment. You never know when fate will hand you a treasure or stab you in the heart."

"Speaking from experience?" he asked softly.

She nodded. The starlight shining in through the window glinted off moisture in her eyes.

He gripped her arms. "Did you lose someone you cared about?"

Again, she nodded without speaking.

His heart wrenched and he asked the question he wasn't certain he wanted the answer to. "Someone you loved?"

KINSLEY HAD SPENT the past two years trying to heal her broken heart and pushing past her fear of losing someone she cared about enough to let herself fall in love again. She thought she was well on her way to doing just that, until she'd hunkered down outside an Al-Shabaab camp, waiting for T-Mac to appear. All that old fear and anxiety had surfaced and practically consumed her.

Now that T-Mac was safe and in her arms, she couldn't let another moment go by without really being with him. She'd spoken her truth about seizing the moment. They might not have tomorrow together. If Al-Shabaab caught up with them, or the rules of Camp Lemonnier kept them apart, they would have only this one moment in time to pack into their memories. Kinsley was determined to make the most of it.

Their military careers would keep them apart tomorrow, but they had the night.

Kinsley held out her hand. "If you'll hand me the protection, we can get this show on the road."

T-Mac shook his head. "Not so fast. You might not think foreplay is necessary, but I want you to be every bit as turned on as I am before I come into you."

A shiver of anticipation rippled across her skin. "What exactly did you have in mind?"

"This." In one fluid motion, he turned her over and pinned her to the seat and cushion of clothing.

She giggled. "Are you always so eager with your women?"

T-Mac kissed her forehead and the tip of her nose, and nibbled her left earlobe before replying. "Just so you know, I don't have women. I'm not celibate, but there's no woman in my life except the one lying beneath me at this moment."

Her body heated at his warm, resonant tone. "I'd understand if you had a female in every port."

"That's nice. But I don't." He trailed kisses down the side of her throat and lingered at the base, where her pulse beat hard and fast.

Kinsley squirmed beneath him, wanting more than just his lips, more than kisses.

Then he moved down her body, trailing his mouth, his tongue and his hands. He slowed to suck one of her nipples between his teeth and rolled it around.

She arched her back off the seat, pressing her body closer, a moan rising up her throat.

He flicked the hardened bud of her nipple with his tongue again and again. Then he moved to take the other nipple into his mouth and gave it the same delicious treatment.

Kinsley's core tightened, coiled and heated. She threaded her hands in his hair, urging him to take more.

He did, pulling hard on her breast, alternating between flicking and nipping at the tip.

Then he abandoned her breasts and moved lower, skimming across her ribs, tonguing a warm trail, stopping to dip into her belly button. When he reached her mound of curls, he parted her folds and dragged his finger across that strip of flesh tightly packed with nerves.

A moan rose up Kinsley's throat, and she dug her fingernails into his scalp. "Oh…dear…sweet…"

He touched her there with the tip of his tongue.

Kinsley moaned again, her hips rising to meet that tongue, willing him to do that again.

T-Mac swept a warm, wet path through her folds and dipped a finger into her slick channel.

Her entire body quivering, Kinsley ached for what came next. She wanted him. Inside her. Now.

But he wasn't finished with her. Apparently, he wanted to torture her into submission, one incredibly delicious lick or stroke at a time.

His tongue worked magic on her nubbin while his fingers teased her entrance and dipped in, first one, then another until three stretched her opening, preparing her for him.

Tension built inside, centering at her core. Her muscles tightened and she dug her feet into the seat cushion, pressing upward. "Please," she begged.

"Please what?"

"I want you."

He chuckled, his warm breath playing across her wetness. "Sweetheart, you have me."

"No. Now. Inside me," she said, her voice breathy. She couldn't breathe, she was so caught up in the sensations he evoked. "I need you."

"But you're not there yet." He blew a stream of warm air across her nubbin and then flicked it with his tongue.

A shock of electricity ripped through her from the point where T-Mac touched her all the way out to the tips of her fingers, tingling all the way.

He flicked again and again, refusing to let up and give her a chance to fill her lungs, think or pull herself together. She came apart at the seams, rocketing to the stratosphere, any modesty left in the dust of the African desert gone. She soared into the heavens, crying out his name as she launched.

For a long moment, she remained suspended, somewhere between earth and heaven, every nerve on fire, her blood moving like molten lava through her veins.

When she finally came back to earth, she tugged on T-Mac's hair. "Now. I need you now," she said, her voice hoarse with emotion.

He crawled up her body, leaned up on his knees and grabbed the foil package he'd set on the dash earlier. He tore open one end and shook out the protection into his palm.

Impatient, and past caring how pushy she looked, Kinsley snatched the item from his palm and rolled it over his distended erection.

When he was fully sheathed, she positioned him between her legs.

T-Mac took over, pressing against her entrance, his gaze meeting hers. "Tell me to stop, and I will." He gave her a crooked grin. "It'll be hard, but I can walk away if you change your mind."

Before he finished talking, she was already shaking her head. "You're not walking away now." She gripped his buttocks in both hands and pulled him closer. He penetrated her, easing in, careful not to hurt her, giving her channel time to adjust to his girth.

The deliberateness was excruciating. More painful than anything, and she could do nothing to stop it. She almost pounded her forehead in frustration. Why did he insist on going so slowly? Gripping his bottom, she guided him in and out, setting a rhythm both comforting and exciting.

T-Mac drove deep, filling her to completely full, stretching her inside and creating a friction so wonderful, it set her body on fire.

She urged him to go faster and faster, until he pounded into her like a piston.

Kinsley rose up to greet each thrust with one of her own. The slapping sound of skin on skin echoed inside the truck cab.

T-Mac's body stiffened. He thrust one last time, going as deep as he could get and froze, his shaft pulsing with his release. His breathing came in ragged breaths, his chest heaving, a sheen of perspiration making his body glisten in the starlight penetrating through the windshield.

When at last he relaxed, he lay down on her, covering her body with his. He gathered her in his arms and kissed her long, hard and thoroughly, stealing her breath away and caressing her tongue.

When at last he eased off to let her fill her lungs again, she let go of a shaky laugh. "Wow."

He chuckled. "That's all? Just *wow*?"

"You so rocked my world, my brain is mush and my vocabulary reduced to one-syllable words. Thus…*wow*."

He lifted her off the seat, removed the condom and settled his body on the cushion, draping her over his chest. "This way I don't crush you."

"I'd die a happy death." She laid her head against his heart and listened to the fast, steady rhythm. "Think Al-Shabaab will find us tonight?"

"I doubt it," he said.

"Good." Her fingers curled softly into his chest. "Then you can stay with me."

He rested his hand over hers. "Someone needs to stay awake in case they find us."

"I'm willing to risk it if you are."

He inhaled deeply, the movement raising her up and then lowering her downward. "Much as I'd like to lay here with you and feel your body against mine all night, I'd better get out there and keep both eyes open."

She sighed. "Wake me in an hour and a half. I'll take the next watch."

He didn't answer, just shifted into a sitting position, levering her across his lap. He cupped her breasts in his palms. "You know, you're beautiful beneath all that camouflage."

She wiggled against his stiff erection. "You're not so bad yourself." Kinsley leaned into his palms. "Care to go for round two?"

"I'd love to, but I only had the one condom."

"It's too bad we're not close to a drugstore." She cupped his cheeks and bussed his lips with a hard kiss. "Thank you."

He smiled. "For what?"

"For not being selfish, and making it just as good for me as it was for you." Kinsley frowned. "It was good for you, wasn't it?"

"Darlin', if it had been any better, I would be passed out or dead from a heart attack." He lifted her off his lap and set her on the seat beside him. He dragged on his trousers and boots and then slipped out the passenger door to stand on the ground.

Kinsley dressed in her bra, T-shirt and panties, her gaze on T-Mac as he covered his glorious body one item of clothing at a time. What a shame that he had to cover all that taut skin and those bulging muscles.

She dragged her trousers up her legs and buttoned them, then pulled on her boots with a sigh. They were back in uniform, back to reality. Soon, they would be back at Camp Lemonnier, where they wouldn't even be able to hold hands or kiss without the threat of an Article 15.

"Sleep. You don't know what tomorrow might bring," T-Mac said. "You'll need your strength." He left her alone in the truck and disappeared around the giant boulder to take up a position where he could watch the road.

With a yawn, Kinsley leaned over the back of the seat to check on Agar.

He lifted his nose and touched her hand.

"At least I will have you after the SEALs redeploy back to the States."

Agar nudged her hand and licked her fingers.

There had been a time when she thought loving Agar was enough. His loyalty was unquestioned, his love unconditional. But he wasn't a man. Kinsley hadn't realized just how much she needed the warmth and physical contact only a man could give her.

Until T-Mac entered her life.

She hadn't known what she was missing.

Now she did. And he would ship out, leaving a giant hole in her heart and soul.

She lay on the seat, her head resting on her bent arm. A single tear slipped from the corner of her eye and splashed onto the seat.

Crying accomplished nothing. So she limited it to the one tear. When T-Mac was gone, she might have to shed a few more. Until then, she wouldn't think that far ahead.

Chapter Twelve

T-Mac didn't wake Kinsley after an hour and a half. Nor did he wake her at two hours. Not a single vehicle had gone by on the road. He couldn't be certain one hadn't passed while he was making love to Kinsley, but he doubted it.

Which meant the Al-Shabaab faction hadn't made it out of the camp at a decent hour, unless they'd slipped by him while he'd been otherwise occupied.

He cursed himself for losing his concentration and focus. Their lives depended on him staying aware and on top of the situation. Sex in a truck wasn't going to keep them alive.

But oh, it had felt amazing. Having Kinsley in his arms hadn't gotten her out of his system. If anything, holding her made him want her even more.

The woman was tough as nails on the outside and all soft and vulnerable on the inside. And she'd fit perfectly against him, their bodies seemingly made for each other.

He found himself trying to figure out how a navy SEAL and an army dog handler could make a long-distance relationship work. Throughout the night, he worked it over in his mind and came to one conclusion.

As long as they were both on active duty, a relationship between them was doomed before it started.

Who was he kidding? They would never be on the same base, and probably not in the same state or even the same continent. Why go through the heartache of separation, as often as he was on call and deployed?

Why was he even thinking that way? He was a navy SEAL. He didn't have any right to expect a woman to give up all she knew and loved to follow him around the country or world, only to be stuck somewhere, waiting for him to come home.

He'd been an idiot to make love to her. Satisfying his base needs could only hurt her in the long run. And make it harder to let go when he left.

A couple times during the night, he'd almost nodded off. Each time, he'd imagine Kinsley wearing a dress, standing in the doorway of a cute little cottage with a white picket fence, sending him off or welcoming him home.

But that image clashed with the reality of what and who she was. She'd trained to be a dog handler. Surely, she would never be content to stay behind and keep the home fires burning.

He admired his teammates' ability to find love and the ways they'd worked out the difficulties of maintaining a relationship even when they were separated. If they could do it, why not him?

Because Kinsley belonged to the army. She had a commitment to serve. She couldn't move around from navy base to navy base and still do what she did. The army didn't care if she was married to a navy guy. They'd send her wherever they needed her.

T-Mac wished Big Jake or Harm were there. He could

sure use some advice, or just a sounding board. He had a lot on his mind and he couldn't seem to push any of it aside.

The first gray light of dawn pushed over the tops of the hills, creating long shadows and warming the air.

They needed to get on the road to Djibouti. The sooner the better. He'd made up his mind that they would take the route through Ethiopia, hopefully avoiding Al-Shabaab all together.

As much as he hated doing it, he got up, brushed off the dust and walked back to the truck to wake Kinsley.

When he looked inside, the truck was empty. His heart leaped into his throat and he shot a glance around the truck, the cliff and the giant boulder. Kinsley was nowhere to be seen.

With his heart pounding and a sweat breaking out on his forehead, T-Mac spun in a circle.

"I'm over here," Kinsley called out, emerging from around another, smaller boulder. "I had to relieve myself."

T-Mac didn't answer, taking a moment to drag air back into his lungs and calm his racing pulse. "You scared me."

She smiled. "I'm sorry. I didn't think about letting you know."

"It's imperative that you let me know where you are at all times. Al-Shabaab isn't above kidnapping women, drugging them and abusing them. They will give you even less slack because you are dressed as a soldier."

Kinsley squared her shoulders. "Bring it on."

T-Mac frowned. "You can't take on all of the Al-Shabaab faction. They have weapons, and they aren't afraid to use them. They don't follow any government. They aren't governed by the Geneva convention and they don't have a code of honor like ours."

Kinsley crossed her arms over her chest. "I can take care of myself, navy guy."

He cupped her chin. "You might think you can. But if these men gang up on you, you have to be ready for the worst."

She pushed her shoulders back and lifted her chin. "Yes, sir." Then she leaned her face into his open palm. "I'll play it safe."

"Good." He bent to kiss her, unable to resist her lips, swollen from his kisses. "What am I going to do with you?"

"I asked myself the same question all night long," she admitted.

He stared down into her eyes.

Kinsley met his gaze, unblinking. "How do two people from two totally separate military branches even dare to get together? You have to be all kinds of stupid to allow it to happen."

He chuckled. "Call me stupid."

"And me." She turned her face and pressed a kiss into his palm. "But we can't get hung up on what's going on here."

"You're right," he agreed. "We have to get back to Camp Lemonnier and report what we found in that Al-Shabaab camp."

"Right." She cupped the back of his hand. "And what happened here, last night, will stay here." Her lips twisted into a tight frown. "It can't go any further."

T-Mac wanted to disagree. He opened his mouth to do just that, but closed it nearly as fast. Kinsley was right. They couldn't go there. Anything between them was doomed. "You're right. We have a job to do. We need to focus on getting it done."

Though he knew it would only prolong the pain, he pulled her into his arms and kissed her hard.

At first she stood stiffly. Then her hands slid up the back of his neck and cupped his head, pulling him closer. She opened to him, allowing him to sweep in and caress her tongue with his. He accepted her offering, greedily tasting her, holding her and giving back all she gave him.

Agar brought them back to their senses. He pressed a warm, wet nose between them.

Kinsley leaned back and laughed shakily. "Hey, boy. Are you not getting the attention you deserve?" She lowered her hand to his head and scratched him behind the ears.

T-Mac dropped his hands lower, cupping the small of her back. He leaned forward and kissed her forehead, then swept his mouth lightly across her lips. Then he stepped away. "We have to get going. The sooner we get back, or find a phone to call for a lift, the better."

Kinsley pressed a hand to her lips and nodded. "I'm ready."

Agar jumped up into the cab of the truck and sat in the middle between Kinsley and T-Mac.

T-Mac would have preferred Kinsley sitting beside him, but having the dog between them was perhaps the only way he'd keep his hands off the woman.

He needed to concentrate on the road ahead, not on the woman. The men from the Al-Shabaab site would be out for revenge and wouldn't stop short of killing the people responsible for setting off the explosions in their camp and offing three of their men.

T-Mac turned the key in the ignition. The engine

didn't make a sound. He did it again with the same result. Damn.

Kinsley held up a hand. "Pop the hood."

"I'll look," he insisted.

"No, you need to turn the key. I had some training in the motor pool. Let me try the usual quick fixes." She hopped out of the truck and ran around to the front.

T-Mac released the hood. Kinsley pushed it up and climbed on the bumper to lean over the engine.

T-Mac tried to see what she was doing, but the hood blocked his vision.

"Try it now," she called out.

He turned the key, and the engine started right away.

Kinsley closed the hood and climbed up into the passenger seat with a grin.

"What was wrong?" he asked as he shifted into Drive and pulled around the big boulder.

"Corrosion on the battery terminals. All I did was wiggle them and break loose some of the crud. If we stop again soon, we need to do a more thorough job of cleaning the posts and connectors."

T-Mac admired the female for her ingenuity. He knew too many who wouldn't have had a clue about engines. "You are an amazing woman, Kinsley."

She shook her head. "Not at all. I just use the brain I have."

T-Mac's chest tightened. The more he knew about her, the more he loved. When the time came to part, he'd have a tough time saying goodbye.

KINSLEY SAT IN the passenger seat with her hand on Agar's back. The dog usually had a way of calming her when she was upset. All she had to do was rest her hand on his fur and the world would right itself.

Not this time. Since losing Jason to an IED explosion, she hadn't thought she'd fall for another military guy. Too much could go wrong and her heart couldn't take another loss like that.

She'd dated Jason for two years and thought she was in love with him, but what she felt for T-Mac seemed much stronger and harder to push aside.

Who would have thought she'd find a man who could rival Jason? Or that she would fall so fast and so hard? She was insane to even consider another relationship with a guy so entrenched in his military career.

No. Just no.

She stared at the road ahead as they angled west toward the border between Somalia and Ethiopia without actually seeing any of the terrain. Her thoughts remained pinned to the man in the driver's seat. In her peripheral vision, she could see him over Agar's head.

T-Mac's lips pressed tightly together, and his hands gripped the steering wheel as he kept the truck on the dirt road, his gaze sweeping the road ahead, the hills to each side and the rearview mirror.

He had a strong jaw and high cheekbones to go with his auburn hair and the dark auburn shadow of his beard.

If they somehow managed to get together, they'd have beautiful redheaded children. She could imagine a little girl with bright hair and T-Mac's startling blue eyes. And a little boy with auburn hair and her green eyes.

Kinsley looked straight ahead. Why was she daydreaming the impossible?

As soon as the SEAL team left, T-Mac would forget she ever existed.

She wouldn't forget him. Not for a long time. But she'd get on with her life, complete her commitment to the army and decide what she wanted to do next. She loved training dogs. Maybe she'd start her own training and boarding facility. And when Agar was retired from duty, she'd apply to adopt him. He deserved a happy forever home. A place with a big yard and lots of room to run and explore.

The truck leaped forward, jerking Kinsley out of her reverie.

"What's wrong?" she asked.

T-Mac's lips thinned and he glanced in the side mirror. "We've got trouble behind us."

Kinsley turned in her seat and stared through the back window, over the boxes and crates. Emerging from the dust cloud behind them were a truck and two motorcycles. The men riding the motorcycles wore the black garb of the Al-Shabaab fighters.

Her pulse banging against her veins, Kinsley fumbled on the floorboard for her rifle.

The truck bounced on the rough dirt road.

T-Mac pushed the accelerator all the way to the floor, but the truck and the motorcycles behind them were catching up.

"Stay down!" he shouted over the roar of the road noise. "They have guns."

No sooner had the word *guns* left his mouth than a bullet hit the back window and exited through the front, leaving a perfect round hole in each.

"Get down!" T-Mac ordered.

"The hell I will." Kinsley crawled over the back seat.

"What are you doing? You're going to get killed."

"No, but I'm going to put the hurt on them." She

hit the bullet hole in the window with the butt of her weapon. The glass shattered, but didn't fall. She hit it again. This time shards spilled outside and onto the seat beside her.

Bashing the jagged shards again and again, she cleared the rear window, pointed the rifle through the open space and aimed at the vehicles following them.

One of the motorcycles raced up to the back of the truck.

Though she was being jostled by the bumps in the road, Kinsley steadied her arm as much as possible and stared down the sights at the man on the motorcycle, who was getting close enough that he could eventually hop into the truck.

She took a breath, held it and caressed the trigger.

Her aim was true. The man on the motorcycle jerked sideways, lying over the bike, skidding along the dirt road for a long way before coming to a stop.

"One down!" T-Mac called. "Good shot."

Kinsley didn't respond, her attention on the other motorcycle and truck.

The motorcycle had slowed to run alongside the truck, both of which were speeding toward them.

Kinsley aimed for the driver's window.

Just as she pulled the trigger, their truck hit a rut, throwing her aim off. The bullet went wide.

Undisturbed, she aimed again and pulled the trigger before they hit another bump.

The bullet must have hit close to the driver. He swerved, sending the truck off the side of the road for a moment before straightening and pulling back into the middle.

The motorcycle stayed on the road, gained ground and headed for the driver's side of T-Mac's truck.

Kinsley took aim, sighted down the barrel and pulled the trigger.

The weapon jammed.

"Damn!"

"What?" T-Mac asked.

"Jam." She slapped the magazine from the bottom and pulled the trigger again. Still jammed.

The motorcycle rider pulled alongside the truck. "Watch out!" she called. "Motorcycle coming up on your side." Kinsley pulled back the bolt and found a bullet lodged at a bad angle. She dug in her pocket for the knife she kept handy. She dug out the bullet, slammed the bolt home and rolled down the window in the back seat as the motorcycle rider pulled up beside the truck, holding a handgun.

Kinsley aimed through the window and pulled the trigger.

The weapon jammed again.

Her heart hammering, Kinsley turned the weapon around, leaned out the window and, holding the barrel, used the rifle like a baseball bat and swung as hard as she could, knocking the handgun from the rider's hands and the rider from his seat. He crashed to the ground, the motorcycle slipping sideways under the truck's wheels.

The resulting bump nearly threw Kinsley out of the truck. She was so concerned about keeping hold of her rifle, she forgot to hold on to something to keep from being thrown from the truck. Thankfully, she had her heel hooked beneath the back seat and was able to pull herself and her rifle back inside.

Just in time for the truck behind them to ram into the rear of their vehicle.

Kinsley slammed into the back of T-Mac's seat.

"Are you okay?" he asked.

She pulled herself off the floorboard and up onto the seat, shaken but not injured. "I'm okay."

Then she cleared her weapon, braced it on the rim of the back window, aimed at the driver's windshield and prayed her rifle wouldn't jam.

The trailing vehicle raced forward, full speed.

Kinsley focused down the sights and pulled the trigger.

The bullet flew through the window and into the truck, directly into the driver's-side windshield.

For a moment, the vehicle stayed its course, heading straight for the back of T-Mac's truck.

Kinsley braced for impact, closed her eyes and held on.

A moment passed. Then two. Nothing happened. The truck behind them didn't hit theirs.

Frowning, Kinsley opened her eyes.

The Al-Shabaab vehicle was going so fast that when it spun sideways, it rolled over and over, coming to a halt on its side. Steam rose from the engine, but no one crawled out.

Drawing in a deep breath, Kinsley stared out the back window until the toppled truck became a speck in the distance. She crawled over the seat and settled in the front, her weapon across her lap.

Agar nudged her hand.

She laughed and patted his head, glad she was still alive to do it.

"You weren't kidding when you said you were a good shot," T-Mac said.

"I'm just lucky you were able to keep your cool and drive on."

"We make a good team," T-Mac said.

"Yes," Kinsley agreed. Too bad the military wouldn't keep them together to see how far they'd go on synergy.

Hell, too bad they wouldn't be together for the long haul. But Kinsley couldn't be too sad. Not after what had just happened. At least they were still alive.

Without a tail following them, they drove into Ethiopia, hoping to find a town of sufficient size and infrastructure where they might find a working telephone.

After two hours on the dirt road, they finally entered such a town. And none too soon. The gas gauge had dipped low. Fortunately, there was a place to purchase fuel, and that station had a telephone.

After going through several operators, he got one who understood how to connect him to an operator at Camp Lemonnier, and he was able to talk with his commander.

Kinsley waited nearby, feeling more hopeful than she had since they got separated from the rest of the SEAL team.

When T-Mac completed the call, he smiled in her direction, making her day brighter. "They're sending a helicopter to collect us. They should be here in two hours."

"What about the motor-pool truck?" she asked.

"I mentioned it to Commander Ward. He didn't give a damn about the truck." T-Mac grinned. "He was just glad to hear from us. They sent a couple of Black Hawks out to the site this morning. Everyone was gone."

"We expected that. They were packing up when you hit them with the explosions."

T-Mac nodded. "The commander figured we might have had something to do with the abandoned vehicles and scorched fuel barrels."

"You did a number on them." Kinsley glanced around the little town. "I don't suppose we could find some food here?" she suggested.

"I'm hungry too, but I'd just as soon wait until we get back to Camp Lemonnier. At least I'll know what I'm eating."

"Agreed." Her belly rumbled loudly. "Where will they land the choppers?"

"On the road headed northeast out of town," T-Mac said. He paid the man for the fuel, thanked him for the use of the phone and held the passenger door while Kinsley climbed up into the cab.

In silence, T-Mac closed the door and climbed into the driver's seat. He sat for a moment with his hand on the key. He opened his mouth as if to say something, but closed it without uttering a word.

Kinsley wondered what he'd been about to say, but didn't ask. Her emotions were still on overload from making love to the man the previous night, followed by the adrenaline rush of being attacked.

If he said anything about forgetting what happened, or pretending it never did, she wasn't sure how she'd react. The only thing she was certain of was that her heart was 100 percent involved.

Dang. She didn't need that kind of complication.

Chapter Thirteen

T-Mac drove a few miles out of the small town and parked the truck in a clear area with only one tree for hundreds of yards. The helicopter would be able to land easily, and T-Mac would be able to watch both directions. If Al-Shabaab decided to send more mercenaries their way, T-Mac needed to see them enough in advance to know whether they should stand fast and defend or run.

For the time being, the road was clear and the sun shone down, burning into the roof of the vehicle, making it unbearably hot inside.

"I'll park in the shade." He positioned the truck beneath the low-hanging branches. Then he climbed down, rounded the hood to the other side and opened the door for Kinsley.

He held out his hand. "We'll be back before you know it."

Kinsley laid her fingers across his palm, but didn't get out of the truck immediately. "About last night..." Her voice was low, husky and sexy as hell.

T-Mac's groin tightened at the mere mention of the previous night. "What about it?"

"We're headed back to camp," she blurted out.

He gave her a tight little smile. "Don't worry, I won't tell anyone. My career is just as much on the line as yours."

She laughed, the sound more nervous than humorous. "No. I mean… I just…" Kinsley flung her hands in the air. "What I'm trying to say is—" She threw herself into his arms and kissed him long and hard.

T-Mac gathered her into his arms and held her in the air, holding her tightly against him, his tongue thrusting between her teeth to sweep across hers.

When he at last lowered her to the ground, he lifted his head and sighed. "We won't get the chance to do that back at the base."

She laughed and leaned her forehead against his chest for a moment. "No, we won't."

He tipped her chin upward. "What are we going to do about us?"

Kinsley shook her head. "I don't think there can be an *us*. Not when we're both on active duty, and we'll be going our separate ways as soon as we leave Djibouti."

"It's hard to believe we've only known each other a few days. I feel like I've known you for a lifetime."

"And I you." She smiled. "And yet, I don't know anything about you. Like what's your favorite color? Do you have any siblings? Are your parents still alive? Where did you grow up?" She cupped his cheek. "None of that matters because I know you here." Her hand moved from his face to his chest. "You're loyal. You care about your team. You take your duty seriously and you love animals. Those are the big things. The rest is just data."

He pressed a kiss to her forehead. "Blue." And kissed the tip of her nose. "You already know I have one sister." He swept his lips across hers. "Yes, my folks are still alive, and before you lost your memory, I told you how I grew up on my father's farm in Nebraska." He held her face between his palms and kissed her lightly. "And I know very little about you, but I know you can fire a rifle, you aren't afraid of going into enemy territory, you can hold your own as a soldier in the army, you care about Agar. You care about your country and you care enough about me to take out a truck driver and two men on motorcycles."

"To be fair, you lit their world on fire with a little C-4." She wrapped her arms around his waist and squeezed gently. "I'll be sad when you leave with your team to redeploy back to the States."

"And I'll be sad when I go." He shook his head. "Maybe we'll see each other back home," he said hopefully.

"The most likely scenario is that you'll be in Virginia, I'll go back to San Antonio or somewhere else equally distant, and we'll get on with our lives and never see each other again."

"Wow, a little negative much?" He brushed a strand of her hair from her face. "I prefer my version."

"I do, too. But reality is, we're both committed to our careers. We've trained hard to get where we are today. Jetting back and forth across the country or around the world isn't realistic."

"I'll tell you what." He rested his hand on her hips. "If we're both still single—and since I'm a SEAL, I'm pretty sure that'll be the case for me—can we at least meet on the anniversary of our night in Somalia?"

She smiled. "Sure. Why not? But only if we're both single."

"Good. Then I'll have a date." He captured her face

in his hands. "But for now I'd like to take advantage of the little bit of time we have alone together to hold you and kiss you."

"I'm in." She snuggled close to him, despite the heat of the desert sun cooking the landscape around them.

Kinsley gave Agar some water from her CamelBak thermos. Then the three of them settled on the ground in the shade of the tree and waited for the helicopter to arrive.

Agar slept while T-Mac kissed Kinsley, held her hand and talked.

While they waited for their transport, T-Mac learned Kinsley's favorite color was red, she had no siblings and her father had passed. She liked watching NFL football but sadly wasn't a Dallas Cowboys fan, preferring the Denver Broncos. She grew up in Colorado Springs, Colorado, and joined the army to earn money for college. She stayed because she enjoyed working with the dogs.

"I like camping and fishing but prefer to shoot animals with a camera, not a gun." She leaned her head against his shoulder. "I don't like to dance, because I'm not very good at it, but I do enjoy slow dancing...with the right person."

"And have you met the right person?"

"I won't lie. I fell in love once. I told you about him. He was a dog handler, too. We thought we might one day have a future together." She sighed. "He and his dog had just identified an IED when the ISIS rebel set it off remotely."

"I'm sorry."

She shrugged. "That's part of the reason why I try not to get involved with military guys. What's the use?

They might die or be transferred. I don't know if I can go through that heartache again."

"Will you go through that heartache over me?" T-Mac asked, his arm tightening around her shoulder.

"I'm trying really hard not to fall for you." She tipped her head upward to stare into his eyes. "You're making it really hard on me. Can we stick to the facts that don't mean much?"

"Sorry." He raised his hands in surrender. "Continue."

"Where was I?"

"You like slow dancing."

"Right." She took a breath. "There's not much more. I favor daisies over roses, and I enjoy a cold beer on a hot day, like today, and I really like walking in the rain."

"As hot as it is today, I'd enjoy a cold beer and a little rain as well."

"What about you? Ever been in love?" Kinsley asked.

"No," he said. *Until now,* he didn't add. He feared he was falling hopelessly in love with the army dog handler. But telling her would only make it harder for him and for her when they parted. He'd avoided relationships, knowing how hard they were to maintain for a guy in his career field. He'd never been in love. Kinsey tempted him to break all his self-imposed rules. Was what he was feeling for Kinsey love? His heart skipped several beats and then jerked like a jackhammer.

"Do you want a family?"

"Someday, maybe," he replied. "When I'm not shooting bad guys for a living." He could imagine Kinsley's round belly. She'd be beautiful pregnant with their child. The baby girl would have bright strawberry blond hair like her mother and a smile that would melt every male heart.

Kinsley stiffened. "There's a vehicle coming."

T-Mac leaped to his feet and jerked Kinsley up beside him. They both grabbed their rifles and took up defensive positions, using the truck for cover.

A dilapidated truck loaded with bags of grain, people and livestock trundled by. The folks on the back of the truck waved as they passed.

Kinsley and T-Mac lowered their weapons out of sight and waved back, not letting their guard down completely.

When the truck disappeared and the dust settled, T-Mac and Kinsley sat beneath the tree again.

The afternoon passed entirely too quickly. By the time the helicopter arrived, they were both hungry and ready to be back at Camp Lemonnier, yet T-Mac was sad to leave their little patch of shade where they'd had the time to get to know each other better.

When the chopper came close enough and T-Mac identified it as one belonging to the US, he stepped out of the shade and waved.

The chopper landed and five men jumped out.

"You old son of a gun." Harm was first to greet him, dragging him into a giant bear hug. "We got a little worried about you when we couldn't find you at the Al-Shabaab camp."

"That's right." Diesel gripped his forearm and pulled him into a hug. "Wasn't as much fun going back to camp without our T-Mac."

"How's the guy who stepped on the mine?"

"It was Stucky. They flew him to Ramstein, Germany," Buck said. "He had multiple lacerations and embedded shrapnel, one piece lodged close to one of his eyes. They're trying to get him to a specialist to save the eye."

"Damn. I hope he'll be okay."

"We all hope for the best." Big Jake limped up to T-Mac. "We saw the damage to the camp. Glad you were able to escape. We were confused when your GPS tracker headed deeper into Somalia."

"I didn't want to lose them, so I sacrificed my tracker. Once I planted it on one of their trucks, I stole one of the vehicles they had in their camp and got the heck out."

"This the truck?" Pitbull called out from where he stood by the vehicle.

"It is."

Pitbull shot a glance toward T-Mac. "Who put the bullet holes in it?"

"Three of the Al-Shabaab fighters caught up to us early this morning."

Pitbull shook his head. "I hope they look worse than this truck."

"They're dead." T-Mac grinned. "Our little dog handler is a crack shot."

Kinsley's cheeks flushed.

Diesel held out his hand to Kinsley. "I'm impressed. You can have my back anytime."

She gripped it and shook. "Thanks."

T-Mac busted through Diesel's grip on Kinsley's hand. "Hey, she's my sidekick."

"Yeah, I get that." Diesel shook his hand. "I've got my own sidekick waiting for me back home."

Harm snapped pictures of the truck and the bumper with the writing.

T-Mac walked to the back of the truck and climbed in. He opened one of the crates and held up an M4A1 rifle. "We can't leave these weapons in the back of that truck. They might fall into the wrong hands."

"Load them into the helicopter," Big Jake said. "We'll take them back to camp for disposal. We need to get back. The commander wants a debrief."

The men loaded the crate of weapons onto the chopper. T-Mac helped Kinsley and Agar up into the fuselage and climbed in to sit beside her. He adjusted her safety harness around her shoulders and lap before buckling his.

"Here." Big Jake handed Kinsley a plastic-wrapped package. "Figured you might be hungry."

"Thank you." Kinsley smiled and opened the package to reveal a sandwich loaded with salami, ham and turkey slices. She moaned.

The sound reminded T-Mac of how she'd moaned when he'd made love to her the night before. His groin tightened and he looked away from her biting into the sandwich.

"We didn't forget you." Big Jake slapped another sandwich into T-Mac's hands. "Eat up. It's a long flight back and the commander won't let you hit the chow hall or the sack until you debrief him on what happened after we left you."

Pitbull faced T-Mac in the seat across from him. He leaned forward and yelled as the rotor blades spun up to speed. "The boss wasn't too happy with us when we came back without the dog handler."

"You didn't have a choice. You had to get Stucky back before he bled out," T-Mac said.

The men settled back against their seats, the roar of the engine and blades making it too difficult to carry on a conversation.

The chopper lifted off the ground and circled back the way it had come.

T-Mac made short work of the sandwich, feeding bits of bread and meat to Agar.

Kinsley ate a third of her sandwich and fed the rest to Agar. Once she finished the food, she stuffed the plastic wrap into her pocket and leaned her head back, closing her eyes. She let her hand fall between them on the seat where T-Mac's rested.

T-Mac captured her hand in his and held on. If someone noticed, too damned bad. That little bit of contact with Kinsley might be the last he would get before they made it back to all the rules and consequences. He'd be damned if he wasted the opportunity to touch her this one last time.

KINSLEY CURLED HER fingers around T-Mac's. Though the past thirty-six hours had been difficult, she hadn't exactly felt scared. Unless she counted the minutes she'd lain in wait for T-Mac to emerge from the rebel camp. Then, she hadn't been afraid for herself, but for T-Mac. He'd walked right into that camp as bold as day and set off those explosions. Anyone could have caught him. Anyone could have shot him on sight.

Kinsley had been more scared than she'd been in her entire life. She felt as if her heart hadn't started beating again until she'd seen T-Mac behind the wheel of that truck.

Her fingers tightened around his. Now she wanted to hold on to his hand and never let go. She was afraid she'd lose him. Which was silly. Their time together was coming to an end. His team was scheduled to ship out in a day or two. They'd leave and she'd be left behind to continue her mission of supporting operations out of

Djibouti. Her deployment was for a full year. She'd been there only a few weeks.

When she'd arrived, she'd been excited to actually put her and Agar's skills to use.

Now that she and Agar had been under fire, she wasn't nearly as excited. More cautious, yes. A little frightened? She'd be a liar if she said she wasn't. Her next engagement with the enemy might be without the SEAL team as backup. She might not be as lucky without them.

She had to face it. T-Mac wouldn't be there every time she went outside the wire, and that made her sad.

Her chest tightened and her eyes burned. A single tear slipped from the corner of her eye, down her cheek.

She raised her free hand to brush away the moisture. Her drill sergeant in Basic Combat Training had assured her vehemently that soldiers didn't cry. Now wasn't a good time to start. Surrounded by SEALs who'd been through a whole lot more, she couldn't show any weakness.

Yet another damned tear slipped down the other cheek, closest to T-Mac.

He raised his hand as if to brush it away, but caught himself before he touched her. Instead, he pushed his hand through his hair and let it drop to his lap.

Kinsley had wanted him to touch her cheek. But she knew any public displays of affection were frowned upon and, in front of his buddies, would be purely awkward. So she sat still, hiding her disappointment, wishing she and T-Mac were alone again where they could hold each other, kiss and touch to their hearts' content.

Kinsley must have fallen asleep on the ride back.

The change in the speed of the aircraft and the gentle squeeze on her hand brought her back to consciousness.

The chopper came down on the tarmac and the SEALs piled out.

Still a little groggy from her short nap, Kinsley took her time climbing down.

T-Mac stood on the ground, holding out his hand.

She stumbled and fell into his arms.

He caught her and held her briefly, perhaps hugging her harder than he would a stranger. Then he set her up straight and gathered Agar's lead from the ground where she'd dropped it. "Steady there," he whispered.

She nodded, her cheeks burning. "Thanks."

"We're all due to report to Commander Ward in the command center," Big Jake reminded them.

Kinsley nodded, all her grogginess wiped clean. They were back. Rules and regulations couldn't be ignored. She couldn't hold T-Mac's hand or steal a kiss whenever she liked. Tired, grungy and ready for a shower and a real bed, she squared her shoulders and marched alongside the SEALs, her hand wrapped around Agar's lead. The vacation was over.

Ha! Some vacation. They'd been shot at, nearly blown up and on the run for the past thirty-six hours. And somewhere in there had been the most magical point of her life. Making love with T-Mac had changed everything. Inside, her heart bubbled with the need to shout out how good he'd made her feel. How he'd lit a fire inside the woman in her. Couldn't everyone see that? T-Mac had made her feel so very different.

And she could do nothing about it.

Kinsley pushed her hair behind her ears and tried to tuck it into the back of her shirt. She'd long since lost the elastic band that held it off her face. Yet she would stand in front of the mission commander, in her dirty uniform, and tell him everything that had happened.

Except what she considered the most significant... what had happened between her and T-Mac.

If the truth got out, neither one of their careers would survive. Time to suck it up and be a professional. In order to do that, she'd have to cut all ties and forget what had happened between her and T-Mac.

Like that would ever happen.

Even if she'd never forget her night with the SEAL, she would have to pretend it never took place.

Somehow, she made it through the debrief. When she left the command center, T-Mac cornered her in the shadow of one of the buildings.

"Kinsley, I can't pretend what we have together means nothing. I don't want this to be the end."

Her heart pinching in her chest, Kinsley held up her hand and shook her head. "Don't."

He gripped her arms. "What do you mean?"

"We're on two divergent paths, heading in completely different directions. We are destined to be apart. The sooner we accept that, the better off we'll both be."

He held her arms for a moment longer. When footsteps sounded on the gravel, he dropped his hands. "Is that the way you want it?"

She nodded, her eyes stinging with unshed tears. "It is."

"Very well." He took a step back. "I'll let you have time to think about it. But I can tell you now... I don't give up that easily. I wouldn't have come as far as I have... I wouldn't have made it through SEAL training if I gave up on what I wanted." He leaned closer so only she could hear his next words. "And I want you, Kinsley Anderson. I. Want. You."

Chapter Fourteen

T-Mac walked away from Kinsley, his chest tight, his fists clenched. He wanted to turn and run right back to her and kiss her until she changed her mind. He knew, deep inside, that she wanted him as much as he wanted her. She couldn't have faked her response to him when he'd held her in his arms and made sweet love to her. And she couldn't have faked how much she enjoyed kissing him when they were waiting for the helicopter.

She was a rule follower, and the rules were firmly in place at Camp Lemonnier. Breaking them would get them in trouble, and T-Mac didn't want to jeopardize Kinsley's career. He'd pushed the limits, bent a few rules and done things that could have harmed his own career, but he couldn't sabotage Kinsley's. She loved working with Agar. He knew a dog handler might not always get to work with the same dog. Kinsley knew it, too. If she were reassigned or got off active duty, Agar would still belong to the army. Until he was retired, he'd have to go back to work. With another handler.

If Kinsley got in sufficient trouble, she could be kicked out of the military or reassigned to a different skill set and no longer be allowed to train with the dogs.

T-Mac's strides ate the distance as he passed the

motor pool. The acrid scent of something burning irritated his nose. A yell made him slow to a stop and glance around.

"Someone help!" a voice cried out. "Man down!"

T-Mac altered his direction and headed toward the sound—and a growing cloud of black smoke.

As he rounded the corner of the motor-pool building, he could see a young marine dragging another man in uniform across the pavement.

T-Mac ran toward them, grabbed one of the inert man's arms and helped the marine drag him out of the smoke.

Harm, Diesel, Pitbull, Big Jake and Buck appeared beside him.

Buck dove in. "Let me check for a pulse."

T-Mac moved aside while Buck put his medical training to good use. He pressed his fingers to the base of the man's throat and stared at his chest. "No pulse and he's not breathing." Immediately, Buck began compressions against the man's chest. "Breathe for him while I work on his pulse." He pointed at the young marine standing by. "You! Get help."

The marine sprinted toward the next building.

Soon they were surrounded by people. A fire truck arrived and an ambulance pulled up. The trained medics took over from Buck.

The firefighters went to work on the fire burning inside the building. The medics loaded the injured man into the back of the ambulance and whisked him away to the medical facility, leaving the rest to pick up, clean up and get on with their own work.

T-Mac found the marine who'd originally pulled the man out of the motor-pool building. "What happened?"

The young man shrugged. "I don't know. One minute, Jones was fine. I went to the base exchange to get us a candy bar, and when I got back, smoke was billowing out of the building. I ran in to find Jones on the floor. If you hadn't come along..." He shook his head, his cheeks smudged with soot. "Do you think he'll make it?"

Buck stood beside T-Mac. "We did all we could. It's up to the medics and the doctors now."

"I don't get it. What would have started that fire?" He stared at the building where the firefighters were winding up the hoses.

"You should head to the medical facility and have them check you out for smoke inhalation."

The marine squared his shoulders. "I'm fine. But I'll go check on Jones."

"Seriously, man." Buck touched the man's shoulder. "Smoke inhalation might not hit you immediately. Better safe than sorry."

"Okay. I'll check in with the doc." The marine left.

The SEALs stood staring at the wreckage of the motor-pool building.

"What are the chances," T-Mac mused, "that we find a vehicle from this motor pool in the hands of Al-Shabaab, and the next thing we know, the motor pool building and all its records are burned to the ground?"

Big Jake shook his head. "Too much of a coincidence."

T-Mac's jaw tightened. "I don't believe in coincidence."

"We still don't know who was after your little dog handler," Harm reminded him.

T-Mac turned away from the building. "You're right."

"Her dog should keep her safe," Diesel assured him.

"Yeah, but he can only do so much." T-Mac left his team and walked toward the containerized living units. His walk became a jog, and then he was sprinting toward the one assigned to Kinsley. When he arrived, he pounded on the door.

When he got no answer, he glanced around wildly. She wasn't anywhere to be seen. He pounded again. "Specialist Anderson!"

A female poked her head out of the unit beside Kinsley's and frowned. "Hey, you might want to keep it down. Some of us work nights."

"Do you know where Specialist Anderson is?" he asked.

"No, but she might be in the shower unit." When T-Mac turned in that direction, the woman added, "I wouldn't go barging in on her. They frown on that kind of thing, you know." She chuckled and closed the door.

"Looking for me?" a voice said behind T-Mac.

He turned to find Kinsley wearing her PT gear and shower shoes. She carried a shower caddie of toiletries and her hair was wound up, turban-style, in a towel. Agar stood at her side, his coat slick and damp.

T-Mac caught himself before he did something stupid, like grab her and pull her into his arms.

She frowned. "Is everything all right?"

He shook his head. "I'm not sure you're safe."

"Why? What happened?"

"There was an accident at the motor pool. A fire and a man knocked unconscious."

Her eyes rounded. "That's awful. Is he going to be okay?"

"I don't know." He explained his concern about the

fire coming on the heels of finding the motor-pool truck in the Al-Shabaab camp.

"You think the fire and attack in the motor pool had something to do with the stolen truck?" She pulled the towel from her head, looped it over her shoulder and finger combed her hair.

"What do you think?" he asked, wishing he could run his hands through her wet hair.

"Sounds too coincidental to me." She glanced down at the ground. "Do you think someone is trying to destroy the record of who checked it out?"

"That's what I'm thinking."

"Are all records stored online now?" she asked.

"I'm pretty sure they are," T-Mac said. "But the fire could have destroyed the computer." He lifted his head. "And the data might be stored on a database at a remote server." T-Mac smiled. "I'll check on that."

"In the meantime," Kinsley nodded toward her quarters, "I have a date with a blow dryer."

"Okay then." He stepped aside.

As she passed, he touched her arm. "I'm still not giving up on us."

She sighed and stared at the fingers on her arm. "Do you know how hard it is not to throw myself into your arms?" she whispered. Her gaze rose to meet his. "Just leave me alone. I can't be this close to you and not touch you. It's killing me."

As it was killing him. He nodded. "Don't let your guard down for a minute. Whoever attacked the guy in the motor pool might still consider you a threat."

"I don't know why. It's not like I remember anything from the attack in that village." She pressed her lips together. "But I'll be careful. And Agar will be with me at all times."

"Good." He nodded toward her door. "Let Agar go in first."

She gave him a gentle smile. "I always do." Kinsley turned toward her unit and stopped. "For the unofficial record, I miss being out in the desert, just you and me."

"Then why won't you consider seeing me again?"

Kinsley smiled sadly. "Because it will make the parting even harder. We're both married to our careers."

He smiled. "Then I want a divorce."

"You can't. You and I both have a number of years to complete our obligations." She lifted her head and stared directly into his eyes. "We can't tell the army and navy to go take a hike just because we might want to be together."

"Why not?"

"Because of all the attributes we've identified we like about each other, including loyalty and patriotism."

"But I don't want to give up on you...on us," he said, and reached out for her hand.

She stepped back and glanced right and left. "We can't be together, and it would be foolish to think otherwise. Long-distance relationships rarely work."

"I'm willing to give it a try."

"I'm not willing to hold you to it."

T-Mac pounded his fist into his palm. "Damn it, Kinsley, why do you have to be so obstinate and...and..." He sighed. "Most likely right."

She smiled, her eyes glistening with what he suspected were unshed tears. "Give it time. You'll forget Djibouti ever happened."

"Nope. Not a possibility. I don't want to forget it, and I suspect you don't either."

"For now, respect my decision," she said, and looked up at him, a tear slipping from the corner of her eye. "Leave me alone."

He inhaled a long, deep breath to calm his hammering heart. Then he let it out. "Okay. For now. But this isn't over. I won't let it be."

"I'm sorry," she said. "It has to be." Then she ducked past him and entered her unit with Agar, shutting the door behind them.

ONCE THE DOOR was closed behind Agar, Kinsley let the tears fall unchecked. She threw herself onto her bunk and hugged her pillow to her face to muffle the sobs. She wanted to be with T-Mac more than she wanted to breathe. But they couldn't abandon their careers. They each had a commitment to uphold. She had three more years on her current enlistment. In three years, they could each find someone else. Someone who wasn't so far away.

Yet Kinsley was certain she wouldn't find anyone she cared about as much as she'd learned to care about T-Mac in the few short days she'd known him. But he had an important job to do. He needed all his focus to be on staying alive and accomplishing his assigned dangerous missions. Trying to work out the logistics of a long-distance relationship would only make him lose focus. And that could be deadly.

After a good cry, she dried her tears, pulled back her hair, dressed in her uniform and went to the chow hall for dinner. She hoped she wouldn't run into anyone from T-Mac's SEAL team. Agar trotted along at her side.

In the dining facility, she collected a tray of food, not really hungry but knowing she had to keep up her strength should she and Agar be assigned to another mission. At the very least, she might be put back on gate-guard rotation. At that moment, she'd almost prefer the monotony of guarding the entrance of the camp. At least then she wouldn't run the risk of bumping into T-Mac.

Her gaze drifted to the door more often than she cared to admit. Part of her wanted T-Mac to walk through. Another part prayed he wouldn't.

"Mind if I sit with you?" a voice said, drawing her attention away from the entrance.

She looked up to find Mr. Toland hovering over her, holding a tray of food. Kinsley shrugged. "Not at all," she said, though she'd rather be alone with her thoughts. But she didn't want to be rude to the contractor.

"I hear you and one of the navy SEALs have been on quite the adventure."

Using her fork, she stabbed the meat on her platter and cut it with a knife. "If you want to call it that," she replied.

"We all thought you and the SEAL were casualties when you didn't make it back with the others."

"We weren't," she said, stating the obvious.

"I was surprised they sent you out again after your last mission resulted in a concussion."

Tired of the man's conversation, Kinsley turned to him and gave him a direct stare. "I'm sorry, sir, but information about missions is classified. I'm not allowed to discuss the details."

He held up his hands. "Of course. I wouldn't want you to get into trouble."

Good. Then maybe you can go away. She wanted to

say the words, but she refused to take out her bad temper on the contractor.

"I was just worried about you. You remind me of my daughter." He smiled. "How are you feeling after the concussion?"

Feeling a little guilty for jumping down the man's throat, Kinsley answered, "Perfectly fine, except for a little memory loss."

"Really?" Mr. Toland nodded. "Sometimes situationally induced concussions can result in memory loss. You don't remember anything before the blow that knocked you unconscious?"

She frowned hard, trying to force the memories out. Finally, she shook her head. "Nothing." *But I feel like I'm forgetting something really important.* She stared into the man's eyes. "You know, like it's right there on the edge of my memory, just waiting to come back." She laughed. "Maybe I just need another knock in the head for it to shake loose." Kinsley shrugged. "At least I didn't forget how to work with Agar or how to hold my fork." She lifted her utensil as proof.

"Strange thing, the brain," Mr. Toland said. "I've heard of people never recalling tragic events. Then I've heard of people suddenly remembering all of it."

"You never know with amnesia." Kinsley wished she could forget how much she cared for T-Mac. Then again, she didn't want to forget, because he was such an important part of her life. He'd shown her how real her emotions could be and how much she wanted that in her life.

She stared down at her tray, giving up on refueling her body. "If you'll excuse me, I think I'll go for a run." She stowed her tray, gathered Agar's lead in her hand and left the dining facility.

The only way she could clear her mind was to run until she was too tired to think. Even then, she doubted she'd forget T-Mac. Most likely, he'd haunt her dreams for years to come.

Outside, she hurried back to her quarters and slipped out of her uniform and into her PT clothes. Agar danced around her, knowing he would be included on her run. The dog needed to blow off steam as much as Kinsley. A run around the perimeter would be just what they both needed.

When she stepped out of her quarters and started for the field beyond, she spotted T-Mac jogging ahead of her.

She almost turned around and went back into her container to hide.

Agar tugged on his lead, eager to get out and run.

Kinsley couldn't disappoint the animal. He needed the exercise, and she had to get used to seeing T-Mac in passing until they left to return to the States. Hadn't his commander said something about them redeploying in four days? That had been a few days before. If they were still on track to return to Virginia, they'd be leaving soon.

Good. At least then she could start down the road to recovery. In the meantime, she jogged behind T-Mac, admiring the way his muscles bunched and how graceful he was when he ran.

Her imagination took her back to when they were lying naked on the front seat of the truck. His buttocks were hard and tight beneath her fingertips.

Her heart beat faster and her breathing became more labored than her slow, steady pace warranted.

When he turned at the far end of the field and circled

back toward the living quarters, he spied her. For a moment, he slowed, his brows dipping into a fierce frown.

Kinsley focused on putting one foot in front of the other, if a little slower. She prayed he wouldn't stop and wait, or run back to her. She wasn't sure she could keep up her adamant refusal to see him again, when all she really wanted was to be with him always.

How did this happen? How did she fall for a military guy after losing her first love? She knew the dangers of death and separation.

Thankfully, T-Mac kept running toward their quarters without slowing significantly. As he neared the living area, five of his teammates met him. They put their heads together and spoke in low tones. Whatever they were saying didn't carry on the wind.

Having been a part of their mission task force, Kinsley was interested in what was going on. She might have input into the next operation, and she sure as hell wanted to know if they'd followed the GPS tracking device to where the Al-Shabaab rebels had moved.

Kinsley picked up the pace, racing to the group of men, Agar running easily alongside.

"Hey, Specialist Anderson." Big Jake held out a hand.

Kinsley came to an abrupt stop and took Big Jake's hand in a firm shake. "What's going on?"

"Got word back from the doc at the medical center," Buck said, his lips forming a thin line. "The guy from the motor pool didn't make it."

"Smoke inhalation?" Kinsley guessed.

Buck shook his head. "Blunt force trauma to the back of his skull. We couldn't have saved him."

Kinsley's chest tightened. "Why?"

"Either he knew something or he got in the way of someone burning the building is my guess," Big Jake said.

"The weapons, the truck, they're all part of whatever is going on here at Camp Lemonnier." Kinsley frowned, pushing hard to remember. "I get the feeling I should know something or that I saw something that night I was shot in the chest." She smacked her forehead, angry at her inability to pull those few minutes of her life, seemingly lost. "If only I could remember."

"Don't worry about it," Harm said. "It's probably your mind's way of protecting you. It had to be pretty horrific to see a gun pointed at your chest and not be able to do anything to stop the shooter from pulling the trigger."

"Still…" She sighed. "If only I were a computer with a reboot button."

"On the bright side," Big Jake interjected, "the commander had the UAV team track the GPS you two planted on the Al-Shabaab truck." He paused dramatically.

"And?" T-Mac questioned impatiently.

"The truck led them to their new camp." Big Jake's eyes narrowed. "Once they determined there were no civilians in the way, the UAV team dropped missiles in their midst. They won't be using our weapons and vehicles against us anytime soon."

Kinsley crossed her arms over her chest and her eyes narrowed. "Good riddance. But what happened to capturing one of them to determine who their supplier is?"

"That decision wasn't ours to make," Big Jake said. "The commander decided it wasn't worth risking the lives of our SEALs and dog handler again."

"And we're still due to redeploy back to home base tomorrow," T-Mac said. His gaze captured hers. "Our transport leaves at seven in the morning."

Kinsley's heart plummeted to the pit of her belly, and her knees wobbled. She'd known they would leave soon, but she'd selfishly hoped they would be delayed a few more days. "What about the supplier connection? Isn't Commander Ward concerned about finding the link?"

"He is, but he's bringing in an investigator and working with the intel guys looking into the motor-pool database. He thinks they'll be able to trace back to the man responsible. And since we were able to bring the weapons back, they might be able to pull a serial number and find out who shipped them in the first place."

"So you're done here?" She smiled, though her heart hurt so badly she could barely breathe. "I know you'll be glad to get back home."

"Some of us will be happier than others," Harm said, his eyes sliding sideways, aiming toward T-Mac. "We'd better go pack our gear." He gave a chin lift to the others. "And leave T-Mac to fill in Specialist Anderson on anything we might have left out."

"What did we leave out?" Pitbull asked.

Harm glared at the man and jerked his head toward T-Mac and Kinsley. "I'm sure we've left off something. T-Mac will fill her in." He gave Pitbull a shove. "Sometimes you can be so thickheaded."

"Oh." Pitbull grinned. "You want to let T-Mac have some time alone with his dog handler. Why didn't you say so in the first place?"

Harm raised his face to the heavens. "I'm surrounded by morons."

"Watch it, dude." Pitbull shoved Harm. "I have feelings."

The five SEALs left T-Mac alone with Kinsley.

"I hope you have a good flight back to the States."

Kinsley refused to look into T-Mac's eyes. Hers were burning with unshed tears, and if she didn't get away soon, she'd lose it in front of him. "Safe travels," she said, her voice catching. Then she turned and would have run but for the hand that grabbed her elbow and held on.

"I want to see you again."

"No," she whispered, staring down at the hand on her arm. "It's better to end it now than to drag it out."

"Will you be there in the morning when we take off?"

"No." She shook her head. "I have to be on duty at the gate," she lied. Since she'd been tasked to aid the SEAL missions, she hadn't been added back to the gate-inspection schedule. But she couldn't let T-Mac see her standing by, watching them leave. She'd be all red faced and tear streaked. And if she didn't get away from him quickly, she'd be that way all too soon. "I have to go." She ducked past him and ran.

Kinsley had marched right into enemy territory, stood face to face with a killer who had shot her in the chest and fought terrorists from a moving vehicle, but she ran from T-Mac because she was afraid.

She was afraid of losing someone she loved. Again. Maybe her reasoning for running didn't make sense, but she had to get away. He was leaving. She was staying. By the time she returned to the States, he'd be off on his next mission or—worse yet—on to his next girlfriend.

Not that Kinsley was ever his girlfriend. Knowing each other for such a short time shouldn't have made her feel this strongly about T-Mac. But there she was, crying like a baby, her vision blurring so much she ran into someone.

Hands reached out to steady her. "Specialist Anderson, are you all right?"

"I'm fine," she said, and then sniffed loudly and blinked enough to clear her eyes and look up at Mr. Toland. "I'm sorry. I'm just…just… They're leaving in the morning," she cried, and the tears fell faster.

"The navy SEALs?" he asked.

"Yes."

"Things always have a way of working out," he said.

She rubbed her hand over her face, knowing her situation with T-Mac would never work and talking it over with a stranger wouldn't make her feel any better. "I'm sorry. I need to go."

With Agar at her side, Kinsley ran all the way back to her quarters, pushed through the door and collapsed on her small cot. She cried herself to sleep, wishing there was another way.

She'd be up early to watch their plane take off, despite telling him she wouldn't.

Chapter Fifteen

Pounding on the door to the unit T-Mac and Harm shared startled T-Mac awake. He glanced at the clock. Two in the morning. "What the heck?"

"Seriously." Harm swung his legs out of his bunk.

"Wake up, T-Mac!" Big Jake called out from the other side of the door. "We've got orders to move out."

T-Mac pushed the door open. "Thought we weren't leaving until seven."

"Plans changed," Big Jake said. "We have one more operation before we bug out. Gear up. We leave in fifteen."

All sleepiness disappeared in seconds. T-Mac grabbed his go bag and upended it onto his bunk. He jammed his legs into dark pants and boots, pulled a dark T-shirt over his head and slipped a black jacket over his shoulders. He knew the drill, knew exactly what he needed, and in under five minutes he was fully dressed, wearing his body armor vest and carrying enough weapons and ammunition to start his own damned war. He settled his helmet, complete with his night-vision goggles, on his head and slung his M4A1 rifle strap over his shoulder.

Harm finished preparing at the same time.

Together they left the unit and headed for the landing strip, where the helicopters sat with rotor blades turning.

Big Jake, Diesel, Pitbull and Buck were climbing aboard when T-Mac and Harm arrived.

T-Mac hopped on board only to find one more person already there with her dog.

He grinned, happier to see her than he could say out loud. He settled his headset over his ears and waited for the others to do the same.

All the while, he couldn't stop staring at Kinsley where she sat beside him. He reached out and scratched Agar behind the ears.

"Comm check," Big Jake said into his mic.

They went around the interior of the helicopter calling out their names.

"You all might be wondering why we were called out without any warning," Jake started as the rotor blades spun faster and louder.

Everyone nodded.

"Commander Ward received a message from intel that our attack yesterday did not take out the leader of the Al-Shabaab rebels. They were able to locate his position. We have the new coordinates and are tasked with taking him out. If this mission goes well, we'll be back in time to ship out. Maybe not at seven in the morning, but at least by noon."

"Good. Marly's supposed to get back from her chartered flight tomorrow," Pitbull said. "She promised not to fly any more gigs until we've had time to really see each other." He patted his flat belly. "And I have a steak with my name on it back at the steakhouse in Little Creek."

"I can't wait to see Reese," Diesel said. "We're finally going out on an honest-to-goodness date. I'm not sure how to act."

"Talia has been busy redecorating my apartment. I can't wait to test out the new king-size bed," Harm said.

"Angela's been too busy at the hospital to care about the furniture in my apartment," Buck said. "I imagine we'll find a house pretty quickly."

"I can't wait to see Alex." Big Jake smiled. "She should be settled into her new teaching job."

Everyone had someone to go home to back in the States. Everyone but T-Mac. He had everything he wanted in the helicopter at that moment. If he could, he'd extend his stay in Djibouti just to be with Kinsley. This extra mission meant he got to see her one more time. He might even get to hold her hand as they flew to their location.

The Black Hawk lifted off the tarmac and rose into the star-studded night sky.

Moments later they were high above the ground. They headed out over the Gulf of Aden and started to turn south.

A loud bang sounded over the noise-reducing headsets. The helicopter shook violently, and shrapnel pierced the shell.

Kinsley yelped and doubled over, grabbing for T-Mac's hand.

The motor shut down and the helicopter fell from the sky.

Over the headset, the pilot's tense voice sounded. "Brace for landing."

As the chopper lost altitude, T-Mac reached his free hand for the buckles on the harness holding him in his seat. They would have only seconds after hitting the water to get out. If the helicopter rolled upside down, the confusion of which way was up and which was down in the dark would be deadly.

He and his teammates had gone through special training on how to get out of a helicopter that had gone down in the water. They knew how to get out. He'd bet Kinsley had not had similar training.

Based on the way she squeezed his hand, she was scared. Her fear was about to multiply.

Right before the chopper hit the water, it tilted, slowed and then slammed into it. As soon as they hit, buckles popped free and SEALs pushed away from their seats.

T-Mac ripped open his seat-harness buckles and floated free.

The helicopter rolled and filled with water so fast, T-Mac barely had time to pull his arms free of the harness. He let go of Kinsley's hand only for a moment, but that moment was too long. He held his breath, his lungs burning, hands reaching in the darkness, searching for Kinsley.

The arms and legs of his teammates floated against him as they struggled to find their way out through the open doors.

Just when T-Mac's lungs felt as if they would burst, a small hand wrapped around his wrist.

T-Mac grabbed Kinsley's arm and pulled her out of the helicopter and swam for the surface, his own buoyancy leading him in the right direction. A moment later, his head breached and he gulped in air.

Kinsley's head popped up beside him. She coughed and sputtered, dragging in huge breaths. As soon as she stopped coughing, she yelled, "Agar!"

Splashing sounded beside them and Agar dog-paddled over to Kinsley, whining pitifully. T-Mac swam toward them.

"Head count and status!" Big Jake's voice boomed across the water. "Buck."

"Alive and bleeding," Buck called out.

"Pitbull," Big Jake yelled.

"Here," Pitbull answered. "Nothing but a goose egg on my forehead from where Diesel kicked me."

"Harm." Big Jake sputtered and coughed.

"Took some shrapnel to my thigh," Harm said. "But I'm alive. Hurts like hell."

"T-Mac and Specialist Anderson?" Big Jake queried.

"We made it. And Agar's here." T-Mac continued to hold on to Kinsley's hand. If anyone wanted him to let go, they'd have to pry his cold dead fingers loose. He wasn't letting go of her ever again. She treaded water with her free hand but clung to him like a lifeline.

"Commander Ward?" Big Jake called out.

A moment went by.

"Commander?" Big Jake repeated.

"I'm here," he said, his voice weak. "I think my arm is broken."

"Gotcha, sir." Buck swam over to the older man and helped him stay above water.

"What about the pilot and copilot?" Big Jake called out.

"Pilot here. We both made it out, but the Black Hawk is toast."

"What happened?" Big Jake swam up to T-Mac and treaded water.

"Didn't you feel it?" the pilot said. "Someone shot us down."

T-Mac's grip tightened on Kinsley's hand. "That's what it felt like."

"Who the hell would shoot us down from Djibouti?" Harm asked.

"Al-Shabaab?"

"Or whoever is supplying them." T-Mac's jaw tightened as he struggled to tread water with one hand.

"Oh, hell." Kinsley rubbed her forehead with her free hand while kicking her feet to keep her face above the surface.

"What's wrong? Besides being in deep water with no life raft?" T-Mac held on to her, helping to keep her afloat.

"My knee hurts like hell, for one," she said. "And I hit my head coming out of the chopper."

"Are you feeling dizzy? Confused?" Buck swam over to where she bobbed in the water.

T-Mac wished he could get her out of the water and to the nearest medical facility. But they'd have to wait until folks at Camp Lemonnier realized what had happened. "It won't be long. They had to have seen the explosion. We'll get you the help you need."

"No. You don't understand." She pressed her palm to the top of her head. "I… I…remember!" She glanced up and stared across at T-Mac.

"Everything?" T-Mac asked, his heart swelling.

She nodded and struggled to tread water. "Everything."

WHEN THE CHOPPER had gone down, Kinsley had braced for the landing. She knew the dangers of landing in the water and had her hands on her seat belt before they crashed into the Gulf of Aden. She'd released her harness a fraction of a second too soon. When they hit, she flew out of the harness and slammed her head against the top of the fuselage, and twisted her leg so hard she'd felt something snap in her knee, accompanied by a sharp stab of pain. She'd seen stars and feared she'd pass out. But all she could think about were T-Mac and Agar. She had to get out to save them.

The knock on her head made her disoriented. When the chopper rolled in the waves, Kinsley went under. Like a movie playing at high speed, her memories flashed through her mind, all the way up to, and including, the current crash. She'd seen her first meeting with T-Mac, the time he had thrown himself into her quarters to protect her from an unexploded package. He'd been so darned sexy.

Memories of her first night out chasing down enemies hung in the background. She remembered leading the SEAL team with Agar. They'd found numerous land mines through the rubble of the little village, Agar doing his thing, following his nose.

Kinsley remembered her jolt of fear when Agar entered that hut. She'd turned the corner and charged into the building before she thought through the consequences.

And then she'd shone her light into the face of someone she recognized. "The man who shot me. I remember who it was!" she said, and dipped below the surface, choking on a mouthful of salt water.

T-Mac jerked her back to the surface. "Breathe," he said. "We'll worry about who it was when we're out of the water."

"But I know who it was. It was that contractor working on the improvements to the camp."

"Which contractor?" the commander asked.

"Toland. William Toland." A gate opened in Kinsley's mind and all the memories flooded in. She pushed through the pain in her knee, relying on one leg and her arms to keep her head above water.

The roar of rotor blades sounded, coming from the direction of Camp Lemonnier.

Joyful relief filled Kinsley. Not only would they survive a crash, she remembered who'd shot her.

"Toland has to be the one responsible for the gun trading and the information leaks," T-Mac said. "Wasn't he involved in renovating the command center?"

"He was," Commander Ward said. "He could have bugged the room with electronic devices."

"Look, when we're taken back to the camp, let everyone believe Specialist Anderson didn't make it. We'll have her delivered directly to the medical facility, but have the doctors announce that she's dead."

"Why?"

"We want Toland to think he's in the clear," Harm said. "The only eyewitness to him being in that Al-Shabaab camp will be dead. He might get careless. At the very least, we'll be able to catch him before he tries to make a run for it."

"Are you game to play dead?" T-Mac asked Kinsley.

"I'd rather be in on the action. That man tried to kill me." She treaded water for a few seconds before adding, "But I have to be realistic. Something's wrong with my knee. I'll play dead, but you have to promise me you'll get him."

"Are you sure it was him?" Harm asked.

"Absolutely," Kinsley said, her arm getting weaker

as her strength waned. "I remember seeing his shock of gray hair before he pulled the trigger." Her eyes narrowed. Yeah, she'd like to be there at his takedown. He'd tried to kill her.

"We'll take care of him," T-Mac said, his face dark and hardened into stone.

When the Black Hawk arrived, Kinsley and Agar went up first on the hoist as the chopper hovered over the water. One by one, the rest of the men were reeled in. Buck stabilized her leg by applying a temporary splint. The pain was so bad, Kinsley passed out several times en route back to land.

By the time they returned to camp, it was late.

Nevertheless, Kinsley was loaded onto a stretcher and into an ambulance to be delivered to the medical facility. She was sequestered in a room at the back of the building, along with Agar. No one was allowed to enter but the doctor and Commander Ward. The doctor suspected she'd torn her ACL or her meniscus. They'd have to send her back to the States to have an MRI. Fortunately, a C-130 airplane was scheduled to leave the next day. She would be on it. They discussed the plan to declare her dead. The doctor set her up with an IV and pain meds before leaving her and Agar alone.

The commander called in the veterinarian to perform a house call and check Agar over. The dog had been limping so badly, he'd been brought into the medical facility on a stretcher as well. He lay on a bed that had been pushed up to the side of Kinsley's.

When the veterinarian came, he gave Agar pain meds and recommended he be airlifted out along with Kinsley and taken to a veterinarian surgical clinic, where they would have the equipment to better treat the animal.

Kinsley couldn't tell how much time had passed. She floated in and out of a cloud of pain, the morphine the doctor had given her barely taking the edge off.

Kinsley lay on the hospital bed and waited for someone to come tell her that Toland had been captured and locked in the brig. At the very least, she wanted to shower the salt water off her skin. A nurse had helped her out of her uniform and into a hospital gown under strict instructions to keep quiet about Kinsley being alive.

Alone in the hospital bed with Agar in drug-induced sleep, whining every time he moved, Kinsley could only imagine what was happening. Every scenario she came up with ended badly. When she heard footsteps in the hallway, she held her breath and prayed it was T-Mac coming to tell her they'd caught Toland.

The pain medication finally took its toll and claimed Kinsley in sleep.

THE GRAY LIGHT of morning edged its way around the shades over the window when Kinsley opened her eyes.

She stared up at the ceiling for a moment, trying to remember where she was and what had happened. Her skin felt sticky, and that's when she recalled all that had happened the night before and all that she'd forgotten from when she'd been shot. She turned her head to see dark red hair lying on the sheet beside her, a big hand holding hers in its grip.

"T-Mac," she whispered, and reached over to smooth her hand through his auburn hair. It wouldn't be so bad to have red-haired children. As long as they looked like the navy SEAL who'd stolen her heart.

He raised his head and stared into her eyes. "Hey, beautiful."

She snorted softly. "Hardly. I'm sure I look like I've been dunked in the ocean and put up wet."

"Which is beautiful to me."

"Did they get Toland?"

"They did. And he confessed to trading the weapons. He was also working with a guy in the motor pool to transport the goods."

"The guy who died?" Kinsley asked.

T-Mac nodded. "Toland killed him to shut him up."

"He admitted to the murder?"

His brows dipping lower, T-Mac pressed his lips together in a tight line. "Toland was more afraid of us than of going to jail. He spilled his guts."

Kinsley sighed. "Good. He'll get what he deserves. The man is a traitor."

"Yes, he is." He leaned across her and pressed his lips to hers. "But all that is done. How are you feeling?"

"Better, now that you're here." She wrapped her arms around his neck and pulled him down to return that kiss with all of her heart.

When they broke away for air, she smiled up at him. "Aren't you afraid we'll get in trouble?"

"I don't really care."

She chuckled. "Me either."

"They should be in soon to load you up into the plane and take you back to the States."

She touched his cheek. "I don't want this to end."

He cupped her hand and pressed a kiss to her palm. "Me either."

"It might not have to." She glanced down at her leg. "I might be medically boarded out."

"The doc thinks you tore your ACL or meniscus."

She nodded.

"And if they medically retire you?" T-Mac looked at her. "What then?"

Her hand slid across the sheet to smooth over Agar's head. The dog whined and tried to lick her fingers.

"I'll probably go on and get that college degree I joined the military for." She met his gaze with a direct one of her own. "If Agar is retired as well, I want to give him a forever home with a yard to run in."

"There are some great colleges in Virginia," T-Mac offered.

"Yeah?" Kinsley smiled, tears welling in her eyes. "Will you want to date a gimpy girl?"

"I'll want you no matter what, my sweet, brave dog handler." He slid onto the bed beside her and carefully gathered her into his arms. "You're amazing, and I want to spend a lot more time getting to know you. Like the rest of my life. Baby, you're the one."

She shook her head. "How do you know I'm the one? We haven't known each other very long."

"A wise old friend of mine told me you don't have to know a person very long to know she's the one for you." He pushed a strand of her hair out of her face. "I didn't believe him, until I met the one person who convinced me."

"And who was that?" Kinsley whispered.

"I think you know."

"Hmm. Maybe I do. You better kiss me before my chariot arrives to take me away. This kiss will have to last me until I see you again." She brushed her lips across his. "Because when you know he's the right one, you just know."

Epilogue

Three months later...

"Need help bringing out that platter of marinated steaks?" T-Mac called out.

"No, I can manage." Kinsley limped out to the patio of the house they'd purchased together in the Little Creek area.

T-Mac smiled at her, his heart so full he couldn't believe how lucky he was to have found the love of his life.

"The gang will be here any minute. Should I put the steaks on right now, or wait to make sure they arrive on time?"

"Wait. The guys like them practically raw." She set the tray of steaks next to the grill.

T-Mac captured her around the waist and pulled her into his arms, kissing her soundly. "I'm the luckiest man alive."

"Oh, yeah, how's that?" She leaned back against his arms around her middle and smiled up at him.

"I have you, don't I?"

"That makes me the luckiest woman alive."

"Even though you had to give up the army?" He kissed the tip of her nose. "Do you miss it?"

She shrugged. "I do miss helping keep our guys safe. But since Agar and I were both injured and retired, it worked out for the best. I can be around to see to Agar's needs, and you and I get to be together."

A damp nose pushed between T-Mac and Kinsley's legs.

"That's right, Agar. You're loved, too." Kinsley reached down and patted the dog's head.

He would walk with a limp for the rest of his life, but he was retired from active duty and would lead the good life with a big backyard to run in and a soft bed to sleep on.

"Hello! Anyone home?" a voice called out. "The gang's all here." Big Jake stepped through the patio doors with Alexandria Parker at his side.

Behind them were Buck and the love of his life, Dr. Angela Vega.

Diesel came out on the patio with Reese Brantley, the former army bodyguard with the fiery auburn hair and mad fighting skills that served her well in her chosen profession.

Pitbull held hands with Marly Simpson, the bush pilot he'd fallen in love with during a vacation in Africa. She'd relocated to the States and was flying for a charter company.

Harm followed Talia Ryan, the former owner of an African resort.

Talia carried a bottle of wine. "I hope you like red. I thought it would go well with the steak."

Kinsley smiled and took the offering. "I'll save it for later."

T-Mac circled her waist with his arms and grinned at Harm. "Nine months later."

"What?" Harm's jaw dropped. "Nine months? Are you saying what I think you're saying?"

"No kidding?" Buck grinned. "Kinsley's got a bun in the oven?"

Angela frowned. "Do people really say that anymore?" She hugged Kinsley. "I'm so happy for you two."

"When's the wedding?" Big Jake asked. "You have to make an honest woman of her now."

"Next weekend. If you all can make it," T-Mac announced.

"Oh, wow!" Marly exclaimed. "That's great. I'm pretty sure I don't have anything on my schedule that can't be pushed off."

"Where's it going to be?" Talia asked.

Kinsley laughed. "We're having a JP perform the ceremony on Virginia Beach. Someplace Agar can be a part of the ceremony."

"Do you need help with the preparations?" Alexandria asked. "I'm really good with decorations and flower arrangements."

"I'd love some help."

"Have you bought your wedding gown?" Talia asked.

Kinsley's cheeks flushed pink. "No, I haven't."

"Oh, sweetie, we have to get on that," Talia said. "I can help you there. How many bridesmaids and groomsmen?"

"None," T-Mac said. "It's just going to be Kinsley, me, Agar and all of our friends."

"Oh, and your parents and sister are coming," Kinsley added.

"What?" T-Mac frowned. "I haven't even told them I'm getting married."

"They know," she said, her face smug. "And they're so delighted you wanted them here to celebrate."

He laughed and pulled her into his arms. "You are the right one for me. Are they happy about their new grandson?"

"I'll let you share that news with them after the wedding." Kinsley lifted her chin. "But I'm sure they'll be ecstatic about their granddaughter."

Reese laughed. "Too early to know whether you're having a girl or boy?"

T-Mac nodded. "Yeah, and we won't until the baby's born."

"Oh, that's not fair. We want to know what it is," Buck complained.

"And you will." T-Mac said. "When the baby comes."

Harm shook his head. "I can't believe you're getting married before the rest of us." He pulled Talia into the circle of his arms. "I just got Talia to agree to marry me."

"Seriously?" T-Mac shook his friend's hand and then hugged his fiancée. "I'm really happy for you two." He turned to Talia. "You're getting a great guy."

"I know." She smiled up into Harm's eyes. "He's been patient with me through my move back to the States. I wasn't sure I wanted to get married again. I loved my first husband so much. But I've learned I can love again, and Harm's the man who showed me how."

The others all gathered around to congratulate Harm and Talia, T-Mac and Kinsley.

"Anyone else holding out on us?" T-Mac asked. "Speak now before I put the steaks on the grill."

"Alex got a job teaching at the elementary school around the corner from our apartment," Jake said. "The kids all love her. And so do I." He hugged Alex and gave her a big kiss.

"I have an announcement," Buck said.

"That you're getting off active duty and going back to medical school?" Diesel guessed.

Buck frowned. "Hey, I was supposed to say that. How did you know? But yes, I was accepted into medical school. I start next spring."

Diesel opened the cooler he'd brought with him and tossed Buck a can of beer. "It's about damned time. You're going to make a great doctor. You and Angela can open your own practice when you're done."

"Anyone else?" T-Mac asked.

"I'm giving up my gig as a bodyguard," Reese announced.

Diesel frowned. "That's news to me. I thought you liked it."

"I did, but it's not really conducive to pregnant women." A smile spread across Reese's face.

"Pregnant?" Diesel's face went from shocked to joyous. "Are you kidding?" He lifted her off the ground and spun her around. "Really?" He lowered her to her feet and stared down into her eyes. "Sweetheart, I love you so much." He dropped to his knee and held her hand in his. "Will you marry me?"

Reese laughed. "You don't have to ask me if you don't want to marry me. I like things the way they are now. Why ruin it by getting married?"

Diesel straightened and gathered Reese in his arms. "Because I love you and would be honored if you'd be my partner, my lover and my friend in marriage."

"To love, honor and swing from tree to tree?" Pitbull joked.

"I'd do it, if she said *yes*," Diesel said, his gaze never leaving Reese's. "Will you marry me, Reese Brantley?"

She smiled up at him and nodded. "I will."

"Next week? Can we make it a double wedding on the beach?"

Reese gave T-Mac and Kinsley a nervous smile. "They might want to have a wedding all to themselves. I don't want to butt in."

"The more the merrier," T-Mac said.

"It's a great idea," Kinsley agreed. "And our babies will grow up together. How wonderful."

"Well, damn," Pitbull said. "We're not keeping up with the rest of them." He started to bend down on one knee, but Marly beat him to it.

Marly held up her hand. "Before you start, let me say something."

Pitbull frowned.

"Will you marry me?" she asked, and grinned. "Beat you to it."

"Damn woman. Is this how it's going to be?" He pulled her into his arms and kissed her on the lips. "Because if it is, I'm in. Yes. I will."

More congratulations were offered.

T-Mac finally got the steaks on the grill, and he stood back with an arm around Kinsley, Agar lying at their feet and surrounded by the men and women who were so much a part of his life, they were like family.

"I'm truly the luckiest man alive," he said.

Kinsley leaned into him and smiled. "I love you, Trace McGuire. I'm glad you didn't give up on me."

* * * * *